Always a MARINE

BOOK FOUR WOUNDED WARRIOR SERIES

Patty Campbell

ALWAYS A MARINE
Copyright © 2019 by Patty Campbell

ISBN: 978-1-68046-772-7

Published by Satin Romance
An Imprint of Melange Books, LLC
White Bear Lake, MN 55110
www.satinromance.com

Published in the United States of America.

Cover Design by Ashley Redbird Designs

This book is dedicated to Curt Rasmussen from the Department of Homeland Security. Curt is a genuine White Hat Hacker working for DHS. He and I exchanged countless emails, so that I would get the details of computer forensics for my character, Joe Hamilton, correct. Thank you for your time, Curt. Any mistakes in the book are mine alone. Keep up the good work protecting America. We need you.

The author donates all royalties from the sale of this work to the Wounded Veterans Relief Fund. Information on the organization can be found at www.wvrf.org.

Chapter One

Joe Hamilton shrugged into his jacket and grabbed his car keys. Why he'd agreed to let Liz talk him into meeting another woman puzzled him. His sister's constant matchmaking was done out of love, he was sure, but he was perfectly happy with the single life.

He gave himself one last cursory glance in the hall mirror, brushed a curl of black hair back off his forehead and left his apartment. He'd never get used to having hair again, not after fifteen years in the Marines. He'd almost forgotten he had thick, curly hair. The last photo of him with a full head of hair was his high school prom picture with the luscious and loose Rita Simmons. He smiled at the painful memory of sexy Rita. He'd been a virgin, but she knew her way around a young man's body that night.

So taken by her, he'd proposed marriage after their hot, satisfying sex in the small hotel room he'd quickly paid for. The prom had been in the hotel ballroom and nobody seemed to notice when he and Rita disappeared. He hadn't been disappointed, not by a long shot. Rita was everything he wanted in a girl. Pretty, funny, sexy and smart. She'd laughed when he asked her to marry him saying, "Sure, Joey, why not? I don't have anything planned after graduation."

1

Rita was royally pissed the next day when he told her he'd joined the Marines. Talk about ruffled feathers. She looked like a rooster that got soaked with a hose. He softened the blow by consenting to spend the last of the money he'd saved to buy her a car and took her engagement ring shopping. They spent every night together until he shipped out for basic training. He saw her twice more before he got deployed to Iraq. He was stupid with love and passion for good old Rita.

Then he got the proverbial *Dear John* letter one month later. He'd become nothing more than a cliché.

That's when the drinking started, and he acquired the name Boozy in his unit. If it hadn't been for Master Sergeant Beachy and Gunny Dempsey, his career in the Marines would have been short and ignoble. They'd whipped him into good enough shape to finish his tour of duty and he'd been one of the few not physically wounded when they got ambushed on their way to Baghdad to ship home.

He became a pretty pitiful and wasted alcoholic after that. Liz had rescued him even though she wasn't much more than a kid. He gave up the booze and the nickname, rejoined the Marines and hadn't had a drop of alcohol since. He lived with temptation. So why had she asked him to meet her and the girl-of-the-month at a bar? Out of the Marines, wounded on two different deployments, and holding a great job with a good future ahead of him, he was finally on the right path. Granted, he was thirty-three, but he felt young and strong. He could put off finding the right woman for quite a while.

If he was lucky, he wouldn't like the latest woman, and the evening would be brief. He'd play the gentleman, satisfy Liz once again then move on. Maybe she'd get the message. He wasn't seeking a wife. He was looking for a solid financial situation and stability. Maybe Liz thought he was just fine, but he knew better. He went to AA meetings twice a week and still had a sponsor to answer to. There was no way he'd jeopardize his recovery by getting mixed up with a woman. Joe welcomed an occasional roll in the hay, but something permanent? No way.

He pulled up to valet parking in front of the fancy bar-restaurant. He wasn't going to park his brand-new Beemer on the busy street. It took too long to finish his education, finally achieve his bachelor's in physics and math, and master's in criminology—and then get to the place where he could justify owning his dream car. He tightened his grip on the steering wheel, gave it an affectionate pat and handed the keys to the valet. This baby was the current love of his life. The only love he needed.

———

Liz Hamilton stared at her friend and co-worker, Sandy Cassidy. "You have got to be kidding me!" Sandy must be joking. She wouldn't really do such a thing, would she?

"No, I'm not kidding. You should try it." The spirited redhead twirled a curl around her finger and took a sip of her Cosmo.

"Sandy! That's dishonest." Liz still couldn't wrap her mind around it.

"Oh, pooh. It's a great way to get dinner out at a nice restaurant, two or three nights a week. It gives me something to do. Who says everybody online is looking for a serious relationship? Anyway, they can afford it."

"How can you know that? Do you run them through a credit bureau ahead of time? If you haven't even met them before, how do you know what they can afford? Anyway, I'm disappointed in you. Like I said, it's dishonest." This conversation was all it took to change her mind about introducing Sandy to her big brother, Joey. She crossed her fingers in hope he'd be a no-show. He got annoyed with her trying to fix him up all the time as it was. He'd never agree to another introduction if she hooked him up with Sandy.

"I don't understand why you're so bent about it. It's not your money, and it's only one dinner out, not a lifetime commitment for crying out loud."

How had Liz not known Sandy was this shallow? They'd worked together for over a year and she'd been completely blindsided by this revelation. "Sandy, is that the reason you're always trolling around on those dating websites? You could get all the dates you want. I was planning to introduce you to my big brother, but not now."

A spark of interest lighted Sandy's golden-brown eyes. "Is he rich?"

"No! He just retired from the Marines."

"Ooooh, a Marine. Tell me about him."

"No way, I love my brother. I only introduce him to the right kind of girls." And Sandy clearly demonstrated she'd be the wrong kind of girl for Joey Hamilton.

"Oh, for heaven's sake, all I do is accept a dinner invitation. I let them pick up the check because they're usually gentlemen and expect to pay."

"When you accept an invitation to dinner with a man you've met on a dating site, and then you don't insist on going Dutch, they're expecting more than a meal with a glamorous girl."

"And that's my problem why? Anyway, if I really like the guy, I'll go out with him again and maybe he'll have his expectations met." She winked.

Liz reached back through her mind for any clues she may have missed in her encounters with Sandy at the advertising agency. She was very pretty, sharp on the job, and had a good sense of humor—but this? She never had a clue. "Don't any of the men you meet wonder why somebody like you is looking for romance on the internet?"

"Some of them ask me." She crossed her legs and the fluttery skirt slid higher on her perfect thighs. The tattooed bartender appreciated the show.

"And?" Liz gestured *gimme* with her fingers. "What do you tell them?"

"I say I'm tired of looking for eligible men at church socials or depending on introductions from friends." She shrugged and squeezed her lips into a pout. "It's out of the question to look at work. That's a good way to end my career."

Liz had to give her credit for having that much sense. As far as she knew Sandy had always been circumspect at the agency. Most all the men they worked with were married, and except for some playful flirting, everyone knew the limitations. She enjoyed some of the good natured back and forth herself.

"Tell me about your brother. What's his name?"

"Joey, but I'm not introducing you to him."

"Why not? We might hit it off and I'll end up as your sister-in-law."

"God forbid! He may be a big strong Marine, but he's tender-hearted where women are concerned. He got dumped by his fiancée

4

while he was deployed in Iraq years ago, and he's been gun shy ever since."

"Why'd she dump him?"

"My opinion? She was stupid." *And Joey was lucky.*

"You say that because he's your brother. How old is he? What does he look like?"

"He's thirty-three, smart, handsome and fearless. Why am I telling you this? I'm not introducing you to him."

"Does he look like you?"

"There's a family resemblance. Why?"

"Because you're sexy and beautiful, in case you hadn't noticed."

"Pffft. I look like a million other women." She heard the bartender snort.

"I won't debate it with you. How tall is he? Does he have black hair like you? Are his eyes blue too? How come I've never seen him before?"

"I told you. He just got out of the Marines. He got his degree and went to work for a private security outfit in Burbank." *Shut up, Liz!*

"You're killing me! I want to meet this guy. When can I meet him?"

Liz made a show of glancing at her watch. "How about an hour from never? I told you you're wrong for him." Oh, boy, she was so wrong. The last thing she'd ever do was let Sandy get her hooks into her sweet big brother.

"Hey, sis." A familiar voice approached from behind. Sandy's eyes went wide with appreciation. "Sorry I'm late." He slung a long arm across Liz's shoulders and kissed her cheek.

"Joey! I didn't think you were coming. You said you wouldn't be finished moving into your apartment until day after tomorrow." There he stood, handsome and smiling, dressed in chinos, a black muscle shirt under his sport jacket.

He grinned. "I got done early." Smiling at Sandy, he asked, "Aren't you going to introduce me to your friend?"

Sandy grinned and thrust out her hand. "Sandy Cassidy. Liz was just telling me about you, Joey."

"It's Joe. I haven't been Joey since high school."

Liz wanted to strangle Sandy when Joey raised his eyebrows and flashed his smile-to-die-for. God, her brother was so good looking! This was a bad idea. Why did he have to show up? He'd told her there was a good chance he wouldn't make it tonight. She clenched her teeth. How was she going to get him alone and tell him to steer clear of this redheaded gold digger?

"Are you playing matchmaker again? We discussed that at length during Thanksgiving dinner." He shook his head and turned to smile at Sandy. "Liz has been trying to fix me up for so long I'm annoyed with her. I'm taking Sis out for dinner and dancing tonight. Why don't you join us?"

Joey, no!

"Oh, I don't want to impose. If I did join you, I'd insist on paying my own way."

The brazen witch! So innocent! It was all Liz could do not to kick her. *I'll fix her!*

"Sandy was just telling me she always pays her own way. She doesn't want to give men unrealistic expectations by letting them pick up the tab. Isn't that a wise thing to do, Joey?" She glared a warning at her co-worker. "Right, Sandy?"

Joe grinned. "I can see where it would avoid awkward situations at the end of the evening."

Sandy's expression was all innocence and wonder again. "You have no idea." She took a deep breath and her ample breasts swelled beneath her clingy silk blouse.

Yes, Liz would definitely strangle Sandy at the first opportunity.

"Too bad you can't join us, Sandy. She gazed at her brother. "Sandy already has plans for this evening."

Joe tipped his head, a look of genuine regret on his face. "Ah, that's too bad. I love Latin dancing and sometimes I'm embarrassed to always have my little sister as my partner." He squeezed Liz's shoulder and planted a brotherly kiss on her head.

"Oh, I'd much rather go dancing with you and Liz than sit through a boring movie with my girlfriend." She snatched her cell phone off the bar and started a text. "I'll let her know I've made other plans."

"Won't she be disappointed that you're blowing her off?" Liz stared into Sandy's face. Was there no stopping this woman?

Sandy waved her hand. "No. It wasn't really firm. She'll understand."

Joe grinned. "Great!"

Liz clenched her teeth to hold back a scream begging to come out. "Um…Sandy, when you finish that let's hit the ladies room before we leave."

Sandy pocketed her phone. "We'll only be a minute, Joe." She stuck out her ample bosom and smiled.

If there was a way to accomplish it without spending the rest of her life in jail, Liz would make sure Sandy never made it out of the ladies' room alive. Liz fumed at the way Sandy made a point to add a little extra swing to her hips then glance over her shoulder to make sure Joey was getting the full effect. He was. From the look on his face he liked what he saw. Maybe Liz would just go home, leave a note of apology to her brother and slash her wrists.

Liz pushed the door open and faced a line of chattering women waiting. Forget laying down the law to Sandy in this crowd. "Do you want to wait in this line?"

"No." They stepped into the now deserted hall. "I can wait."

Liz stopped her. "Sandy, I'm warning you. Keep your hands off Joey. You are so wrong for him. Wrong. Wrong. Wrong."

Sandy raised her eyebrows. "In case you haven't noticed, *Joe* is a big boy. A very big boy. He doesn't need his baby sister looking out for him." She made a beeline back to the bar and tucked her hand inside his elbow. "We're ready to go, Joe. I'm no expert in Latin dancing, so you'll have to teach me." She pressed her big boob against his arm.

Joey, the big dope, raised an eyebrow and said, "I'd love to."

———

Sandy insisted Joe order for her. "I'll ask for separate checks, of course."

Joe couldn't miss the fact that his usually sweet little sister glared at Sandy's every remark. Something was going on with Liz. "You all right, sis?"

"I'm fine, Joey. Just a little tired. Sandy and I had a very busy day.

We'll probably have to leave soon after the dancing starts. Staff meeting early tomorrow."

"Oh, I don't have to attend tomorrow morning. So, I can stay as long as Joe wants." Her coy smile was replaced by a painful, "Ouch!"

"Oh, sorry, Sandy, did I step on your toe?" Liz patted Sandy's clenched fist.

Joe gave his sister a sidewise look. He'd have to call her tomorrow and find out what was up with her. He smiled at Sandy. "That's great! I usually like to stay on Friday nights until they close the place. There'll be plenty of time to teach you all my favorites. You'll be a pro by the end of the evening."

"I'm so looking forward to it." Sandy made a space for the waiter to put down her plate. "Um, this smells delicious!" She rolled her eyes and inhaled deeply, wriggling with anticipation.

Joe loved a woman with a good appetite. There was nothing more boring than a picky eater who went on and on about her diet. Sandy was a refreshing change. He'd have to thank Liz for finally introducing him to a woman he could click with.

Liz left shortly after one dance with him. She was grumpy and out of sorts, scowling through the entire salsa. Not like her at all.

Joe led Sandy onto the dance floor for a samba. She caught on real fast. He hadn't danced with such a natural dancer since the annual military fund raiser. Cluny McPherson's tall and willowy Brazilian wife, Graciella, had enjoyed every Latin dance with him. They'd had a great time that evening. He smiled at the memory of Cluny cutting in with a friendly warning.

Sandy was a head shorter than Joe and very well endowed. He found himself responding physically to her delicious body. The long number ended, and the band took a break. "I'm pooped." Sandy put her hands on her heaving chest. "Let's talk for a while. I'd like to get to know you better."

Joe led her back to the table and ordered another glass of wine for her and a Pepsi for himself.

Sandy cocked her head? "You don't drink?"

"Nope. Here's one thing you should know about me. I'm a recovering alcoholic. Haven't had a drop in a dozen years." He raised his eyebrows waiting for her reaction.

"Well… that's fantastic, Joe! A man I don't have to worry will get wasted by the end of the evening and then insist on driving me home." Her cute nose wrinkled. "As if I'd get in a car with a guy who couldn't walk a straight line." She fluttered her long beautiful fingers. "Pah!"

Joe's mouth quirked up at the corner. "I do have to take you back to your car when we leave here."

She raised her glass. "Ah, yes," took a sip of the ruby red pinot noir, and abruptly changed the subject. "Liz told me you're an ex-Marine."

He chuckled. "It sounds like a cliché, but there is no such thing as an ex-Marine. Once a Marine, always a Marine. Corny as it sounds."

"Is that really true?" She pursed her lips in a doubtful pout he found very sexy. Blood from his brain boarded a rocket and shot straight south.

"On my honor as a recon Marine. I retired because I was finding it harder and harder to compete with the kids. It was time I had a place to put down roots."

"Recon Marine? Ooh, tell me more." She put her elbows on the table and leaned closer.

He reluctantly tore his eyes from her chest and looked into her eyes. "Most of the first guys in the USMC Special Operations Command were raiders. The last four years of my service were spent with MARSOC."

"Is that like Delta or SEALs?" Her golden-brown eyes sparkled.

"Pretty much, but every service brags about being better than the rest." He flashed his best grin at her wide-eyed appreciation. He wanted to be on the dance floor with her. Wanted to touch and hold her.

"So, are you going to tell me who *is* the best?" The tease in her words had him tingling.

"The Marines, no question." He returned her smile, his insides warming at the idea of getting his hands on her again. "Come on, I'll teach you the steamy tango." He reached for her hand and led her to the center of the now sparsely populated dance floor.

He winked at the bandleader. "Your sexiest tango, Mauricio." He held Sandy close and took a step with the first musical note. Halfway through the dance he dipped her, and she wrapped her leg around his thigh. "You've done this before, chica, haven't you?" A tiny warning jangled in his brain. Why had she lied?

She smiled. "Yes, José, I have, but never like this. Are you disappointed?"

As an answer, Joe pulled her close and kissed her on those luscious red lips he'd been salivating over all evening. Man, oh man, all he could think of was getting her naked and in his bed, but he'd been down that path. Sleeping with a woman before he got to know her hadn't worked out for him in the past. He'd take his time. "No, I'm not disappointed." He was disappointed that she'd lied to him, but not disappointed that she'd done it because she wanted to dance with him.

———

The minute Joe Hamilton had put his arm around his sister and kissed her cheek, Sandy had the sensation of being immersed in a warm spa. He was the best-looking man she'd ever seen, and his smile would stop a train. She'd always been a sucker for a genuine smile, and Joe's smile lit up the room. She couldn't take her eyes off him. Her physical reaction to him shocked her, a pleasant shock. How could this guy be single? It didn't seem possible. He probably had a string of women a mile-long panting after him, or several ex-wives, but he didn't come across as a player.

He exuded power even though he wasn't bulging with muscles. He wore the sport jacket like a male model, but relaxed, self-assured. She closed her mouth, afraid she was drooling. Come heck or high tide, she'd find a way to see what made Joe Hamilton tick.

Were the Hamilton brother and sister just late bloomers? Liz was twenty-nine. Tall like Joe, and beautiful, even though she denied it to herself. So, why was Liz still unattached?

Sandy wasn't interested in a serious relationship. Not after the disaster she was still dealing with, but it would be so nice to enjoy herself with a nice and interesting man, to have some fun. To feel desired, but respected. To delay going home after work every evening to face Phil.

Chapter Two

THE SILENCE IN JOE'S CAR WAS AWKWARD. SANDY RACKED HER brain for an intelligent answer after his question, "Can I see you again?"

"Joe." She wanted to see him again. Very much. "It's just—"

"No, it's okay if you don't want to, there's no need to explain." He pulled into the parking lot of the restaurant. "Point out your car to me."

"Joe, I do want to see you again, but I have a temporary problem I need to resolve. It's something I've put off far too long." A lump of ice formed in her stomach. How could she, or should she, explain?

"It's another man. I get it." His response was cool.

"That's my car. The red one." He stopped when she nodded at her small Honda.

"Yes. It is another man, but it's not what you think, Joe. I don't have a boyfriend, and I do want to see *you* again. I have a situation I've put off resolving. Give me your phone number and I'll be in touch." She wasn't handling this well.

He faced her. "Tell Liz when you've got whatever it is squared away. I don't want complications. I need to concentrate on my new job and settle into my apartment. I've done drama, and I don't like it." The set of his jaw daunted her.

Heat suffused her cheeks. She'd messed this up already, and whose fault was that? She created the mess and it was time she did something about it. "I don't like drama either. But I'm not in a position right now to go forward with you. I can't imagine you as no more than a casual date. I don't want to be your casual date. I'm trying to be as honest as I can, Joe." Perhaps it might be best if this never got off the ground. Joe was an alcoholic. He was clean, but it was a matter of concern. She couldn't bear the thought of dealing with another alcoholic.

"Fair enough." He got out of the car and walked around to her door and opened it. "Good night, Sandy. I had a good time." He made no move to kiss her good night but extended his hand as if closing a business deal. "I'll wait until you get your car started. Make sure you're safe before I leave." He returned to the driver's door and got in.

"Good night, Joe. I loved dancing with you. I'll be in touch." She closed the door and stepped away. He moved his car a short distance, idling his engine, waiting. She sighed. He'd make sure she was safe instead of dumping her off. She'd never met such a gentleman.

Her feet were rooted to the ground and she had to shake herself to open her door and get in the car. She backed out and passed him. He blinked his lights and followed her to the exit, turning left when she turned right. Her heart thudded disappointment. She hadn't been ready for their night to end, especially on such a disheartening note.

———

The living room light was on and the TV flickered like a broken beer sign when she parked in her driveway. She sat for a few minutes to get her thoughts together. She hated it when he waited up for her.

"Where have you been?" he snarled in a beer slurred voice when she entered the house.

"Good evening to you too, Phil." She set her purse on the small shelf on the coat rack and entered the living room. His walker was propped against the end of the sofa where he sprawled.

"You said you were going out to dinner. It's after two a.m."

"I didn't know I was required to seek your permission to stay out late. It's not a *school night*, is it? Oh, sorry, I forgot, it's been years since either of us was in school."

"Don't be nasty. I was worried."

Why, because your two-legged ATM machine might not be coming back?

"I went dancing with Liz Hamilton and her brother. We stayed until the club closed, not that it's any of your business."

"As long as I live here, it's my business."

"Yes, well, we're way overdue to discuss that again, aren't we? I'm going to bed."

"It's your fault!" he shouted at her back. "It's your fault I'm in this condition, you know!"

Yes, my fault. Will I have to pay for the rest of my life?

———

This time when Joe kissed her, they weren't on the dance floor, but on a cliff overlooking the Pacific, the full moon bright, but not bright enough to obscure the blanket of stars. He held her in his arms while they stood at the very edge. His hands slid down her back as he pressed her closer. She'd burst into flames like a California brushfire if he kept this up.

Finally, he released her, looking deep into her soul with his piercing blue eyes. "Lie here with me, Sandy." He tugged her hand and lowered her onto a thick blanket he'd laid on the dry grass. She went willingly, eagerly. Stretched out alongside her, he rolled to his side and kissed her again, long, lingering, hot. "Let me make love to you, my beautiful girl. Please say you'll let me make love to you."

"Yes, Joe, yes!"

She bolted upright, startled into wakefulness by the sound of her own voice in the dark room. Groaning, she lowered her head into shaking hands then glanced at the lighted dial on her digital alarm. Five a.m. Only three hours since she'd gone to sleep. She fell heavily on her back.

Something moved in the shadows of her room. "Who's Joe?"

She screamed, "Phil! You scared me. What are you doing in here?"

He moved closer to the edge of her bed, his walker clumping on the floor. "You were moaning. I thought you were sick. Who's Joe?"

"I don't know what you're talking about. Go away and leave me alone. I have to get up at seven for an early meeting at work." She rolled on her side, hoping he'd leave without any more of his endless interrogations.

"On Saturday? You don't work on Saturday."

"You're right. I don't, but the boss is leaving town and we have a minor crisis to take care of before he returns. The whole management staff is expected to attend."

He grunted, and then thankfully, shuffled out and closed her door.

She fell back and pressed a pillow to her face. *What am I going to do?*

She'd been asking herself this question for almost four years. Stymied, she tossed and turned knowing she wouldn't get another minute of sleep. A flickering light glowed beneath her bedroom door. Phil was watching TV. She didn't know what else he did with his time when she was at work, or on another boring dinner date with a lonely man she had no intention of encouraging, just to stay away from Phil as much as possible.

She knew the speculation about her at work. The men and especially the women often glanced at her as she moved about the office. It wasn't her fault she had the body men lusted after and women envied. She was careful to dress appropriately. No mixed signals coming from her quarter.

She overheard a couple of married men joking as she was about to enter the break room one morning. "How do you suppose Barbie stands upright with her fabulous rack? You'd think gravity would topple her. I overheard a couple of those bitchy secretaries refer to her as 'Two melons on a broomstick.'" He chuckled.

The other guy laughed. "They'd kill for her slim hips and legs. Hell, I'd kill to get my hands on her ass."

Barbie. That's what they called her behind her back. To hell with them! She was a complete professional at work. The top boss, Jordan People, appreciated her and treated her with respect. She brought more new business into the agency than the next two sales agents combined. They could say what they wanted, think what they wanted. The only person at People and Productions who was consistently nice to her was Liz Hamilton. Gorgeous herself, Liz had been fair game for some of the office talk, too. But Liz was so classy and smart it never got out of hand. She'd laugh and joke with them in a friendly way as if she didn't care, but Sandy knew it rankled.

All those jealous witches who envied her and Liz had no idea how difficult it was for a beautiful woman to compete in a man's world. To be taken seriously without having to constantly prove their worth. There were times Sandy wished she'd been born plain as a dormouse, respected for her brain and her abilities, not her oversized breasts and dewy skin. She knew what men wanted, had known since she was thirteen. Her career demanded more, and she was providing more.

She'd always been careful to dress in modest business attire when calling on customers. In the five years she'd worked there, never had she used her physical assets to get ahead. Sure, her looks didn't hurt when soliciting new business for the agency, but she conveyed a professional off-limits attitude. She was valuable to the firm and she'd never do anything to jeopardize that. Her personal living expenses were through the roof. Keeping her good paying job had to be her top priority.

She showered, dressed in a casual pantsuit and dabbed concealer on the dark smudges under her eyes. The smell of coffee lured her to her kitchen. Phil stood at the stove laying strips of bacon in a big cast iron pan. One of the nice things he did for her was to prepare breakfast every morning. He insisted she have breakfast before leaving for work and made sure of it by setting a plate in front of her every day. She hated herself for thinking it was just another way he subtlety manipulated her.

"Smells good, Phil." Sandy took two mugs from the cupboard. "Shall I pour you some coffee?"

"Nah. I'll wait until I'm done here. You go ahead."

She carried her filled cup to the table and opened the folded newspaper at her usual place. He always put the WSJ on the breakfast table for her. She had the humorous notion that Phil was somehow playing the role of dutiful and neglected wife. Cooking for her. Cleaning as well as his physical limitations would allow and waiting up for her late returns to greet her with an injured expression. She shook her head at her silly thoughts and gave a cursory glance at the first page. The usual.

She turned to the Life section to see if any of the print ads produced by People and Productions were to be found. Sure enough, there was Liz's clever design for the Healthy Homemade Yogurt Maker prominently displayed to entice WSJ women readers.

Sipping coffee, she began to feel her brain waking. The lack of sleep would hit hard by early afternoon, but she'd be bright as a baby chick for the duration of the staff meeting.

Phil set the plate in front of her. He'd made a bacon and cheese omelet and a toasted garlic bagel today. Returning from the stove with his own plate, he sat across from her and glowered. "I don't suppose you remembered I have a therapist appointment this afternoon at four?"

"Yes, I remember. I'll be home in time to take you. Why are you so grumpy?"

As if she didn't know. Grumpy was a good day. Snarly the rest of the time.

"I'll ignore that." He picked up his fork and dug into the perfectly made omelet. "Eat. It's one of my best."

She pasted a smile on her face and took a bite. "You're a great cook. I always enjoy whatever you make. Thanks."

"I make supper too, if you'd ever bother to show up. I don't understand why you have to be out five evenings out of seven. It doesn't add up that you're required to entertain potential customers for People and Productions so often. Why can't you take them to lunch?"

"I do go out with *friends* once in a while. I enjoy the relaxation after a long day of making sales calls and conferencing with the creative department to come up with what the customers expect from us. It's not exactly a nine to five job." She didn't add the obvious; she avoided him as much as decency would allow.

"So you say." He sent her a sharp look through the cloud of steam rising above his coffee.

"What's that supposed to mean?" She put down her fork and stared back.

He mimicked her voice, "Yes, Joe, yes!"

"Oh, for the love of…I told you Joe is Liz's brother. We went to dinner and dancing at Caliente Latino. He offered to teach me the Bachata."

"Never heard of it."

"You never heard of the Merengue either. So what?" She resumed eating and glanced at her wristwatch.

"I'd love to learn those dances, but obviously I—"

"Don't start. Just for once…please don't start. You never showed any interest in dancing before the accident." She put down her napkin and picked up her coffee mug. "I have to get my laptop." She left the kitchen before saying something she'd regret.

She emerged from her bedroom with her hair arranged in a subdued twist. Dangly earrings with amber stones her only jewelry. After the staff meeting, she'd be calling on an agency that provided adult home care and child care. They'd decided it was time to hire a professional ad agency to stimulate new business. She'd spoken to the owner on the phone several times. Today would be the first in-person meeting. Sandy would make the right impression. She'd secure the account for P&P.

"I'll be here to take you to therapy. As of now, I have no plans for later." She stood inside the kitchen doorway. Phil was washing dishes.

He looked over his shoulder. "We need to stop at the store on the way home from the therapist."

"Make a list and I'll do the shopping while you have your session."

"Yep," he said to the kitchen window.

How does he do that? Fill me with guilt to start my day?

Sandy sighed and picked up her briefcase and keys, oblivious of the beautiful day. She started the little Honda and backed out of the driveway, wishing she'd taken the time to get it washed and the oil changed. She needed new tires too. Driving on bald tires was one reason for the fix she was in with Phil.

―――――

Sandy didn't miss Liz's scowl when she passed her on the way to the sales office. There was no reason they had to be enemies. They worked together and until last night they liked each other. Sandy needed to clear the air with Joe's sister.

"Liz? Can we talk for a minute?"

Liz turned, her arms filled with folders and drawings. "Look,

Sandy. Joe's love life is not my business, so there's really nothing to talk about." She hugged the folders to her chest like a battle shield.

"Please put those down for a minute and come with me." She watched as the hard look in her co-worker's eyes softened slightly. "Please?"

With a pained sigh, Liz put the files on top of the nearest shelf and shrugged. "Let's get it over with." She spun around and headed for the break room.

A man on Sandy's sales team was getting a cup of coffee and waiting for a pastry warming in the microwave. She reached for disposable cups and handed one to Liz then peered in the refrigerator like she was looking for something, all the time wishing the guy would leave before somebody else came in.

"How are the two most beautiful girls at P&P this morning? You two make showing up for work worth it." The microwave beeped and he pulled the paper plate gingerly forward. "Damn, I overheated this again."

"Stan, how many times have I said ten seconds is plenty, fifteen at the most? You must enjoy using a steak knife to eat a Danish." Liz rolled her eyes and rewarded him with a smile.

"I'd love it if you'd take care of me, baby." He waggled his eyebrows and backed toward the door.

Sandy thrust her finger in the direction of the outer office. "In your dreams. Now do us a favor and get out, Stanley,"

"Yes, ma'am, anything you want, beautiful."

"Oh, lord, just go already!"

He chuckled and left them alone in the small room.

Liz picked up the coffee pot. "I don't have much time. What do you want?" Her back was stiff, her movements wooden.

"Just relax, would you? I really like Joe and we had a great time dancing. Nothing else happened. He asked if he could see me again and I told him it wasn't a good idea. End of story."

Liz's mouth dropped open and her eyes went wide. "You—why?"

"My life is complicated. It wasn't fair for me to encourage him, even though I'd like to. He deserves someone with a clean slate and less baggage."

"Sandy...I...I'm sorry. I misjudged you."

"Yeah, well you wouldn't be the first." She pursed her lips and added a packet of sweetener to her cup then reached for the pot. "So? Are we good?"

"Yes, I'd like to stay friends."

"Me, too. Now—After my meeting with the care agency, I'm depending on you to back me up with some great creative ideas if they give us a trial."

"You can count on it." Liz's expression said the wheels in her head were already turning.

"I never doubted it."

She hadn't been sure how Liz would feel about her after last night. She sighed with relief and headed to her office. Time to put her fantasies about Joe aside and get back to work. Maybe someday she'd find a way out of her situation, and a man like Joe would be waiting for her. She could dream, couldn't she?

Chapter Three

Joe enclosed his mother in a hard hug. Bernice Hamilton was tall and willowy like Liz, but her dark hair was shot with strands of gray, her eyes dark chocolate brown. He stepped back and gazed into those eyes he loved and that loved him back without reservation. "You're still the most beautiful woman in the world, Mom."

Don Hamilton laughed and slapped him on the back. "We didn't raise a fool, Mother. There were times I wasn't so sure but looks like we did a good job."

Joe hugged her again. "Why do you let him get away with calling you Mother? He looks old enough to be your grandpa." He grinned at his father. Don's blue eyes were all he'd inherited from him, except maybe the black hair. Dad had been bald for so long he couldn't remember what he'd looked like with hair. The only photo that gave him away was the wedding picture taken forty years earlier in front of the officer's club at Camp Pendleton. Colonel Donald Hamilton grinned broadly at his new wife who stood a good two inches taller than him, even in low heels.

His parents were made for each other. Joe had known that every day of his life. "Where's Liz?" He looked around. "I didn't see her car."

"I asked her to stop at the store and pick up something. She should be here any minute. Don, get Joe a soda and you two get out from under my feet. I'll bring the steaks out when the grill is ready." She gave Joe a little shove in the direction of the back patio. "Major's going to dig his big clumsy paws right through that screen if you don't get out there and throw that ball for him."

"I'd like to take him off your hands, but they're dead set against big dogs at my condo complex." Joe had brought Major back with him from his last deployment. The dog had received an honorable discharge from the Marines and was happy to be a pet instead of a soldier.

"Don't you dare think of taking that big baby away from me and Clint. Your brother would never forgive me. At the rate you and your sister are going, Major's the only grandchild I'm likely to get. Now scat! You're in my way."

The front door opened. "Hi, Mom. I'll just put this on the kitchen counter. Got any beer?"

"Are women really from Venus and men from Mars?" Joe grinned at his beer loving sister and raised his eyebrows in question aimed at his little brother.

Clint followed Liz into the house. "I'll have a beer."

"Like hell you will." Joe playfully punched his thirteen-year-old brother. Clint jumped back and raised his fists in a boxer's stance. The kid was tall for his age. Like Joe and Liz.

"Easy, boy! Down!" Joe motioned the powerful dog back from the sliding screen. Major dropped the slimy, chewed up, green tennis ball and grinned. The minute Joe stepped out the door, he went up on his hind legs, put his oversize paws on Joe's shoulders and lapped his face. "Yuck!" Joe laughed and pushed the big mixed breed mongrel away. "Your breath smells like a gym locker. What the heck are they feeding you?"

Don joined him, handed over a can of cola and closed the screen. "Anything he wants. He earned it when he saved your sorry ass."

Joe grinned into his father's teasing eyes. He never doubted who was top dog in the family. Don Hamilton had been a demanding, tough, but loving father to his children. Joe and Liz, and later Clint had known all their lives that their dad would be there for them no matter what. They may get a well-deserved dressing-down, but they never for a second doubted their father's bottomless love. If Joe could be half the father his dad was, he'd count himself very lucky.

Liz peeked through the screen. "How's the temperature in the grill, Dad?"

"I was just about to check it. Hold on." Don opened the top of his pride and joy. Joe didn't even want to know what his dad had spent on this tricked-out Cadillac of grills. He and Liz exchanged an exaggerated eye-roll.

"It's ready any time Mother wants to bring out the steaks, Lizzie." He shoved Major back with his leg. "For Pete's sake, Joseph, throw that goddamned ball before this mutt drives me nuts."

Bernice carried a cookie sheet with five huge top sirloin steaks and set it on the tray extension of Don's everything-but-the-kitchen-sink barbeque grill. She smiled and kissed his cheek. "Make mine medium, honey."

Don huffed, "Haven't I known that since the Jurassic period." He pecked a kiss on her cheek and smacked her bottom. "Medium rare for you, Joseph? I'll put Clint and Lizzie's on first, they like theirs cremated. Goddamned waste of a good steak, if you ask me."

Bernice patted his chest. "Nobody asked you, Colonel. Get cooking. I'll bring the salad and the squash. If you behave yourself, you can have a piece of the ricotta cheesecake Liz made especially for her daddy."

Joe chuckled at the interplay of his parents. He picked up the slimy tennis ball and threw it clear to the back of the long lot. Major took off like a rocket. Joe's arm would wear out long before the dog tired of the game. He trotted back to Joe and dropped the disgusting thing at his feet. "Hey, sis, your turn."

"If you think I'm going to touch that icky thing, you've lost your mind. Ugh!" She set a bun warmer on the table next to the Waldorf salad. "Just tell him no."

"You tell him no. He scares the crap out of me."

"How did I ever raise two complete wussies?" Don grumbled as he turned two steaks over and added his and Bernice's. Joe's would go on last.

The laughter never stopped on those one-Sunday-a-month family brunches, and today was no exception. Don brought out a chessboard and slammed it on the table where Liz had picked up some dishes. "Time to face the music, son."

Joe stood and brushed off the seat of his jeans. "You wish. Get Clint to play while Liz and I do KP. Shouldn't be long." Clint gave him the finger behind his back and sat across from Don. Joe grabbed the few remaining serving pieces and joined Liz in the kitchen. "Come on, sis, let's get cracking." He enjoyed their tradition of kitchen police since childhood. They seldom used the dishwasher.

Liz smiled and joined him. She was silent, up to her elbows in soapy water. She placed dish after dish on the rack so Joe could dry them and put them away. He felt pretty sure the silence had something to do with Sandy. After a few minutes, he stepped back and snapped her on the butt with his damp towel.

"Ouch! You brat!" She threw a handful of suds at him and he jumped back in time to avoid getting them in the face. They landed smack in the middle of his T-shirt. "What's the matter with you?"

"The question is, dear baby sister; what's the matter with you? Spit it out." He flip-rolled the towel again and squinted a warning.

"Don't you dare! I'll sic Clint on you. He's almost got his black belt now." Her beautiful lips twisted in a warning smile.

"Nothing happened between me and Sandy. We danced. That's it."

Liz nodded. "That's what she told me." She snatched the towel out of his hand. "I'll dry. You get to wash the pans for being such a smart aleck jerk, Joey." She took a handful of dripping silverware and plopped it in the towel she held in her other hand. "Get to work."

Joe wrapped a dry dishtowel around his waist and plunged his hands into the sink. They made short work of the rest of the kitchen cleanup. "Hey, sis, remember when Dad grabbed the front of my shirt and slammed me back against the wall that 4th of July when I got shit-faced and insulted McPherson's girlfriend, Graciella, at Dempsey's house?"

"How could I forget? He gave you his scary commanding officer glare and said, 'The drinking stops now!' I thought he was going to lift you right off your feet and throw you through the window with one hand."

"Yeah, you were just a kid, about Clint's age." Joe grinned. "I rejoined the Marines the next day. Dad saved my life."

"That and the fact Mr. Dempsey threatened to throw you out of his house or beat the stuffing out of you."

He nodded. "And now you're trying to manage my life by picking out which women I should date. Commanding officer genes must run in the family."

Liz gave him a little shove. "Okay, I get it. I resign as your matchmaker."

"And as my babysitter?" he added with a rakish raise of an eyebrow.

"That too. I'll concentrate on Clint." She turned to leave then spun around. "Hey! Let's take Major for a walk and drop in on Cluny and Graciella. I'm dying to see their new baby. They only live about three long blocks away from here, near the park. You wanna?"

Every retired Marine in his unit from Fallujah had married and were having children. He wanted a family of his own. When he'd asked Rita to marry him years ago, he looked forward to returning from the Iraq war and starting a family with her. She was the one—until she wasn't. He'd never laid eyes on her after he deployed. The Dear John letter had destroyed him. She dumped him from the other side of the world while he was in that sand-pit-hellhole. Joe was nineteen and on top of the world. His girl was waiting for his return. She'd run to him and throw herself into his arms. Except she wouldn't. She'd married another guy and disappeared.

That would never happen again. He'd had women since then, some of them he really liked, but nothing ever amounted to more than casual fun, and sometimes, if he got lucky, friendly sex. They weren't looking for anything permanent. He was an active duty Marine, so neither was he. Now it was a different story. Thirty-three years old and not getting any younger. He hoped he'd find someone in the next five years, or he might as well accept permanent bachelorhood.

"You think we should just drop in on them?"

"I told Graciella I'd be in Spring Grove today, and she said she'd be glad to show off their little Maureen. Come with me. You and Cluny can catch up. When was the last time you saw them?"

Joe searched his memory, twisting his brows with the effort. "She was pregnant when I left for Germany. So that kid must be what? Five or six?"

Liz's face dimmed and she looked at her feet. "The baby boy, Ronan, died when he was two days old. It was horrible. I know I told you."

"Oh, Christ, yes, I remember you sent me a letter. Man, that must have been awful for them."

"It was awful for everyone." She sighed. "No—now I remember. You were here when Misty Beachy and Jack Hawk got married. Graciella was pregnant then, that's probably why you're confused. They had another boy, Ricardo. He's three, and he's the image of Cluny. I think he lives on top of Santos's shoulders. It would take a pry bar to separate those two. You should see them together."

Santos was Graciella's son from her first marriage. "How old is Santos now?"

"Sixteen, maybe? I'm not sure. Come with me and you'll find out."

Yes, it was about time he started getting reacquainted with all his old buddies and their families. They stepped outside. "Dad, the chess game will have to wait until we get back from McPherson's."

Clint stood and told Don, "I'm going with them, Dad. I haven't seen Santos for a while."

The instant Joe snapped the leash on Major, the dog's behavior went from exuberant puppy to disciplined adult dog. "He'll love visiting Queen and Happy." Liz was shrugging into a bulky sweater and Joe paused to give her a hand.

"That's the other sad news. Cluny had to put Queen down a few months ago. She was really old and had very painful arthritis in her hips. It got so he had to carry her in and out of the house to do her business. One night she gave him a look as they were standing in the glow of the porch light in the backyard. Queen knew it was time and so did he. She was fifteen. Old for a big dog."

"Yeah," Clint added. "It totally sucked. I never seen Santos cry before, but he was totally craptasticked."

Joe looked at Liz. "Does he speak English?"

"Only when Dad's around." She put her hand around Clint's elbow. "We'll keep your secret."

Joe'd never been a big dog person until he was introduced to

Major. Then everything changed when he saw the devotion and loyalty the mutt gave him. "I wonder what God's grand plan was when he made us love our pets so much, but gave them very short lives compared to ours?" He remembered Misty Beachy had trained dogs for ICE. "Is Beachy still involved with dogs?"

"She's Misty Hawk now, remember? Yes, but not as a full-time occupation. She and Jack's daughter, Ellen, train therapy dogs. Their place is huge. They work from home. You wouldn't recognize Ellen. She's no longer the sullen teenager who did everything possible to keep her dad and Misty apart."

"Yeah," Clint offered. "She's totally hot for an old babe."

"Old babe? She can't be more than twenty. What's she up to?" He zipped his light jacket against the chill of early evening.

"She just got accepted into veterinary school at U.C. Davis. She still lives at home with them, but she's got an active social life."

Joe chuckled. "That must drive Hawk nuts. He was an overprotective father, as I remember. He glowered the entire time I danced with Ellen at their wedding reception. I could see she was going to be a stunner. I hope any kids I ever have will all be sons."

Liz elbowed him in the side. "Misty is pregnant, she's out to here." She made a big circle in front of her stomach. "It's another girl."

Joe and Liz laughed as they walked up the driveway to the McPherson residence and knocked on the door.

"Joey!" Graciella squealed and grabbed him, "my favorite dance partner. Dios, when did you get so handsome?"

"Hey!" Cluny walked up and put a possessive arm around his wife's shoulder. "I thought I was your favorite dance partner."

"You're my favorite everything else, querido, but you can't hold a candle to Joey on the dance floor. Your singing makes up for it. Hello, Major!" She patted the dog then took Liz's hand. "Come in, all of you, come in."

"Are you still serenading the ladies, Cluny?"

"Just one lady." He kissed Graciella's cheek.

A tall, large, dark skinned young man with a tow-headed little boy on his shoulders ducked through the dining room doorway and approached them.

"My God." Joe stopped short and stared. "Is this Santos?"

"Yes, and Ricardo, his favorite brother." Cluny took Santos's elbow. "Do you remember Joey Hamilton, son? The last time you saw him was at the Hawk wedding."

Santos extended a manly hand. "Sorry, sir, I don't remember."

Joe shook his hand. "No problem." He looked the young man over. "I remember your father. You look like him."

Santos grinned and slung an arm around Cluny's shoulder. "You mean my late biological father, Marv Jefferson. Dad is my father." He lifted Ricardo off his shoulders. "My brother, Ric. He looks like Dad, doesn't he?"

Joe couldn't help smiling, then winked at Graciella. "You sure you're his mom?"

"Very sure. I was there." She tousled the young boy's hair. His fair skin and bright blue eyes left no doubt who his father was. Ricardo lowered his eyes shyly and clung to Santos's leg. "He looks exactly like Cluny's baby pictures. Wait till you see Maureen. You'll recognize my hand in that one." She beckoned them. "Let's go in the kitchen. I just put on a pot of decaf. The baby will wake soon."

"Mom. Ric, Clint, and I'll take Major out back to visit Happy." He lifted the boy to his shoulders again. "Let's go supervise the dogs, buddy." The three boys and Major went out the back door.

"Holy smokes. I can't believe how he's shot up. His resemblance to Marv brings back a lot of memories."

"How did you know him?" Liz asked as she helped Graciella place mugs and plates on the table.

"Marv was part of the Navy SEAL Team that came to our rescue when we were ambushed on our way to Baghdad on the last day of our deployment. Those guys saved our asses. Marv was killed just a few days after we shipped home."

Liz put a hand on Graciella's arm. "That must have been very hard for Santos."

"No, he was born while his father was deployed. He never knew Marvin. All he ever knew was a small faded snapshot of a big black SEAL in camos. Cluny is the only father he's ever known." The look of deep love and trust she bestowed on her husband was enough to melt Joe's heart.

"So, Joey, what have you been up to?" Cluny put his arm around

Graciella's hips and pulled her close. She kissed his forehead then went to get the coffee pot.

"First off, let's dispense with Joey. I'm all grown up and Joe's the name. Only Liz is allowed to call me Joey, and I'm working on breaking her of that."

Cluny laughed. "Joe it is."

"I'm with Worldwide Security Partners. My specialty is cyber-crime. I've barely started with them, but it's the job I belong in. Once I discovered technology when I was with MARSOC, I knew what I wanted to do after I retired from the Corps. I just moved into an apartment in Glendale, not far from work. I'd like to have you guys over for dinner once I'm settled." He pursed his lips in an ironic smile. "I can cook. Don't know why the women aren't falling at my feet."

Cluny grinned at Liz. "Why haven't you found the woman for him?"

Liz smirked and raised her hands. "Not me. I resigned about two hours ago. He's on his own, the dumbass."

They laughed at Joe's expense. Cluny squinted and cocked his head. "I hear my little princess." Graciella started to rise from her chair. "No, baby, I'll get her. I'll make sure she's fit for company." He hurried from the room.

"Cluny changes diapers?" Joe chuckled.

"It's a good thing he's got a demanding business to run otherwise I'd never get either of the babies to myself. Sometimes he spends so much time with them in the morning I practically have to shove him out the door." She smiled and shook her head. "He's a wonderful father."

Graciella turned in her chair to face Liz. "How's the job, Liz?"

"I love it and we're really growing. Every day brings new challenges."

"There must be some young women there who'd be good prospects for Joe."

Liz exchanged a look with Joe. "Nope. Not a one." Cluny entered the kitchen holding their new daughter, effectively changing the subject. "Oh, what a beautiful child! Please, let me hold her." Cluny put the baby in Liz's outstretched arms. "Look at you, you little angel. I can see why your daddy is so crazy about you."

Joe took in the infant's olive complexion and milk chocolate eyes in startling contrast to a mass of dark blonde curls. "Oh, man, you are in such deep doo-doo, pal."

Cluny chuckled. "Any guy will be lucky to get past me and Santos."

Chapter Four

"Dad's probably pacing like a caged lion waiting for you to attack that chessboard." Liz elbowed her big brother. "Glad I never learned how to play."

Joe chuckled. "Every now and then I realize you're a lot smarter than I give you credit for. Who played chess with him when I was on active duty?" Don Hamilton was competitive in the extreme. He'd never let Joe win just to make him feel good. Every time Joe said *checkmate*, he'd earned every move. Dad would grumble and mutter, but there was a proud gleam in his eye when he got trounced by his sons.

"He has a group of cronies who like to play and trash-talk. Mom says he gets together with them once a week, but mostly he plays with Clint. The cronies can only talk their wives into taking turns providing their dining rooms, snacks and beer about once a month. It's a moving feast. But I know he loves playing with you the best. Don't tell Clint. You might as well resign yourself to it for every Sunday brunch."

"I'll share a secret with you. I love playing chess with Dad. I just pretend otherwise."

"You weren't fooling me or Dad."

"True. But keeping up the deception is fun." He took Major's leash. "I'll put him out back. Dad's probably already pacing and cursing. Don't leave without saying goodbye." He tipped his head and opened the gate on the side of the garage.

"Hey, Dad. I'm here."

"About Time. Where's your brother?"

"He's hanging out with Santos for a while. Said he'd be home by nine."

———

The game didn't last long. Don whipped him soundly and shook his head. "You didn't have your head in the game tonight, Joseph. Something on your mind, son?"

Joe couldn't concentrate on the game. Images of Sandy bombarded his brain. He had plenty on his mind, but nothing he cared to share with his father. He and Sandy had ended their evening on a sour note. The encouraging signals she'd been sending him all evening were in sharp contrast to the abrupt rebuff at his request to see her again. What the heck was going on with the woman? Did she have a boyfriend? A husband? If so, why was she going out dancing with him in the first place? This kind of complication he did not need in his life right now.

"No, Dad, just thinking about the job tomorrow. There are lots of people I haven't yet met at the company. I'll be doing an all-day orientation and may have to spend a few days at headquarters in Dallas soon. It's a lot to take in."

Liz stepped out onto the patio. "I'm taking off, Dad." She hugged him when he stood to kiss her goodbye. "See you later, Joey."

Joe hugged her too. "You want to have dinner later in the week? It's going to take a while before I get the kitchen organized and stocked. I've been eating too much pizza and frozen junk."

"Sure, call me and let me know where you want to meet."

"You know the territory better than I do. Pick a place and give me a call."

"Thursday then?" She went back through the sliding screen. "I'll text you."

"You probably should head home and hit the sack too, son," Don said. "You've got an hour drive back to your place. Call if you need any muscle. Retirement is driving me nuts. Your mother, too. She'd welcome a chance to get rid of me and your brother for a couple of evenings."

"You might wish you hadn't offered. I haven't even started moving my crap where it belongs or put my bed together. I'm still sleeping on a mattress on the floor."

"Ah, the joys of bachelorhood. How well I remember. Find yourself a good woman." Don urged him inside the house. "Mother, where are you? Joseph's heading out."

A good woman. Not so easy.

Clint sauntered down the front walk as he was going to his car. Joe bumped shoulders with him. "Seeya, bud."

"Shove it, Joe." The kid was becoming a real smartass. He was too much like him at that age, and there was a very good reason for it.

He thought about Sandy during the drive back to Glendale. He'd hoped to forget how good she'd felt in his arms and how much fun they'd had together. Even though Liz had tried to discourage him from going out with her, he'd been immediately intrigued. Liz was to blame. If she hadn't been dead set on fixing him up, he'd never have met her in the first place. He still couldn't figure out why his sister had changed her mind at the last minute and was so upset when he'd invited Sandy to dinner and dancing with them. He'd grill Liz when they went out for dinner on Thursday.

Women—they'd always be a mystery, so it was best he put them out of his mind and concentrate on work. Except that single kiss they'd exchanged on the dance floor still burned deep in his gut.

———

EARLIER, SAME AFTERNOON, SANDY'S RESIDENCE.

Sandy was unsuccessful at erasing the memory of Joe's kiss even though she threw herself into a frenzy of house cleaning. She ignored Phil's complaining when she asked him to move once again so she could vacuum the carpet.

"Chrissakes, you did than an hour ago! Why do I have to turn off the TV and move?" He pulled himself up on his walker and grumbled all the way out to the back patio. "Bring me a beer."

Yes, Master.

"You've downed almost the entire six-pack. I'm not going to the store again until after work tomorrow. What will you use to drown your sorrows until then?" Not that she cared even a little what he did all day. Just once it would be so nice to come home and find him gone. He had friends who'd offered to take him drinking at the sports bar. He usually put on the face of a martyr and found an excuse not to go.

Sandy turned on the vacuum and went over the living room carpet with a vengeance. At this rate, she'd have to replace it before she'd ever gotten a chance to wear it out. Screeching to a stop, she turned it off, retracted the cord and stuffed it in the hall closet. She opened the refrigerator, grabbed a can of beer and took it out to the patio and thrust it in his hand. "I'm going to the movies." Before he had a chance to complain, she added, "I'll be late."

Since she had no plan and no particular place to go, how did she hope to fulfill her promise that she'd be late? It would be beyond stupid to drive aimlessly just to kill time. Not in the mood for a movie or shopping, she racked her brain. What to do for five hours? Where to go? She had to get away from Phil. There were too many angry words aching to be released. Words she'd no doubt regret the minute they leaped from her tongue. No good could come of her dumping on him. They'd been playing this game far too long.

There had been opportunities for her to change their living situation several times in the past few years, but she'd foolishly let them pass in hopes Phil would be the one to make the decision to strike out on his own and make the best of it. It now looked suspiciously as if he took for granted their living situation was permanent. It was her fault; she'd let that happen.

What a coward you are, Sandy!

She'd used many coping mechanisms the past couple of years. A treadmill of dating men she had no interest in, finding reasons for being away from the house as much as possible, grasping at any excuse to work late or travel for the company.

Phil wasn't stupid. He knew what she'd been up to. Instead of giving her any kind of break from the endless routine of listening to his constant stream of complaints and recriminations, it fueled his determination to pile on the guilt, to solidify his endless presence in her life.

He couldn't get away with it if she hadn't enabled him. Her thought processes had swerved in an unexpected direction when she met Joe. He mattered to her. None of the others did, they were nothing more than distractions. No strings. No expectations. In her heart, she knew Joe wasn't that kind of man. He was someone she could very easily care for. Not like the others who'd done nothing more than fill up the empty holes in her existence. Yes, she'd misrepresented herself to the men she'd gone out with. Given them hope that she was available and willing, but all they were to her was an escape, a momentary distraction from gritty reality. It had been so long since a man, any man, had touched her in a loving, affectionate way.

Could Joe be that man? The way they'd laughed together and the way he'd held her when they danced had ignited a spark of hope deep in her heart. They'd come together so naturally, they seemed so right in each other's arms. She conjured the warmth of his big hand on her back as he supported her during their dramatic dip at the conclusion of the tango, but most of all the memory of his sincere and happy smile still had the power to warm her like a rising sun on a cold morning.

No, she couldn't go there. She was locked into the plight she'd made of her life. It would not only be unfair to Joe to encourage him; it would be disastrous. God, how she wished she had somebody she could really open up to. She'd lost touch with former friends, especially those mutual friends of hers and Phil's. Nobody knew what had really happened in their lives before the car wreck. She'd buried herself in work and career advancement to escape, even for short periods, the muck and mire of her secret and lousy private life.

She could always have called her brothers, Damon or Greg, but she was ashamed of how long it had been since she'd reached out to either of them. Damon would understand and forgive her, but Greg, was another story. As the oldest of the three, Damon had more or less taken over the job of looking out for them when their father deserted the family after his wife was diagnosed with MS. Damon was sixteen at the time, Sandy was twelve and Greg eleven.

Sandy stayed in touch with her mother, Beverly, through frequent phone calls. Mom's MS was so bad now that she required full time care. Deeply chagrined that she hadn't been to Portland to visit her in the past three years, she reached for her cell phone then stopped. Mom knew nothing of Sandy's situation with Phil. She'd never had the heart to tell her that her *perfect* son-in-law was a total jerk.

Sandy drove for several minutes before she realized she had no idea where she was or where she was going. Pulling to the curb, she turned off the engine and gripped the steering wheel. She stared at the phone in her right hand but dropped it on the car seat instead after touching her mother's icon. *Coward!*

She grabbed the phone again and pushed the dial command.

"Hello, baby, how nice to hear from you again so soon." So far, the MS hadn't noticeably affected her Mother's warm, sweet voice.

Sandy attempted to answer but found herself choking back tears. She cleared her throat.

"Sandy, dear, are you all right?"

Getting a firm grasp on her racing heart then swallowing back the pending tears, she said, "I miss you, Mom. Can I come and visit you?"

"My goodness, honey, you don't have to ask me that. Of course you can come. Please do, I'd love to see you and give you several overdue hugs I've been saving. Is Phil coming with?"

Mom's mid-western roots came through every now and then in the way she phrased some of her sentences, bringing a welcome smile to Sandy's lips. "Um, no, he's not able to travel right now, but I have some vacation time coming. I suddenly realized how much I've been missing you and the boys."

"Honey, you've made my day. Call Damon and let him know your flight number and he'll pick you up at the airport. The boys will be so happy to see you."

"I'm going to drive up, Mom. Flying these days is such a hassle and I need the road trip to decompress. I'll leave this afternoon and overnight in Sacramento. I should be there before dinner time tomorrow."

"Goodness, the drive here is almost a thousand miles. Are you sure? I'll be worried with you on the road all those hours by yourself."

"Are you always going to worry about me, Mom? I'm a big girl, you know."

Sandy's heart almost broke when her mother said, "Yes, but you'll always be my Little Sweet Pea. I'm so thrilled you're coming, honey. I can't wait to see you."

"Me too, Mom, it's been too long."

Much, much, too long.

She was way past due to reconnect with her family. Why she ever thought she could handle everything on her own without their support, was a mystery. "See you tomorrow."

"I'll call your brothers and let them know you're coming. Please stay in touch along the way, just to keep me from imagining every possible thing. I can't help thinking of you and darling Phil in that awful crash a few years ago."

Darling Phil.

Mom didn't need to know the truth about Phil. Sandy wouldn't do that to her. No matter what misfortune ever befell her mother, she'd always given the benefit of the doubt and believed the best about everyone. She even made excuses for their father for deserting them when they needed him the most.

"Love you, Mom. I'll be on the road within the hour."

Sandy wondered how many florists she'd have to inquire with to find her mother's favorite old-fashioned flowers, purple sweet peas. She could almost smell the sweet fragrance from the vines covering the side of her childhood home every spring.

Thankfully, Phil was out when she got home, so no explanation was demanded as to why she was packing a bag. She swept the few cosmetics that were essential into a small clear plastic zipper case she used for business trips and hurried to the car so she'd be gone by the time he came back from wherever he was.

Bleary-eyed from driving for hours, she pulled into a small roadside chain motel and crashed for the night. And dreamed of Joe Hamilton.

She relived his spontaneous kiss on the dance floor, felt how her heart had momentarily stuttered, and of his compelling masculine scent. She conjured a hot, sweaty love scene between them that had her waking with a start just as the sun rose.

"Whew, Sandy, get a grip." She threw back the covers and stretched, groaning at the stiffness from the less than comfortable motel mattress. Staggering into the stark white, basic bathroom she started the two-cup coffee brewer and turned on the shower. Today's drive would be a repeat of yesterday, but the northern California and southern Oregon scenery would be different.

An hour later, because it took almost that long to dry her thick head of hair, and after quickly dressing in jeans and a sweatshirt, she sipped another cup of coffee in the motel dining area and stared balefully at the unappetizing bowl of instant oatmeal. *Eat the sticky stuff, Sandy.* Two long days of driving called for oatmeal to do the trick of keeping her body on track. The silenced TV hanging high on the wall showed a reporter standing at the scene of a massive pileup on I-5 near Medford.

Flashing lights of the emergency vehicles reminded her of the night she and Phil had crashed through the low guardrail and landed in a culvert. That night had changed the direction of her life. She was hopelessly trapped in the misery of a future with Phil. She was responsible for his crippling injuries. She hoped there'd been no serious injuries in the scene she now watched and crossed her fingers they'd have it cleared away by the time she got that far.

On a deep sigh, she picked up her spoon. There was no way out. She had no business dreaming of Joe Hamilton, or any other man. It wasn't going to happen.

———

Weary but excited about seeing her mother after so long, Sandy pulled into the long bumpy driveway leading to the home where she'd spent her childhood with two annoying brothers she loved beyond words. A gray Audi was parked in the driveway and she pulled onto the grass at the far side to avoid blocking it in. She had no idea who the car belonged to. Her mother didn't drive. Perhaps it belonged to her caretaker. That seemed unlikely. Home care workers couldn't usually afford pricey vehicles.

Her question was answered when Damon stepped out the front door and waved. "You like my new car?"

Damon. Her big brother. The image of their father. Tall, hefty, large head covered in a thick thatch of very dark auburn hair. She'd always loved the freckles sprinkled liberally over his nose, cheeks and arms, but thankful she'd been blessed with her mother's flawless, ivory skin. An unexpected knot formed in her throat nearly choking her. Tears pooled in her golden-brown eyes, mirror images of his.

Sandy scrambled out of the car and straight into his strong arms. Tears flowed freely when she rested her forehead against his wide chest.

Damon kissed the top of her head. "I'm glad to see you too, Muttface." His childhood endearment brought a laugh bubbling up.

She pounded her small fist into his shoulder. "I'm happy to see you, Stinky." Damon always smelled so good, now more than ever the woody scent of his cabinet-making shop clung to his hair and skin. She'd always loved his elemental aroma. Damon had been sawing, sanding and shaping wood as far back as she could remember.

He subjected her to a bone-cracking hug. "It's been too long, brat butt."

"It has." She cupped his bristly cheek. No matter how often he shaved, he'd have stubble within an hour. "How's Mom? And why hasn't some brilliant, sexy woman snagged you yet?"

His answer was a rakish waggle of his eyebrows.

"Tell me," she demanded. "Tell me right now!"

"Nope. Don't want to jinx it." He took her hand. "Come inside. Greg's helping Mother put dinner on." Damon had always called Beverly Cassidy Mother, never Mom the way she and Greg did. He pulled open the screen door.

"Wait, I brought Mom a bouquet of sweet peas. I can still smell them after you closed my car door." She turned but he tugged her toward the side of the house.

"You sure about that?" He pointed to the massive, fragrant tangle of sweet pea vines climbing the side of the wide covered porch.

Sandy groaned. "I should have known. When were these planted?"

"Greg and I put the seeds in the ground just before the spring equinox. The weather has been just right. Aren't they something? They should last till at least July. Mother says they're the best ones she's ever seen. Or smelled."

"Mercy, I'm not even going to bring mine in the house!"

"Don't be silly. She'll be thrilled you thought of them. Come on." They went back to the car and Damon opened the passenger door, retrieved the florist box and handed it to her, just as Greg stepped out onto the front porch.

"What's the holdup? Why does dinner always have to wait for you two?" He grinned and came to give her a hug. Barely two inches taller than Sandy he raised his chin to kiss her on the forehead. "Sandy, you get more beautiful every year."

"You're just saying that because we look like twins, handsome." Greg played for the other team. She could imagine him swooning after a good long look at Joe Hamilton.

"You got a point." He threw his arm around her shoulders and glanced at the box. "Sweet peas?"

"I feel silly bringing them in the house."

"Mom will love them." Greg stepped aside and led her inside. "Mom! Sandy's finally here and she brought you a present." He winked at Sandy and pulled her into the dining room where her mother was seated in a wheelchair at the heavily laden table.

Beverly Cassidy had changed dramatically in the past three years. The wheelchair was new, and her lovely black hair had gone gray. Her body moved noticeably with the excitement of seeing Sandy again, or was it the MS? Mom's sharp blue-green eyes looked the same as always, as did her loving smile. "Sandra. How nice to see you, darling. Come here and give me a hug."

Sandy went to her mother and knelt. Her mother leaned forward and embraced her. "Mom, I love you so much. Please forgive me for staying away so long."

———

Later she and Damon were loading the dishwasher while Mom and Greg worked on one of her beloved twelve-hundred-piece puzzles covering a card table.

"I thought you took Phil's last name when you married him." He eyed her while drying a large platter.

"I did. What brought that up out of the blue?"

"Your driver's license says Sandra Cassidy."

Shock, tinged with anger, jolted her. "You went through my purse!" She whipped around and glared at him.

"No, I didn't! When you dropped it on the table in the hall some of the contents spilled out and I picked them up to put them back. Your driver's license was on the floor." It had always been impossible to hide anything from Damon. That's one reason she'd stayed away for three years. "What's going on, Muttface?" He put his hand on her shoulder when she turned back to the sink. "You and Phil are divorced, aren't you?"

She turned and pounded a fist into his hard chest. "Damn you, Damon!" She collapsed in his powerful arms. "Damn it," she choked on a sob.

"Shhh." He squeezed her. "Come out back with me. They don't need to know." Instead of taking her hand, he picked her up like a small child and pushed the back screen-door open with his foot. He set her on her feet, and with his arm around her shoulders, led her to the very back where he and Greg had planted a large vegetable garden for their mother.

She couldn't remember a time when they hadn't had fresh vegetables on the table every night. She put her arm around his waist and dropped her head on his shoulder. The shoulder that had always been there for her, even when they'd butted heads like bold elks and hated each other.

He remained silent and waited for her to speak, all the while rubbing a big callused hand up and down her arm. He pulled up a young carrot, brushed off the soil and handed it to her. It had been a wonder any of them had made it to the table when she was a kid.

She took it from him and bit off the end, breathed deeply against his woody scented shirt. Why had she denied herself Damon's comfort? "Yes. We're divorced. I can't keep anything from you."

"Why should you?" He stepped back so he could study her. "What happened? I always despised that dirtbag you married. If he hurt you, I'll beat him within an inch of his useless life."

An involuntary smile played across her lips. "You despised him? I thought you and Mom and Greg loved Phil."

Damon's eyes sparked love—and anger. He made no attempt to mask his emotions. "Mother loved Phil. Greg and I never understood what either of you saw in him, with all his greasy charm. He reminded us too much of Dad, and how he'd fooled us with his false love, then deserted us when we needed him the most." Damon shook his head, his fists clenched at his sides. "I see that bastard every time I look in the mirror."

She reached for his hand. "Let's take a walk, you annoying, bossy big brother. I'll tell you everything. I *need* to tell you everything. I just realized that's why I came here."

Chapter Five

LIZ HANDED HER MENU TO THE WAITER AFTER PLACING HER order and asked Joe, "So when are you leaving for Dallas?"

"Sunday evening. My orientation sessions start Monday morning." He nodded to the waiter and pointed to his half-full iced tea glass. "Do you want another beer, sis?"

"No thanks." She waved her hand. "I thought you'd already been trained at the Worldwide Security Dallas office."

"That's right, but since then they had a major computer software upgrade. Now their investigators need training in the new technology. I'll go next week, then when I'm done, the woman I work with will go for hers. Everybody needs to be proficient on the new system." He tore a piece of sourdough bread apart and dipped it in the seasoned olive oil.

"Woman?" Liz cocked her head and gave him one of her perfected probing stares.

"Yes, woman." Joe sniggered. "You've got that interrogator face down pat, sis. And no, there's no chance of anything developing with her."

"Why?"

"She's a sweetheart, but she's older than Yoda, looks like Yoda, and about the same height. She comes to here." He put his hand mid-chest and smiled at Liz's sour face. "But since you brought up the subject of women…"

She leaned back and crossed her arms. "I should have known you didn't invite me to dinner because you love your little sister. You want to grill me about Sandy, don't you?"

"Check. But you happen to be a woman and whether you believe it or not, I am interested in *your* love life, or absence of one." Joe raised an eyebrow. "Planning on being a spinster?"

Her sigh was big enough to inflate the sails of a small boat. "I'm not planning on it, but I haven't met a man worth a second date. Someone I'd bring home and introduce to Dad, if you get my meaning."

"That's no excuse. Dad doesn't believe there's any man worthy of his Lizzie. If you use that as a reason for not putting yourself out there, I'll never get to be Uncle Joe. Would you do that to your big brother?"

"Wow, talk about being between a rock and a hard place. You and Dad allow no room for me to maneuver. I probably should have taken that job as an art teacher in the private school in Seattle. I'd have had half a dozen red hot lovers by now and be unable to choose just one." She dropped her chin on her fist and grinned.

"Too much information!" He playfully covered his ears. "I won't play matchmaker, but I do have single men friends. A couple of whom I wouldn't be tempted to kill if they made a pass at you. How could they not? I'm your brother, but I'm not blind." He reached across the table and patronizingly patted her head. "Poor Lizzie."

"Oh, shut up." She took a sip of beer. "So, tell me about these guys you know."

"I'll make you a deal. You explain to me why you tried to set me up with Sandy, and then attempted to back out and acted like a sour-puss all evening. Then I'll decide which guys I know I'll allow to ask you out."

She smacked his hand away, crossed her arms and bounced back in her chair. "Why do you care about Sandy? She blew you off."

"She's beautiful and smart and I really liked her. She's a terrific dance partner. We had a lot of laughs. What happened between the time you two went to the bar and I arrived? If you didn't want me to show up, you had plenty of time to call."

She rolled her eyes. "If I'd had time to call you, I would have. She didn't tell me until a few minutes before you got there, so I didn't have a chance."

He leaned forward and opened his eyes wide encouraging her to go on. "Tell you what?"

Sighing again, Liz shrugged. "I thought I knew her better. She's very professional and friendly at work, so when she launched into her story about all the dating websites she's on and how she goes out with different men two or three nights a week, alarm bells started clanging in my head. She told me it was a great way to get dinner at a nice restaurant. Some poor guy she had no intention of going out with again would pick up the check."

Joe's stomach clenched with the old burn of betrayal. "Wow, pretty cold. She actually told you she was using men for free meals? That's weird. She doesn't strike me as the type."

"I didn't think so either. Why would I want to get you involved with somebody who would do that? Exactly why I made a big deal about how she always insisted on paying her own way. I thought that would stop her in her tracks. How wrong I was. I'm sorry."

"Don't apologize. How would you know?" He shook his head slowly. "Now more than ever, she's one big mystery. I can't get her out of my mind. It's a good thing I'm leaving town for a while and getting my head deep into work."

The waiter brought their order and they made room for their plates. Liz said, "In spite of what she said I still can't help but like her. She did the right thing by not encouraging you. We both want to stay friends."

Joe shrugged and dug into his southwest chili pot pie. "I forgot how good this is."

Smiling, Liz nodded. "That's why I suggested this place. Let's just enjoy a good meal and find something else to talk about, okay?"

"Sure." He smirked. "Let's get back to your looming spinsterhood. I may have a couple of men you might like. But I don't want you to come back to me complaining if you don't."

He gazed across the table at her. He was five when she was born.

They'd always been close even when sparring like a wet cat and a singed dog. Liz deserved the best. If there was any truth to the old aphorism—*what goes around comes around*—she would follow in their mother's footsteps and find the right man. Dad wasn't always easy to live with, but no marriage was perfect. They'd defied the odds and stayed together forty years through thick and thin, setting a good example for Joe, Liz, and later Clint. They knew they were winners in the parent lottery.

Joe mulled the names of two men friends. One was a co-worker at the Burbank office. He worked as an old-fashioned investigator–boots on the ground. Aptly named, Sam Hunter was divorced, was a straight arrow, and had joint custody of his ten-year-old son. He didn't have a steady woman in his life as far as Joe knew, but they'd barely discussed their private lives. He'd make some discreet inquires at work.

The other man, Captain Cole Brandon, was a career Marine who laughingly claimed to be married to the Corps. When they'd served together, Cole's love life was hit and miss. The same age as Joe, he'd been known to complain about the dearth of available quality women. Currently stationed at Camp Pendleton, Cole worked with and selected young Marines for Special Ops advanced training.

Joe would ask his parents if he could invite Cole for Sunday brunch in three weeks. Even if he and Liz didn't hit it off, Joe and Cole would have a good weekend catching up, going to a Dodgers game, maybe hitting a couple of sports bars to troll for female companionship.

Liz's question brought him out of his thoughts.

He focused. "Sorry, what?"

"I asked for the names of those men. You said you had a couple of names."

"Yeah, I do, but in order to fulfill my responsibilities as a good big brother, I need to think about it some more. Vet them."

"Forget it. You're just as bad as Dad. I'll ask Sandy which dating websites are the best."

"What's the big hurry? Give me a few days after I get back from Dallas." There was something creepy about his sister resorting to the internet to find a good man. "One of the men I'm thinking of is right here in my local office, but I won't have time to talk to him until I get back."

"What does he look like?"

"And here we go, all this time I thought only men were that shallow. You surprise me, sis."

"Oh, stuff it. I'm tall. I don't want you to introduce me to some short guy. I can't wear heels when we go out."

"Rest easy, he's taller than me and he's about my age. Both of the men I have in mind are tall enough to meet your picky criteria." He smiled inwardly. Liz loved to wear heels and she had great legs. He sympathized with her minor vanity. If he were honest with himself, he'd have to admit that physical attributes were also important to him, even though they didn't add up to who and what the person actually amounted to.

Liz signaled the waiter. "It's on me tonight, Joey. If neither of those potential dates turns out to be to my liking, I'll ask for a refund."

"When did you get so tough?" He grinned and put his wallet away.

"I prefer strong and plucky." She smiled. "Anyway, you picked up the check the last time and that blind date didn't turn out so well."

"I consider us even." His cell phone buzzed. "Now what? I'm not expecting any calls." He glanced at the caller's name, and his eyes went wide. "I have to take this, sis. I'll meet you out front."

Holding the phone to his ear he said, "Hold on, Sandy. It's noisy in here. I need to step outside." He made his way around the tables, through the entrance and stepped out the door, pleased and unsettled that she was calling him.

"Hey. I didn't expect you to call after the other night. Where are you?"

"I'm on my way back from Portland. I just got off the freeway and I'm near Fresno, looking for a place to crash for the night."

"Were you traveling for business?"

"No, I was visiting family." She hesitated. "Look, Joe. I'm sorry our evening ended on a sour note. I wanted to apologize."

"Not necessary."

"No, it is. I've been thinking of you on this endless drive back to L.A. If you're interested in giving me another chance, I'd really like to see you again. At least have lunch or dinner so I can explain myself. Will you be around next weekend?"

"No."

"No problem. Sorry to bother you."

"Wait! Don't hang up. I wasn't blowing you off, I'm leaving for Dallas next weekend. I'm attending an advanced software training class at my company headquarters." He asked himself if it was wise to see her again. "I'd love to have lunch with you after I get back. Is this phone you're calling me on the best way to reach you?"

"No. Would you call me at work? If I'm not in, I'll call you back as soon as I can. You'll be gone for a week?" He detected a note of regret in her question.

"At least. It could be longer but tell you what—if I'm going to be longer, I'll call you at work and let you know." Joe didn't want to leave any doubt in her mind. He wanted the air cleared between them. "I promise, Sandy."

"All right. I need to get checked in. I'm nearly asleep and I have another long drive tomorrow. I look forward to your call."

"Great. I'm just leaving the restaurant. I had dinner with Liz."

"Joe, don't tell Liz, okay? I'll tell her. There are some things I need to explain to your sister. I want her to know I'll be seeing you, but I would rather tell her myself."

"No problem. I'm glad you called." Liz joined him in front of the restaurant. "I gotta go. See you soon."

"Bye, Joe."

He dropped the phone in his pocket. "I'll walk you to your car. Unless there's someplace else you'd like to go?"

"No. It's almost my bedtime."

"Come on, sleepyhead." He took her arm and they crossed the street to the parking lot.

———

Dallas company headquarters, Monday morning

The young man who'd sat next to Joe during the early briefing session stretched his back. "My brain can only absorb what my butt can endure. How about some coffee?"

"Great idea." He put his hand out. "Joe Hamilton, Glendale office."

"Barry Roberts, D.C. How long you been with the company?"

They strolled to the coffee setup in the back of the conference room. "About six months. You?"

"Three years. They hired me right out of the Army Signal Corps."

"USMC." Joe grinned. "They hire a lot of military. How long were you in? Where were you stationed?"

"Eighth Army, five years, South Korea near the 38th Parallel for the last two years. Before that I was at Fort Lewis. When did you join the Marines?"

"My dad was a career officer. I joined right out of high school. I thought he'd kill me. He wanted me to go to college before making any decisions about the military. But I wanted to be a hero. I was in for fifteen years and got my bachelors and masters during that time. So—he reluctantly forgave me."

Barry laughed. "I joined halfway through my junior year at Sac State. It was the only way I could escape from my scary girlfriend."

"That's rich. My fiancée used the military as an excuse to ditch me while I was deployed in Iraq. You married now?"

"Nope."

"Me neither."

They enjoyed a good laugh and a cup of coffee that revived them enough to make it through the next session.

By the time the afternoon rolled around, Joe's head was bursting with all he'd learned. He was in his element and looking forward to the rest of the week. The new software amazed him. He hoped he'd get a chance to meet the team who'd designed it. Joe had fooled around with some of his own code and programming but had to admit he was nowhere on the level with the people who'd put together this new stuff.

Joe wanted to work a full-time job, have a *life*, and take the courses he'd need to advance. He had no idea how he'd manage. He'd fall back on an old Marine mantra: Git'er done!

He had to share his day with somebody. Too revved up to relax in front of the motel TV, he picked up the phone and called Liz. She answered after the second ring. "Hey, sis."

"Hey, Joey. How's the class going?"

"Oh man, I'm really enjoying the new training and wanted to talk about it with someone. You're the lucky recipient." He had a picture of her crinkling her nose. Liz's talent was art and design—but creating software required artistry. And design was a given. He'd explain it in a way she'd appreciate it.

"Will I need a glass of wine to get through this?" she teased.

"If I can't have one then neither can you." He leaned back against the pillows propped against the motel headboard. "Look at it this way —if it's really boring, you'll fall asleep and wake up refreshed to face a new day at the agency."

"Well, when you put it that way."

They were on the phone for almost an hour. He relaxed as he described what he'd learned and his sister asked a lot of pointed questions, which told him she'd been listening.

"I should let you go, sis. We both need sleep. I still have at least four days ahead of me. My brain is swimming already."

"Call me again tomorrow night if it will help you defuse, Joey. I've always found that repeating something I've learned helps to reinforce it in my mind."

"You're right about that. Goodnight, baby sister."

"Goodnight, big brother."

He'd find a way to squeeze in a call to Sandy during the day, when the advertising agency was open. At the very least he'd leave a message. That way she'd know he was thinking about her.

Joe double checked the alarm clock, brushed his teeth and turned out the lights. The second his head hit the pillow he was out.

———

At lunchtime the next day he held his cell phone in his hand ready to call her. A rushed conversation wouldn't do it. Needing to be sharp for the afternoon session, he put the phone back in his pocket and headed to the employee dining room for lunch.

Chapter Six

EXPLAINING HERSELF TO JOE WAS THE RIGHT THING FOR SANDY to do. She worked with Liz and wanted to be her friend. Enough was enough, she would plan a way to extricate herself from the domestic situation in the best way possible for herself and Phil. Obviously, they couldn't go on indefinitely like they had been.

Joe sounded pleased and surprised when she'd called. Liz explained how he'd been hurt badly when his fiancée dumped him while he was deployed in Iraq. His engagement ending and ugly combat led to a drinking problem that nearly destroyed him. He'd overcome it and remained sober. Liz's revelation said a lot about what kind of man he was.

She hoped they could develop a friendship that would end up being more, but she would tread carefully. Liz had made it clear he was focused on his career, having put any pursuit of a personal life on the back burner. She hoped Joe would open his heart to her. She regretted the stupid, flippant remarks she'd made to Liz in the bar the night she met Joe. Concealing her miserable private life had driven her to put up a false front, effectively hiding her true self from her co-workers.

She approached the office reluctantly the next morning, dreading her pending conversation with Liz. At least they had mutual respect for their professionalism on the job. "Unhh," she groaned as she pushed open the shiny glass doors of People and Productions. She'd head straight for the Creative department. There was no sense in putting it off.

"Morning, Ms. Cassidy," the security guard at the lobby desk greeted her. "Promises to be a beautiful day." He smiled and nodded his snow-white head.

"Good morning to you, Thomas. When are you going to let me treat you to lunch?"

"Today would be good, if you really mean it. I clock out at one." He gave her a skeptical wink.

"Today is fine. I'll come down and meet you at one." She grinned at the pleased and surprised look on his weathered face.

Thomas reminded her of the grandfather she fondly remembered. Gramps and his beloved pear trees. What wonderful memories she had of helping him pick, grade and size them before they went in the cooler. Later they'd pack the finest ones in shredded paper into fiber boxes for shipment to Harry and David. Gramps was one of their most valued suppliers of top-grade fruit.

The office hummed with activity. Sandy nodded to several co-workers on her way to Liz's department. She heard Liz's voice behind a partition.

"Use this color wash on the background, so the product box pops off the page. The eye should be drawn to the contrast between the color of the box and the product name, and not drawn to the background. Got it? Great. Find me when you have the first draft ready, then we'll see how it looks."

Sandy waited for Liz to step into the main office. She smiled when Liz appeared.

"Sandy. Good morning, do you have another project for me?"

"No, but I'd like a moment of your time."

"Sure." Liz proceeded to her corner office. "Have a seat. I was just planning to finish this coffee before it went cold. Is everything all right?"

"Yes. I called Joe Thursday evening as you two were leaving the restaurant. I'd like to see him again, but I owe both of you an explanation. Would you have lunch or dinner with me tomorrow? I'd like things between us to be out in the open." She bobbed her foot nervously.

"Oh." She'd clearly taken Liz by surprise, but she recovered quickly. "I couldn't meet you for lunch tomorrow, but we could do dinner after work.

"Thank you, Liz, yes. I'll meet out front shortly after six. She rose from the chair and smoothed the front of her skirt. "I'll let you get back to your coffee and try to grab one for myself before the sales meeting."

"I'll see you tomorrow, Sandy, we—" Her phone rang, and she tipped her head with a look of regret.

Sandy shrugged and smiled, then went for coffee.

Promptly at one, Sandy stepped off the lobby elevator. Thomas greeted her with a wide grin. "Where would you like to go, Ms. Cassidy? I know you only have an hour or so."

"How about the Mexican joint on the next block?"

"Love that place. Hope the wife doesn't catch me having lunch with the most beautiful girl in the building."

"Oh, pooh, I was planning on taking a selfie of us hoisting a Corona and emailing it to her. You're no fun." The walk to Gordo's was a mere five minutes, and the bulk of the lunch crowd had already been and gone, so they had no trouble being seated immediately. "This is my treat, Thomas. No arguments."

"My lucky day." He laughed and picked up the simple one-page menu.

———

Still laughing when they left the café, Thomas said, "Go ahead and send the selfie to Florence. She'll never believe it and swear I had to pay you to pose with me."

Sandy held up the doggie bag. "Take this to her and say dinner is on me." When they reached the building, she waved goodbye to him as he turned toward the garage and she pushed open the front door. Thomas brightened her day every morning with his friendly greeting. He told her at lunch that he and 'his Flo' had been married for fifty-two years, and they had twelve grandchildren. Would she ever have such a wonderful achievement? She'd foolishly thought she and Phil might have had such a marriage.

———

Following her round of sales calls the next day Sandy had time to stop at home and change into a more comfortable pair of shoes. The garage door rolled up and the back door into the laundry room was just closing. That was strange. Who'd been in her garage? She left her purse on the passenger seat and carried her briefcase and laptop inside.

Phil flopped in front of the TV, one of his cronies acknowledged her by holding up a can of beer. Another man folded a card table and propped it back against some chairs.

"What are you doing home?" Phil asked in an accusing manner. "You said you were having dinner with a co-worker and wouldn't be back until about eight. Are you checking up on me?"

She stopped on her way to her bedroom. "Do you need checking up on? I finished early and came home to change my shoes. Don't let me spoil whatever plans you had." He'd told her this morning that he'd be spending yet another boring evening alone, but that was not the case. The two men in the living room were his old card-playing posse. Phil said he'd given up on the card games because these guys invariably left with all his money. Considering he was on disability, it couldn't have amounted to much.

Sandy went to her bedroom and closed the door. The murmuring voices of the men were indistinguishable. Phil had his friends at her home, expecting her to be away until late evening. It wasn't the first time she'd discovered he hadn't spent the time she was gone exactly as he'd described it.

She changed her shoes, made a quick pit stop, and walked back through the house on her way to the garage without speaking or acknowledging the guilty looking men watching sports on the TV. She definitely had to find a way to extricate herself from this unhealthy situation.

Sandy and Liz arrived within minutes of each other and took a seat in a quiet booth in the rear of the busy deli. They ordered dinner and sat in awkward silence for a moment.

"Liz, because I want to see your brother again, it's only fair that I let you in on what's really going on in my life. I'll tell Joe too, but if having any kind of relationship with him isn't in the cards, I'll accept that."

"I'm very protective of my big brother, but Joey will make his own decision." Liz shrugged. "I promised him I'd stay out of his private life." She took a sip of water. "If you want to reveal personal information to me, I'll keep it confidential, but you don't owe me any explanations."

"I disagree. I've given you a false impression of who I am, and how I live my life. I like you, Liz, and I'd like to be friends, but you'll decide that after I set the record straight."

The server put their sandwiches and drink orders on the table and asked if there was anything else they needed. Liz and Sandy shook their heads and said, "No, I'm fine," and then laughed because they'd simultaneously given the same answer. The laugh lightened the tension between them.

After a few bites, Sandy said, "My ex-husband has been living in my house for a few years."

Startled, Liz set her glass down. "Ex-husband? Why is he still in your house?"

Sandy shook her head. "Years ago, after we'd divorced, I got a call from the bartender in one of Phil's favorite hangouts. He knew we were divorced but didn't know who else to call. He said Phil was drunk and making noises about getting in his car to drive home. He asked me if I'd come and drive him. I only lived a few blocks from the pub, so I walked over there and took Phil's keys. He put up a stink, but still had enough sense to know he shouldn't be driving. I told him I'd take him home and get a taxi back to my place.

"By the time we headed for the parking lot it had started to rain. It was coming down so hard we sat in the car for several minutes waiting for it to let up. We had a brief respite and I headed in the direction of his apartment. The rain became a deluge. It was so intense the windshield wipers couldn't keep up with it. We were creeping along when the vehicle in front of me slammed on the brakes. I tried to stop, but Phil's tires were in such bad shape we hydroplaned right for it. I swerved to the right and we slid in a ditch and rolled over."

"Oh, my god! Were you hurt, Sandy?" Liz stared across the table at her.

"No, I escaped with bruises and cuts, but Phil received severe injuries to his lower back, pelvis and legs. It was touch and go for several days. They didn't know if he'd survive." She took a breath. "I was drowning in guilt because the accident was my fault."

"But, how was that your fault? He was responsible for the condition of his own car. Why did you blame yourself?"

Sandy raised her arms helplessly. "I could have sent him home in a cab, or I could have stayed home."

"Did you get back together, try to mend the relationship?"

"There was no way that was ever going to happen, but he had nobody other than me. His nearest relative, a cousin, lives in Alaska. She hadn't seen Phil since they were kids, and she wouldn't leave her family to come to California to care for him. I didn't blame her. The doctors said he had years of therapy ahead if he was ever to regain his mobility. His medical expenses were through the roof. He couldn't go back to work, so he declared bankruptcy. I felt responsible for him. I rented a hospital bed and the necessary equipment so I could care for him and hired help during the day while I was working. I expected it to be temporary, but..." Sandy pushed away the other half of her sandwich; her stomach rebelled against one more bite.

"Is he better now? Is he still disabled? What's the outlook?" Liz shook her read and placed her hand on top of Sandy's.

Swallowing back tears, she answered, "He's much better now. He's regained enough mobility to move around with the help of a walker. I drop him off at therapy twice a week. I don't know how much more they can do for him. He's a genius at playing the guilt card. When we were married, he'd be sweet and solicitous one day and hateful the next."

"What about your family?"

"I kept it from them. I didn't even tell them about the divorce. My mom and my two brothers live in Portland. I visited them last week. My big brother, Damon, suspected something was up. I finally confessed my situation to him. He surprised me by saying he'd never liked or trusted Phil but had kept his mouth shut for my sake. Phil charmed my mother with his good looks and engaging personality, but he didn't fool my brothers. She still doesn't know the truth. Mom has MS. There's no point in adding to her troubles. She believes we're happily married. I've dug myself in so deep I don't know how to get out, Liz."

"Oh, Sandy, what a mess. I don't know what to say. You're in quite a predicament."

"Exactly." Hearing Liz's words brought home the truth. Sandy may not have been directly responsible for Phil's accident and resulting condition, but she'd built a web of lies, a trap in which she'd ensnared herself.

"Do you think it's fair to Joey to get him in the middle of this? It's his decision, I realize, but I can imagine any number of problems that might crop up if you two become involved. He really likes you."

"And I like him, Liz. What horrible timing, but it has spurred me on to find a solution and get on with my own life. One I feel I deserve. You will find this hard to believe, but I haven't been with another man since Phil was injured. Nobody who thinks they know me would believe it."

"I believe you now that you've told me the whole story."

"You do?" Sandy's heart pounded.

"Why would you lie about it now? There'd be nothing to gain by making up something this bizarre. I'm just sorry you didn't confide in me earlier. I probably couldn't have done anything substantial to help you, but wouldn't it have been a relief to share the burden? Have someone who knew the truth?"

Sandy's chin trembled. She swallowed the lump in her throat. "You have no idea how much it means to me to hear you say that, Liz. All this time I've needed a friend and you were right there in front of me every day."

"Let's put our heads together and do some serious research on what resources are available to your ex-husband and get him out of your home and your life. You've already gone above and beyond what any other ex-spouse would have done for him. Have you had a private talk with his physical therapist? Or are you only getting feedback from Phil on his progress? It sounds to me like the man has been and is still taking advantage of you."

"And I'm obviously not only allowing it, I'm enabling it. The first

56

thing I plan to do is talk to his therapist. The man will probably have some information about resources for the disabled who have need of them."

"This is probably going to take a long time to resolve, Sandy. I hope you don't get discouraged and give up on it."

"If I hadn't met Joe, I'd most likely have gone on with the situation indefinitely. Your brother made me feel things I'd convinced myself were out of my reach. He and I may never get together, may never be anything more than friends or dance partners, but I know I need to make some drastic changes, quit closing myself off from enjoying my life." For the first time in years, Sandy began to believe in a better future for herself. She wasn't past the age where she could find love again, dream of having a family of her own.

Liz signaled for the check. "I need to get going. I promised my mother I'd help her with alterations to a formal dress she hasn't worn for years. She and my dad are attending a fancy charity affair to benefit homeless veterans. No Marine ever gets out of the Corps." She gave Sandy an ironic smile.

"That's what Joe told me. Their loyalties run deep, no doubt about it."

As they departed in the company garage, Liz said, "Any time you need to talk, let me know. I want what's best for you and for Joey. He's big and tough, but he has a very soft heart."

Sandy sighed. "What a wonderful combination, don't you think?"

"He's the kind of man I'm looking for." Liz pointed her finger. "Don't tell him I said that."

"It's in the vault." Sandy waved and headed for the aisle in the company garage where she'd parked. As she fastened her seatbelt, the phone sounded off. Her heart pounded. Caller ID told her - Joseph Hamilton.

Chapter Seven

JOE'S PULSE QUICKENED WHEN THE CALL CONNECTED. HE reclined against the headboard of the bed in his motel room.

"Joe?"

"Sandy. Hi. You asked me not to call you on this number, but I'm slammed during the day with training. I can't catch a break to call you at work. Sorry it's so late. Is this a bad time?"

She laughed softly. "No, in fact your timing couldn't be better. I just had dinner with Liz and was about to head home. It's nice to hear from you."

"Great." He released a pent-up breath. "So, you had dinner with my sister?"

"Yes, and to answer the question you're dying to ask, we talked about you."

He grimaced. "Do I want to know what was said?"

"Your sister is very protective of her big brother. I'm sure that comes as no surprise."

"Damn! I want to see you again, Sandy. I hope it isn't going to cause problems between the two of you at work. I'll talk to her." It was past time his sister backed off and let him conduct his private life as he chose.

"I don't anticipate any problems, Joe. We had a good talk. She's reconciled to our meeting again, on the condition I tell you everything I told her. If you call her don't assume she was meddling. I'm the one who invited her to dinner."

"So, tell me what you told her." Had Sandy come clean with Liz? Explained why she'd given him an abrupt brush-off? Had she been truthful? He hated lying and hoped she could explain herself.

"I'd rather talk face-to-face. I haven't been completely forthcoming, and if we're going to be friends you deserve an explanation of why I dumped you before we even got past the first evening."

"Are you going to explain, and then dump me again?" He lightened his voice in an attempt to make his question come off as a joke. Even then, his gut tightened. "Is that why you want to talk in person?"

"If there's any dumping done, it will be by you and not me. After I lay it all out for you, it will be up to you. I really like you, and I want us to get off to a good start."

"Okay, I'll take your word for it. I'll be home next Wednesday. Let's have dinner. If you come to my place, I'll cook."

"You can cook? I'm impressed. Oh, wait, Wednesday's not good for me, but Thursday would work."

"Works for me." His pulse quickened. She was coming to his place. He recited his address in Glendale. "It's easy to find. There's a big Rite-Aid on the corner next to the building."

"Got it. I'm looking forward to seeing you."

"How's six-thirty?"

"Sure. I'll come straight from the office. What shall I bring? I know wine is out."

She was all he needed. He hoped the night turned into a kiss, maybe more. He wouldn't rush her but itched to take her into his arms. "There's a Trader Joe's right around the corner from your office. I went in there with Liz once. Could you pick up a French baguette and a boule of soft cheese? We can snack on that while I get dinner going."

"Baguette and cheese, it is. See you Thursday evening, Joe."

"I'm counting the hours, gorgeous."

Joe hoped he could keep his head in the software training and think less about Sandy now that they'd made a firm date. There was no point in speculating about her great revelation. He'd know soon enough.

Rising from the bed, he went to the bathroom to shower. Showering tonight would give him an extra few winks of sleep in the morning. He'd had enough up-before-sunrise mornings to last a lifetime while on active duty.

———

The week was intense. Management wanted Joe to stay a few more days for advanced training. He asked if he could go back as scheduled, put what he'd learned into practice and then return a couple of weeks later. His co-worker was scheduled for training next week. He said they'd get up to speed faster once they'd had a chance to work on it together. Management agreed.

Wednesday finally rolled around and he was more than ready to get back to California. Not only was he anxious to meet with Sandy, he'd promised Liz he'd introduce her to a couple of men he knew. As soon as he arrived at LAX he called his parents.

"Dad, it's Joe. I just got back from Dallas."

His father snorted. "When you open with 'Dad' you don't need to identify yourself, son. You're the only man who calls me Dad."

"Clint calls you Dad."

"Yeah, well he thinks he's a man, but he has a way to go yet."

Joe laughed. "I wanted to ask you and Mom if I could invite a pal of mine who's stationed at Camp Pendleton to join us for our next Sunday family day."

"Sure. Is it anybody I know?"

"I doubt you've met him. He and I were in Special Operations Command at the same time. We've stayed in touch. I might as well tell you—I'd like him to meet Liz. He's single and they might hit it off."

"Be careful there, son. Lizzie has a mind of her own. She might have tried to run your love life, but she'd get her back up if you turned the tables."

"I mentioned it to her. She's in. I haven't brought it up with him yet. I wanted to clear it with you and Mom first."

"What's the young man's name?"

"Cole Brandon. He's active duty, a captain. Ring a bell?"

"Nope. Hold on. I'll clear it with the General."

Joe smiled at his dad referring to his wife as *General*. "Always a wise tactic, Dad."

"I haven't lived this long by accident."

Joe waited curbside for the shuttle to the offsite parking lot where he'd left his car ten days earlier. The dry California air was a welcome change from the humidity in Texas. Less than a minute later, his Dad was back on the line. "She says the more the merrier. Let me know after you talk to him so I have enough steaks. I'm making teriyaki marinated rib-eye next time."

"Sounds good, Dad. My shuttle is here. I'll call Cole tonight and let you know. Give Mom a kiss from me." He shoved the phone in his pocket and hefted his bag onto the bus.

Joe stopped at the supermarket on the way home to pick up a couple of items he needed to make his specialty, cheese and bacon twice-baked potatoes, for Sandy. He also grabbed fresh salad greens and a small package of grape tomatoes. The supermarket's bakery had a selection of mini cheesecakes, so he picked up a raspberry-marble sample and tasted it. Satisfied it would fill the bill, if they ever got around to dessert, he purchased one.

He had no intention of making a move on her unless she gave a clear signal, but he wouldn't deny he'd given it thought. He'd had the occasional one-night encounters in his past, but Sandy and his sister were friends. Casual sex probably wasn't on her radar. Or on his, for that matter. He wanted more. At thirty-three he'd begun to think more clearly about what he wanted and expected for his future. He was a man, a normal, healthy man. Not a swinging bachelor in any sense of the word. That life held little satisfaction for Joe.

At work early Thursday morning he got everything ready for a briefing session with his co-worker, *Yoda*. Not that he'd ever call the sweet lady that to her face. He smiled every time he made the mental comparison and wouldn't have been surprised if others had made the same connection. He'd be the last one in the office to ever say it.

"Good morning, Mr. Hamilton." She took the desk across from him. "I assume you have a wealth of information to impart before I leave for my training Sunday. Shall we start?"

"Good morning, Yvonne, please call me Joe." Her formality was office legend.

She grinned. "Employee fraternizing is strictly prohibited, you realize. I wouldn't want to start tongues wagging if we're too familiar."

Joe laughed and rocked back in his chair. "I love you, Yvonne. You've made my day."

She put her purse under her desk. "Mission accomplished. Shall we start?"

Joe and Yvonne worked steadily till lunch time, barely covering a quarter of the material he'd brought back from Dallas. He had an hour for lunch and caught a break when he located Cole with his call to Pendleton.

"Cole, old buddy. Joe Hamilton here, how are you?"

"Good, and you?"

"I called to see if you'd be able to get leave Saturday after next. I'd like you to come up for the weekend. My parents have a family barbecue the last Sunday of every month."

"Hey, that sounds great. I'm already scheduled off for four days, starting that Friday. Maybe we can catch a Dodgers game on Saturday?"

"You read my mind, Flash."

"Christ on a crutch, man, you're the only one who continues to call me that. What do I need to do to get you to stop? Other than beating the crap out of you."

"Good luck. I can take you down in under a minute. I'll stop if you'll do me a favor."

"Yeah, what?"

Joe had no problem imagining the skeptical expression on Cole's face. They'd played many practical jokes on each other over the years and were always wary they were being set up once again. "I'd like you to meet my sister."

"Your little sister? The one in the picture you used to carry around? Or do you have an ugly one stashed in the attic?"

Joe chuckled. "I only have one sister. Liz. And it's her picture. I still carry it."

"You always were a pathetic loser. What's the catch?" Cole's voice reeked with suspicion.

"No catch. Truth. I told her she might like to meet a friend of mine, no strings attached. If you didn't hit it off, no hard feelings on either side. You in?"

"How old is she?"

"Twenty-nine next month."

"Oh, man, she's seven years younger than me. I'm not sure this is a good idea. Why now?"

"She's spent the last ten years trying to set me up, so I told her I was turning the tables. We reached an understanding and had a good laugh over it. She's beautiful, pal. She's knows you've got a face like a chimp. What have you got to lose?"

"So, why's she still single?"

"She's uber-selective."

"Great, that lets me out, so I'll agree to meet her. Should be short and sweet. At least I'll get a baseball game and a good meal or two out of it."

"Come straight to Glendale that Friday night. You can grab the train if you don't want to drive. I'll email you the address and get tickets to the game. I'm looking forward to touching base. It's been too long, bud."

They spent another five minutes bringing each other up to date on what was happening in their lives, and then Joe hurried through lunch. He and Yoda had a lot to cover today and tomorrow. Sandy would be at his place for dinner tonight. He was itching to see her.

———

Joe had little to do to make his place look presentable before Sandy arrived. He checked his watch. He still had half an hour, so he took a quick shower and changed from his suit into jeans and a polo shirt. Dinner was nearly ready to go in the oven. He put out placemats and what passed for his good dishes, a set of stoneware his Mom no longer used. After placing the utensils, he searched his cupboards for the candles he knew he'd packed but came up empty. *Oh, hell.* He wanted to add a romantic touch.

The buzzer sounded. "Sandy? You here?"

"Hi, Joe."

"I'll be right down." He buzzed open the locked entrance. "The door's unlocked." Anticipation got his pulse rate up. Avoiding the elevator, he took the stairs down two at a time. "Hey, beautiful. Good to see you. Who died?"

She held out the bouquet. "Why should women be the only ones to get flowers?" She handed over the yellow mums and the small plastic grocery bag containing the bread and cheese. "Hug?"

Joe laughed and held out his arms, his hands full. Sandy gave him a quick, hard hug.

"I'm so happy to be here, Joe." Her golden eyes shimmered with unshed tears.

"No tears. I want to see a smile on those pretty lips." He placed a quick peck on her cheek. "Let's go up. You good with the stairs?"

Sandy pushed her bag strap higher on her shoulder and walked ahead of him to the stairs. "What floor?"

"Two. Turn left at the top." He followed, admiring her sweet ass in the casual denim skirt, and slender legs in low heel shoes. Some of the shoes women wore looked as if they'd been designed by a medieval torture deviser. "Number 221, third door down."

Sandy stopped at his door and smiled. Her eyes were clear now, the brief hint of tears gone. "Is it locked?"

"Nope. Go on inside." He slid past her as she held the door for him. She closed it and followed him to the small kitchen.

"Something smells good. Bacon?" She tipped her head back and sniffed. "Definitely bacon." She reached for the flowers. "Do you have a vase?"

"Not a one. Use that utensil holder by the stove. The one with the wooden spoons." He set the plastic bag on the workspace next to the stove. "I'll slice some bread and get it on a plate. The potatoes will take about thirty minutes, so I can hold off on putting them in the oven while we talk for a while."

Sandy lifted the spoons and spatulas out of the tall holder and placed them on the counter. She filled the old-fashioned ceramic container with water then peeked under the foil resting on top of the aluminum baking tray. "Oh, those look tasty."

"I haven't made them in a while. First time in this little kitchen." He set about slicing the baguette and placed the small rounds on a plate. Opening the packaging around the cheese, he sniffed the pungent goat cheese spiced with garlic and herbs. "Oh, wow. We may never make it to dinner."

"I hesitated about the garlic but caved. It's too good to pass up. What are we drinking?"

"There's a jug of iced tea in the fridge. Glasses are in the cupboard over the sink." The easy camaraderie between them warmed his chest. They were comfortable with each other in this small space.

Sandy opened the cupboard and examined his motley collection of glasses. She removed two and turned to face him, grinning. "Let's use these." She held two inexpensive mismatched stemware glasses. "We'll pretend the iced tea is champagne."

Joe stepped around the island, took the glasses from her hands and set them on the counter. "I gotta do this first." He took her into his arms and kissed her. A nice, almost casual kiss, not one filled with the passion he held in check. He released her. "I've wanted to do that since we went dancing."

Sandy closed the gap between them. "Hmm, I seem to remember it more like this." On tiptoe, she crossed her arms around the back of his neck and kissed him with a lot more oomph than he'd allowed himself.

He drew her tight to his chest and deepened the kiss. He gasped as they moved apart and took a breath. "We moving too fast?"

"Yes, we need that conversation first." She took her hands from his neck to cup his cheeks. Her smile was tentative, but her eyes sparkled as she held his gaze. She turned and picked up the glasses again. "Shall we?"

"Yep." He pulled the jug of tea from the refrigerator, but not before he pecked a small kiss on her forehead. "Let's sit in my sumptuously furnished living room. I'll grab the tray and some paper napkins."

Sandy laughed when she crossed the narrow hallway and stepped into Joe's living room. The only furniture he had was a bright red sofa facing a giant, man-sized TV. Three empty plastic crates turned upside down, covered with an unpainted door, served as a coffee table. "Gee, I don't know if I can stand all this luxury. You must be loaded." She grinned over her shoulder and set the glasses on the door then sank into the couch cushions.

"Yeah, I don't like to look too flashy. Sends the wrong message to the dozens of women I bring here." He put the tray holding the bread and cheese plate, two small knives and a stack of paper napkins between the glasses of tea. He gestured to the plate. "Ladies first."

Sandy opened a paper napkin on her knee and placed a piece of bread there. She loaded one of the knives with cheese and spread it on the bread. "Your turn, unless you're waiting to see if I've poisoned it." She grinned and took a bite.

Joe sat back and sipped iced tea and watched her eat the bread. Every move of her lips fascinated him. An image of watching her mouth as she ate dinner with him, and Liz at the Latin club returned. She'd fascinated him that night with her laughter and quick wit between bites of food she'd clearly enjoyed. He remembered the feel of his lips on hers at the conclusion of the tango. She'd lost none of her appeal. If he didn't quit thinking like a love starved teenager, how was he to be objective when she revealed what she'd come to tell him?

"Okay, since you're still breathing, I'll try some." He helped himself, groaned with pleasure at the burst of flavor on his tongue and closed his eyes. "God, this is good. I'll have to remember the brand so I can find it again."

Sandy prepared another piece. She handed it to him and fixed another for herself. "Liz turned me on to this. She brought it to an office retirement party a while back. Trader Joe is probably selling a lot of it to our staff members. It is good, isn't it?"

Joe nodded and enjoyed his second piece. He sat back against the sofa cushions again. "Tell me what you told Liz, Sandy. Whatever it is, we can still enjoy dinner and a friendly evening together. We're adults here."

Chapter Eight

Sandy took a swallow of tea and looked around the room. "You don't have any books or music?" She needed a minute.

"Packed in boxes, in my bedroom. I don't have any shelves to put them on yet."

"How long have you lived here?"

"Six months. You're stalling."

She set the glass down. "You're right. It was hard enough to tell Liz. It's even harder with you."

"What's the worst that can happen?"

"I don't want to think about that." *No more stalling.* "Here goes."

She crossed her arms and tucked her feet up on the couch under her skirt and told him the dismal story. Joe's handsome face was unreadable. He listened intently and nodded when she looked into his deep blue eyes, encouraging her to continue, but made no comment. Putting a napkin to her eyes, she dabbed away annoying and frustrating tears. She would not hold anything back if they had any chance to have a relationship, she had to bare all. Every last detail. She took a deep breath and waited.

Unable to stand his silence any longer she asked, "So what do you think?"

"Come here." Joe held out his hand. Her fingers in his, he pulled her close. "You were dealt a lousy hand and probably could have handled it better, but I didn't live it. You did."

Sandy drew in a deep breath and leaned into his side. His strong, warm side. Drawing strength and comfort from him, she began to feel the slightest inkling of hope.

Joe gave her another squeeze and rose. "I'm going to put the potatoes in the oven. We can talk more while they're cooking." He picked up her empty glass. "I'll give you a refill."

She followed him to the kitchen with his glass. "I'll fill the glasses while you put those in to bake."

"You got it." He checked the temperature of the oven, placed the pan on the middle shelf and set the timer.

She got a glimpse of what it might be like for the two of them to bustle around in this small space night after night. His small apartment already felt more like home than the house she shared with Phil. This was a place she'd look forward to coming to every evening after work, not dreading it and looking for excuses to stay away.

Joe's movements were sure and efficient. He was comfortable in his body, in his space.

"I'll take these glasses back to the living room."

"I'll be done here in a minute." There was no tone of dismissal in his voice. It was merely a statement of fact.

Sandy felt lighter for unburdening herself to Joe, but she couldn't get a read on where to go from here in the conversation. To keep her hands busy, she spread cheese on another slice of bread and nibbled at it.

Joe sat next to her and did the same thing. He leaned back and gave her a penetrating look. "So, what's your plan moving forward?"

She cleared her throat. "I...um...I'm going to take Liz's advice and go to the physical therapist and speak to him. I'll have him give me his best guess on Phil's prognosis and ask him what resources are available to him when I move him out of my house."

"Sounds like a good plan." He put the entire piece of bread and cheese in his mouth and chewed silently. "What else?" He wasn't letting her off the hook.

"After Liz's reaction in the bar the night we met, I regretted the cheap way I'd used those poor guys from the websites who took me out to dinner. I did lead them to believe I might be available for... um...you know. That's not who I am, Joe."

Her hand shook when she lifted the tea glass. She took a sip and set it down. "I'll track down every one of them and apologize. God! I still can't believe I did that."

"I don't think that's necessary. They might get the idea you'd go out with them again. It's time to put it behind you." He squeezed her hand. "Please don't give Liz any of those dating site recommendations. I have a couple of good men she's agreed to let me introduce to her."

"She already told me she wasn't interested in going that way. I had second thoughts about it later, anyway." She sighed. "Liz will do what she wants without help from either of us."

He grinned. "Yes, she will."

"Joe, please tell me what you think of me after I told you my story."

"I'm in no position to judge, but it's what we all do, isn't it?" He leaned forward with his elbows on his knees. She couldn't take her eyes from his beautifully muscled forearms and long tapered fingers. He was perfect, and she'd probably lost any chance she'd had with him.

"Here's what I think." He surprised her when he turned and dragged her onto his lap. "I'm very attracted to a complex woman who's had a rough time of it and is looking for a decent way out." He stroked her cheek. "I want to kiss you again. I want a lot more, but the timer just went off." He gave her a squeeze and slid her off his lap. "Let's eat. You can take the salad out of the refrigerator and toss it. I have three or four different kinds of dressing. Pick the one you like best."

The small kitchen was filled with the delicious aroma of bacon and cheese when Joe opened the oven door and slid the baking pan out. "Perfect." He set the hot tray on the stove top and removed the potatoes with a spatula onto a serving plate. "You're gonna love these, gorgeous. I guarantee it."

Sandy snickered. "Pretty sure of yourself, aren't you, Marine?"

"Look at it this way. If I'm not sure of myself, why would anybody else be?" He set the plate on the table next to the salad. "Let's eat."

They avoided discussion of Sandy's predicament during dinner, opting for small talk about their jobs and their favorite activities and music. At the conclusion of the meal, Sandy reached for their plates. "I'll load the dishwasher."

"I won't argue." He pushed his chair back. "While you clear the table, I'll search through the music channels on the TV and see if we can find something we both like to listen to while we continue our conversation."

It only took Sandy about five minutes to load the dishwasher. She returned to the living room in time to hear the beginning of Patsy Cline's *Crazy*, which pretty much defined her life. "That's one of my favorite songs," she remarked as she took her seat. "What channel is this?"

"Vintage Country Western. I'm glad we both like it." He patted the spot next to him. "Move closer."

She slid across the couch and he put his feet up on the makeshift coffee table. Joe dropped a long arm around her shoulders. "This is nice, Joe." She let her hand rest on top of his hard thigh. "I hope you and I can move forward. That's important to me."

"I want that too and I'd like to kiss you." He pulled her closer and dropped his head. "Okay?"

"More than okay." She held his deep blue gaze, and then let her eyes close. She placed her hand on his cheek and savored the rough, end-of-the-day stubble growing there. When his mouth came down on hers she held her breath and drank in every sensation. Even though she'd thought herself in love with Phil all those years ago, she couldn't recall ever feeling a kiss that warmed her in every crevice and muscle of her body. An involuntary moan escaped her lips, and his groan followed an instant later.

Joe pulled back and gasped. "I told myself to take this slow. It's difficult, but we have to take it slow." His warm hand brushed up and down her back in contradiction to his words. The muscles of his jaw jumped beneath her fingers.

Words refused to form in her mouth or her mind. One kiss and she was on fire. He kissed her again and a small whimper escaped her lips as he went deeper. Finally, he pulled back, and she was still too stunned to speak.

"God Almighty, this is killing me. You should go, but I want you to stay." This woman was touching him so deep, so fast, he could barely breathe. He was at war with himself. After what Rita had done, he swore he'd never rush into a relationship again. But all he could think of was the way her hand felt that very moment, on his chest, her fingers twisting the fabric of his shirt, her warm breath on his neck. Was he going to spend the rest of his life being overly cautious? Afraid to take the risk of loving again?

"Ah, to hell with it." He clutched her to his chest and kissed her in a way that said he meant business. If she pulled away, or resisted in the slightest, he'd back off. She didn't.

Sandy took a breath and dived into his next kiss. She fell back and Joe followed her lead. Looking up into his face, she said, "Joe. This is crazy, it's not why I came here tonight, but, oh, God, I want you to make love to me. Send me home. Tell me to leave."

"Don't leave." He brushed hair back from her face. "Let's just stay like this for a minute. Think—we need to think. All I can do right now is feel."

"What's happening, Joe? Help me. I don't know what to do."

Her beautiful face pleaded with him. She lay on her back, one leg hooked around his on the too small sofa. "I know what's happening and so do you, Sandy. But we're not kids. We need to stop, to give this more time. It's the last thing I want to do, believe me." He pushed himself up and stood before her, the evidence of his arousal unmistakable. He took her hand and pulled her to her feet. She looked good enough to eat. Hair mussed, clothes rumpled, lips swollen from his kisses.

She straightened her blouse and pushed hair back from her face. "Thank God one of us still has a few functioning brain cells." She looked around. "Where's the bathroom?"

Joe gathered her in his arms and kissed her forehead. "In the bedroom. I'll stay here. I'd better stay here."

"Yes." She grabbed her purse off the floor in the hall and disappeared into his bedroom.

Joe raked his hands through his hair and walked in a tight circle. "Too close, that was too close," he muttered, "much too close."

She took a while. He turned off the music and went to the kitchen and took a long drink of cold water and waited. When she returned her hair was combed and her clothes straightened. She'd applied fresh lipstick on her luscious mouth. He was so tempted to kiss her again.

"Walk me to my car, Joe." She reached in her purse and took out her keys.

They left the building in silence. When they reached her shiny red Honda, she pushed the remote unlock button. Joe held the door open for her, leaned close and kissed her with a feather-light kiss. "Goodnight, sweetheart."

"Goodnight, Joe." She smiled. "Buy a bed."

"First thing Saturday morning." A hand on her neck, his thumb caressed her ear. "When can I see you again?"

"Let's play it safe. Call me in a few days and we'll plan dinner out and a movie."

"You got it." He was about to close the door, then remembered. "Thanks for the flowers."

"Buy a vase." She fastened her seatbelt. "Goodnight, Joe."

He stood on the sidewalk for a long time after her car disappeared down the street. It was still early. The drugstore was open and there were a few customers inside. Joe wandered in, went to the magazine rack and picked up the latest copies of Wired and Connected World. He headed for the cash register to pay then whirled around and went to the pharmacy section and picked up a box of condoms. At the checkout counter, he threw a big chocolate bar on the magazines. That's when he remembered the cheesecake they'd never gotten to and put the candy back.

He knew where this *thing* with Sandy was headed and he knew where he wanted it to go. He'd plan, he'd prepare, and he wouldn't let his libido get ahead of his brain. Not like it nearly had tonight.

The young clerk grinned when he rang up Joe's purchases. He picked up the condoms, pretending to look for the bar code. "You planning to get lucky, Joe?" He wiggled his eyebrows at the tech magazines. "Or just catching up on your porn reading?"

Joe pulled out his wallet. "Anyone ever tell you, you're a real smartass, Seth?"

"All the time." He held up the condoms. "You want a plain brown bag for these?"

"One of these days, kid." Joe grabbed the magazines and the box and left the store. He chuckled as he strolled back to his building. He played handball with Seth from time to time. The kid was good and gave him a real workout. He'd only been in the area six months but already recognized most of the faces in the neighborhood. Back inside, he dropped the box and magazines on the kitchen table, cut half of the small cheesecake and plopped it on a plate. He carried it to the living room and turned on the TV. The last few holes were finishing up in the qualifying round of the LPGA golf tournament in Orlando. A minute passed and he switched channels. He didn't want to watch any women doing anything. Maybe he'd get lucky and find an old Rocky movie or some classic Clint Eastwood on the movie channel. It was worth a shot. Anything to get his mind off Sandra Cassidy.

That search proved worthless so he turned off the TV and went to the kitchen to grab the magazines, purposely not looking at the box of condoms. After flipping through pages while eating the cake and not finding an article he felt like concentrating on, he gave up and went to the twenty-four-hour gym three blocks down the street to sweat off some frustration. He needed to get his head straight. Get his brain in front of his dick. There was too much he didn't know about her yet.

———

The house was dark when Sandy got home. It wasn't like Phil to go to bed this early, and he always left the porch light on until she returned. She pulled into the garage, parked and sat for several seconds before going inside. She flipped on the kitchen lights. Dirty dinner plates cluttered the table and several empty beer bottles littered the sink. It wasn't Phil's poker night, so what was up with the mess?

She walked through the house turning on lights as she went. Phil's bedroom door was open, and his bed hadn't been slept in. "Phil?" She nearly jumped out of her shoes when his answer came from *her* bedroom.

"Yeah? Whaddya want?" He was drunk and he was in her room.

Voices? Feet hitting the floor. Scrambling around? Who's in there with him?

"What are you doing in my bedroom?" Sandy threw open the

door. Phil reclined across her bed, and a blowsy looking woman was in the far corner dragging on her clothes. "What the hell is going on here, Phil!" She pointed at the woman who looked like she'd had a bucket of cold water thrown in her face.

Phil slurred, "What's it look like?" He pointed to the woman who was searching for a way to get out of the room without bumping into Sandy. "This is my ex-wife, Sandy. Sandy, this Jerri. Where you going, honey? No reason to run off."

Sandy recognized the woman as one of the barflies who hung around the place she'd picked Phil up on the night of the accident. She stepped inside the doorway and pointed. "Get out of my house, Jerri, or whatever your name is. Don't ever come back here." The woman ran past her and pounded out the front door.

"Get out of my room, Phil! This is the last straw."

"What are you bitchin' about? You're never here. I got a right to a life, too, you know."

"Yes, you do, but it's time you found someplace else to live it. Now move!"

"I can't make it out by myself. You'll have to help me."

"Where's your walker?" The last thing she wanted to do was touch him.

"How the hell should I know? Come and help me." He struggled to a sitting position, totally naked and surprisingly fit. She stared at his oddly small feet wondering what she'd ever seen in him.

She stared, disgusted. "You got in here."

"Lila helped me."

"You said her name was Jerri."

"Lila, Jerri, what's the difference. She's just a worn-down whore."

Sandy shook her head, her lip curled. "And you're just a lying bastard. You'll have to figure a way to get out by yourself. I don't care if you have to crawl."

He raised a fist and yelled, "You heartless bitch. It's your fault I'm like this!"

"That won't work anymore, Phil." She turned on her heel and went back out to the garage, got in her car and drove. And drove. As her rage lessened, she took stock of the situation. There was no way she would go back there tonight. She remembered a Ramada Inn a few miles down the road and headed for it.

I'll figure out what to do tomorrow.

At eight the next morning, she called in sick, dressed in the same clothes she'd worn to Joe's, and walked to the coffee shop next door to the hotel. She'd go to Kohl's department store down the street, buy something fresh to wear and go to the physical therapy location where she dropped off The Philanderer for his bi-weekly appointments. There had to be a way out for her, and she was determined to find it.

Shortly after ten-thirty Sandy pushed open the double glass door at the rehab center and asked to speak to Phil Rice's therapist.

"He's finishing up with a client. If you'll have a seat, I'll tell Zack you're here. May I give him your name?"

"Sandra Cassidy. I'm Phil's ex-wife. I just need a moment of his time."

The young man smiled and walked through the swinging doors into the treatment rooms. In a minute or so he returned. "He'll be about ten minutes. May I get you some coffee or a bottle of water?"

"Water would be welcome, thanks."

She picked up a copy of Men's Fitness from a small table and leafed through the pages. The magazine featured a photo array of military veterans with various amputations. They all looked like male cover models, proudly showing the results of physical therapy and weight training on their bodies. Some had numerous tattoos, some none. She winced at the thought Joe could have been one of these men. He'd been wounded while on deployments, but not seriously enough to prevent him from returning to the battlefield.

Sandy was overcome with gratitude for these beautiful young men who'd given so much through their service to the country. Men like Joe. Men who wouldn't hesitate to put their lives on the line to protect what they loved.

A muscular, gray haired man entered the waiting room. "Ms. Cassidy? How nice to meet you. How is Phil doing?"

Blindsided by his question she hesitated, and then said, "That's what I came to ask you. How much longer will his therapy last? I'd also like to talk to you about what social services and resources he might take advantage of, to help him get out on his own."

He held out a gnarled hand, "I'm Zack Graham." He shook her hand and cocked his head, "Are we talking about Phil Rice?"

"Yes. He was injured in an auto accident three years ago. I'd like some kind of estimate from you on how much longer he'll need therapy."

Zack jammed his hands in his pockets. "We should step inside where we have more privacy. Will you follow me to our conference room? We can talk in there."

Puzzled by his hesitancy, and especially his question to clarify they were speaking about the same patient, Sandy rose and followed him. They walked down a short hallway. He stopped in front of an open door to a rather small meeting room and gestured for her to enter ahead of him.

He closed the door. "I admit I'm puzzled by your questions, Ms. Cassidy."

"Why? Is it something you can't discuss with me without Phil's prior approval?"

"No, I'm puzzled because I discharged Phil about seven months ago. He'd made a remarkable recovery. There was no need for continued therapy. I gave him instructions for exercises and stretches he can do on his own to maintain his level of fitness."

"I don't understand. He still uses a walker."

"I can't imagine why. He hadn't been using one for months when he was discharged."

She frowned. This made no sense. "I drop him off here twice a week."

"This is troubling. He hasn't been in for therapy for months. Perhaps he needs to be reevaluated. Would you like to make an appointment for me to do a new assessment?"

Slowly Sandy comprehended the extent of Phil's deception. "May I sit for a minute?"

"Certainly." Zack pulled out a chair for her. "Are you feeling all right?"

"I don't believe this. How could he do this?"

"What's going on, Ms. Cassidy?"

"Phil's been lying to me for the better part of a year. All this time he's hobbled around with a walker and blamed me for his injuries. We were divorced before the accident. He talked me into letting him live in my house—convinced me he had no alternative because his disabilities were my fault. I feel utterly violated." Tears came unbidden, tears of frustration and a deep sense of betrayal.

Zack dispensed cold water into a paper cup and carried it to her. "Take a breath and drink some of this." He grabbed a chair, moved it in front of her, and then sat facing her. "We'll get to the bottom of this."

Sandy nodded numbly and drank some of the water. Dozens of questions competed in her mind, but she couldn't think straight enough to ask one.

"Take your time. I don't have any other clients coming in this morning. I'm just going to step out for a minute to make sure this room isn't slated for a meeting in the next hour. I don't want us to be interrupted." He scooted back the chair and walked out, leaving the door open.

These hideous, stressful months!

The depth of Phil's deceit was nearly impossible to come to grips with. The man was a chameleon. Fixing her breakfast in the morning, and then manipulating her emotions in the evening. Questioning her relentlessly about where she'd been and what she'd been doing. Piling on the guilt. There were terms for that—*Sociopath, narcissist.*

Zack returned and sat in front of her. He'd left the door open. The main therapy room was quiet. One man was working with a patient, and it appeared as though they were about to finish. "We'll have as long as you want to discuss this, Ms. Cassidy. I'll help you in any way I can."

"Thank you, Zack. You've been a big help already."

They spoke for nearly an hour. The last question he asked her was, "Is he still collecting disability checks?"

"I don't know. He brings in the mail and handles his own bank account. Why?"

"Part of the process of discharge from treatment is to give the patient paperwork and instructions on how to notify the benefits provider, whether it's the state or an insurance company, that they are no longer eligible to receive payments. They're ready to reenter the workforce. The only benefit due them after discontinuance of therapy is unemployment for a defined period of time."

"He can work? All I want is to get him out of my house and out of my life. The last few years have been a nightmare." She dug through her purse, found a tissue, and blew her nose. "Sorry."

"No need to apologize, Ms. Cassidy. I hope I've been of some help to you."

She thanked him again and took her leave.

Where do I go from here?

Chapter Nine

JOE'S CELL PHONE CHIMED AS HE WAS LEAVING HIS OFFICE THE next day. Caller I.D. identified Liz. "Hey, sis. What's up?"

"Sandy had dinner at your apartment last night, right?"

"And that's your business because?" Was there no end to her meddling?

"Oh, stuff it! I'm worried about her, Joey. She called in sick today and I haven't been able to reach her on her cell phone or her home phone. I'm going to her house and make sure she's all right."

Cold dread filled him. "No, wait! I'll go with you. I'm just leaving work. Where are you?"

"I'm still at my office. You can pick me up here."

"It'll take me about forty minutes to get there."

"Sounds good. I'm glad you're coming with me, Joey. I wasn't sure going there and running into that creep of an ex-husband of hers was a good idea. Call me when you're close and I'll wait in front of the building."

"I'm on my way." He retrieved his car and headed across town to Liz's workplace. Sandy seemed fine when she left him last night. Rattled, sure, they both were, so something must have happened. Liz said Sandy had never missed a day of work as far as she knew. She'd laughed and said that besides being beautiful and smart, Sandy was disgustingly healthy.

His left knee bounced incessantly. The 210 was bumper to bumper. Joe checked his watch, but not as much time had passed as he'd thought. As soon as he saw his off ramp, he got into the exit lane. He'd have to take surface streets for a couple of miles. He was glad his sister had called him from work and not from her home. It would have taken a lot longer. His concern for Sandy grew with every mile. Her ex-husband must have had something to do with her absence from work. Why wasn't she answering her phones?

"I'm a block away from your building, Liz." Joe waited for a traffic light to change.

"I'm out front and ready to go, Joey."

Joe slowed when he approached her building. She was chatting with a scruffy looking guy. They shared a laugh then she waved goodbye to him and opened the passenger door of the car and got in.

"Who in heck is that bozo? He looks homeless."

"He is homeless. He's here every day, and in spite of his looks he's a good man. I share a cup of coffee with him every now and then."

"Not good judgment, sis."

"And you would know that how? He's a veteran of Afghanistan. His wife left him while the Army had him deployed. Sound familiar?" She poked him in the shoulder. "The difference is he hasn't seen his two kids in over ten years. She told them he was dead. He can't get over it. He's a friend of mine, Joey."

Feeling remorse for his snap judgment of the man, Joe had a *There-but-for-the-grace-of- God* moment. "All right, I accept that. Maybe I'll join you and him for coffee one day."

"There's the big brother I love." She fished a piece of paper from her pocket. "I'll program Sandy's address into your GPS. I don't think it's far. She told me once it only took her half an hour to get to work during peak traffic." She tapped the address in then sat back in her seat.

"I hope to God she's all right, and I didn't poison her last night." He racked his brain for anything in the food that could have caused her to get sick.

"I have a feeling it's something personal. It really bothers me that she's not answering either of her phones. I left voice messages on both numbers. Several."

They rode in silence. Joe became aware that she was staring at him. "What? Do I have dried shaving cream in my ear?"

"You're a good brother, Joey."

"Now you're scaring me."

They exchanged a brief glance and burst into laughter, easing the tension and worry over Sandy.

The GPS indicated they were less than a mile from her address. Joe turned into an old, tree lined neighborhood of California ranch-style houses set back on wide lots. He drove another few blocks and turned again. Sandy's house was in the middle of the block. He pulled to a stop at the curb. "What the hell?"

The front porch of the house was a jumble of boxes, bags. Heaps of clothing were strewn across the boxes and in the grass. A man's loud voice broke the silence. "You bitch! What do you think you're doing?"

Joe bolted out of the car and ran toward the scattered piles of books, clothes and boxes. He yanked open the screen door. "Sandy? You all right, honey?"

"Honey?" A large man with his face twisted in anger sneered at Joe and took an aggressive stance, blocking his way into the house. "You referring to the whore I used to be married to?"

Joe clenched his teeth and fisted his hands. He was this close to putting the guy on his ass, when Liz came in.

"I'm here to see Sandy." She shoved Phil in the chest and pushed past him into the house. "Sandy? It's Liz. Joey and I came to make sure you're all right. Sandy?"

"I'm in the kitchen, Liz. Keep going straight." A choking sob followed the statement.

Joe ran past his sister into the kitchen, where he found Sandy sitting on the floor in the corner of the kitchen. She had an angry red handprint on her cheek. Her face crumpled when he knelt beside her. "Did he do this to you?' He crushed her against his chest, and she sobbed against his neck. "I'll kill that bastard!"

"No, Joe, the police are on the way." She held up her hand, her iPhone clutched in her fist. "I never thought he'd react this way." She clung tight to him and sobbed again when Liz knelt next to her.

"I thought so!" Phil barged into the room. "You've been screwing this guy all along, and from the looks of it, he has a clueless wife." He gave Liz a sneering once-over.

Joe pushed Sandy into Liz's arms and leaped to his feet. Phil took a step back but not fast enough to keep Joe from grabbing him by the shirt collar and slamming him against the doorframe.

Two uniformed LAPD officers burst through the front door, guns drawn. "Everybody stay where you are. Check the living room, Mac. Is there anybody else in the house? Any kids?"

Sandy struggled to her feet. "No. I called you. My friends came to help me." She pointed at Phil. "He threatened me."

The officer looked her over. "Looks like he did more than threaten you, ma'am."

The second uniform, Mac, entered the room. "The house is clear."

The policeman with Sandy pointed to Phil. "Cuff him."

"Turn around. Hands behind your back. I advise you to keep your trap shut. Everything is being recorded." Phil was cuffed and transferred to another black and white arriving on the scene. The officer in the kitchen took Sandy's statement. Mac, asked Liz and Joe to step into the living room and give their statements.

An hour later, Sandy, Liz and Joe were alone in the house. Sandy sat close to Joe on the sofa while Liz busied herself in the kitchen filling glasses with ice water, and then carried one to Sandy along with a bag of frozen corn. "Put this on your bruise. Joe and I will take you to the ER when you've had a chance to take a breath." She returned for the other two glasses and handed one to Joe before taking her seat in a chair across them.

They sipped water in silence. Joe put his arm around Sandy and pulled her close. His hand drifted to her head where he found a good-sized lump. "What happened here?" He set his glass down and turned her so he could get a look at her head. Gently parting her hair, he saw the purple knot. "You're hurt, sweetheart." He stood and pulled her to her feet. "Let's get this checked out. Liz, you drive."

On the way to the local hospital, Joe sat in the back seat with Sandy, her head drifting to his lap. "Don't fall asleep, honey. We'll be there in a couple of minutes. You might have a concussion." The words hadn't left his lips when Sandy lurched forward and vomited on the floor of his car. For a man who'd made it clear he didn't want drama in his life, he'd stepped in a massive dose of it today. He heard Liz gag involuntarily.

Sandy retched over and over. Gasping an apology, she cried, "Joe, your car, I'm sorry."

"Don't worry about my car. We're here, let me help you out." He opened the door and stepped out. Sandy reached for his hand, but he lifted her in his arms and carried her through the double doors of the emergency entrance. Liz pulled away and looked for a parking space.

An attendant rushed forward with a wheelchair, and Joe placed Sandy in it. "She has a head injury."

"I'll take her in to the doctor. You can wait out here. Take care of her information with the admitting clerk if you have what they need."

Just then, Sandy fell forward, and Joe grabbed her before she pitched onto the floor. "I'm coming with her. My sister will talk to the clerk." The man nodded and pushed her into the first examining room.

The attending physician entered seconds later. "What do we have here?"

"Her ex-husband belted her. She hit her head."

The doctor cast Joe a suspicious look. They'd probably heard every story in the book when battered wives showed up in emergency rooms.

"Don't give me that look. The cops arrested him!" Joe raised his hands and dragged them through his hair. "I brought her here. She almost passed out on the way."

"Sorry, we've seen everything in here, Mr....?"

"Hamilton. I get it. I'm going out to wait with my sister. Please keep us informed." He whirled around, and then stalked back and kissed Sandy on the forehead. "I'll be right outside."

"What happened?" Liz turned to him when he reached the desk.

"The medic gave me *the look*."

"The look?"

"Yeah, the one that says: you did this, you creep. I was ready to deck him."

Liz pulled him down into the plastic chair and sat next to him.

"Take it easy, Joey. They're suspicious because of what they see in here."

"It still pisses me off." He balled his fists on his knees, wanting to hit something.

"Sandy will be fine. We got there before her ex could do anything worse." She rubbed his hand. "You've got it bad, big brother."

He snorted. "Tell me about it."

She sighed. "I do have some good news. Sandy threw up on the floor mat. I pulled it out very gingerly and threw it away. The back seat and floor are clean."

"Thanks, sis. I'd have spent a fortune having the car detailed and they still wouldn't have been able to get rid of the smell. Remember the time Dad had to sell the family car because you got carsick when we were on vacation?" He held his nose and gave her a cross-eyed grimace.

"You're never going to let me off the hook on that one, are you?"

"Nope." He got to his feet. "Here's the doc."

"Ms. Cassidy has a mild concussion. I advised her to stay the night, but she's very adamant about leaving. She shouldn't be alone for the next several hours."

Liz stepped forward. "Liz Hamilton, doctor. Sandy and I are co-workers. I'll take her home with me. We don't want her to go back to her place alone."

"Or, she could come to my place," Joe added. "We'll let her decide. When can she check out?"

It would probably be best if she went with Liz, but Joe was anxious to make sure she was all right. The truth was, he didn't want her out of his sight until he knew what the cops had done with Phil Rice.

"We're just waiting for the neurologist to read the CT scan and we'll have the blood work back any minute now." He nodded and returned to the examining room where they'd taken Sandy.

"Joey, why don't you and Sandy both stay at my place tonight? I've got a spare room and you can sleep on the couch."

"Sounds fine with me, sis, but it's up to her." Joe walked back to the reception desk to make sure there'd be no paperwork snafu when they were ready to leave. His stomach complained from lack of food, or stress. He wasn't sure which. He stretched and rubbed his side. The old bullet wound acted up when he was mentally tense.

"Joe?"

He saw Sandy in a wheelchair being pushed by the same attendant who'd met them at the door a couple of hours ago. He rushed to her side. "You okay, honey?"

She nodded; her eyes seemed oversized in her pale face. "I have a super-duper headache, but the doctor says I'll live." She blushed. "How embarrassing, huh?"

Joe squeezed her arm. "None of that."

Liz met them halfway to the door. "You're coming home with me, Sandy. No arguments. We've got all weekend to sort this out. I asked Joey to come, too."

"I'll need some clothes. All I have is what I'm wearing and my purse."

"I'm sure I have plenty of things that'll fit you. Tomorrow's Saturday. If you want to pick up some of your clothes over the weekend, Joey will drive us over to your place."

Sandy swiped away a tear and blinked. She put her hand over her mouth and shook her head. "Thanks," passed her lips, barely audible.

"We're friends. You'd do the same for me, so it's no big deal."

Joe drove straight to Liz's apartment. They'd retrieve her car sometime before Monday, but there was no reason to do it tonight. He saw the women inside then said, "I'll make a quick run over to the German deli and pick up something for dinner. Any special requests?"

———

Sandy sat across the table from Liz. Joe had brought a delicious roast brisket with red sauerkraut and potato salad. She hadn't realized how hungry she was until he walked in the door and the delicious aroma filled the apartment.

Liz had set her up in the spare bedroom and given her a nice running outfit, pants and sweatshirt in bright green and yellow. After her shower, Sandy blew her hair dry with little concern about styling and didn't apply any makeup except lip gloss. She stepped out of the room and nearly bumped into Joe, who'd apparently been waiting for her.

He touched the bruise on her cheek. "My, God, you are beautiful. Your hair—I love it like that." He leaned forward and placed a soft kiss on her lips. "Mmm, you taste good too."

"Careful, you'll turn my head, and may even put Clinique out of business when I stop buying all their expensive beauty products." She grinned. "I'm starved."

"Me too." He took her hand, and they strolled to the kitchen.

A purr of heat warmed her all the way to her toes. Head pounding, she was still full of anxiety, so why was she thinking how much she wished she could fall asleep tonight in Joe's strong arms?

During dinner, Sandy began to nod. "Gosh, I'm so sleepy all of a sudden."

Liz got up and reached for her. "Let's get you to bed. Joe and I'll check on you every now and then to make sure you're all right." Liz led her back to the guest bedroom, got her settled and left the door open a crack.

Sandy drifted off but woke later to see Joe sleeping on the floor next to her bed. "Joe?"

He was instantly awake. "You all right, sweetheart?" He came to the side of the bed and sat next to her. "You need anything?" He smoothed the duvet and pulled it closer to her chin. "Cold?"

"I should call Damon."

"Damon?" An odd look flashed briefly in his clear eyes.

"My big brother. I told him I was throwing Phil out. He'll be worried if I don't call him. What time is it?"

"It's after eleven. Will he still be up?"

"He's a night owl. Can I borrow your cell phone? I must have left mine home because it's not in my purse."

"Sure." Joe grabbed his phone from a small pile of his belongings next to the air mattress he'd been sleeping on. "Do you remember his number? I'll dial it for you."

She squeezed her eyes shut in concentration. "It's...uh...I don't remember, but I have it in my wallet." Any other day she could have rattled off Damon's number with no hesitation. It upset her not to remember it now.

Joe handed her the small purse. "Do you want me to open it and get your wallet for you?"

She couldn't help herself, she smiled. "Joe, you're so considerate. Yes. Open it. But first kiss me, unless I look too hideous for words." She stroked his cheek.

He lowered his head and gave her a soft kiss on the lips. "You're stunning." His warm smile made her sigh with contentment.

"Careful. You'll make me fall in love with you. Must be my head injury speaking."

"There's nothing wrong with *my* head. I'm already there." He threaded his fingers through her hair and lifted it away from her forehead, and then kissed her bruised cheek. After a long, penetrating look into her eyes, he opened her purse and found her wallet.

"Thank you." She took a small laminated card with half a dozen numbers on it and handed it to him.

He identified Damon's number and tapped it on the screen. "It's ringing." He handed the phone to her.

It rang several times and went to voicemail. "Damon?" She glanced at Joe and grimaced. "Damon? Pick up if you're there. It's Sandy." She was about to disconnect when he answered. "I'm all right! No, really, Damon, I am. It's a friend's phone." She nodded. "The brother of a co-worker. I'm at her house for the night." She saw Joe watching her intently and put a hand on his arm. "You're what? Why? But—." She handed the phone to Joe. "He wants to talk to you."

"Hello." He pinched the bridge of his nose. "Joe Hamilton. We're at my sister's house in L.A." His eyebrows went up. "You're halfway here?"

The bedroom door opened. Liz peeked in. "Is everything good? I heard you talking."

Joe motioned her in. "Yes, my sister. Her name? Elizabeth Hamilton." He grinned, shook his head and handed the phone to his sister. "He wants to talk to you."

"Who wants to talk to me?" Liz asked.

"My brother, Damon. He's on his way to L.A. He was worried because I didn't call him like I promised." She sighed and pushed herself into a sitting position. "Sorry."

"Hello, Damon. Sure, it's..." Liz recited her address. "Sandy is staying here because my brother and I wouldn't take her back to her place tonight." She sighed and rolled her eyes. "Phil, he, um, he was arrested right after Joe and I got there. Yes, here she is." She handed the phone back to Sandy. "Boy, he's really fuming. He wants to talk to you."

Chapter Ten

Sandy shook her head and sighed. "They're both coming. Damon *and* Greg."

Joe took his phone and chuckled. "Both your brothers? Sounds like Phil might be in trouble." He could handle Phil by himself, but it never hurt to have somebody watching your six.

"I should probably tell you. Greg is gay."

"So what?" Joe had never felt threatened by gay men. There were plenty of them in the Marines. Some of the fiercest fighters he'd served with were gay. No big deal.

"Well, mostly I wanted to warn you, Liz. Greg is beyond handsome, he's gorgeous. I thought you should know he's, you know, not available. I'm trying to save you from getting a broken heart." Sandy's grin was full of the devil. Joe could tell she was definitely on the mend.

Liz cocked her head and smiled mischievously. "It will be nice to have a man in my apartment who isn't sprinkling his conversation with what he assumes are clever sexual innuendoes. There's nothing more boring. I can't wait to meet both of them. Am I safe from Damon?"

"Can't promise anything, but I think he's in a pretty serious relationship."

"Good, I won't be the *other* woman."

Joe crossed his arms and tsk-tsked. "Is this how women abuse us behind our backs? I'm shocked."

Sandy pointed a finger at his nose. "We don't want to know how you guys talk about us when we're not around."

"Beat it, Liz. Enough fun and games. Sandy needs to sleep. I'm on the job."

"See you at breakfast." Liz smiled and left them alone.

Sandy slid down and sighed. Joe rearranged her blankets and turned off the small lamp.

"Joe? Would you sleep up here with me?" Her voice sounded unsure and childlike. Probably lingering anxiety from her nasty encounter with Phil.

"Sure, sweetheart." He climbed onto the bed and lay on his side next to her then slid his arm across her body. "I've got you."

"Will you be warm enough outside the covers?"

"Don't worry about me. If I get cold, I'll crawl under the duvet." He tucked a curl behind her ear. "Go to sleep now."

"Yes." Big sigh. "Night."

"Night." Joe got comfortable. Sandy turned on her side facing away from him. He snuggled tight against her. Yes, he was in the middle of drama on steroids. He'd watch his step. Think things through where this woman he cared for was concerned. No easy task.

———

Joe's eyes fluttered open as early light made its way slowly across the room. The door clicked open and Liz drew in a breath. "Oh!" she backed out, a horrified look on her face, hands crossed over her chest.

"Shhh." Joe gently lifted the duvet and slid off the bed. Liz saw his bare torso, but he was wearing the Dockers he'd worn to work yesterday for casual Friday. He grabbed his Henley shirt off the floor and motioned her out the door.

"Jeez, sis!" Joe hissed, "What's with that look? You think I'm some kind of pervert?"

Liz whispered, "What was I supposed to think, finding you in the bed with her."

"Correction: On the bed with her. Sandy asked me to sleep next to her. She was anxious."

Liz threw up her hands. "Look, I'm sorry. Are you sure it's all right to leave her alone? Did you check her?"

Joe pulled the shirt over his head and crossed the hall to the bathroom. "She's fine. I'll join you in the kitchen in a minute. Did you make coffee?"

"Yes, it's ready. How long should we let her sleep?"

"She'll wake up on her own, or when her brothers get here. Did they say what time to expect them?" He glanced at his watch.

————

Joe and Liz were draining their coffee cups when he heard a rap on the door. He went to open it. Two men who couldn't look more different stood in the hallway. Joe put a finger to his lips. "Come in, Sandy's sleeping." He put his hand out, "Joe Hamilton."

The big guy grabbed his in a strong grip. "Damon Cassidy, this is my brother, Greg."

Joe's eyes widened. "Greg, you and Sandy could be twins. Come in. My sister has a fresh pot of coffee brewing. Have you had breakfast?"

Damon stopped at the edge of the white carpeting. He toed off his boat shoes and carried them inside. Greg did the same. "We didn't stop to eat, but you don't have to feed us."

"Not a problem. I have the waffle iron heating. The guest bath is the first door on the right. There's another one in the back bedroom."

"Thanks." Damon nodded and both men went down the hall.

Joe returned to the kitchen. "They're here. I directed them to the bathrooms. Wait till you see Damon. He's a guy I'd never pick a fight with. Greg's a dead ringer for Sandy. He's a good-looking man. She wasn't kidding."

They spoke quietly at breakfast hoping to avoid waking Sandy. Joe and Liz alternated the narrative of yesterday's events. Sandy's brothers thanked them for looking after their sister.

"Greg and I never did like that crap-master. He was her choice, so we kept our mouths shut figuring she'd come to her senses sooner or later. She finally divorced him, but he found a way to keep her under his thumb. I hope she'll come home with us. Get away from here for a while."

Joe's heart sank. The thought of Sandy being so far away when they'd just discovered each other left a cold hole in the pit of his stomach. "Sandy has a life here, friends, and a good job. Maybe it would do her good to have a change of scene, but I hope she'll stay here."

"I'm not leaving you, Joe."

Their heads turned at the sound of Sandy's voice. She stood in the doorway, pale and disheveled, the bruise on her cheek an ugly purple and black against her flawless skin. Damon rose from the table and embraced her, he was so large she virtually disappeared in his arms. Greg joined them and shoved Damon back so he could hug his sister. The three of them stood huddled together.

Liz put a trembling hand over her lips and grabbed Joe's arm with the other. She sniffed and he handed her a paper napkin to catch the tears welling in her eyes. He nodded and brushed his fingers over her silky black hair. "Yeah."

Damon touched her cheek. "Jesus H. Suffering Christ! Did Phil do this to you, Muttface?"

"Yes, but I'm fine, Stinky. You know me. Can't keep me down." Her affectionate smile was wobbly and genuine. "You're the best brothers in the world for coming to rescue me."

Joe stood. "Come sit, sweetheart." I'll make a waffle for you, and, uh, maybe Stinky and Greg would like seconds now it's clear you're a survivor." Joe motioned them back to the table.

Damon smiled menacingly and pointed an accusing finger in Joe's direction. He wouldn't make the mistake of calling him Stinky again. He smiled back and shrugged, pulled out a chair for Sandy, leaned down, and kissed her. Damon, Greg and Liz exchanged glances, but he didn't give a damn if the entire world knew how he felt about her.

"I'll have another waffle too, Joey." Liz grinned. "Being surrounded by handsome men does wonders for my appetite. Especially if one of them is waiting on me."

Joe gave her a fake glare. "Don't get used to it."

"I'm hungry too, and I sure could use a cup of coffee." Sandy added with a sigh.

"Comin' right up." Joe took another mug from the cupboard, filled it and set it in front of her. He busied himself with the waffle iron and mixed another batch of batter.

———

Sandy sighed and rested her chin on her fist. "That hit the spot, Joe. You're hired." She turned to Damon. "Who's looking after Mom?" A twinge of guilt pricked her. She hadn't thought of their mother until this moment.

"Greg and I dropped her off at Uncle Orlie's place. We told her we got a last-minute invitation for a fishing trip. We didn't say anything else. You know she'd be frantic. She's frail and doesn't need the worry."

"You did the right thing, Damon. There's no reason to drag her into this soap opera." Sandy didn't want to be a cause of her mother's distress.

Greg turned to Joe. "When will we learn if Phil is still in custody? I think Sandy should press charges and swear out a restraining order after what he did."

Joe pressed his lips together and nodded. "You guys should catch some sleep. There's a Comfort Inn not too far from here. I'll do some checking with the cops and we can meet here again this afternoon. If Phil's not in custody, I'm not letting Sandy go back home unless she consents to me staying with her, or she can stay here with Liz until we know what's going on."

"Joe, that's not necessary, I—"

Damon cut her off. "Listen to the man. Greg and I can only stay until Monday morning. For our peace of mind, let Joe and his sister offer you a helping hand."

She raised her hands helplessly. "All right, I'm too tired to argue."

Liz came to her end of the table. "You need to lie down for a while, Sandy. Come on." She urged her to her feet and walked her back to the bedroom.

Sandy reclined on the comfortable bed and closed her eyes. "I should probably brush my teeth."

"Your teeth will survive one day of bad hygiene." Liz checked to make sure she had water in her glass and closed the blinds. "Joe or I will check on you in a while."

"Liz, I don't know how to thank you."

"Easy." Liz squeezed her hand. "Be very good to my big brother."

———

Joe went to the LAPD precinct closest to Sandy's neighborhood. He recognized the uniformed officer when he approached. "Officer, glad you're in. Ms. Cassidy's family drove down from Portland this morning. I told them I'd get an update on Phil Rice's status while they caught some shut-eye."

"Rice was released on his own recognizance, but we'll pick him up if Ms. Cassidy presses charges. It would wise if she did, and also obtained a restraining order."

Joe nodded. "Yes, her brothers want her to go for the order. They'll most likely bring her by this afternoon. Should they ask for you?"

"No, I'll be on patrol until late. Have them check with the desk sergeant when they get here. He'll know who they should speak to. Off the record, Hamilton—Cassidy shouldn't go back to her house unescorted. These situations have a way of going sideways. You understand?"

"Yes, officer, we've discussed that. Thanks for the update."

Joe left the police station, got in his car, but instead of going directly back to Liz's apartment he drove by Sandy's house. He parked at the curb and stayed in his car. The piles of boxes and clothing had disappeared. The front door stood open. There was no car in the driveway. He thought of calling the police, but he'd do a quick recon first. Cell phone in his hand he walked up the walk and stood at the open front door. "Hello? Anybody here?" He was greeted by silence.

Tapping Liz's number on his cell he put the phone to his ear and took one step back from the door. "Liz? Are Sandy's brothers there yet? No, that's OK, I'll call the motel. Everything all right on your end? Good. I'll be back in an hour or so." He clicked off, stood there for a minute then leaned on the porch railing. He called the Inn and asked to speak to Damon or Greg Cassidy.

Greg answered, groggy voiced, "Yeah?"

"Joe Hamilton here. Sorry if I woke you. I'm at Sandy's house. I think you and Damon should come here. Phil's belongings are gone from the porch and yard, but the front door is open. Nobody answers from inside. It's not a good idea for me to go in there by myself. Half an hour? I'll wait in my car."

Joe checked his wallet to make sure the patrol officer's card was there. He sat in the car and lowered the windows. It was a nice day in a nice neighborhood. Half an hour passed and no Damon and Greg. He was about to call again when he spotted Damon's gray Audi turn the corner. He stepped out of his Beemer and waved. They parked behind him.

Damon pointed. "I see the door is open. Shall we take a look?"

The three men proceeded up the front walk to the house. Damon entered first. "Oh, shit!"

Greg and Joe pushed in beside him. The house was trashed. Black spray paint streaked the walls and floor, furniture and light fixtures.

Joe's stomach clenched. He went down on his haunches and tested the paint on the floor. "It's dry. Come on; let's see what else has been done."

"Where's all the water coming from?" Greg asked when his shoes squished on the carpet. "I'll check the kitchen." He shouted a vile expletive and stepped rapidly to the sink. "Whoever did this plugged up the sink and left the water running."

Damon stood in the kitchen doorway, hands on hips. "Look, the jerk left all the appliance and cabinet doors open and sprayed black paint on everything he could see. Wait until I get my hands around that lying bastard's neck!"

Joe had the same reaction. "Me first." He backed into the hall and followed the path of destruction to Sandy's bedroom. If it were possible, even more of the surfaces here were vandalized. The closet slider was open. Even her clothes had been sprayed.

Greg followed him into the room. "Jesus God!" He indicated the vanity and dresser. All the contents had been dumped on the floor. Nothing had been spared. "How could anyone but a total nut job do this? Let's get the cops here."

Joe was already tapping the number. "Joe Hamilton here. Sandy Cassidy's brothers and I are at her house. You need to come here. Yes, we're inside. Got it. We will. Thanks." He dropped the phone in his pocket. "They're on the way. We're supposed to wait outside and not touch anything else." He dreaded telling Sandy what had happened here. Gorge choked against a knot in his throat. Air—he needed air.

The three men sat on the front steps, alternately mumbling, cursing and clenching their fists. Joe couldn't adequately express his outrage.

The police arrived in less than ten minutes. They put up crime scene tape, called in a forensic team and documented the damage with photographs. Joe let Damon take over with the cops, discussing what was to be done, what they were allowed to touch or take after the forensics guys were finished, and the name of the detective to call for follow-up.

Damon joined Joe and Greg as they leaned against the Audi, arms crossed, glaring helplessly at the unfolding scene. "They said not to expect anything much to get done until Monday. Murder and assault take precedence on weekends. Greg and I have to pull out Monday by mid-day. Let's exchange phone numbers so we can keep in touch."

Greg stepped away from the car. "You're not going to tell Mom anything about this, are you?"

"Absolutely not." He turned to Joe. "Make sure you don't call Mother's home number. She has steadily advancing MS. Greg is there much of the time and he has his own cell number."

Once they were given the go-ahead by the police, they went inside the house, took a few pictures on their phones and left.

Damon told Joe. "We'll join you at your sister's. If you don't mind, I'd prefer if I was the one to tell Sandy what's happened."

Joe raised his hands. "No problem. That's a job I don't want. I'll tell Liz so she can be prepared when you break it to Sandy."

Greg put his hand on Joe's shoulder. "I'm so glad you and your sister are here for her. She doesn't deserve any of this. We'll take her to press charges against Phil and put the wheels in motion for the restraining order. We'll pick up something for dinner tonight and bring it to Liz's house. You're a good man, Joe."

"Thanks. There's no way that scum-bag will get near her as long as she lets me hang around."

He waved when their car pulled away. Now, as much as he dreaded it, he had to go back to Liz's and tell her what they'd found before the brothers got to her apartment. He hoped Sandy would be up to going to the precinct today. Of one thing he was certain, he'd feel a whole lot better once he could put his arms around her again.

Chapter Eleven

SANDY WOKE TO DAMON'S VOICE COMING FROM LIZ'S LIVING room. She dragged herself to the bathroom. "Ack." The bruise was uglier than ever. Liz had left a jar of moisturizer on the sink in the guest bathroom, a new toothbrush and some gentle facial cleanser. She washed her face and sighed at the way her hair went every which way as if she'd styled it by sticking her finger in a light socket. Back in the bedroom, she swiped on a little lipstick, just because it made her feel better, not that it would improve her appearance.

"Here I come, ready or not." She put on a smile and joined them. The expressions on their faces said all she needed to know about how lousy she looked. Except for Joe. He was grinning the way he had when they sat across the table at Caliente Latino. He came to her and wrapped his strong arms around her.

"I'm going to kiss you whether your brothers like it or not," he whispered.

She sighed and draped her arms around his neck. "Go for it, Marine."

"Break it up. Break it up. We have business to take care of," Damon groused, but there was a tinge of amusement in his demand. "Come over here, Muttface. We have bad news and worse news." He smacked the space on the sofa between himself and Greg.

She plopped down. "Phil's out of custody. What else?"

Instead of answering, Greg handed her his cell phone.

She gasped, dropped it in her lap like a hot potato, and slapped her hands over her mouth. "Phil did this?" she squeaked through clamping fingers. She raised her eyes and looked around. She couldn't stand the sympathy in their expressions. "Oh, God," She moaned. "Everything I own is ruined. What am I going to do?"

Damon pulled her hands away from her face. "There's no proof he did it yet, but before it gets any later Greg and I are escorting you to the police station to press assault charges against Phil. Once you make it official, they'll put out a warrant for his arrest. And if it's possible to start the process before Monday, you need to obtain a restraining order."

"I want to go to my house." She was numb with cold. "I have to see it."

"I don't think that's such a good idea, but it's up to you." Damon squeezed her knee. "Liz wants you to stay here for a few days while things get sorted out."

Sandy cast a bleak look at Liz. "I can't impose any longer."

"Sweetheart," Joe knelt before her. "It's either here or my place, because there's no way you can go home until the crime-scene investigation is completed and the destruction has been cleaned up."

"Do you want to come home with us?" Greg asked. "You can stay at Damon's. Mom doesn't need to know."

Sandy slumped and sighed. "If Liz is okay with it, I'll stay here for a while." She couldn't bear the thought of being hundreds of miles away from Joe.

Holding her face in his hands, Joe whispered, "Good girl. Are you ready to go to the police precinct with your brothers?" She nodded, and he tugged her up. "All right, troops, let's put this operation in action. While you're gone, I'm taking Liz to the advertising agency to retrieve her car. We'll see you back here later."

He kept his arm around her until he opened Damon's car door and she took the passenger seat. Joe and Liz waved goodbye. Sandy relaxed, surrounded by their wall of support and love. *I'll get through this, I'll get through this.*

The desk sergeant rang the squad room for the officer who'd take her statement for the second time and complete the formalities necessary for her to press assault and battery charges against Phil. The friendly, but tired looking man came to the foyer and escorted Sandy to his desk then took her photo for the file he'd assembled on the case. All this while her brothers waited outside. She could do this on her own; she was strong and determined and would take the steps required to change her life.

She wasn't blameless. By her misplaced sense of guilt and responsibility she'd turned herself into a world class enabler. She'd known the pitfalls of such action but had ignored her best instincts and continued the behavior destructive to Phil, and to her. That was over now. Time to move forward. She sighed inwardly, grateful she'd kept her costly premiums for homeowner's insurance current, while hoping she'd never have to use it.

To cut the cost, she'd elected a one thousand dollar deductible and compared with the total destruction done to her house and its contents, it was a drop in the bucket. The nightmare of completing the claim would be a small price to pay to recoup most of her losses.

She rejoined her brothers. "That's done. I made a decision while I was going through the motions in there. "I'm going to restore the house once I get the insurance settlement and put it on the market. I don't ever want to live there again."

"Good decision," Damon said. "Let's get you back to your friend's apartment."

They piled in Damon's car and headed back to Liz's place. He dropped them off and went for take-out. Greg stayed behind with his sister. "I'll help you with the insurance filings. A friend recently went through a house fire. I helped him with all the required documentation. It's a mountain of paperwork. Do you have the policy in your house?"

"No, all my important papers are in a safe deposit box at the bank. I'll retrieve my laptop and my car when we go to the house. It's in the garage. Did you check to see if it was there? God, I hope it's still there and not damaged." Her stomach churned. She needed to rest.

"We couldn't get access to the house after the police arrived and closed us out. Maybe Liz or Joe will find time to drive you over there once they finish with the investigation."

Liz and Joe weren't home. It was a good thing Liz had given her a key. "I wonder why they aren't back yet." She opened her purse and removed her phone. "My battery is dead, darn it! I hope they didn't try to call."

Greg turned his head at the sound of the door opening. "Maybe that's them."

Sandy could tell by the look on Liz's face that something wasn't right. "What happened?"

Liz sighed and slumped on the couch. "Tell them, Joey."

Joe shoved his hands in his pockets and rolled his eyes. "When we got to the parking garage, we discovered that all four of Liz's tires had been slashed. We called the cops and after they took the report, the car was moved to the dealership to see if the tires can be repaired and also make sure there's no other damage."

This can't be happening to Liz because of me!

"Oh, my God!" Sandy lowered her head in her hands. "I can't believe I've gotten you mixed up in this!" Tears welled in her eyes. "I'm so sorry, Liz."

"What did the police say?" Greg directed the question to Joe.

"They took a report and asked the company that has the garage contract to preserve all the surveillance tapes for the last twenty-four hours. We gave them the contact number for the detective investigating the vandalism. I can't believe Phil would be stupid enough to pull something like this right after being released. It has to be unrelated." He looked around. "Where's Damon?"

"He dropped us off and went for take-out. I thought he'd be back by now."

Liz got up from the couch. "Joe, help me set the table. Damon probably won't be long. Sandy, relax on the sofa or lie down until dinner's ready."

Joe whispered to Sandy, "She's a regular drill sergeant, isn't she?"

"I suspect it runs in the family." She ran her hand down his jaw. "Follow her orders then come sit with me till Damon gets here with dinner."

Greg joined them. "What orders?"

"Liz wants me to set the table, but Sandy wants me to sit with her." Joe smiled and raised his hands. "I'm in the crosshairs."

"Stay with Sandy. I'll set the table. That way I can spend some quality time with your gorgeous sister." Greg winked and headed to the kitchen.

"Are you sure he's—?"

"Positive, but he's a man, and he appreciates feminine beauty." She crooked her finger and whispered, "Anyway, he knows I want to be alone with you for a little while."

Joe hugged her. "Did you clue him in?"

"You haven't exactly kept it hidden, anyway I never have to tell Greg anything. He's always been able to read my mind."

"That could be inconvenient."

"Oh, yes."

He tugged her to the sofa and pulled her close. Lowering his head, he kissed her. "Let me know if I'm coming on too strong." He touched her bruised cheek. "I'm dying to get you alone."

"When my brothers leave Monday, we'll have to put our heads together and make it happen, Joe. I want to be alone with *you*."

She did want to be alone with him, but at the same time she also wondered if they were in too much of a hurry. She trusted Joe but questioned herself about whether or not she was ready to enter into a serious relationship with any man. She'd made a big mistake with Phil. She needed to be more level-headed now. To look beyond their strong physical attraction. Maybe that's really all it is. Physical attraction.

———

Lust smoldered in Joe. It was all he could do to keep from picking her up, carrying her to the bedroom—and damn the consequences. That wouldn't happen. He had plans about the way he'd advance their relationship. No teenage wrestling. No mindless sex. When he finally got her in his bed, he'd be laser focused. Pleasing her and assuring her she was safe with him was paramount. And, he had no plans to set himself up for disappointment with another woman he cared for.

"When does the ER doctor want to check you again?" Joe stroked her arm. Her velvet soft skin beneath his palm stole his breath.

"He doesn't need to see me. He suggested I make an appointment with my family doctor. The hospital has already transmitted my record to her office. I'll give her a call on Monday." She gazed into his eyes. "I'm fine, Joe. I haven't had any of the danger signs since you brought me back from the ER. One more night of good sleep in your arms will be all I need."

"Do you have any idea what torture that is for me?" He shook his head and chuckled.

"You're strong. You're a war fighter. I trust you." She poked a finger in his chest.

The doorbell rang.

"That's Damon." Joe rose from the sofa. "I'll let him in." Damon waited with several bags balanced in his arms. "Something smells good. What'd you get?"

Damon handed him a couple of the bags. "It's a cliché, but I got Chinese. A variety of almost everything they had. Careful, they're on the warm side. How's Sandy?"

Sandy joined them. "I'm doing great, Stinky. Let me have a couple of those."

"Okay, I have to know," Joe said. "Why do you call him Stinky?"

'Because he always smells so good. Like a big Teddy Bear who's been rolling in a pile of cedar chips."

"I suppose that makes sense, in some perverted way." Joe shook his head as they followed Damon to the kitchen and placed the bags on the counter.

"Hi, Damon," Liz called. "What do you have for us?"

"Chinese, but I forgot the chopsticks."

"Good. We can use forks and not have to pretend we love eating with those pesky things."

"A beautiful woman with an honest and functioning brain." Greg faked a swoon. "I'm in love at long last."

Damon, Joe and Sandy laughed when Greg gave Liz a moony-eyed stare.

"Sandy warned me you'd break my heart, Greg. You don't happen to love Latin dancing, do you?"

Greg raised his eyebrows. "I'm more of a *swing* dancer. But, I'm a fast learner."

"Lesson number one coming up right after dinner."

Dinner winding down, Joe was glad the light banter and laughter they'd enjoyed during the meal had avoided any further reference to Sandy's situation or the police investigation. She clearly enjoyed the company of her brothers and Joe was glad the five of them were compatible. Greg and Liz volunteered to clean up the kitchen, and she gave Joe orders to roll back the rug on her living room floor and dig the salsa CD's out of her rack. She was serious when she'd threatened Greg with lessons.

"Sandy, let's take a walk," Damon suggested to his sister.

"Want to join us, Joe?"

"Just the two of us, Muttface. I'd like a private conversation."

Joe speculated her brother wanted to caution her about embarking on a relationship with him. "Go ahead. If I don't want to end up in the stockade, I'd better get the living room ready for Liz. She's hell bent on teaching Greg her favorite dances. Maybe you're up for a couple of turns around the room?"

"You know I am." She pecked a kiss on his cheek then took Damon's arm and they headed out the door.

———

"I know what you're up to, Damon. Yes, I'm fond of Joe. Very fond. I'm a big girl, and he's a good man, so save your breath on the fatherly advice." She squeezed his arm against her side and leaned her head on his brawny shoulder. "You're a good brother, but I don't have blinders on this time."

"This time?"

"Don't be cagey. You know exactly what I'm saying."

"Are you sleeping with him?"

She was accustomed to his bluntness. "No. Not that it's any of your business. But I won't take offense because I know where you're coming from."

"He wants to. I can see it."

"What you don't see is this; Joe's the one who's been cautious. He knows all about me and my history with Phil, and he's kept me at arm's length, and not taken advantage of my situation. He could have. I was more than willing. He knew it."

"I don't want you to rush into anything."

104

"Rush? Damon, I've been divorced for years. I haven't been sleeping around, nor have I met a man I was attracted to, other than Joe. Liz originally tried to set us up then changed her mind when she decided I wasn't good enough for her brother. She was correct. I wasn't, but I'm working on it."

"You weren't good enough? What made her think that? You work together. She knows you. She likes you. I don't get it." He faced her, his brow creased with the question. "I don't like her sticking her nose into your business one bit."

Sandy shrugged then told him the sordid story of her online dating activities, how she'd used several men under false pretenses, and how Liz had reacted when she told her about it.

Damon stopped walking and put his hands on her shoulders. "I'm disappointed in you. I'm trying to understand why you acted that way. I can't condone it. I see why she wanted to keep you away from Joe."

Sandy nodded regretfully. "After I bragged to her about all those free dinners out at nice places, she was shocked and disgusted, but it was too late. Joe walked in to meet us, and I wormed my way into going ahead with the blind date despite her. It took some doing on Liz's part to believe me when I told her I regretted my past and had brushed off Joe's request to see me again at the end of the evening."

"You brushed him off? That didn't last long."

"After I drove up to Portland to visit you and Greg and Mom, I thought I should take the first step and come clean with him. He's very special, Damon. Joe has his own demons to contend with, but he's cautiously willing to give us a chance. I hope there's more beyond physical attraction. And even if it turns out it *is* only physical, I'll have no regrets because of the man he is."

"Well, they're certainly up to their necks in your mess. I hope the incident with her car is unrelated. If it isn't, the menace to you and them has escalated to a dangerous level."

She was reassured when her brother put his arm around her shoulders and hugged her to his side. She'd lost count of the times Damon had been there for her and Greg, how he'd assumed the role as head of the family at such a young age, putting his dreams on the back burner to take care of them and keep the family together.

"So, tell me about the mystery woman in your life, Stinky." She nudged him with her elbow. "Who is she?"

He couldn't keep the smile off his face. "Her name's Janeen, she's a widow with a three-year-old daughter. I hired her to handle the office so I can concentrate on doing what I love. She's only twenty-five, but she's convinced I'm the man she wants to be her little girl's dad. We've been intimate for over a year, but I've kept it to myself, afraid if I confided in my family it might be bad luck. Stupid, I know." He shrugged and gave her a silly grin.

"You're only seven years older than her. I don't see the problem." She nudged him. "You once told me you wanted a big family. What are you waiting for? Mom will be thrilled. Does Greg know?"

"Doesn't he know everything? He has a sixth sense where you and I are concerned."

"You're right. That's part of the reason I stayed away from Portland for so long after I divorced Phil. How did he react when you told him about her and the child?"

"He's already planning the wedding and has picked names for our first two children. He won't keep it from Mother much longer. So, when we get home, I'm going to ask Janeen to cook dinner for Mother and Greg and invite them to our house." He grinned. "Yes, our house. We've been living together for the past five months."

Sandy stopped and put her forehead on his wide, solid chest. "I'm so glad. I might be prejudiced, but she's the luckiest woman in the world to be loved by you. What's the little girl's name?"

"Isabella. I call her Belle and she calls me Daddy. I'm crazy about her."

"You're going to make me cry. I can't wait to meet them. Are you going to marry her?" It was high time he got on with his own life.

"Oh, yeah. I hesitated, because of Mother's MS, but then we decided we shouldn't wait until it progresses any further. We want her to have time to enjoy Belle. Janeen has gone off birth control. We want lotsa kids. I'm working on making it happen." His smile was full of mischief.

"Nice work, if I do say so." Sandy wanted a family too, but she was grateful she'd never had children with Phil. "I'll keep your secret for now. We'd better get back so we can watch Greg's dance lesson. Liz is in for a surprise."

Sandy and her brother strolled back to Liz's building. When they came abreast of Damon's new Audi, she stopped and gasped. "Oh no!" She stared at the deep, jagged scratch marks gouged from the front headlights all the way past the back door.

Damon blanched. "That's one too many coincidences for one day." He used his phone to photograph the damage from two different angles. "I'm calling the detective on your case. He needs to see this."

Somehow Sandy had involved and hurt everyone she cared for by getting them in the middle of her rotten, repulsive situation with Phil. Wretchedness overwhelmed her. Tears clogged her throat.

Chapter Twelve

THEY HEARD JOE'S LAUGHTER AND THE MUSIC WHEN THEY GOT close to Liz's apartment and opened the door. Liz and Greg were dancing in the small space in the living room where Joe had rolled back the area rug.

"Come in. My sister got sandbagged by Greg. There isn't a dance he doesn't know and now he's teaching her—" He stopped talking when he saw Sandy's troubled face and Damon's black expression. "What's the matter?"

"Somebody keyed my car. I'm calling the detective. Liz's slashed tires, and now this, is no coincidence. He needs to know what's going on."

Liz and Greg bolted to the door trying to squeeze outside at the same time. Greg bowed and stepped back letting Liz go first.

Sandy grabbed Joe's arm. "Show him the pictures, Damon."

Joe reached for Damon's phone at the moment Liz's rang. He picked it up and didn't recognize the caller ID, so let it go to voicemail. When Liz came back inside the apartment wearing an expression that would make a warrior quail, he handed it to her. "You missed a call."

Liz looked at the screen. "Hmm. I wonder who this is?" She put the phone to her ear and listened to the message. Color drained from her face.

Sandy touched her shoulder. "Liz? Who was that?"

"You tell me." She put the phone on speaker.

"You'll stay out of my business you meddling bitch if you know what's good for you."

"Oh, my lord, what will he do next?" Sandy reached for Damon just as Joe caught her. He led her to the couch.

"I'm taking this to the detectives to listen to, along with the photos of my car." Damon pulled his keys from his pocket. "Liz, it's your phone. Why don't you come with me?"

Sandy spoke up, "I think we should all go."

"I agree." Joe helped her up. "Liz, go with Damon in his car. Sandy and I'll follow in mine. Take your pick, Greg."

"I'll ride with you and Sandy. This is serious. They need to get that psycho behind bars before he does more than property damage."

———

Monday morning Sandy got a call from the detective. "I hope I'm not calling too early, Ms. Cassidy."

"No, not at all. Do you have something good to tell me?"

"We've arrested Phillip Rice on the assault and battery warrant. He's cooling his heels in jail and waiting for a public defender to be assigned to his case."

She let out a pent-up breath. "What a relief. Thank you for letting me know. If he gets out on bail again, will you call me?"

"Absolutely." He ended the call.

Joe smiled. "That's very good news. Now all of us can take a breath."

Liz gave her a hug. "Once that bruise fades you can get back to work and nobody will be the wiser." She slung her bag over her shoulder. "You ready to leave, Joe? You have to take me, remember?"

"Oh, yeah." He grabbed his keys. "Call me if the dealer doesn't have your tires fixed or replaced and you need a ride home."

After Liz and Joe left for work, Sandy turned to Damon. "Would you tell Mom about my divorce from Phil, and explain that I kept it from her because I didn't want to worry or disappoint her?"

Damon gave her a solid hug. "Don't worry. I'll tell Mother. I'll leave out the nasty details. No need to upset her. She'll be fine."

Greg kissed her on the cheek. "Good idea. Mom will take it better from Damon. Update us with a text every few hours while we're traveling."

"I promise."

"You be very careful, Muttface. Watch your surroundings and keep your cell handy. Call the police even if you're unsure you're in jeopardy. They've got Phil in custody, so you should be all right. Stay alert. I don't like what you've told us about his sleazy friends."

She promised to be careful, said goodbye and watched them through the open door until their car turned right at the busy intersection. She went back inside the apartment and locked the doors then took a long, soothing bath and washed her hair, relieved to have some time alone to think and plan. She donned the same underwear she'd laundered the night before. Liz had told her to go to her closet and chest of drawers and select anything she wanted to wear. Having only the flat shoes she'd worn when she left home, Sandy selected a casual pair of jeans and a pullover cotton sweater.

She tapped her handyman's number on her phone. "Jerry? This is Sandy Cassidy. Do you have time to meet me at my house Wednesday? You saw the yellow tape? Yes, you won't believe the mess inside. After the insurance adjuster does his thing, you and I need to sit down and see what needs to be done to get the place in shape to sell. No, we can't go in there until they conclude their investigation. It took longer because of the weekend. Thanks, Jerry. I'll call you Wednesday to set a time."

Next, she contacted her neighbor, the insurance agent. He'd been expecting to hear from her. They made arrangements to meet early Wednesday morning. Things were moving along. She felt a great sense of accomplishment as the cab arrived to take her to the Enterprise agency. She decided to rent an inconspicuous compact car for now instead of attempting to retrieve her red Honda.

First on the agenda—shop for a few clothes to get her through the next week. As for a place to live? She'd enlist Liz's help.

That evening, tired but relaxed, she was putting dinner on the table when she heard Liz's key in the door.

"Sandy?"

"In here. I hope you like Mexican, because I just took my chili relleno casserole out of the oven."

Liz walked in the kitchen. "Look what I brought home." She held aloft a fluffy yellow kitten with green eyes.

Sandy put her hands to her face and shrieked, "Oh, how precious! Where did you get it?"

"Remember the feral cat that hung out around the agency? The one Thomas used to feed on the sly?"

"Raggedy Ann?"

"Yes, the poor thing got hit by a car and left three orphans by the dumpster. Thomas rescued them and this was the only baby left without a home. He said she was the runt of the litter. I couldn't resist. Isn't she the sweetest thing?"

Sandy grimaced. "Yes, but she's probably covered with fleas and God knows what else. Maybe we should give her a bath." The adorable kitten couldn't have been more than six or seven weeks old. Far too young to be without a mother.

"I have a carrier, a bed and some flea shampoo in the car. I'll put her in a box, and she'll be all right while you help me carry it up. She's probably hungry. I don't know if she can lap cream from a dish yet." She made a face. "I'll probably regret this."

Sandy took the hot dish from the table and placed it on the warming plate on Liz's stove. "I'll keep the casserole warm. We should bathe her right away to make sure you don't get fleas in here. Let's set her in the bathtub instead of a box. She won't like it, but she'll be safe there. I'll pour some half and half on a saucer and put it next to her."

They put the kitten in the bathtub with the saucer and went down to the parking garage to retrieve the supplies Liz had purchased.

"Holy mackerel! You must have spent a fortune at the pet store, Liz. What is all this?" Liz's trunk was crammed.

"A carrier, bed, fresh pureed kitten food, a cat pan and litter, and some toys. I got carried away." She held up a slender book. "The Kitten Bible."

"No kidding. I hope we can haul this up in one trip." Sandy grinned at Liz's extravagance.

By the time they'd bathed the reluctant kitten and had scratches on their hands and forearms from her needle-sharp claws to prove it, they hand-fed her some of the food the store had recommended. Liz put a big, fluffy towel in the carrier and tucked her new baby inside and closed the door. It never stopped crying during their dinner and wouldn't quiet down until Liz released her and cuddled her on the couch.

"I thought of a good name for your baby." Sandy scratched the tiny chin. "Madame Butterfly."

"Perfect! She hasn't stopped belting out her arias since I brought her home. Butterfly it is." She held the kitten in front of her face. "You like?" In answer Butterfly emitted a purr loud enough for a wildcat. Liz and Sandy laughed and startled the new reigning queen of Liz's apartment.

―――――

At nine that evening Joe thought of calling Sandy, picked up his cell then decided not to complete the call. He'd back off for a few days. He'd told her he was available to help if she wanted him.

He and Yoda had been very busy at work with the new software. Not only perfecting how to use it but training the other two investigators. By the time he got home from the office and warmed up a tasteless frozen entrée, he was at loose ends. He went to the gym and picked up a couple of handball games with other members to kill a couple of hours.

His phone buzzed. "Hamilton."

"Hi, Joe."

His heart rate soared as his mouth turned up in a smile. "Hi, sweetheart."

"My mother often lectured me that girls didn't call boys. The girl had to wait for the boy to call, otherwise she'd look eager and cheap."

"Nice talking to you, Eager and Cheap. What took you so long?" He grinned into the phone. "I was just fantasizing over you."

"Me too. You." She sighed. "Can I come over? I rented a car. Liz is busy with her new baby, a yellow kitten. I can't get in my house until day after tomorrow, and I've got the yips."

"Don't come unless you plan to spend the night. Once I get my hands on you, I'm not letting go." Excitement ignited in his gut. "So, you might want to re-think this." If he were honest with himself, he should be re-thinking this.

"Are we moving too fast, Joe?"

"I'm not sure, but I don't want you to have regrets. I was ready the first night we met." His skin tingled everywhere, from his scalp to the bottoms of his feet.

"I'm on my way." She hung up.

Joe's heart raced. He flew through the apartment, changed the sheets on his bed, the towels in the bathroom, and then left a message on Yoda's office phone. "I have some urgent personal business to take care of, so I won't make it in tomorrow. I'll get it handled and be back on Wednesday. Call my cell number in case of emergency. I'll miss you, gorgeous." He grinned imagining the vexed look on his colleague's face.

He barely had enough time to run to the market down the street and buy a can of gourmet coffee and English muffins for breakfast. He was about to leave the store, changed direction, and grabbed a bouquet of yellow roses, a bottle of chilled sparkling cider and package of tea-lights. He planned a romantic evening he hoped would strike the right mood for both of them.

He lit the tea-lights in his bedroom and pulled apart two of the rosebuds, scattering petals on the bed and throughout the room. The other ten went in the vase he'd purchased after Sandy had teased him about the lack of essentials in his apartment. He'd spent a pile of dough on the new, extra-long queen bed. It was a good investment because it turned out to be the most comfortable mattress he'd ever slept on. Other than the bed, the bedroom still had no other furniture except for a lamp table and a used chest of drawers. Nothing he could do about the Spartan look now.

While he fussed putting out glasses for the cider and selected some music, he dimmed the lights in the living room then realized he'd bought nothing to go with the *champagne*. "Dammit!" Joe rooted through his cupboard, found a package of Oreo Thins, put several on a plate, and set it on his coffee table.

He rushed downstairs to the foyer of the building and paced, waiting for her. Five minutes later she walked through the door carrying a TJ Maxx shopping bag. Before she had a chance to say anything, he pulled her close and kissed her. "Hey."

"Hey." She stroked his cheek. "Kiss me again then I'll share the bad news."

He wasted no time. Thrusting his fingers through her hair he kissed her more deeply. When they came up for air he said, "What's the bad news?"

"I forgot to bring something to sleep in."

Joe raised his eyebrows. "That's a damn shame." He grabbed her shopping bag and nudged her toward the stairs. "But don't worry about it. I wasn't planning on sleeping."

Sandy turned and grinned over her shoulder. "That's a damn shame." She took two stairs at a time and he had to hurry to keep up with her, catching her at the door to his apartment.

He reached around her and pushed the unlocked door open. "Come in. I dare ya."

She grabbed the front of his shirt and backed into the apartment. "You don't scare me." Inside the doorway, she linked her fingers around the back of his neck and jumped up, locking her legs around his waist. "Close the door. We don't want to scandalize the neighbors."

He grinned from ear to ear. "You're starting to scare *me*." He dropped her shopping bag on the floor and reached back to close the door. Both hands free now, he gripped her bottom and pulled her tighter. "What am I gonna do with you, lady?"

"Whatever you want, big guy."

Joe laughed and walked to the couch. He pried her legs free and set her on her feet then kissed her before pulling her arms from his neck. He held her hands close to his lips and caught his breath on a jolt of alarm. "What the hell happened here?" It looked like she'd been fighting off somebody. He would kill whoever it was.

"Liz and I gave her new kitten, Madame Butterfly, a flea bath. I don't know who hated it more, the kitten, or us."

"You girls gave a cat a bath? Where were you when I was behind enemy lines?" He made it his mission to kiss every tiny cut, then sat and pulled her down next to him. "Let's relax and talk for a while."

Sandy grinned at the bottle of cider and cookies. "Classy! Just like the best bistro in town." She picked up the bottle. "You're not going to try to get me drunk and take advantage of me, are you?" She poured some into the mismatched glasses, set the bottle back in the bowl of ice and took a cookie.

Joe raised his glass. "Here's to you taking advantage of me."

"Hmm. Were you always a dreamer?"

"From day one, according to Mom." He took a sip. "Colonel Dad can never know. He busted my chops real good once and young Joey learned his lesson."

She leaned back and crossed her legs. "Only once? Tell me."

He smiled, munched on a cookie, and embarked on the story of his father's method of convincing him to stop drinking and get his shit together. "It didn't take long for me to realize I'd wallowed in juvenile heartbreak over my cheating fiancée long enough." He'd tried to get a job at Gunny Dempsey's construction company but was told he still had some more growing up to do. He didn't bother applying for a job at Cluny's plumbing outfit, after the fool he'd made of his drunken self at the barbecue, insulting Cluny's wife. "That's when I re-upped in the Marines. They made a man out of me. Or so the story goes."

"Are you still mad at her, your fiancée?"

"Nah. That song, the one about girls just wanna have fun was written with her in mind. She wanted to marry me. I must have caught her in a moment of weakness. I was a big naïve kid with way too much testosterone. Even if I hadn't joined The Corps and gotten deployed, the marriage would have been doomed from day one."

"Did you ever try to look her up? Reconnect?"

"No, she was killed in a freak accident during one of my deployments. Gotta be almost fifteen years now." He set his glass down and slid close to her side.

"Oh, that's sad. Tell me what you do at work, Joe. How you got interested in it and what you like or don't like about it. You've learned everything about me in the past couple of weeks. I want to know everything about you."

He loved the way his name sounded when it rolled off her tongue.

"One thing you should know—I want you, Sandra Cassidy." He took her hand and placed it on his thigh.

"How do you want me, Joseph Hamilton?" She squeezed his leg. A rush of pure lust surged through him when she slid her hand to his lap. She had the ability to turn him on in an instant.

He groaned and kissed her. "Any way and every way I can."

"Do you want to make love to me?"

"Oh, yes, I do." He smiled at her question. "You know I do."

"How do you like it Joe?"

He was dizzy with desire for her. "Slow, very slow, real slow."

"Mmm, me too." She shifted, raised herself, and straddled his lap, her knees clamping his hips. "Show me." Her lips captured his, her fingers threaded through the hair at the back of his head. He couldn't take much more. Her mouth rested on the sensitive area of his neck below his ear. "You smell so good, Joe." Her lips trailed across his jaw to his mouth.

Joe kissed her deeply and thrust his tongue between her soft, incredibly sensuous lips. He'd been waiting for this woman for a long time. He just hadn't realized it until this moment. He pulled his head back, sucked in a deep breath and tightened his hands on her ass. Crushing her against his torso, he kissed her again, slowly, deliberately.

"Take this off," She tugged at his shirt. "I want to see you."

"That makes two of us." His fingers fumbled with the buttons. He was thrilled when she pushed his hands away impatiently and finished the job. Her soft palms caressed his shoulders as she slid the shirt off.

"Your turn." She raised her arms so he could pull her sweater up and off.

He stared at her magnificent breasts and tentatively traced the edges of the barely-there bra, marveling at its ability to support her cleavage with nothing but sheer lace. "I have to take my time here, sweetheart. I want this moment seared in my memory for the rest of my life."

She smiled and ran her hands over his chest and upper arms crooning, "So strong." Feeling the muscles of his chest and sides, she stopped abruptly. "Oh, what's this?" She leaned back and looked at the place where her thumb had stopped. "A scar? Is this a scar?"

"You know I was wounded. Twice. There, and then later I took one in the ass. This one went clean through." He took her wrist and slid her hand around to feel his back. "My red badge of courage." He grinned. "This one, not the other one."

Her eyes went wide. "And you went back again?"

"I guess I hadn't learned my lesson. But, to give myself credit, I did switch from a recon grunt to the school for cyber-spooks."

"Spooks? You mean spies?"

"No, just advanced training in computer tech for the purposes of keeping track of the bad guys. The Marines in my former MARSOC unit named it the school for spooks, but they gave me a pass because I'd already been shot twice." He drew her hands to his face and kissed her palms. Taking her wrists, he moved her arms around to her back. "Undo this, but please don't take it off."

Chapter Thirteen

Sandy held her breath at Joe's deliberate and excruciatingly slow removal of her bra millimeter by millimeter. He traced the edges of the lace with his fingers and followed their trail with his lips and tongue. Burying his nose in her cleavage he slid the straps off her shoulders.

"So sweet." He raised his astonishing blue eyes and smiled. The smile guaranteed to melt her heart.

She gasped when he nipped her neck and trailed kisses down from her collarbone. "Joe, I knew it would be like this with you." She placed her hands over his to stop them so she could slow her heart rate. "So good, oh, so darn good."

He shifted and laid her on her back to tug off her jeans. She raised her hips when his mouth found her stomach and began exploring her skin with his tongue. As much as she loved slow and gentle lovemaking, she found herself needy with impatience. "I want you, Joe."

He moved back on his knees and stared at her nakedness. Shaking his head, he sighed, hands trembling as he lifted the bra from her chest and dropped it on the floor, then softly ran fingers over her bare skin. "I have to see you first, sweetheart, soak you in. I want to memorize every curve and texture. You're so incredibly lovely and smooth. I'm the luckiest man on earth tonight."

Sandy trembled with anticipation.

He kissed her on the mouth taking his time exploring her lips, teeth, tongue then breasts. He gazed into her eyes and raised his head. "You taste as good as you look. Let's move this to the bedroom." His eyes were filled with boyish wonder. He took her hands in his and helped her to her feet, turned her around and pulled her back against his chest. Kisses rained down on her shoulders when he kneaded her breasts, gently then stronger. He tested their weight. "Look how magnificent you are. I'd imagined what you'd look like and feel like, but I wasn't even close. Words fail me."

"You're doing just fine." She giggled and pressed her naked bottom against him. "Get out of these pants, Marine. Don't make me hurt you."

He laughed and turned her to face him and kissed her hard. "You can do anything you want to me. *Please* do anything you want to me." In no time, he'd lost the pants and stood before her in his rangy, muscled, proud splendor.

"What a lucky girl I am. I'm in Liz's debt forever." She ran her hands down his chest and arms, lingering on his wound for a second. "Turn around." He complied, and she bent down to kiss the jagged scar on his bottom. Desire enflamed her as he trembled beneath her lips.

He grabbed her hands when she slipped them around to the front of his legs. "I might have to re-think *slow,* sweetheart. I don't know how much longer I can be strong. Being this close to you is destroying my resolve to make our first time together special."

"What could be more special than this? Release my hands. Let me touch you, Joe. Let me realize the fantasy I've been living since the first minute we met."

He didn't release her hands but guided and pressed them as she held him. "Oh, man." He sucked in a breath. His knees shook. "Go easy or we'll never make it to the bedroom. I'm ready to throw you over my shoulder and do the Tarzan thing."

She bit his bottom hard enough to leave teeth marks. "Another of my fantasies."

He jerked, turned and embraced her. His heart beat strong against her breast. "Careful what you wish for." His big hand encasing her slender fingers, he led her to the bedroom. "I went to some trouble. Let's enjoy it for a moment."

As they stepped through the bedroom door, her eyes rounded with delighted surprise. The candles flickered and shadows danced on the walls. She stepped on something soft and tender. "Rose petals? You scattered rose petals?" Her lips trembled in a smile and she fought tears. "Joe, this is the most romantic moment of my life. I never dreamed. I never imagined. I feel like a queen." Tears sparkled on her lower lashes in spite of her attempt to stop them. She turned her face to him. "I don't know what to say."

"Sweetheart, you just made my day again." Hands on her cheeks, he rasped softly, "Now let me make yours."

She melted into his arms when he lifted her. Her bones disappeared. She'd never experienced a moment like this, even though as a young girl she'd harbored her prince charming dreams. Here was Joe, her prince in the flesh. What had she ever done to deserve such a man? What strange string of events had brought them together here and now? No matter what happened down the road, this would be a night she'd always remember.

He woke when her hand smoothed across his belly.

"Again, Joe." Sandy's wild honey eyes challenged him. Her fingertips traced a path downward. She caressed him, smiling when he responded lightning fast. "Oh, my, yes."

He rolled on top and crushed his lips to her mouth. "You're a very bad girl."

"And you're a very good boy." She squirmed beneath him and flung out her arm, reaching blindly for the scattered condoms on the bedside table. "I hope you bought enough of these."

Joe barked a laugh. "Enough for the next twenty-four hours, after that, no promises." He grabbed one and handed it to her. "You do it." He shifted back on his knees. "Good thing I took today off for personal reasons, isn't it?"

"What could be more personal than this?"

"Maybe I'll ask my boss to switch me to part-time," he teased. "I had no idea how much personal time off I needed."

———

Joe rolled over, automatically reaching for Sandy. He was alone in the bed that now looked like a war zone. He sniffed. Coffee! Moaning, he staggered to his feet. Rubbing his face briskly he wandered into the kitchen. She stood in front of the sink, naked as the day she was born, pulling apart English muffins and arranging them on the rack of his small toaster oven. "Need any help?"

She rewarded him with a brilliant smile and a toss of her hair. "I can handle it."

"Of that I have no doubt." Joe nestled up to her back and put his arms around her waist. "Coffee. I need coffee, woman."

"It's ready, master." She turned in his embrace and draped her arms around his neck. "You certainly earned it."

"Yes, I did, didn't I?" He bumped her nose with his. "But I'm not certain what to do for an encore."

"Let's discuss it over breakfast. I'm sure we can dream up any number of things if we put our minds together." She pushed him back. "I need to put something on. It's chilly this morning. Don't go away, I'll be right back."

"You couldn't get me out of here with a grenade." He smacked her bottom gently when she turned to leave then took a quick step forward and did it again before she could get out of his reach. "I'm already coming up with a couple of good ideas."

"Watch those muffins. I like mine when the edges just start to burn."

Thinking himself the luckiest guy on the planet once again, he grumbled, "Down boy," opened the refrigerator and removed half and half, whipped cream cheese and a partially used jar of blackberry jam.

Sandy returned rolling up the sleeves of a favorite threadbare denim shirt he'd left hanging on the back of his closet door. "Do you mind if I wear this?" She smoothed her hands down the front of his old shirt in a slow and deliberate way meant to inflame him and he didn't disappoint her.

He straightened to give her the full Monty. "You look a hell of a lot better in it than I ever did; besides I'm sure I can talk you out of it when I want it back."

"I'm helpless against your power of *persuasion*." She sniffed. "Don't burn those muffins or I'll have to pack up and leave."

He whipped around and yanked open the glass door on the toaster oven, and then using the tip of his finger he slid the smoking muffins onto a waiting plate. "Dammit!" He stuck his scorched finger in his mouth.

Sandy rushed forward. "Oh, honey lamb, sweetie pie, sugar baby; did you burn your pinky winky? Let Mama make it all better." She pulled the finger out of his mouth, kissed it on the tip, and then stuck it in her mouth. "Better?" she mumbled around his long digit.

Like an enraged silverback, Joe let out a roar and slapped his hands on his chest. "Me Tarzan. You my woman. Eat later." With that he ran back to the bedroom with Sandy shrieking over his shoulder. He tossed her unceremoniously on the rumpled bed and launched himself after her. "No slow! Jungle sex!"

Sandy screamed, giggled and pounded his hard shoulders.

———

Around two that afternoon they sat across from each other at 24/7 Diner, three blocks from Joe's apartment. He'd already Hoovered down their signature farmhand breakfast and was working his way through a plate-size, strawberry-topped Belgian waffle.

Sandy had quit eating fifteen minutes before and watched him, grinning and shaking her head. "How can you eat so much?"

"Marine training: Eat all you can when it's available because you never know when you might have to go back in action." He squinched his eyes. "I'm prepared for anything."

"Good to know." She slid from the booth. "Be right back. I'm going to powder my nose then text Liz. She asked me to stay in touch. She worries about me."

"Or she's just being nosy. Please don't make me the subject of your text."

"Don't worry. She wouldn't believe me anyway because you're her KISA big brother."

"KISA?" He stopped with the fork halfway to his mouth.

"Knight in shining armor—but we both know better, don't we?" She gave an extra sway to her hips when she strolled away.

"Oh, man," he muttered under his breath and signaled the waiter for more coffee. He set a coaster on top of Sandy's cup to keep it hot.

She approached the table wearing a big grin. "Want to see her answer?" She held out her phone.

He took it, not sure he wanted to see what his sister had to say.

He read: *Big bro any good?*

Glaring at Sandy he demanded, "What was your answer?"

"Scroll down."

Luv u but my lips are sealed.

He smiled and handed the phone back. "Good girl." He lifted the coaster. "I'm keeping your coffee hot."

A sultry smile covered her face when she lifted the cup to her lips. "And that's not all."

They finished their last cup of coffee, returned to Joe's apartment and flopped on his couch to watch a movie. Within minutes they'd both conked out and continued to sleep until Joe's phone buzzed. He gently moved Sandy's head from his shoulder. "Hamilton."

"We still on for Friday?"

Confused, Joe rubbed his face. "Uh."

"Were you asleep, Joe? It's Cole Brandon. Hope I didn't interrupt anything." He chuckled.

"Cole, buddy, yeah I fell asleep watching TV."

Sandy groaned and sat up. "Joe? Is that Liz?"

"No, sweetheart, it's a friend." For no justifiable reason, he felt his face go hot.

"What time is it?" She looked around, still groggy. "It's dark outside."

Cole hooted. "I did interrupt something, you dog. Call me later." He clicked off.

Joe tossed the phone on the coffee table and pulled her to his side. "We should probably hit the sack. I have to work tomorrow, and you've got to meet with your handyman and the insurance adjuster."

She raised her head and kissed his jaw. "I'm going back to Liz's place. I won't get any sleep if I stay here." She punctuated the remark with a poke in his chest. "Neither will you."

He groaned. The two fantastic nights had to end sooner or later. "I don't want you to leave, but you're right. The call reminded me I invited a Marine buddy, Cole Brandon, for the weekend. He's coming Friday. We're going to a Dodgers game on Saturday and then my parents' home on Sunday. I'm trying to set him up with Liz." He held up his hand at the look on her face "She knows about him. I want you to come too. You could ride over to Spring Grove with Liz. I'd love you to meet my parents and flaunt you before Cole." He grinned and kissed her on the nose.

"I can't show up there uninvited. I have better manners than that."

He laughed at her reticence. "Any of our friends are always welcome. All I have to do is let Dad know in advance, so he'll have enough steaks for the barbie. He's in hog heaven when he's grilling for a crowd. Come. Please. I want you to."

"You sure?" He could see her wavering.

"Positive." He stood and pulled her up. "I'll walk you down to your car when you're ready. I'd rather have you in my bed, but you're thinking more clearly than I am. I'll call Cole back while you get your things together."

"Okay, but first text Liz to let her know I'm on my way."

He crushed her in a bear hug. "You got it." She left to retrieve the few things she'd brought with her, and he texted his sister to watch for Sandy in about forty minutes. He called Cole back. "Hey, bud. I gave my woman the heave ho, so I'm all yours. Friday is a go."

"You gave me the heave ho?" Sandy called from the bedroom. "Too bad this is your apartment, or I'd give you the heave ho!"

Momentarily dismayed by her comment, Joe realized she was playing with him.

Cole laughed so loud, Joe had to jerk the phone away from his ear.

"Man, you are so whipped! I'm glad I've lived long enough to witness it."

"Bullshit, you're just jealous. I'll meet you at the Glendale Amtrak station on Friday evening. Now go to hell." He grinned and disconnected.

Sandy sashayed into the living room. "Is that the way you talk to your friends? I'd hate to be an enemy. You—,"

He silenced her with a hard kiss. "Don't sass me, or I'll be forced to take you back to the bedroom and teach you a lesson. A hard lesson." His eyebrows took turns bouncing up and down.

"I'd hold you to that, but right now I have to get going, Tarzan. Call tomorrow night and your eager and cheap woman will discuss plans with you."

"I want you to move in with me." The words were out of his mouth before he had a chance to consider them. He stared at her, his mouth hanging open.

For Christ's sake Joe!

Sandy laughed and put her hands on his chest and shoved him. "I should do it just to teach you a lesson." She gazed into his eyes. "Take it back."

He raised his hands, grinned sheepishly and stepped away. "Okay, I take it back, but next time I say it, I'll have given it a lot of serious thought and I'll mean it."

She jingled her keys. "I'm ready for my heave ho, Marine."

They walked arm in arm from the apartment to her rental car. He opened the door for her, kissed her goodnight and waited on the sidewalk until she was out of sight. He turned and bumped into Seth who was zipping up his hoodie. "Hey, Seth, just get off work?"

"Yeah, man. I'm gonna grab some dinner. I didn't have time to eat before my shift. You wanna join me?" He rolled his eyes at the fast food place across the street.

Joe realized he was hungry. "Don't mind if I do. I didn't get dinner either."

"Couldn't have anything to do with the gorgeous redhead with the shiner, could it? Wink-wink."

"It has everything to do with the gorgeous redhead, smart mouth. And don't even think I had anything to do with the shiner." He looked both ways. "There's a break in the traffic, let's haul ass." He took off running with Seth laughing and dodging close behind.

They gasped for breath after their death-defying jog through the heavy evening traffic. Joe leaned forward with his hands on his knees, shaking his head at his foolishness.

Seth nudged him. "Come on, old timer. I'm buying."

Joe straightened up and followed him inside. "Damn right you are." He walked to the counter and ordered a double cheese burger with a large order of fries and a root beer. He stepped out of Seth's way and told the teenage clerk. "He's buying."

The girl smiled shyly, her cheeks pinking. "Hi, Seth. What'll you have?"

"Besides you?"

"Oh, stop it." By now her cute pixie face was blazing. "Order something before you get me fired."

He placed his order, took the plastic tent with their order number on it and headed for the drink dispenser.

Joe staked out the last table and waited for him. When Seth got there, Joe went for his own drink and grabbed some napkins and ketchup packets. He brought them back to the small table and took his seat. "Don't you love the oppressively greasy, fast food smell in here? No matter what the health cops say, I'll never give up burgers and fries."

"Me either." Seth took a big sip through his straw. "Is she hot?"

"Blazing, but don't' ask me anything else unless you want to lose those teeth your parents spent a fortune on."

Seth nodded. "No sweat, just glad you got your money's worth outta the condoms." He dodged back as Joe raised a fist. "You'd be scaring me if you weren't grinning like an idiot."

Chapter Fourteen

EARLY WEDNESDAY MORNING SANDY MET HER INSURANCE adjuster at her vandalized house. They walked through together. "It's ruined." Seeing it again turned her stomach. She shuddered with discouragement. "I doubt there's much to be salvaged."

He nodded and took notes and pictures with his smart phone. "It won't look so bad after you get a clean-up specialist in here. It looks to me like the real damage is to the contents, structure's solid. I'll do a thorough inspection inside and out and make sure it's limited to cosmetic." He smiled and put his hand on her shoulder. "It's not as bad as it seems, Sandy."

"If you say so." She struggled to work up some optimism. "I'll get a breath of air outside while you finish in here. Then if it's all right I'll start sorting through my personal belongings and see if I can rescue anything." She took another glance around then went back out the front door and sat dejectedly on the porch steps. Seeing the damage again overwhelmed her just when she thought she was strong enough to face it and do what needed to be done.

After a while the adjuster joined her outside. "I'm going to have another look inside once I assess any exterior damage but go ahead and see what you can salvage. I've already documented everything with photos and voice recording."

She sighed and got to her feet. *Time to quit babying myself and get to work.* She started in her bedroom closet picking through her clothes hanger by hanger to see what she could save. To her surprise many of the garments had been untouched by the spray paint. Removing them one at a time she made space at the end of the closet bar and began selecting and placing them there.

Sandy heard footsteps in the hall then recognized Joy, the lady from across the street. "Sandy? Oh, there you are, sweetie. Is there anything I can do to help? I've been watching the police while they worked here and wondering when you'd be back. I'm brokenhearted for you. The whole neighborhood is upset." Joy walked forward and opened her arms.

Sandy fell into her embrace and the flood of tears she'd been holding back began. Joy held her quietly, stroking and patting her back. Anger gave way to pain and frustration over all she'd lost financially and emotionally. She pulled away and wiped her face. "Wow! Where did that come from?"

Joy reached into her pocket and handed Sandy a tissue. "Honey, this makes *me* cry. You didn't deserve this. What do you want me to do? I'm here to help you."

Sandy mopped her eyes. "Um…we could…," She threw up her arms. "I don't know where to start."

"If we both pitch in you'll see progress in no time. I see you've been sorting through the clothes in your closet. If you like, I can do that while you go through the drawers. I have a couple of mover's wardrobe boxes left over from my daughter's move to Colorado. She didn't need them after all, and I saved them. You can hang your things in there. How does that sound?"

Sandy had never had more than a nodding, waving acquaintance with Joy, and other than chatting with her at the annual 4th of July block party, they were virtual strangers. Hard to believe they'd lived across the street from each other for five years. "I hardly know what to say, Joy."

"Just put me to work. We'll make a big dent in this mess in no time." A determined look crossed her face. "Let's go fetch those wardrobes. I also have some unused moving boxes of various sizes. You can use whatever you need. You'll be helping me by getting them out from underfoot in my garage."

For the first time since she'd left Joe's apartment, Sandy's mood went up several notches. "Okay, let's do it." They walked across the street to Joy's garage.

While they were struggling with the cumbersome, cardboard wardrobe boxes Joy's elderly neighbor entered the garage pulling a dolly. "Just like a couple of women," he fussed. "Move out of my way and I'll haul these across the street one at a time, otherwise you'll be stumbling around like a couple of drunks and have the darn things in tatters by the time you get them there."

Joy and Sandy stood back and let Grouchy Bennett take over. The old man had a heart of gold, but he intimidated every kid in the neighborhood. They'd cross the street to avoid his barbs if he was sitting on his front porch when they came home from school. He was famous for telling the boys to pull up their pants and turn their base-ball caps around and quit parading like a bunch of knot heads.

The two women carried as many boxes as they could and followed him.

"Mr. Bennett, I really want to thank—"

He cut her off short by scowling and holding up a gnarled hand. "Hush and get on about your business. I got work to do. Where do you want me to put this flimsy piece of cra… junk?"

Before he had time to react, Sandy leaned in and kissed him on the cheek. "You don't scare me, Grouchy. This way—my bedroom."

He winked. "I ain't been in a good lookin' gal's bedroom in more years than I care to remember. Lead on."

With Joy's indefatigable help and Mr. Bennett's grousing, it was noon before they realized it. Joy slapped her hands together. "I'm going home. Tuna sandwiches. My kitchen. Ten minutes. Coffee or Coke?"

"Coffee!" Sandy and Mr. Bennett answered together. It got a reluctant grin out of the old curmudgeon.

"What you going to do with all these boxes, young lady?" Mr. Bennett pointed to the growing array in the hallway.

"I suppose we should move them to the garage. My car's at the dealership, but they're waiting for my auto insurance agent to inspect it before they do anything. I hope it's mostly cosmetic, like here." Every time she looked at the walls and floors her stomach churned.

"I knew those scalawags was up to no good." He shook his head with disgust and rolled the dolly toward the boxes.

"Who?"

"Your husband and those bums he hangs around with. Bunch of knot heads if you ask me."

"Did you see them do all this?" If Mr. Bennett could identify the vandals, the police would have more to add to the complaint she'd filed against Phil.

"No, I only seen them move some things out of the house and load it into that old red pickup one of them bums drives. After that they was in the house for over an hour before they left. Your front door was hanging open, so I took a peek inside and seen what they done. I was about to call the police when your friends came."

Sandy sighed and shook her head, the blues threatening to overtake her again. Her cell phone rang. She took it out of her shirt pocket and checked the caller I.D. *Joe.* "I have to take this call. Why don't we leave this for now? I'll meet you and Joy at her house in a few minutes."

He nodded and shuffled out the door.

"Hi, my honey lover." She smiled into the phone. Just knowing he was on the other end of the line made her happy. "I miss you."

———

Joe had counted the minutes until his lunch break to call her. If he hadn't been so busy trying to catch up on the lost day's work, he'd have been tempted to take another day off and go help her. "Hi, my naughty sweetheart, I miss you. What's it been? Six hours? I got it bad."

"Glad I'm not the only one," she answered, the smile in her voice warming his heart.

"How's it going?" The thought of her having to face that mess alone, made him heartsick. "I wish I was there to help you."

"My neighbors across the street, Joy and Mr. Bennett have been here all morning helping me. I was about to go over to Joy's house.

She's fixing sandwiches for us. They've been a godsend. But, Joe, it's not as bad as it looked when we first walked through here. I've salvaged a lot of my personal items."

"Did you find your laptop?"

"I called the dealership. They told me it was on the backseat of my car."

"Hey, that's great. What did the insurance adjuster say?"

"The damage is all cosmetic and what's been lost in the contents will all be covered by my homeowner's policy. I have a thousand-dollar deductible, but that's not a problem, because most of the furniture and carpeting are a total loss."

"When's your handyman due to show up?"

"He'll be here in about an hour. After I clear out my stuff, he'll have a better take on what needs to be done. I don't know where to store these two wardrobe boxes and all the other cartons we'll have packed up by the end of the day. I'm just beginning to understand what it must be like for people who've suffered through fire and floods. I never thought it could feel so personal, but it does."

"Sweetheart, can you leave them in the garage for tonight? I'll search the internet this afternoon and find a small storage unit for you in Liz's neighborhood. That will give you some breathing room."

"I should have thought of that, honey."

Both times she called him honey, his heart had given a painful squeeze. Pain, but it hurt so good. He wanted to have her in his arms tonight, tomorrow, forever. He couldn't come to grips with how fast his mind was streaking in this direction. All his straight talk to himself wasn't working.

As if she'd read his thoughts, she said, "Joe, I want to stay with you again tonight."

Hope zinged through his brain. "Go to Liz's when you leave there. I'll come over and take you both to dinner and we'll tell her you're going to stay with me for a couple of days. Will you? With me?" Two days wouldn't be nearly long enough, and his brain screamed, *slow down, slow down.*

"Yes. I'll come home with you, but your friend is getting there on Friday, so I'll leave Friday morning and go back to Liz's. Face it, honey. I need to find a place to live. I hate being a vagabond. I want to settle in somewhere. A place where I can go inside, lock my door and feel at peace. Do you understand?"

Remembering how important it was for him to get out of staying temporarily with his parents and Clint when he returned to California, and to find a place of his own, he knew exactly what she was saying. "Absolutely, I understand. We'll talk about it tonight. I'm running out of time to grab some lunch before I have to get my head back in the computer. I'll see you and Liz later."

"Bye. I can't wait to be back in your bed with you. You make me feel treasured and safe. I don't know how you do it, but don't stop."

"That's not gonna happen. I want you with me, sweetheart. You make me whole. In a few hours, then we'll be back together." He hung up the phone and closed his eyes. Unaware that Yoda had sat across the table from him until she spoke.

"So, I guess that means I'm not the only woman in your life."

His eyes flew open and he had the urge to round the table and give her a big hug. "It'll be difficult keeping both of you happy and in line, but I'm up for it, beautiful. What's for lunch?"

She grinned her Yoda grin and held up a small package. "This wonderful tasty Weight Watchers frozen entrée, as soon as the microwave is available. I'd share it with you, but it's barely enough to keep me alive, so you're on your own."

Joe opened the small padded cooler he carried in every day. "Don't worry about me. I've got PB&J, potato chips and an apple. Every good boy's favorite lunch." He winked. "Don't take off too much weight. I like my women soft and squeezable."

"I'll pretend you didn't say that, Mr. Hamilton." She grabbed her package and dashed to the microwave before anybody else had a chance to claim it. "Don't start without me."

———

On his way to Liz's place that evening he replayed his conversation with Sandy. They wanted to be together but respected each other's need for space. He'd be patient and hang in there for however long it took for them to reach the same place in their minds and hearts. They had plenty of time. She'd meet his parents this weekend. He had no doubt they'd love her. And they'd understand the significance of him inviting her. He'd never brought a woman home. Not even Rita, his short-lived fiancée. Their engagement was a fait accompli before his parents had a chance to know her. Hell, *he* hadn't even had a chance to know her. He shook his head at his young naivete.

Don't go down that road again, Joseph Hamilton. You're one lucky bastard that something great came out of it.

Mom and Dad would immediately discern his feelings for Sandy and since he had no plan to rush anything, they'd all have plenty of time to get acquainted. He didn't want to consider it, but if things didn't work out for them in the long run; they'd still have this time together. Time to become friends, and lovers. It was important to Joe that they become friends who trusted each other and could depend on each other. Friendship would enhance and deepen the meaning of their intimacy.

And face it, Joe, the intimacy is absolutely dominating your thoughts from morning till night.

He found a parking spot in front of his sister's building and hurried up to her apartment. He hit the doorbell and in seconds Liz opened the door. She pressed her lips together then poked her tongue in her cheek. "Do come in, big brother."

"What are you up to, Liz?" He brushed past her into the living room. "Where's Sandy?"

"My, oh, my, aren't we frothing at the mouth. She's showering. Sit down and have a soda. I'm sure the wait won't kill you."

He turned and shoved his hands in his pockets. "Why are you being so weird? What'd I do?"

She made a how-would-I-know face and placed her hand on her heart. "Do? You tell me. Sandy is giving me the Mt. Rushmore treatment."

A yellow blur streaked across the room and sharp claws nicked his leg as a fluffy kitten climbed her way up his pants, stopped at his belt and mewed pitifully and loud with her big eyes imploring him. "Ouch! And hey there, fluff ball." He lifted her the rest of the way and held her against his cheek. Joe laughed at her ear-splitting purr.

Liz slapped her hand on her hip and glowered. "I don't get it.

What is this mysterious power you have over females? Even my cat. Explain it to me."

Joe leaned forward and kissed Liz's cheek. "I love you too, sis." He carried the kitten to the couch and settled into the cushions, murmuring and petting her into sheer ecstasy.

Liz disappeared into the kitchen and returned shortly with two ice-filled glasses of sparkling brown liquid. "Have a root beer. Sandy just got here half an hour ago, so she'll be a while." In spite of her scowl, a small smile pulled at the corners of her lips. "Where are we going for dinner?"

"You pick." He tickled Butterfly's belly.

"Oh, stop it."

"Stop what?"

"Being so darn nice when I'm being a witch."

"Quit being a witch." He grinned at her. "Shit, sis, you're acting like a jealous ex. What's up?"

"Darned if I know. Now that you're nuts over each other, I feel like a third wheel. I've been replaced."

Joe chuckled and pulled her to his side. "Not possible, baby sister. I need you now more than ever. You're my irreplaceable wing man. I'm depending on you to keep me from messing up. Be my compass. Keep me on the straight and narrow. I'm wandering into completely new territory and I need somebody who's never been afraid to talk sense into me."

She sighed and lowered her head to his shoulder. "Okay, I'll try. Maybe I'm just jealous because I don't have a man in my life who's crazy for me."

"I'm working to remedy that. My buddy, Cole, is getting into Glendale on Friday evening. He'll be with me when I come to the barbecue with the Colonel and his commanding General on Sunday. You're going to do me the great service of bringing Sandy with you."

She nodded and reached for Butterfly. "You're coming too, precious. Dad will pretend he doesn't like you, but we'll both know better. He won't let Major eat you."

"Mom asked me to pick up dessert. I planned to pick up a few kinds of ice cream at the specialty shop, unless you have a better idea."

"No. You can't miss with ice cream. Pick up some waffle cones and we'll eat it the old-fashioned way. That'll be fun."

"Now you're talkin'."

Sandy leaned over his shoulder. "What's a good idea?"

Joe handed the kitten off to Liz and threw his arm over the back of the couch and reached for her. "Ice cream cones for dessert on Sunday."

She stepped around and sat at his other side. "Sounds wonderful." She put her hand on his cheek and moved forward for his kiss. "Hi."

"Hi." He grinned into her face and tried to keep his libido from slamming into overdrive.

Liz grumbled and stood with Butterfly clutched to her chest. "Let's get out of here, cuddles. These two are making me ill."

Joe said to her back, "Stick around, you might learn something."

"Stuff it, Joey!"

"Be nice to your sister, honey. She's provided me a temporary home." Sandy brushed her lips against his. "Mmm, more please."

More was exactly what he gave her. Kiss after kiss. He groaned into her mouth when she stroked his chest and pressed closer. "It's a good thing my sister is in the apartment, or we'd never make it to dinner. The last thing on my mind when I've got you in my arms is food. You're all I need, sexy woman."

"I'm hungry!" Liz yelled from the kitchen. "Feed me or die!"

Chapter Fifteen

HALFWAY THROUGH HER GREEK SALAD, SANDY NODDED TO LIZ. "Yes, that's right. I have a thousand-dollar deductible. I wish it were less but when I took out the policy, I was trying to save money. It was the right decision. I'm not complaining. Most of the furniture is a total loss and I'll have to replace all the carpet and flooring before I can put it on the market."

"Before you throw out some of the furniture, you should have Joey take a look at it. He and Dad have refinished a lot of furniture." She sent Joe a pointed look.

Joe nodded. "She's right. Dad has an entire shop setup in his garage. It's one of his retirement hobbies. I'd love to lend a hand saving your favorite pieces if you like, sweetheart."

Sandy sent a moon-eyed grin to her Joe. "Thank you, honey." Was there anything the man didn't have a talent for?

Liz banged her fork on the table. "Oh, for the love of...will you two stop it!"

Sandy reached across the table and patted Liz's hand. "We're teasing you! It's your fault after all. Without you setting it up, I never would have met your smart, handsome, wonderful, sexy, brother. Thanks, by the way. I'm forever in your debt."

Joe sat up straight and preened. "Yeah, thanks, sis."

Liz rolled her eyes. "I'm trying to eat here."

Sandy was happy to see Liz couldn't help laughing. "Anyhoo—Joe tells me his Marine buddy, Cole Brandon, is perfect for you. I have my fingers crossed that you'll like him. We'll provide backup, if you're not sure. We'll insist on double-dating if he asks you out."

Rolling her eyes again, Liz said, "I'm beginning to think this was a bad idea, Joey."

"No pressure, sis. I have a hunch he won't want to pursue it. He thinks you're too young for him. Let's just have a nice family barbecue with our friends Sandy and Cole on Sunday afternoon."

Liz's forehead creased. "Too young? Did he say that?"

Sandy enjoyed the banter between brother and sister. She loved to savor Joe's mouth when he spoke. He had an expressive face and it didn't hurt to know he was a great kisser. Kissing wasn't the only talent he had with those lips. As if he'd read her mind, he looked at her and cocked his head. His heart-stopping grin aimed at her.

"What's that smile all about, sweetheart?"

"Nothing. I'm just enjoying the conversation between the two of you."

"Joey, answer my question! Did Cole really say I was too young for him?"

Joe raised a shoulder. "Maybe he said he was too old for you. Same difference." He winked at Liz's grumpy expression and faced Sandy. "What are your plans for tomorrow while I'm at work?"

"I have a realtor friend who's also a rental agent. She's lined up about six places to show me tomorrow morning. I'll be listing the house with her when it's ready."

"What neighborhood, Sandy?" Liz queried. "Close to your house or someplace else?"

"Tomorrow the places I'm looking at are all within five miles of People and Productions. As long as I'm moving, it makes sense to be closer to work. If I find something I really like, and the rent is doable, I'll take both of you to see it before I sign the lease."

Joe wiped his mouth and put the napkin next to his empty plate. "That hit the spot, sis. Glad you chose this place. I'd forgotten all about it, it's been so long."

"I second that," Sandy added. "This salad was so big I'm going to have them box up the rest for my lunch tomorrow."

Liz held her plate aloft. "Here take these last two dolmades. I'm beyond full."

"Ah, stuffed grape leaves. Thanks, Liz." Sandy used her knife to slide them onto her plate. This would definitely not be the last time she enjoyed the tasty Greek menu here. The fact that Joe liked it meant they'd be coming again.

Joe signaled the waiter. "I'll get the check so we can be on our way. I have an early meeting tomorrow. I'll be up at the crack of dark."

"I'll be snoozing while you two drudges are slaving away. I'm not meeting my realtor until ten." Sleep would come after some earth-shaking sex. Joe wouldn't know what hit him. A melting heat coursed through her most sensitive body parts. Yes, her Joe was in for some surprises.

She handed her plate to the server. "Box this up for me please?"

———

Joe dropped the women at Liz's apartment and headed back to Glen-dale. Sandy would get her things and follow him in her rental car. His neck tingled as he thought of having her in his bed for the next two nights. But, besides that, he loved talking to her, laughing with her, sharing a meal with her, or just lounging in front of the TV eating popcorn while her back rested against his side and chest. They fit together perfectly. Sandy was the best thing to ever happen to him in this life.

He parked his car in the apartment garage, and then paced the sidewalk in front of his building. The evening was balmy even though the day had been typical California June gloom. He grinned, waved, and went to meet her when he spotted her walking in his direction with her overnight bag. His heart rate ticked up just watching her walk.

"Hi, sweetheart. Let's walk to the corner store and pick up some half and half for your coffee in the morning." He took her bag and kissed her. "Glad you're here." And wasn't that an understatement?

Sandy smiled and took his hand. "I'm glad to be here."

The small errand was accomplished in a few minutes. On the way back, she stopped and pointed to an advertisement for a much-anticipated movie. "Let's go see that when it comes out. I read the book and I really liked it."

"I read it too. Some of the packages troops got from USO had paperbacks in them." He chuckled. "Don't tell anyone."

"Another thing I didn't know about my man. He reads romance. I love that." She raised her face to him. "Kiss me, and we'll go up to your place and recreate my favorite love scene. I know you're up to it, Marine."

"Ooh rah, woman. We'll do them one by one. I still have the paperback on my bookshelf." Those 'girlie' novels were chock full of Romance 101.

"Then we'll make up some of our own. You may never get to sleep tonight." She raised her brows and directed a sultry stare into his face. "Did I ever say how hot you are, Joe Hamilton? Did I ever say you set me on fire whenever I think about you, which is every few minutes?" She tugged his hand and speeded up. "Don't make me wait."

His blood boarded that southbound rocket from his brain again. "I promise you won't even have time to get your clothes off." He laughed and broke into a run, tapped his code in the lobby door and hurried her up the stairs. "Come on, slowpoke." Laughter rippled off her as she bounded up the stairs with him.

She tugged him through the open door before he had time to remove his key. He hooted and yanked at it until it was free. Inside he dropped her bag and the small grocery sack, kicked the door shut and pressed her back against the wall.

She put her hands against his chest. "Do you want to talk first?"

He jerked back. "Are you kidding me?"

"I am." She put her arms around him and slid her hands beneath his shirt and up his bare back. "Get this off. I want my mouth on your pecs. Quick, Joe."

"I want you, baby. I want you like I've never wanted anything." The shirt didn't stand a chance. Buttons flew in every direction as he ripped it open. "Go for it." He slipped a hand under her skirt and nearly passed out when he discovered the absence of panties. "My, God." Unable to utter another word for lack of breath, his mouth came down on hers hard and fast. He tasted blood when her teeth sank into his bottom lip. His grip on her backside tightened to the point he feared leaving bruises on her silky soft flesh, but he couldn't stop himself.

She whimpered against his neck. "Bed, Joe."

He wouldn't remember later how they got to his room, but he'd never forget how his heart soared when she cried out in gratification under his hand before he'd had a chance to lower his zipper. He covered her mouth with his to lower the volume of her cries. She finally went limp, a huge smile, full of the devil, on her face as she tugged at the button on his trousers and shoved him off and onto his back.

The room spun, time lost all meaning. The groan he heard was his own when she took him in her hand. *Hang on, Hamilton. Hang on.*

"Look at you, Joe. Mine, all mine. I'm the luckiest woman in the world to have you all to myself." Her hand moved.

It went fast. He gritted his teeth and gasped for air. *Sandy, I love you.* The words were on the tip of his tongue. Had he said them out loud? He didn't know. He didn't care. He wanted her and he loved her. More than he'd thought possible. The realization both exhilarated and terrified him.

She sighed, dropped forward and kissed his chest then melted at his side, one leg thrown across his hips. They were both fully clothed. He chuckled. "I kept my promise."

"So you did." She hummed and stroked his cheek, rough with five o'clock shadow.

———

The next morning at six he dragged himself from her arms. He smiled when she mumbled, rolled over and snuggled in. He covered her nakedness, made his way to the small kitchen and got the coffee going then headed for the shower. Ten minutes later, his hair still damp, he retrieved the small grocery bag from the entry floor, opened the cream and sniffed. *Still good.* His sweetheart would have her coffee just the way she liked it. He placed it in the refrigerator, slipped into his shoes and tiptoed out the door.

His boss did a double take when Joe entered the conference room unconsciously touching his bruised lip. "Jesus, Hamilton. What happened to you?" He caught the gleam in Joe's eye. "Ah. Well. I'm glad you made it in. Grab some coffee then go to the men's room and wring the blood out of your eyes. You can explain later."

Like hell he'd ever explain. He was on time for work; he'd do his job and contribute to the meeting, but explain? Not in this lifetime.

Glad the meeting was brief, he got caught up on paperwork. He glanced at his watch. *Two already.* His cell vibrated with a text and he checked the screen.

Found a condo. Renting furniture from Rent-A-Center this aftn. U-n-Liz see tomoro. move in nxt Mon. I fix dinner 2nite. Hurry home. S. xxxx

He grinned and dropped the phone back in his shirt pocket, looked up and saw Yoda eyeing him over the top of her glasses.

"I'm worried about you, Mr. Hamilton," she teased in a whisper.

"Don't you worry about me, Yvonne. I've never been better." Hell, how could he ever be any better?

"Maybe, but you look like they just Medivaced you from the front lines." She opened her drawer and took out a bottle of eye drops that had bright red words on the label, *Get rid of red!*

"Try some of this and you might not look like you're bleeding out."

He accepted them and flinched when the first drops burned like molten lava. "Ow! Goddammit!" He reached for a tissue and dabbed. "What's in here? Tabasco?"

"Don't be a crybaby." She took them from his hand and dropped them in her drawer. "You look better already, but if you show up tomorrow with the same thousand-yard stare, I'm calling the blood bank."

"I'll get a few winks tonight." He grinned. "Hey, did you get a copy of that long list of new companies who've signed with us? My sister, Liz, works for one of them in their art department. It's an advertising agency. I wonder what they need us for."

"Could be as simple as new-hire background checks. I just processed a ton of them for Pasadena First Bank. You'd flinch at the things people fail to reveal on their employment applications."

"Yeah. Not much escapes this new software, does it?" He'd love to ask Liz or Sandy if they knew anything about their agency hiring his security firm, but he was strictly forbidden personal communication with any company they had under contract.

"I'm just about done for the day, Mr. Hamilton." Yoda shut down her computer and gathered her purse and briefcase.

"Right behind you, gorgeous." He grinned at her unrelenting formality.

"I didn't hear that, Mr. Hamilton."

"Sure you did."

———

Joe opened his front door to a bouquet of delicious aromas. "Mmmm."

"Joe! In here, honey."

"Wow, something smells wonderful." He came up behind her and put his long arms around her slender waist. He'd love to come home to this every night.

"I made you something very tasty." She dropped her head back to receive his kiss.

"Nothing could ever be as tasty as you, my lovely." He covered her breasts and sighed at the pleasure of touching her. "Nothing. Ever."

"You haven't tasted my beef bourguignon yet, so I'll leave you some wiggle room on your statement."

"Umm, wiggle, my new favorite word." He rotated his hips against her small, curvy backside, stoking a fire that needed minimal help.

"Go change out of your suit and let me get this on the table." She pushed back against him. "I expect your unwavering attention to my cooking. Don't break my heart."

"Never." Even as he said it, he recognized life was unpredictable, and anything could happen. "Not if I can help it, my sweetheart."

"Thank you, my honey. Now scram." She poked an elbow into his side. "You're going to love this. At least you'd better. I made enough for tonight and tomorrow night."

Joe laughed and stepped away. "Back in a flash." He grabbed his jacket from the back of the chair where he'd dropped it and went to change into comfortable sweats.

She was on the phone when he returned to the kitchen. "Thanks,

Stinky. Keep me posted. Hug, hug."

"Everything all right in Oregon?" He couldn't read her expression.

"Yes, Damon wanted me to know they'd filled Mom in on my secret, sordid life. She was sorry I'd kept it from her, but she's taking it well. I told him I'd be up for a visit on Labor Day weekend. Would you like to come?"

"Sure. I get four days off. We could make a little vacation trip out of it going up and back. But, maybe it's too soon to bring me into the picture. Until a couple days ago your mother thought you were happily married to Phil Rice."

"Ugh. Don't remind me." She handed him plates and flatware. "Here, set the table while I toss the salad and dish up my specialty."

Joe sighed through every bite. Sandy's cheeks went rosy with pleasure over his unabashed enjoyment of her cooking. "This is one of the best dishes I've ever eaten. You weren't kidding—or bragging. This is my new favorite meal, sweetheart. Tell me—what's your secret?"

"The beef is simmered in red wine." She grinned at him then her face registered horror. "Oh, my, God, Joe, I put wine in this!" Her hands flew to her mouth, appalled at what she'd done. Tears welled on her lashes. "I wasn't thinking. I don't know what to say."

Joe put down his fork and scooted his chair back. He rounded the table and knelt beside her. "Sweetheart, it's okay. I'm sure the alcohol was all cooked out of it, leaving only the flavor. If it makes you feel better, I'll call my AA sponsor and check with him."

Sandy pushed away from him and snatched up the casserole dish. She carried it to the sink and dumped the contents then switched on the disposal. Frantic, she lifted the pot from the stovetop without a potholder and dropped it with a bang into the sink. Her shoulders shook with sobs while she held her hand under the cold faucet.

Joe rushed to her side, lifted her seared thumb and gently kissed it. "Sweetheart, stop! You didn't do anything wrong." He put his hands on her trembling shoulders and pulled her into an embrace. Her legs gave way and she sagged against him. "Sweetheart. Sandy. Please don't." He held her tight and felt like crying for her. "Baby, I love you." Hands on her cheeks, he tilted her head. "Look at me." Her tragic eyes fluttered open, pupils huge in her honey brown irises. "Listen to me. I. Love. You."

"Joe," she blubbered. "How could I have done that to you, the man I love?"

He smiled and lifted the dishtowel to her face and wiped her tears. "I'd walk through fire for you, sweetheart." He pressed the damp towel to her hand and led her to his small living room where he reclined on the sofa, pulling her down on his chest. Never taking his arms from around her, he stroked her hair and her back while crooning reassurances.

"Call him, honey. Call him now."

"Tell you what. There's an AA meeting at First Presbyterian tonight." He glanced at his watch and patted her fanny. "It hasn't started yet. Let's walk down there. We both need some air."

She scrambled off him. "Yes, please, I want to go with you."

"Okay, go splash some water on your face then I'll rub an ice cube on your thumb. There's plenty of time."

She hurried to the bathroom while Joe dumped some ice from the refrigerator dispenser into a cup. She joined him at the kitchen table and held out her hand. "It's not bad. I probably did more damage to the sink than I did to my hand. Did you check to see if I chipped it?"

He brushed a light kiss on her knuckles. "I don't give a rat's ass about the sink." He rubbed a quickly melting ice cube over the small red mark. "This will be fine. How does it feel?"

"It stings a little. Can we go?" She stood and he dabbed her hand dry with the clean towel he'd flipped over his shoulder.

"Sure." He hugged her and she retrieved her sweater off the rack on the way out his front door. They strolled the few blocks in the rapidly cooling evening. Joe draped his arm over her shoulders. "You warm enough? We're almost there."

She nodded to the large, modern, glass-clad building. "Is that it?"

"Yep." They approached the side of the structure where a door had been propped open. An easel announced, "Friends of Bill W. meet here tonight. 8:00 p.m."

"Who's Bill W.?" She stopped. "Are we in the right place?"

"Bill Wilson was one of the original founders of AA way back in the nineteen-thirties." Joe nodded to a couple of people when they stepped inside. "Let's sit over there. I'll keep an eye out for Brian, he's usually here."

144

Sandy's eyes swept the room. "Are all these people alcoholics? They look so...um...normal." Her cheeks blazed. "Sorry. What a thing to say. I'll just keep my mouth shut."

Joe laughed. "We're all 'normal' and we're all here to talk about it. That's the point, sweetheart. You don't have to be afraid of offending anyone. Just relax and enjoy the fellowship." He picked up her hand and kissed the burn again, just as an elderly gentleman with a head of snowy white hair and a beard took the seat next to Sandy.

"Evening, Joseph. Introduce me to your friend."

"Brian, this is my sweetheart, Sandy Cassidy. Sandy, meet my sponsor, Brian. Go ahead; ask him the question that's burning a hole in your tongue."

"Um...hi, Brian. I...um...made beef bourguignon for dinner tonight. That's why we're here. I'm afraid I might have...you know... Joe...he can't have any alcohol. I wasn't thinking."

"Beef bourguignon? One of my favorite dishes. My late wife, Francis, used to make it for special occasions. I didn't know young ladies today still knew how to prepare it."

"But it's made with wine! Joe didn't know that until after he'd eaten two helpings." The pained look on her beautiful face ripped at Joe's gut. He loved her more every minute.

"I told her it wouldn't be a problem, Brian. That's why we're here tonight. Please put her mind at ease."

"Certainly." His smile was wise and kindly. "While the slow process of cooking beef bourguignon dissipates the alcohol in the wine, AA cautions its members against having alcohol in the house. You can substitute tomato juice with a splash of red wine vinegar and achieve a very satisfactory result. In fact, there are several websites and cookbooks with great tips on substitutions for wine, beer and other alcohol." He smiled and patted Sandy's hand. "In the meantime, I'm sure no harm was done."

Joe squeezed her shoulder. "See, sweetheart? No problem."

She expressed a deep sigh. "I'm sorry for throwing out tomorrow night's dinner." Her eyes rolled with relief.

"Tell you what. After the meeting, I'll take you out for cupcakes as your reward for worrying about me." He kissed her forehead and again counted himself a very lucky man.

Chapter Sixteen

SANDY LISTENED TO JOE'S BREATHING AS HE DRIFTED OFF TO sleep around midnight, after he'd loved her his own special way. Slow. Real slow. She smiled with satisfaction and softly rested her hand on his belly, savoring his strength. Strength tempered with marvelous sensitivity and gentleness. She'd never dreamed of finding such fulfillment with a man. She hadn't dared dream after her disappointing marriage disintegrated. She'd allowed Phil to use her, take advantage of her. More than anything, she wanted to trust a man again. To love this man.

Joe didn't use manipulation and lies to get what he wanted from her. She went willingly into his arms and his bed, motivated by one simple fact—she needed what Joe wanted. Making him happy filled her to the brim.

She moved closer to him and placed her arm on his chest. His heart beat strong against her wrist, his breathing deep and contented. She'd never, ever do anything to hurt him. Joe was more than worth the investment of her body and her soul. This man who openly declared his love for her. This man who treasured his family. This man who often spoke of the Marines he'd served with, admiration and respect infusing every word.

She rolled over. He growled, "Get back over here, woman."

Sandy giggled and put her arm and leg across him again. "Yes, master."

He crooked his elbow around her neck and pulled her closer. "Very good. If you're having trouble sleeping, I can remedy that."

She nestled into his side. "I'm sure you could but give me about a minute and I'll be out cold." There was something special, something steadfast about sleeping in Joe's arms. He joked about dominating her while displaying the most sensuous tenderness with every touch. She sighed deeply and drifted off to his whispered endearments.

―――――

The stimulating aroma of coffee drifted past her nose. She reached for Joe and patted the empty spot in his bed. She sighed and tugged his pillow to her face, sucking in his unique masculine scent, a blend of pheromones and spicy pine forest. She had a busy day ahead, so she dragged herself out of their warm nest and padded to the kitchen for coffee. She had less than an hour to get to her ruined house to meet with her handyman. A jolt of caffeine would jump start her. They'd start dragging out the unsalvageable furniture and carpeting today. This evening Joe and Liz would have a look at the condo she planned to lease.

Her cell chirped. She didn't recognize the number. "Hello?"

"Is Phil around?"

Hair rose on her scalp. The tips of her fingers went cold. Why would anyone call her number and ask for Phil? "Who is this? How did you get this number?" The line went dead. Her stomach took a sickening dive.

―――――

Joe drove to the address Sandy had given him for the condo complex. It was in a mixed neighborhood, small stores advertised their offerings in the windows of a mini-mall, next to an LAPD substation. The new complex was just next door. He nodded to himself. *Police right next door. Good.* He spotted Liz's rental car and pulled into the curbside space behind it.

He got out, did a threat assessment at the entrance and street on either side then went through the front doors into the small lobby where locked mailboxes covered both walls. He spotted working security cameras at three strategic locations.

The front door of her unit stood wide open, and he heard the two women talking as he approached. "Knock, knock." Sandy, dressed in jeans, running shoes and a loose T-shirt ran to hug him.

Liz motioned him over. "Joey, look at this place. I might want to move here myself. Isn't this kitchen fantastic?" She walked past the granite counter and smoothed her hand over the glass cook top. "I love this!"

Sandy stood tiptoe and dropped a light kiss on Joe's mouth. "Liz loves it. I told her they have two more available. One on the ground floor and one across the courtyard from me. I can't wait to move in."

"Nice, sugar. Real nice." He dropped an arm around her waist. "How'd it go today at your house?"

"We got more done than I thought possible and I'm completely pooped! The painters are coming tomorrow afternoon, so we'll need to pack up the kitchen in the morning to be ready for them. I'm sending everything that's unopened to the food bank. I'm starting over."

"No furniture you want to save?" Joe cocked his head. "You sure?"

"I don't need the memories. I'm considering buying some unfinished pieces that I'll paint."

"We can do that together." Liz gave a little hop. "It'll be fun. Where will you get the pieces?"

"There's a small store in the mini-mall. You probably thought it was an X-rated video store if you saw the sign. "Bare Naked? I walked through there when I got here ahead of you."

"Oh, I want to see it! Let's walk over there after you sign the lease."

Joe smiled at his sister's enthusiasm. "Have you ever painted unfinished furniture, sis?" He tugged her ponytail. "It's work."

She made a sour face. "I work with paints all the time. I'm an artist, remember?" She turned to Sandy. "What pieces would you buy?"

Joe figured he might as well have not been in the room, both women were off in their own world.

"They have this oval kitchen table and chair set that would fit perfectly in this little nook area." She walked to the windowed corner and turned in a circle. "I picture it in glossy Wedgewood Blue with the table and chair legs white like the plantation shutters."

"Perfect! I could paint some decorative scroll work in white and on the center of the table and the chair backs. Personalize it to your taste."

"Liz, that would be great! I'll order it tomorrow afternoon after Rent-a-Center delivers the pieces I chose for the living room and bedroom. I'll leave the second bedroom empty for now."

"That's wise to rent, Sandy. You'll have plenty of time to shop. It takes me forever to make a decision on something as important as furniture. Joey knows." She smiled at her big brother.

Joe's lips twitched a rueful smile. "Do I ever. You'd think world peace depended on it." If Sandy waited long enough to buy furniture, they might be sharing this place and he'd bring what he already owned. Two could live here very comfortably. There was even a small alcove off the hall that would make a great place for a desk and some bookshelves. Both bedrooms were spacious, and each had its own bathroom. A powder room for guests, off the hall, had a stacked washer/dryer combo in it. He really liked the floor plan.

He stood behind Sandy and put his arms around her. "You made a good choice, sweetheart." He'd rather she'd move in with him, but he had to be realistic. She needed to feel free of Phil once and for all. A complete change of scene would help her make the adjustment. "How about dinner, ladies? I spotted a Taco Bell down the block."

Sandy laughed. "Another reason I liked this place. I'll lock the door and put the lease papers in the rental agent's box downstairs."

———

Sandy wondered if she should tell Joe about the strange call, the man asking for Phil? She sighed and rolled her eyes. She was making way too much of it. There had to be a plausible explanation. It would come to her if she'd quit worrying about it.

The call was the prod she needed to get herself to Verizon tomorrow and ask for a different number, one Phil or any of his loser cronies wouldn't have access to. It was past time to upgrade to a newer phone.

"Joe?"

When he turned to face her and smiled, her heart nearly melted. How could a single female on the planet resist that smile?

"Yes, sweetheart?"

"I'm going back to Liz's tonight. I have so much to do tomorrow, and you're collecting your friend, Cole, after work. I'll come over when we finish here and make sure all my stuff is cleared out, so you don't have any explaining to do." She bit into her crispy steak taco and sighed with contentment.

Joe laughed. "Do you think there's a man alive who wouldn't love to tell another guy he's been lucky enough to have a woman in his apartment?" He shook his head and sipped root beer. "Never happen, sweetheart."

Liz shook her head. "Men are a lower species of animal."

Sandy grinned. "Okay, macho guy, but I am going to Liz's. I'll be up late with the claim forms, and then I have to take them to the main insurance office in downtown L.A. in the morning. After that, I'll swing by the Honda dealer and retrieve my laptop, then talk to my boss to catch up on what I missed this past week." She pointed to her cheek. "The only time the bruise is visible is when I wash my face before bedtime. A little makeup artistry, and nobody will be any the wiser."

Joe leaned close to her ear and whispered, "Bedtime—my new favorite word."

Liz kicked him under the table. "I'm not deaf! Heavens above, I loosed a monster when I brought the two of you together. I'm telling Mom what a very bad boy you are, Joey." She locked eyes with him. "Oh, no. What's that look? What are you thinking?"

Joe grinned, mischief dancing in his eyes. Sandy knew he was up to something. She cast him a suspicious glance.

"Sis, Mom has been married to a very bad boy for almost forty years. You really think she's clueless? Here I am, sitting between two gorgeous women, the envy of every man in this joint, and especially the kid behind the counter."

Sandy smiled. "Don't get a big ego boost. He probably thinks an old man like you is a volunteer for Big Brothers, and we're your charges."

"Ouch."

———

Sandy followed Joe to Glendale. She parked on the street and waited for him to get from the garage to the lobby to let her in. The street was quiet, just one young man, hands in his pockets, wearing a hoodie, walking in her direction. Joe opened the door when he came abreast of her.

He grinned and waved at Joe but said nothing.

Inside, Sandy asked, "Do you know him?"

"Yeah. That's Seth. He works at the Rite Aid on the corner. We play racquet ball once in a while. I met him in an IT class at Pasadena City College right after I moved back to California."

"What could they teach you that you didn't already know?"

"Not much, but we met a couple of cute coeds Seth and I took out for coffee after classes. I was just killing time waiting to start my new job."

She raised her brow with skepticism. "Really."

"Really, sexy. Don't think you're getting out of here in a flash. I crave some physical time to tide me over till next week."

"Why are we standing here?" She squeezed his butt, and he jumped with surprise.

"You're in for it now, baby."

———

An hour later she gathered her few cosmetics from the bathroom sink and cabinet. She reached to the top of the shower door for a pair of lacy, green bikini panties she'd rinsed out that morning.

"Leave'm." Joe pulled her hand back. "I intend to move them to the guest bathroom, hang them on the showerhead, and pretend I didn't know they were there. Give old Cole something to think about."

She snorted. "Men!"

"Yeah, isn't it great?" He crushed her in a bear hug. "Sure you have to go?"

"Yep." She thought again of telling Joe about the unsettling call for

Phil but changed her mind. There had to be a simple explanation. *You're getting paranoid, Sandy.*

———

Joe laid a sizzling kiss on her lips at her car door and stood on the sidewalk, watching until she turned the corner. Back in his apartment, he took the green panties, placed them on the guest bath showerhead and closed the curtain. He chuckled, imagining Cole's ribbing.

The apartment seemed quiet and empty without Sandy. He'd become comfortable with her being there. They were natural and good together. He looked forward to introducing her to his parents on Sunday. They were going to see a lot of her in the future.

———

Friday morning, Sandy braved the awful traffic to the downtown L.A. location of the insurance headquarters. She passed her claim forms to an assistant adjuster. "I'm Sandra Cassidy. I'd like to file these."

The lanky young man, wearing black-rimmed glasses asked her to wait. "I'm Peter Williams. I'll review the paperwork to make sure it's correctly submitted. I wouldn't want you to have to return or have any unnecessary delays in the settlement of your claim."

"Thank you. I'm happy to wait. Anything to avoid driving all the way here again." She took a seat in the small waiting lobby and picked up a magazine. Her eyes always went to the display advertising first. She scanned the pages for ads produced by People and Productions. A full-page ad for the baby products company, her largest acquisition, caught her eye. Liz and her department had come up with fantastic artwork and photo arrays. The creative guys enhanced the message with great tag lines. A warm thrill of satisfaction brought a smile to her face. The results of her many months of sales calls and meetings with the client had really paid off.

Young Mr. Williams approached. "I've checked your forms. There shouldn't be any delay in settling your claim. Thank you for coming in."

She shook his hand and smiled. "I appreciate your help, Peter."

"Anytime," he said, giving her hand an extra squeeze.

She thanked him again and headed to her office. Her boss, Jordan People, was expecting to meet her for lunch at the deli near the agency. She was anxious to get back to work. To get a greater degree of normalcy in her life.

Her heart plummeted when she entered the deli. Jordan dropped his cell phone on the table, a black scowl growing on his face. He spotted her and motioned her over. "Shit and double shit!"

"Nice to see you too, Jordan." She sat across from him.

"Sorry for the language. I just got a piece of very bad news." He rubbed his temples.

"Is everything okay with your wife and kids?" She'd never seen him so perturbed. "What is it?"

"All Things Babies? The account you spent almost a year bringing to us? They just bailed."

"What! Why?" This was very bad news. ATB was their largest account and put P&P squarely in the profit margin this past year. All indications signaled they were happy with People and Productions. The beautiful display ad in the parenting magazine she'd been scanning in the insurance office had to be ramping up their sales significantly. "I don't get it. What did they say?"

"Some crap about realigning the company, moving advertising dollars etc. etc."

"In other words, they're not giving a valid reason. I don't get it. I check their stock prices in the Wall Street Journal every morning. They've been rising steadily, ever since we took over their advertising.

"Jordan. I should call on them right away. We need to know what went wrong, especially if it was something on our end." She closed her mouth when the server approached the table and asked for their order. Her appetite was evaporating rapidly.

Jordan People stared morosely into his coffee mug. "You're due back Monday, right? I'll call this afternoon and try to set up an appointment for you with their marketing department for Monday afternoon. We need to get to the bottom of this. There was no inkling of a problem."

"Yes. I hope they haven't moved their account to one of our competitors. I'll do my best to talk them out of leaving us." Sandy took this personally. ATB was the largest account she'd brought to P&P. It affected Jordan's bottom line, not hers, but he was the best boss she'd ever had and great to work for

He leaned back and shook his head. "I hope you at least had a nice vacation. I could use some good news."

If he only knew.

This, added to the past two week's events tested her ability to remain optimistic about her future. If it weren't for Joe, she'd really be down in the dumps.

Did Liz know about ATB? How could she? Every indication was Jordan had received the bad news just before she walked in the restaurant.

The arrival of their sandwiches gave her a chance to work on a logical response. How was she going to eat any of it, after what he'd just told her? She racked her brain. She had to offer something to ease her boss.

Chapter Seventeen

JOE UNLOCKED HIS DOOR AND STEPPED ASIDE SO COLE COULD enter. "Bathroom's down the hall to the right. Den with a Hide-a-Bed directly across from it. Here, let me have the doggie bag and I'll stow it in the fridge."

Cole hauled his overnight bag down the short hall. "I'll be a minute."

It had been over a year since Joe had spent any time with Cole. He'd almost forgotten he was such a funny guy. They'd reminisced and laughed non-stop during dinner. Joe enjoyed getting caught up on the doings of some of the active-duty men he'd lost touch with. He placed the Styrofoam container between a six-pack of root beer and a carton of eggs, then filled the well on his Mr. Coffee, and dumped some decaf in the filter. The pot made a racket when he switched it on. He kept forgetting to run white vinegar through it to get rid of the calcification. It still made good coffee.

"Hey, pal." Cole stood in the doorway twirling Sandy's green panties on the end of his finger. "You left a pair of your briefs in the shower."

Joe faked surprise. "Oh, man, I hate when that happens." He

155

grabbed the lacy nothing and stuffed it in his pocket, enjoying his buddy's pursed lips. A touch of envy glittered in Cole's sea-green eyes.

"Yeah, sure." Cole shook his head sadly. "You're one sorry-ass, lousy liar. Anything you care to share?"

Joe turned his back to hide a smile. "Oh, look. The coffee's ready."

"If you're rubbing up against a woman on a regular basis, and she leaves her Victoria's here, I want details."

Joe handed Cole a steaming mug of coffee. "I confess, but no details. You'll meet her on Sunday." He grinned. "She's the one." He'd found the one woman he could trust and love from now on.

"As I recall, that's not an original concept for you. Watch yourself, buddy." He blew on the coffee and took a sip.

Joe forced an unwelcome fragment of doubt from his thoughts. Sandy wasn't Rita.

Cole leaned back against the sink. "So, how'd you hook up with her?"

"She's Liz's friend and coworker. We met a couple of months ago. Her name's Sandy. We're enjoying each other but taking it slow."

Cole's lips twitched. "Oh, yeah, now I remember. You like it slow, real slow."

"My sister says all men are shallow, transparent twits." He had to admit; men were pretty simple creatures.

Cole cocked a brow. "This is the sister you're trying to palm off on me?"

Joe snorted. "Watch it! You'll be lucky if Liz even gives you a second glance. She's gorgeous and very smart and talented."

"And you're completely objective. No doubt about it. So, why's she still single?"

"I told you, she's very choosy. You probably won't make the cut."

Cole grinned and sipped coffee. "Now, back to the owner of the lacy green panties."

"Dream on, Brandon."

———

They had a blast at the Dodgers game on Saturday afternoon, even when a woman sitting behind them dodged a foul ball and bumped into Cole's back. Cole's entire cup of beer dumped in Joe's lap. The nice-looking woman apologized profusely, grinning at Cole the entire time. Joe inhaled deeply. Beer. God, he'd almost forgotten the heavenly smell of a glass of cold, foamy beer. He'd have to walk out of the stadium looking like he'd pissed himself, and then stand in the shower for an hour once he got home to rid him of it before they hit his favorite pasta joint for dinner.

Before lights-out that night, he called Sandy's cell, and heard a recorded message—the number was no longer in service. 'Huh?" He tried again and got the same flat-toned speech.

EARLIER, LIZ'S APARTMENT

Sandy was grimy and pooped when she got to Liz's. She opened the door and was assailed by chili spices. "Liz? Whatever it is you're whipping up in there smells more than good enough to eat." She dropped her purse on the floor and threw her sweater in the direction of the coat rack.

Liz held up an icy margarita. "Join me. After today's news, I needed alcohol and comfort food." She lifted the lid on the pot and sniffed. "Almost there."

"Do I smell chili?"

"Chili macaroni and beans drowning in queso blanco. Mom used to make this for me and Joey."

Sandy picked up the margarita, licked salt from the rim, and took a healthy swallow. "This hits the spot. I couldn't get my mind on anything else all afternoon. I imagine P&P is in an uproar."

"That's putting it mildly. Jordan called a joint meeting of the sales and advertising departments right after lunch. We spent the afternoon brainstorming. He's already laid off two recent interns. Everybody looks like they're standing in line for the guillotine."

"That bad?' Sandy's stomach knotted. She told herself she had nothing to worry about. She'd brought in more new accounts than anyone in the past year.

"Jordan told us he had a heck of a time getting ATB to consent to meeting with you on Monday. How are you planning to handle it?"

"Will you to go with me?"

"Me?" Liz put a hand over her heart. "What could I possibly add?"

"Besides offering moral support, I was hoping you could do some gentle probing on their decision to bail. You're so well versed in the actual production of their ad campaign, maybe we missed something? Have they been lukewarm about what we're doing for them, and we just didn't pick up the clues?" She sighed, finished off her margarita and poured another. First Phil's betrayal, and now she worried her job could be in jeopardy. And she'd signed a one-year lease on her expensive new place. What next, finding out Joe was a serial bigamist?

"Nobody at P&P can think of anything negative we missed. We were completely blind-sided." She turned off the stove. "Pour me another one of those and we'll sit down and cry in our booze for a while before dinner."

A little after ten, Liz's phone rang. "Joey, hi. Yes, she's right here." She held out the phone for Sandy. "Joey, said your cell phone number isn't working."

Sandy smacked her forehead. "Oh, heck. I forgot." She took her new phone out of her pocket and set it on the table. "Hi, honey lover." She grinned when Liz rolled her eyes. "I got a new phone today and forgot to call you to let you know. Yes, I'm fine. Everything's done, but now there's a new wrinkle." She told him about the turn of events at P&P. "Liz and I are in total shock. We're going to call on them Monday and try to salvage it." She listened, nodding.

"Yes, our biggest account. The boss already let two interns go." She sighed. "Oh. Why a different number? Mostly because it cuts the final tie with Phil. It was time to upgrade anyway. "It's…" She turned on the new phone and recited the number. "How's your weekend going so far? Good. I'll warn Liz. See you tomorrow, honey."

"Warn me about what? Do I need another margarita?" She went to the stove and took a big ladle to spoon the chili-macaroni concoction into shallow soup plates. After she added a sprig of fresh cilantro, she carried them to the table, then went back for a bowl of grated white cheese. "More queso if you want it."

Sandy sniffed appreciatively. "No, he said you won't be able to resist Cole. He's the man for you. Assuming he gives you a second look."

"We'll see about that."

"He also asked me to say; now you know how it feels to be set up." Sandy laughed. "Relax. You might actually like the guy. What's the worst that can happen?"

"Take that back! After what happened today, I'm not in a very optimistic mood."

———

Sunday, the senior Hamilton's home in Spring Grove

Joe parked in front of his parent's house. He looked at both sides of the street. "The girls aren't here yet. Let's go in so I can introduce you to my brother and my parents." He opened his car door at the same time as Clint walked out of the house. "You going somewhere?"

"Like you care." He stared down at his battered Nikes and kept walking.

"Hey, wait up! Clint, I'd like you to meet my friend, Cole Brandon. He's stationed at Pendleton."

"Hey, man. See you later." He shoved his hands in his jeans and walked away from them.

Cole shrugged. "What is he, thirteen, fourteen? Rough age."

"He's been pissed at me about something. I can't figure it." Joe shook his head. "Let's go in."

"Nice house. How long have they lived here?"

"Since just before I reenlisted. Liz was in junior high." He strolled up the front walk, knocked once and opened the door. "Mom, Cole and I are here. Are we too early?"

"Come in." His dad called from the kitchen. "The women went to pick up something at the grocery. Your mother always forgets an item she needs at the last minute." He smiled and walked forward with his hand extended. "Captain Brandon, it's an honor to meet you."

Cole smiled and shook his hand. "It's my honor to meet you, Colonel Hamilton, sir."

"Now that we've dispensed with the bullshit, please call me Don. How about a beer?"

"Love one, Don."

"Careful, Dad. Cole's clumsy. He dumped an entire cup of beer in my crotch at the Dodgers game yesterday. I almost fell off the wagon inhaling the fumes."

Don Hamilton grinned. "We'll make sure he's sitting down."

"He was sitting down yesterday. In his defense, it was probably the blonde with her huge rack hitting him in the face that caused the accident." Joe laughed at Cole's scowl and followed them out to the back patio.

Cole stopped and stared. "That grill is one big mother. If you put tires on it, it would serve as a second car." He grinned with appreciation. "How long you had this baby?"

Joe enjoyed his dad's flash of pride. Kudos to Cole for finding just the right words to make his father a friend for life. He loved that monster grill almost as much as the flag, and that said a lot.

"Had her about six months." He stood with his hands on his hips and a loving expression on his commanding officer's face. "Wait till you see what it does for a steak. Best you've ever had. Guaranteed."

Major bounded around the corner of the house when he heard the men talking. He gave Joe a joyful greeting and dropped a knotted rag at his feet. Joe knelt and let the dog lave his face with kisses while he tugged at his ruff. "Hey, boy. How's my buddy?"

Don leaned close to Cole's ear. "Joseph thinks the dog is his, but you'll hear a different story from his brother and my wife, Bernice. That mutt is totally devoted to them. There's no way in hell he'll every pry that cur away from here."

"Major," Joe waved the knotted rag. "Dad called you a mutt and a cur. He wouldn't dare say that if General Mom was within earshot. We'll file that away for future reference." Joe gripped one end of the rag and Major the other. The tug of war began.

Cole shook his head. "I can see where that could get old fast."

Don nodded. "Whatever you do, don't toss the ball if he drops it at your feet." He chuckled and checked the temperature gauge on the grill. "Those women better get back here soon. This baby is ready to roll. I'm going to go ahead and put in the potatoes. Joe, would you bring them out? Your mother left them on the kitchen counter."

Cole raised his hand. "I'll get'em. You play with your doggie." He took the few short steps to the sliding screen door and stepped inside. A woman staggered in carrying two grocery sacks. "Let me get those for you, ma'am." He reached for the bags and was momentarily speechless when Liz lowered them. They stared at each other.

Liz said, "Oh…uh…"

"Uh…I…I'm Cole Brandon." He set the bags on the counter. "I… uh…came in to get the potatoes. Don is ready for the potatoes. So I… came in to get them. The potatoes. Are you…?"

She took a breath. "I'm Liz. Joey's sister."

"Okay, I'll just… take these potatoes to Don. He's ready for them." He grabbed the tray holding the foil wrapped potatoes and stepped through the open slider to the patio.

Joe tossed the ball across the yard, laughing at the dog. "Major, don't you ever get tired?" He turned at Cole's approach. "You look like you just saw a ghost. What's that about?"

"Yeah, I just met your sister."

Joe raised his eyebrows and stared. "That bad?" He'd never seen such a gob-smacked look on his friend's face. "What?"

Cole handed the potatoes to Don. "Here you go." Then he motioned to Joe and pulled him aside. "A word."

Joe had no idea what to think. He followed Cole to the back of the yard, where Major assumed they'd come to play with him. "What the hell, Cole? So, you met my sister. So?"

"You didn't tell me she was drop-dead beautiful." He rubbed a hand on his bristly, military haircut.

"I sure as hell did."

"If you did, I didn't believe it. Her being your sister, you know?" He scrubbed the hand down his face. "My God. She's hot. What's wrong with her? Why are you setting her up?"

"What's wrong with her? She's ten times smarter and more accomplished than most men who want to get in her pants, and that's a total turnoff for her. The pool of men she'd be interested in is limited."

"That begs the question. Why in hell did you want to introduce *me* to her? I was so stunned I couldn't even utter a coherent sentence." He glanced up. "Oh, my God. Who is that?"

Joe glanced at the patio just as Sandy stepped out. She was stunning in a bright yellow sundress that stopped just above her knees. She'd caught her wavy red hair behind her ears with sparkly, orange barrettes. "That, my man, is my sweetheart, Sandy, owner of the green panties."

"Jesus, you got any more beautiful women stashed around here?" He no more than got the words out of his mouth when Joe's mother stepped outside. "Are you going to claim that's your mom?"

"Take a breath, buddy. Come with me and I'll introduce you to mom and the girls." Joe smiled broadly at Sandy and walked straight for her.

She returned the grin and stepped in his direction. "Hi, honey. I was wondering when you'd get here. Liz introduced me to your parents. They're great. Your shy little brother, Clint, looks just like you. Got a kiss for me?" She stopped and gave him a challenging smile and fluttered her lashes coquettishly.

Joe growled and put his arms around her and swung her in a circle. "All you want and more. But, I'll go easy because my parents are watching." He gave her a quick kiss on the lips. "Come over here, I'd like you to meet Cole. He's trying to recover from his clumsy encounter with my sister. Have pity on the poor guy."

"He's built like a tank. Does he chew nails for fun?" She sent a little finger wave in Cole's direction. "Did he model for the G.I. Joe doll?"

"No, sweetheart, that was me. Cole modeled for Captain America." He grinned at her reaction.

"I'm sorry you have such a low opinion of yourself, God's Gift." She gave him a two-handed shove. "Maybe I picked the wrong man."

Joe studied Cole appraisingly as they walked to meet him. "He's all Marine, no mistake about it. Hey, Cole! I'd like you to meet Sandy Cassidy. Sandy, this is my old buddy, Cole Brandon."

Cole put out his hand and was surprised when Sandy took it, then kissed his chiseled cheek. "Any friend of Joe's is automatically a friend of mine. He's a great judge of character. Come and meet Joe's mother and sister." She took his hand and pulled him to the patio. "Bernice, this is Joe's friend, Cole."

Bernice stepped forward. "How nice to meet you, Cole. We don't often have the pleasure of meeting Joseph's friends. Have you met our daughter, Elizabeth?"

"Yes, ma'am." A deep blush stained his rugged face. He cast a desperate look in Joe's direction.

Liz took pity on him. "Cole helped me unload the grocery bags when he came in to fetch the potatoes for Dad." She smiled encouragingly. "Cole, join me in the kitchen? You can squeeze some lemons while I make the simple syrup for lemonade. We do it the old-fashioned way here." She tilted her head toward the house, and he followed her like an eager, abandoned puppy.

Joe walked over to his father. "Hey, Dad. What's with Clint? He barely spoke to me when we got here."

"Who knows? He's had a bug up his ass for a couple of weeks. Nearly got suspended for a shoving match at school. He'd better be back here in time for dinner or I'll ground him for life."

Chapter Eighteen

EARLY EVENING, SAME DAY

"I'M GOING TO TALK TO CLINT." JOE STOOD AND BRUSHED OFF his pants. "He's acting weird, and I want to know why."

"He's very sweet." Sandy gazed across the yard where Clint sat in an old tire swing, Major resting nearby, Butterfly asleep on his shaggy head.

"Sweet to you, maybe. He's been treating me like a leper."

"Take your time. Liz and I are going to help Bernice in the kitchen."

He gave her a light kiss, and strolled to the back of the yard, not missing his brother's deliberate avoidance of eye contact. "Hey, pal."

"I'm not your pal." Clint hopped off the swing and headed for the side gate. Joe followed him when he proceeded along the side of the house and out to the front.

"Hold up! What is your problem?"

"I hate you! Get lost." Clint hunched his shoulders and headed down the street.

"I said hold up, goddammit!" He grabbed Clint's arm and hung on when he tried to jerk it away. "I don't know what got into you, little brother, but we need to settle it now."

164

"I'm not your brother!" Clint's face was a picture of fury and hurt.

A chill shook Joe to his bones. He couldn't breathe. Clint had somehow learned the truth. This was inevitable. Unable to speak for a moment, he swallowed. "Get in the car."

"No!"

"Get in the goddamn car! We can do it the easy way or the hard way." He thrust out his arm in the direction of his Beemer. "Now!"

Clint stomped to the car, yanked the passenger door open and plopped on the seat. He hunched his shoulders and crossed his arms. Joe got in and jammed his key in the ignition.

"Where are we going?"

"Anywhere from the house. Fasten your seatbelt and shut up." He hit the automatic door lock in case the kid had any idea about jumping out. Joe peeled away from the curb, drove a few blocks to the park and pulled into a shaded space at the edge of the lot. His shoulders and neck ached from tension. Taking a few slow breaths, he relaxed and turned to face Clint.

"All right, son, let's talk about it." Joe had known for years this moment would come.

Clint's head whipped around, surprise flashed in his wide blue eyes. "You admit it? You're my father."

"Yes. I'm your father." He nearly reached out to touch the angry kid, then thought better of it. "I'm not ashamed of it. I'm proud of you. I always have been."

"Why'd you throw me away then?" Clint's face, a mirror image of his own, was blotchy and red with an effort to hold back tears. He knew the budding teen would rather die than cry in front of him.

Joe raised his arms, shook his head, then dragged his fingers through his hair. "I did not throw you away. I gave you to the best parents on the planet. Believe me, I wanted you. Mom and Dad wanted you. They love you. So do Liz and I."

"You're a bunch of liars!" Clint glared. "If you wanted me so much, why did you give me up for adoption?" He turned his head away and stared out the window at nothing. "How come nobody ever told me?" His knuckles were white, the muscles in his skinny forearms knotted.

Joe groaned and dropped his head back on the headrest and rubbed his eyes. "We always planned on telling you. It's complicated."

Clint whirled on him. "Don't give me that 'it's complicated' bullshit, asshole! I don't need any more of your lies!" He yanked the door handle to no avail. "Let me out."

"Settle down. I'll explain." He took a breath.

"You're going to tell me more lies. I don't want to hear it."

"We never lied to you, we just didn't tell the whole truth." Joe sighed and shook his head. "Look, I didn't even know you existed. I swear to God, son." *Son* felt foreign on his tongue even while he recognized how often he'd wanted to say it. "Rita never told me I had a son. She dumped me for somebody else while I was on my first tour in Iraq."

"Why'd she dump you? Because you're an asshole? Because you were mean to her?"

"No! I was crazy in love with your mother. I'd have done anything for her. I bought her a car and an engagement ring before I shipped out. We were supposed to get married when I got home. She must have found out she was pregnant after I left and grabbed the first guy who was willing to marry her. I didn't know. How would I know?" Joe pounded the steering wheel. "Shit!"

"If you didn't know, how did I end up with Mom and Dad? They knew."

"You're wrong. None of us knew about you. Rita never told anyone. After you were born, she divorced whoever the guy was. Her great-aunt, who was caring for you after your mother was killed, found your birth certificate when she cleaned out Rita's place.

"She tried to find me but found my parents instead. Mom and Dad wanted you the minute they knew about you. They didn't hesitate for an instant. They couldn't imagine not taking you."

"So what? Even after you found out, you didn't want me."

Joe placed a tentative hand on the boy's shoulder. "It wasn't like that."

Clint flinched away from his hand. "So, what was it like, asshole?"

A slap in the face couldn't have hurt Joe more deeply. "Can we dispense with the name calling?"

Clint didn't answer. His jaw muscles twitched, and he stared straight ahead.

Joe balled up his fists and held them tight in his lap. "I was a messed up, brokenhearted kid in the middle of a combat zone seven thousand miles from here. We were getting shot at day and night. I was in no shape to be anybody's father. I was still busted up over being dumped by your mother and on my way to becoming a drunk. It's a wonder I didn't get thrown out of the Corps. A couple of Marines in my unit took me in hand so I could finish my tour and get an honorable discharge. One of them was Santos's step-dad, Cluny McPherson."

The kid blinked and his eyes went wide at that revelation.

Joe took the chance and placed his hand on Clint's shoulder again. This time he didn't pull away. "Mom and Dad loved you the minute they laid eyes on you. They didn't need a birth certificate to recognize you as my kid. They knew what a mess I was. They begged me to let them adopt you." Joe sighed. "I didn't know what else to do, so I agreed. I knew you'd have a much better life with them and Liz. A life I wasn't in any shape to provide. I wish it hadn't happened that way. But it did.

"By the time I got home I… for months I was a useless, shit-faced drunk. You were too little to understand any of that. Dad laid down the law. I had two choices. Shape up or ship out. I re-upped with the Marines and the next thing I knew I was back in that stinking hellhole getting shot at again. It was during my second deployment I finally decided it was time to grow up. When I saw you again, you were a happy, well-adjusted four-year-old. You were well loved and well cared for. I believed I'd made the right decision for you. I'm sorry you found out on your own before we could sit down as a family and talk about it. I was protecting you. We always planned to tell you when you were old enough to understand, but we didn't. That was wrong. I love you, Clint. You're my brother and you're my kid. You can believe that or not. Your choice."

Clint made no response, but he did relax his arms and let them fall to his sides. He turned his head away, but not before Joe saw how hard he was working to choke back tears. After several minutes of silence,

Joe said, "What say we get back home and help polish off that ice cream I brought over?"

"I guess." He didn't flinch when Joe squeezed the back of his neck.

"I'll arrange a time when we can all sit down together for a family conference. You're big enough to decide what *you* want to do." Joe started the car and drove the few blocks back to the house. They'd been gone about forty minutes. Clint allowed Joe to put a brotherly arm around his shoulders when they walked back to the house.

———

Joe rose from his lawn chair and tugged Sandy to her feet. "I'd love to cop a few feels and kisses, but I've got to get home. Cole has an early morning train." It was pure torture to be so close to her and unable to touch her intimately. No matter how often he told himself to be patient, his blood betrayed him by flowing south instead of north.

She sighed and crossed her hands over her heart. "You blow me away with your flowery, romantic, poetic phrases." She stood and brushed at the wrinkles on the front of her skirt. "How early is Cole leaving in the morning?"

"I'm taking him to the Amtrak station in Glendale around six and heading straight for work. We've got a big project to start tomorrow. Want to come to my place for dinner?" He needed to tell Sandy about Clint. The sooner the better. There was no way he wanted her to find out some other way. The family secret wouldn't be kept much longer.

She shook her head on a resigned sigh. "Better not plan on it. Liz and I have the crisis to take care of with P&P's most important customer first thing tomorrow. After we meet with them and hopefully smooth the problems, we'll be heading back to the agency for a conference with all the department heads. No telling how long that will last. Rain check?"

He raised his eyebrows in a loving smile. "You never have to ask."

"What's *your* big project?"

Joe needed to be careful what he said here. The project was a forensic investigation of P&P's in-house computer files and system analysis. They'd expressed concerns about data tampering and loss of proprietary information. The last person he could discuss it with was any employee of the advertising agency. Fortunately for him, access could be accomplished remotely. He'd remain anonymous.

"A Los Angeles firm hired us to check their electronic data files for possible outside intrusions."

She rolled her eyes. "Sounds boring."

"Boring?" He gave her an offended and stern look. "Think of me as a skilled cybercrime detective on a mission to save our customer— not a tiresome computer geek."

She smiled. "Geek is a word I'd never use to describe you, honey lover. I can't say what the others are, because we have an audience."

"Sure you don't want to come over tomorrow night?"

She ducked and yelped when he batted a big moth away from her hair. "Wow. You're fast."

"That's what all the ladies say."

"Speaking of ladies, Liz has been moony eyed over Captain Brandon all afternoon. You may have started something. She told me on the way here, how she dreaded meeting a guy she'd have to be polite to for hours while wishing she could make a quick exit without being rude. I can't wait to get to her place for an intense interrogation."

"I'll see what I can wring out of Brandon, and we'll compare notes. If they've hit it off, I'll be the one in the hot seat if it goes sour."

"Historical hazard of matchmaking. You didn't learn much from Liz's relentless quest to get you off the market. I'm moving into my own place in the next couple of days. The rental furniture is arriving tomorrow. The building manager will let them in. I left her a sketch of the placement and she's happy to direct them. Tomorrow night I need to buy a box spring and mattress. I'm not sleeping on a rental bed." She made a small shudder. "After that I'll be spending every evening after work buying supplies, new linens, and stocking the kitchen. It'll cost a fortune, but it's worth it to make a clean start."

"If I'm invited, I'll spend a couple of nights at your place and help you organize. So make sure you get a bed big enough for both of us," he whispered close to her ear. "And long enough for me. Don't worry about cooking, we'll get takeout. I'll move the heavy stuff if you don't like the original placement. You'll be settled in before you know it."

"Thanks, honey. I'll round up Liz and we'll head out."

Cole and Liz had their heads together. Joe noted him writing something on his mother's shopping list. He tore off the sheet and handed it to Liz.

Sandy grinned and nodded. "Good night everyone. Liz and I are leaving. Big day tomorrow and we're starting early." She walked to Clint, hugged him, and kissed him on the cheek. "Nice meeting you, future heartbreaker." His face blazed.

After thanking Don and Bernice, Cole and Joe walked the ladies to Liz's car. Joe kissed Sandy, and growled in her ear, "Call me first chance you get, sweetheart." He'd have a hard time tackling that investigation of P&P with Sandy on his mind. He tapped her nose. "No more changing phone numbers without letting me know." Once both women were seated, and buckled in, Joe slapped the top of the car and stepped back.

"Wow." Cole stared after the departing ladies. "I owe you big time, buddy."

Joe raised his eyebrows. "I assume you're referring to my little sister?" He was glad they'd hit it off. "I saw you conspiring at the kitchen counter just before we left the house. Anything you care to disclose?"

"She's agreed to a weekend in San Diego next month." Cole flashed a wink and a grin. "I'll be counting the hours."

"Whoa. That's fast, even for you." He felt a little twinge of concern, but knew Liz was a big girl, and more than capable of making her own decisions about men. Still…

"I didn't invite her to sleep with me, if that's what you're thinking. We discovered we have a mutual passion, and we're going to have some fun exploring it."

"I'm afraid to ask, but what is this mutual passion?" He doubted Cole would answer the question, but it was worth a shot.

"Astronomy." Cole laughed and punched him in the shoulder. "I wish you could see the look on your face." He sauntered toward Joe's car, his shoulders shaking with laughter.

Astronomy?

———

"Astronomy!" Sandy studied Liz's profile. "You mean all that smiling, intimate talk was about astronomy?"

"Yep. He's fascinated about it the same way I am. Not only that, he's really smart. All those tasty muscles are from the shoulders down. None residing between the ears. He's my ideal of sexy. A man with a brain."

"It can't hurt that he looks great. I admit it's a to-die-for combination." Sandy shifted in her seat. "When did you get interested in astronomy?"

"When we were kids, Dad was stationed at Pendleton for a couple of years. On weekends we'd visit Balboa Park, the zoo, and Mission Bay. One Saturday he took us to Mt. Palomar observatory. It's run by Cal Tech. They had a special program for kids that day, and I got hooked."

"Was Joe interested too? He's never mentioned it."

"He was already in the Marines. He was having fun completing basic training at Parris Island, South Carolina."

"I've heard it's anything but fun."

"He loved it! The more pain they put them through, the more he loved it. He was proving to Dad and Rita that he was a man." She raised her arms, fists turned in.

"Tell me about Rita." Joe hadn't done more than gloss over that part of his life. But Sandy knew what devastation the woman had caused with her Dear John when he was in Iraq.

"I didn't really know Rita. I was a freshman and they'd graduated by the time I set foot on the high school campus. Joey took her to senior prom, spent the night with her afterward, and proposed the next day. From what Mom's said, he'd have had a worse life with Rita than he'd suffered during his struggles with booze."

"Was that Spring Grove High School?"

"No, we lived in Twenty-Nine Palms. Dad was stationed at the Stumps. That's the Marine Corps Air-Ground Combat Center."

"You both went to high school in Twenty-Nine Palms?"

"Yes, that's where Joey got his first taste of computers. He joined their Cyber Patriots Competition. He probably would have pursued it in civilian life if he hadn't joined the Marines right before graduation."

"I thought he got the bug in MARSOC. He told me he got his

cyber specialist training then." Sandy realized how much she didn't know about Joe. He knew little about her life before they met too. She hoped they'd have many years to discover each other. "But, back to your and Cole's mutual fascination with astronomy. Any chance the two of you will explore that?"

"As a matter of fact, we agreed to meet in San Diego for a long weekend next month. He wants to visit the new planetarium at Palomar College. It opened in 2012. I told him I'd like to go up to Mt. Palomar too. So, we'll take a couple of days, and maybe he'll take me to Mission Bay, and teach me paddle-boarding."

"Sounds like the two of you have a lot in common. At least enough in common to have some fun."

"We'll see. He's planning to make the military his career. That definitely wouldn't fit in with my path. Like life with Dad, the service moves them around a lot. But, hey, he's a great guy and I'm not going to spoil it by worrying about a future that probably wouldn't materialize anyway."

———

Very Early Monday Morning.

"Civilian life is making you lazy, Joe. I don't recall you being such a grouch because you had to get up early." Cole laughed at Joe's sour face and handed him a paper cup of strong coffee.

Joe scrubbed his hand over his bristly chin. "I'll be lucky if I have time to shave before I go in this morning. My partner will think I've been partying all night." His eyes swept the early morning crowd in Perk Up, and he took a sip of the coffee. "Aaaahh. Strong."

"Well, drink up, buddy. You can drop me off at the Amtrak station and head back home. I don't need you to sit around holding my hand while I wait for the train. While you're slaving away in front of your computers all morning, I'll be snoozing all the way south."

Joe yawned and stretched. "So, what weekend are you and Sis getting together?"

"I'll know after I check when Mt. Palomar will be open to visitors. Also, the planetarium lecture at the college requires reservations. I'll give Liz a call. She's going to drive down so we'll have her car available to run around town."

"I thought you had a car."

"I do, but the old beater's on its last legs. I'm planning to trade it in one of these days. That's why I chose the train instead of the drive. What? She offered." Cole grinned. "She said if I'm a dud, she'll have her own transportation to leave. She didn't mince words."

Joe chuckled. "Sounds like something she'd say. No wonder she's still single."

"Hey, I like that about her. She's blunt and honest. No playing around unless it's on her terms. I'll do my best to keep her interested all weekend." He pushed the top onto his cup and rose from the table. "We better head out. My base pass expires at four this afternoon. I'm too old to risk raising the ire of my commanding officers. That's a kid's game."

"As I recall, we were pretty good at cutting it close." Joe took his jacket from the back of his chair.

"Can I drive the Beemer? On my pay level, it's likely as close as I'll ever get to one."

Joe grinned and tossed him the keys. "Live it up, Sparky. Civilian life has its advantages."

Cole slitted his eyes and pointed a finger. "No more Sparky, Boozy. Deal?"

"Deal." Joe climbed in and made a big show of fastening his seatbelt.

———

After dropping Cole off at the Glendale station, Joe went back to his apartment for a quick shower and shave. It was early when he arrived at Worldwide Security Partners, so he had time to grab another cup of coffee and a bagel in the employee lounge. His partner, Yoda, entered shortly after he did.

"You're looking chipper this morning, Mr. Hamilton."

"And you, Yvonne, are my ray of sunshine as usual." He winked at her sour smile, sure they both enjoyed the game. It amused him that she adamantly refused to address him by his first name.

"Are you ready to plunge into the new job?" She sat across from him and added sugar to her black coffee.

"I'm going to ask the boss to exclude me from this one. I have a conflict of interest."

"Is that right?"

"Yes, my sister works at People and Productions. It's a bad idea for me to be doing the investigation." The woman he was in love with worked there too, but why complicate the situation by adding that? It should be enough that Liz worked there.

"I've never known Chambers to excuse a specialist from any project. But, your situation is unique. He may make an exception in this case."

"It would certainly make my life less complicated. Liz would be fuming if she knew I was delving into their confidential files, and kept it secret from her. There's no way she's involved in any shenanigans, but all the same…" He'd have the identical issue with Sandy after the fact. It seemed dishonest to be investigating behind the scenes in their place of employment. His dad would understand the need for secrecy, but he wasn't so sure about his mother, sister and Sandy.

"I suggest you get in to see him early, Mr. Hamilton. He's leaving the city for a meeting in the Dallas headquarters sometime today."

Joe stood abruptly. "I'll go to his secretary now and see if he can make time for me before he leaves."

"While you're there, ask her to verify our contact before we get started. I looked up the man's name on their employee roster and couldn't find it. Perhaps it's misspelled."

"I'll do that." He strode out of the room and took the stairs, two at a time, to the executive suites. The boss's office was still dark and there was no sign of the secretary. He scribbled a hasty note and left it on her desk. Yoda had left the break room, so he proceeded to their workspace.

"Any luck?" She glanced at him briefly then went back to staring at her screen.

"Nobody's in yet. I left a note. I suppose it wouldn't hurt to get started on the preliminaries in the meantime."

"I'm way ahead of you as usual, Mr. Hamilton." She dipped her head to hide the foxy smile, but not before he noticed.

"You after my job, Yvonne?"

Her answer was a disdainful snort and flip of the hand.

At ten, Chamber's secretary called to tell Joe the boss would give him five minutes, no more, and to get upstairs pronto. The man was leaving earlier than he'd planned. Fifteen minutes later, Joe sat across from Yvonne. "No dice. I got a lecture on being a professional, as if I were a raw recruit. What an ass."

Yoda's predictable response, "I didn't hear that, Mr. Hamilton."

Chapter Nineteen

LATE MONDAY NIGHT. JOE'S APARTMENT.

JOE SAT BACK AND FROWNED WHEN THE LOBBY DOOR BUZZER sounded over his intercom. "What the hell?" He walked to the door and pushed the microphone. "Hamilton."

"Hi, Marine. Want some company?"

"Sandy?" His heart raced.

"So…I'm not the only woman who rings this bell late at night?"

"No, the women drive me nuts," he teased. "But I'll make an exception and let you in." He unlocked the lobby door and raced down the stairs. He let out a welcoming whoop and lifted her up before she put her foot on the first step. "I miss you every time we're not together, sweetheart. I thought you weren't coming here tonight." He thought it was an odd coincidence she'd come over the very day he'd plunged headlong into the investigation of P&P.

"I wasn't, but you're what I need after a perfectly demoralizing day."

"You'll forget all about your bad day in about five minutes." He rushed her upstairs and through his open front door, slammed it behind them and drew her into a bear hug. "Can you stay the night? Please, say you'll stay the night."

"If you promise to make sure I'm up and out of here early enough to get to work on time." She placed her hands on his cheeks and gazed into his eyes. "Kiss me, Joe."

He smiled because he loved it when she told him what she wanted. He lowered his head and brushed his lips against hers, gently at first, then went deeper. She draped her arms around his neck when he gripped and lifted her bottom. "I want your legs around me." He loved the way they fit together. He gasped at the intensity of his passion for this woman.

"Joe, I want…"

"Yes, sweetheart," He pulled back and smiled. "Tell me what you want."

Sandy sighed around a rosy blush and dropped her head on his shoulder. "I want you to step back and let me watch while you remove your clothes piece by piece. I want you to do it slow, real slow."

Joe set her on her feet. "You have the USMC to thank for how well I can execute orders." He locked his front door. "Your wish is my command, ma'am." He began unbuttoning his shirt collar. "Then what?" He couldn't contain the grin that was twitching at the corners of his mouth.

Sandy pressed her lips together to suppress her own smile. "Then you'll watch me do the same. And after that…"

"Yeah… And after that?" He removed his shirt, first one shoulder, then the other, and dropped it on the floor like Magic Mike.

"Put on our favorite piece of Latin music and dance with me."

"Ah." He nodded. "Naked tango. I like the sound of that. Then afterward we could advance it to a naked tangle." He toed off his loafers. Slow, real slow.

"The odds of that happening are excellent." She pointed to Joe's waistband and wiggled her fingers. "More."

———

SUNSHINE CAFÉ, TUESDAY MORNING

"They certainly didn't give you much insight about their decision to leave, did they?" Joe checked his watch to make sure they weren't running late and blew on his coffee. He figured Liz's face would probably mirror Sandy's. To lose their biggest account and not have a handle on why was brutal.

"No. All they said was they were concerned about P&P's in-house cyber security. Some of their executives had recent identity theft problems which were coincidental with when we started doing their advertising. They wouldn't be more specific. For the life of me, I can't imagine how it would be possible for that to happen, but they weren't willing to give us another chance. Jordan is in a very black temper."

"Was Liz upset when you left last night to come to me?"

"She went to bed early and cuddled up with Butterfly. She probably didn't miss me until this morning. I'll be completely moved out by Thursday night anyway. She'll be glad to have her apartment to herself again."

"I'll call her later today. Let her cry on my shoulder. Gotta look after baby sister." He winked and pushed back his chair. "And we need to get a move on." He helped her into her jacket. "Last night will have to hold us for a while. Yoda has a brief trip to Dallas, so I'll need to get a handle on this new investigation. I'll be burning the midnight oil for days."

She tilted her chin for his kiss and glanced around to make sure nobody was looking before she squeezed his butt. A woman at the next table snickered and Sandy got an attractive pink glow under her red hair and honey brown eyes. "Oops."

Joe laughed. "That'll teach you to take liberties with my person in public." He put his arm around her shoulders and pushed open the door, hoping there'd never be a day when she couldn't help touching him.

He'd planned to clue her in about the situation with Clint, but they'd been so *busy* from the moment she'd arrived… He'd tell her next time they got together. No matter how busy he was at work today, he'd call his parents and fill them in on his encounter with Clint. They needed to come together as a family and handle the matter quickly.

PEOPLE AND PRODUCTIONS, MID-MORNING.

Sandy peeked in on Liz. "You ready? Jordan is gathering all his essential employees into the emergency meeting. At least we're still considered essential." But for how long? The loss of ATB was developing into an ever-growing calamity.

Liz picked up a folder and followed Sandy to the conference room. "I had to lay off a very promising graphic artist this morning. It made me sick to my stomach to watch him go. Do you feel like you're standing on quicksand?"

"Securing ATB's business turns out to have been a double-edged sword. They're so big Jordan took on extra employees and overhead costs to service their account. Now everyone is distressed about who will get the ax next."

"Surely he won't consider either of us. My department is more than essential. You're the top producer on the sales team." The expression on Liz's face demonstrated the feeling of doom pervading the entire company this morning.

"He needs every person in the IT department to get to the bottom of ATB's claims of a data breach. I just hope Jordan doesn't panic. If he cuts too many people, it will impede our ability to take care of our other customers. We have to maintain our reputation of excellence."

"We can take comfort in the fact he didn't build this company to where it is today by being stupid and impulsive. He's always had clear-cut goals and a solid business plan."

"I wish that made me feel better." Sandy gestured to the conference room door. "Here we go."

Fifteen minutes into his dismal dialogue, Jordan said, "It gets worse. One of ATB's competitors has started a negative ad campaign claiming their disposable diapers have a chemical used during production that may cause a severe allergic rash on babies. I'm the only one in this company who had knowledge of this information. I was assured by their head of manufacturing that they were working to get ahead of the problem and resolve it quickly and secretly. I, sure as hell didn't leak the information.

"My only conclusion is that someone in this company has hacked into my private data or the UPnP on our router. The universal plug and play feature was to have been disabled months ago." He glared at the head of the IT department. "Clemmons has assured me it was removed. So, the confidential information about the chemical had to have been accessed prior to the UPnP program being taken down."

He looked around the table. Locked eyes with each person at the meeting individually, for what seemed an eternity to Sandy when it was her turn. She had no reason to feel guilty and she hoped she didn't look guilty when she met his eyes. She wasn't even familiar with the term UPnP and had certainly not been the facilitator of the data breach. She had to say something.

"Jordan. Their head of marketing didn't breathe a word of this to Liz and me when we called on them." She raised her hands in a helpless gesture. "Why wouldn't he have said something?"

"He's on a need-to-know basis and was unaware of the lab's crisis management. The only reason the owner of the company informed me of the potential problem was so that I'd be in a position to put all of you to work to come up with a quick response if the information got leaked at their end."

"But, have they done a thorough investigation of their personnel to make sure it *wasn't* one of their own employees who was the source? We can come up with a counter campaign now, can't we? We can nip it in the bud."

He crossed his arms and slumped back in his chair. "They've hired a security firm with cyber specialists, white hat hackers if you will, who are conducting an investigation of their data and employees as we speak. They weren't encouraging about whether or not they'd let us handle the response to the negative advertising."

Joe had told her he'd just got a new assignment to conduct such an inquiry. He must be working with ATB to get to the root of their data breach. She'd talk to him tonight if he called Liz as promised. In the meantime, she racked her brain for anyone at P&P who could possibly be involved and came up empty. She remembered a questionable character who'd left the company for a competing agency, but that was months ago. Sandy doubted it was her. Letty Garcia had left under a cloud, apparently disgruntled when she was passed over for promotion a couple of times, but no—she'd left quietly.

"Jordan, this is probably out of left field, but what about Letty Garcia? Where did she go when she left here?"

He stared at the table, his brow heavily furrowed. "I have no idea."

He looked at the head of personnel. "Jillian, do you remember if anyone asked for a referral?"

"No, but I'll check into it as soon as I get back to my desk, Jordan." The white-haired woman scribbled a note to herself. "I'll let you know the minute I do."

Jordan pushed back from the table and stood, signaling the meeting over. Everyone filed out of the room without further comment, but Sandy knew the break room would be abuzz with speculation and gossip until this crisis was at an end.

———

WORLDWIDE SECURITY PARTNERS, 7:00 P.M.

Joe stared at the array of computer screens on his desk. He'd made a lot of headway, and when Yoda got back they'd probably be able to conclude the investigation of P&P's cyber security in a month max.

"You're working late, Mr. Hamilton."

Joe jumped at the sound of Yoda's gravelly voice. "You trying to give me a heart attack, Yvonne?"

"Goodness, no. That's the last thing I'd try, considering you're my partner. How's it going?" A devilish smile graced her wrinkled, elfish face.

Joe was very fond of this interesting and brilliant woman. "That's good to know, but the question is: what are you doing here? I wasn't expecting you back until tomorrow afternoon."

"Always a good idea to keep the men in one's life on their toes, Mr. Hamilton." She dropped her battered briefcase on her desk and stood behind him. "I bailed early. Looks like you've made good headway with the preliminary accesses."

"How was your meeting at the home office?" He scooted over. "Roll your chair over here and have a look."

"It was a waste of my time. I already knew more than the *specialist* they'd brought in to conduct the seminar." She sat in her chair and rode it around to Joe's side of the desk. "What have we here?"

"So far I have access to every employee's office computer and laptop. Just started working on the phones and BlackBerries. They've got a crapload of them. Employees are identified by their names. I'd prefer they'd given us employee numbers only."

"Yes, I agree. So, will we start tonight, hacking into each device one by one? Or do you have a hot date with *Sweetheart?*"

"Sweetheart is busy this evening, so you're my hot date."

"My heart flutters, Mr. Hamilton." She grinned and rolled back to her side of their facing desks. "Start shipping me individual phones and BlackBerries. You keep on the computers and laptops. We should have this knocked out in two weeks."

"Let's start our *hot date* in the break room. I'm starved and I need coffee. I'll make a fresh pot while you call out for pizza delivery."

LATER AT LIZ'S APARTMENT.

"I could have slept at my own place tonight, but I don't have any sheets or pillows for my new bed. You're stuck with me for at least one more night." She tripped around the kitten doing figure eights between her ankles. "Watch out, baby. I don't want to step on you."

"I'm used to you now and Butterfly isn't much of a conversationalist. Hopefully she's a fast learner. All she does is sing." Liz nuzzled her kitten's fuzzy yellow head.

Liz dropped her purse and coat in the entry. "Count your blessings. My mother once had a cat who never stopped talking. Problem was—we never learned cat-speak. She disappeared for two weeks once and told us all about it for two days straight. She had wonderful, long stories, but they were wasted on us. One night, without any preplanning, Damon, Greg and I looked at her and yelled, 'Shut up!' She was very insulted and left the room."

"Hmm. Sounds like she spoke *people* even if you didn't speak *cat.*"

"Mom was mad at us for hours. She insisted we'd hurt her baby's feelings." Sandy sat across from Liz and kicked off her shoes. "Did Joe call?"

"No. He either forgot or was too busy. I guess the project he's working on is pretty big."

"I wonder if his firm is working on the investigation for ATB."

"I thought of that too after Jordan said they'd hired someone to investigate. Good luck in ever getting Joey to reveal anything. He's a human clam."

"Gosh, if he is working for ATB that could really help us win back their business."

"Like I said. Clam."

"Can I ask you something?"

"You can ask. What?"

"Do you know why there was so much tension between Joe and Clint on Sunday?"

Liz got a wary expression on her face. Sandy had the feeling she knew something and wasn't about to share it with her. She hadn't intended to put her friend on the spot.

"Forget it. It's none of my business. Probably just brother stuff."

Liz sighed. "Clint's thirteen going on thirty-three. Mom told me he's had some trouble at school and has Dad pissed at him. Believe me, none of us like it when Dad gets pissed. I asked Clint what the problem was and he clammed up, just like Joey. They're two peas in a pod, those two."

"Joe is twenty years older than Clint. Your parents must have been surprised when he came along." Something in Liz's eyes told Sandy to drop the subject. It was obviously a private family matter. She had no business prying. She stood and raised her hands. "Sorry, none of my business. I'm pooped out. I think I'll turn in. Jordan gave me a list of customers to call on, starting tomorrow. My *vacation* is officially over."

"Some vacation." Liz smiled sadly and shook her head. "I'm turning in too. Joey won't call this late, so there's no need for me to stay up any longer. I can help you at your new place tomorrow night if you need me." She held up Butterfly. "If I can bring my baby, that is."

"I'm going to shop for bed linens and towels right after work tomorrow. Joe said he'd sleep over if I want him to." She grinned at Liz. "Of course, I want him to. We can celebrate my first night in my new home." She started to leave the room then turned. "You're invited too, of course."

"Oh, yes, of course." Liz wrinkled her nose. "Three's a crowd. I'll have a look at your place on Sunday."

———

Joe leaned back in his desk chair, groaned and rubbed his eyes. "Night, Yvonne."

"See you in the morning, Mr. Hamilton." She picked up her battered briefcase. "Get some sleep for a change."

He glanced at his watch. "Damnit!"

She cocked her head. "Miss a date?"

"No, I promised to call my sister. Now it's too late." He stood and pulled on his jacket. "Can't do anything about it now. I'll walk you to your car."

"I have my pepper spray, Mr. Hamilton."

"Great. Just don't use it on me."

"Don't give me cause, and you have nothing to fear."

"You're a unique woman, Yvonne."

"Must be why you're so wildly attracted to me, Mr. Hamilton."

"I think you're on to something, you're such a sharp investigator." He switched off the office light and walked to the garage with her, waited till she started her car, then walked to his Beemer.

On his way home, he promised himself he'd tell Sandy the truth about Clint tomorrow. He couldn't keep such a big secret from her if there was any chance for them to be a couple. And that's what he wanted more than anything. Trust was a two-way street.

Chapter Twenty

Sandy ran to the door when she heard Joe's knock. He'd called to tell her he was on his way with dinner. A glance in the small mirror near the door told her it was too late to repair her disheveled appearance. His reaction would be a true test of his love. She pulled open the door. "Honey lover."

"Hello, gorgeous." His arms were full, so he lowered his head for her welcome kiss. "I brought corned beef sandwiches from Abe's."

He passes with flying colors.

"Bring them in here. I'm starved. I haven't sat down once since I got back from the mall. It doesn't look like it, but I've made a lot of progress."

Joe kicked off his shoes, followed her to the kitchen and set the plastic bags and soft drinks on the counter. His gaze swept her condo. "Wow, sweetheart, your place looks...it looks...like hell." He grinned. "A hell of a mess." He gave her an irresistible, very sexy smile.

She sighed and leaned into him. "The more I do the worse it looks. Kiss me and make it all better." She put her arms around his waist and smiled into the face she loved.

"Happy to oblige." He gave her a sizzling kiss. "Um, maybe a shower would be in order before we eat."

She gasped, horror-stricken, and pulled away from him. "Oh!"

Hands at her burning cheeks she shook her head. "Joe, I'm so embarrassed. Do I stink?" She'd been working hard for the past three hours, had been on her feet since early morning. She went straight from work to purchase the linens, bring them home, wash and dry them, make up her bed, stock the bathroom with towels, soap and shampoo. Now she…oh, God. *Let me disappear, please!*

Joe stepped toward her as she stepped back. He growled and took another step. "I never said that. What I said was a shower is in order before we eat." She shrieked when he grabbed her and lifted her off her feet, then hurried down the short hallway. "A shower with you is always at the top of my priority list."

"You rat!" She giggled and squirmed out of his arms. "You'll pay for that; I swear to you. You'll pay and pay." She moved away from him. He was already pulling off his clothes and dropping them as he stalked her. "Get away from me! I'm warning you, Joseph Hamilton. Don't take another step." She laughed when he kept coming. There was no retreating from his mission. She tried to reach the bathroom door before he hopped out of his pants, but he was too fast for her. He grasped her wrist and pulled her into a super-hot kiss and slid his big hands from her shoulders down to her bottom.

"Are you getting naked, or shall I drag you into the shower the way you are?" He grazed her neck with his teeth. "Hmmm?"

Sandy obediently tugged her old T-shirt over her head at the same time Joe slid her sweatpants below her hips and put his lips on her navel. He had her on fire when he gazed up into her face. Passion burned in his eyes, nearly bringing her to her knees. "Joe, oh, God," she gasped as her legs threatened to give way. She dug her fingers into his hair and pressed him closer.

———

"It's a good thing you brought sandwiches." She pointed to the tail-wagging cat-clock on her wall, a gift from Liz. "Anything else would have been spoiled by now." Nodding to the card table, she handed him two plates and two glasses. "Sit, we'll probably both have heartburn eating this late."

She unwrapped the sandwiches and followed him to the table.

"Oh, look at these heavenly green pickles. I could eat a bucket full of these."

"Abe makes the best fresh dill pickles in town. I don't know how anyone could resist them. Just so you know how much I love you, I'll give you mine."

"Don't be silly, honey. I love you too much to take it from you." She sat across from him. "But next time you go there, get extra." She cut her sandwich in half and rewrapped the rest of it. "Lunch tomorrow."

Joe chewed a mouthful of his corned beef and followed it with a swallow of root beer. "Unless I eat it when I'm done here. Somehow I worked up quite an appetite."

"Hmm, wonder how that happened. All my lovely rental furniture is still exactly where it was when you got here. A big help you are." Her belly still tingled from his *help*.

"Whaddaya mean? I nearly killed myself moving your bed." His blue eyes sparkled with mischief.

"That's bound to happen when you try to move it while you're on top of it. Maybe they didn't teach physics where you went to school?" She clamped her lips together to keep the satisfied smile off her face but rewarded him with an eye roll.

"After what I managed in your shower, I'm disappointed you'd question my knowledge of physics, Cassidy." His hot gaze burned into her. He twisted his lips and poked his tongue in his cheek.

"You've got me there, Hamilton." *No question about it. None.* She grinned and raised her hands. He was nearly finished with his sandwich. She held up her wrapped leftover. "Want this?"

"Indeed, I do, beautiful. Too bad we finished the pickles. Got any chips?"

"I remember putting some expired, sell-by-date Pringle's in the pantry. You that hungry?"

"Nicely aged. Just the way I like them. The most requested item Marines wanted in their USO packages." He cocked an eyebrow. "Do not doubt me. That's the truth." He patted the table next to his plate. "Put them right here, woman. Chop-chop."

Sandy slid her chair back and rose. Pointing her finger about an inch from his nose, she warned, "I'm about this close."

"You know I'm teasing, sweetheart. I can't resist watching your feathers ruffle when I play the macho card." He leaned forward and kissed her finger. "Anyway, there's something important I need to discuss with you before I head home."

"Home? You're not staying?" She reached in the pantry, grabbed the tube and set it next to his plate. "Why?" She'd been looking forward to spending the night wrapped around him.

"I'm meeting Yoda at the office at six. We need to get some work done on our investigation before the staff meeting at ten. Chambers is arriving back in town late tonight. We hear there're some company policy changes to be passed along to the investigators before the ongoing contracts are finished."

She sat across from him and leaned forward on her elbows. "Are you conducting the investigation at All Things Babies?"

He gave her a steady, non-committal look. Took a swallow of root beer and opened the chip container, withdrew a small stack, and put them in his mouth. "Mmm, good."

She sniffed and sat back. "Okay, I get it." Crossing her arms, she added, "Forget I asked."

"I'll do that."

Liz was right. Clam. "What do you want to talk to me about?"

"My…uh…Clint." Joe's face took on a peculiar expression.

A lightbulb switched on in her brain. Eyes agog, she put her hands to her mouth and drew in a sharp breath. "Oh, my God! You're Clint's father."

That stopped him mid-chew. He swallowed, coughed, and then wiped his mouth with the paper napkin next to his plate. "Did Liz say something to you?"

Silently she shook her head then placed a hand over her heart. "No, but you are his father, aren't you? He's a young version of you, Joe. I was startled by the strong resemblance when I first met him."

"Brothers often have a strong family resemblance. He looks like Liz too."

"Are you denying it?" She reached across the table and squeezed his clenched fist. "Joe? Talk to me."

He stood abruptly, pointed to the living room. "Let's get comfortable on your lovely rent-a-sofa." They went the short distance and sat close together.

"Rita was pregnant when I shipped out. She probably didn't know. I sure as hell didn't. Four months later when I got her letter, she told me she was pregnant and marrying another guy. I assumed the kid was his. That's the last I ever heard from her."

Sandy leaned heavily against his side. "Oh, honey, that's so sad for you and for Clint. How did he come to live with your family? Did she give him up? How long has he known? Why has your family let him think he's your brother all this time? Is that why he was so surly with you on Sunday?"

Joe sighed. "Settle back. It's a long story."

It was a long story. Afraid his revelations would have unknowable consequences for their relationship, Sandy had listened silently for several minutes, a deep chill in her chest. The man she loved was being torn in opposing directions. There was no doubt in her mind that he loved her, but he carried burdensome baggage, clearly capable of dividing his loyalties. The Hamilton plight was about to come to a head. A family crisis meeting was scheduled in two nights. Clint would have a say about his life. He was still a child, but Joe felt he had a right to the entire truth, and where they'd all go from here.

"Joe, what if Clint decides he wants to live with you?" She hated herself for feeling jealous of the man's son, but she couldn't help it. What would that mean for them?

He tightened his arm on her shoulders and kissed her on the head. "Sweetheart, I can't speculate on it until we sit down and discuss every possible outcome. He's my son. I love him."

"Surely, you must have known the truth would come out?"

"We made a mistake by not telling him from the time he was old enough to understand. The years passed too quickly. He found out on his own when he stumbled across his school records in Dad's desk. His birth certificate was in there. He's justified in feeling betrayed by all of us."

"Were you ever planning to tell me?" She hated the plaintive tone in her voice.

"Of course. I would never keep anything that important from you."

"You did though." She stroked his arm in an attempt to soothe both of them. "You have to find a way to make it right with him. You have no other choice."

"I'm so sorry to drag you into this."

"Joe! I love you. He's your son. Let me in."

She pushed back and gazed into his anguished face. The man she loved suffered, and the only thing she could think to do was back away and give him room. "It's late. You'd better go. I think it would be best if we didn't talk again until you've had your family conference."

He stood and jammed his hands in his pockets. He turned a steady gaze on her. "I'm not giving you up, sweetheart. No matter what happens, I'm not giving you up."

She had to face the awful possibility of Joe choosing the role of father to Clint over his commitment to her. He was a man of integrity who would stand by his responsibilities over all else. His steadiness and deep ethics were qualities she'd admired from the first evening they'd met. She'd never considered those very qualities could signal an end to their love affair. He meant every word, she had no doubt, but sometimes painful decisions caused people to do things they never intended. His vow was a knife in her heart.

She rose and he embraced her as if it were the last time they'd be together. Tears clogged her throat and burned the back of her eyes. The sense of impending loss was nearly too much to bear. She clung to him while steadying herself. She would not pressure him. She would not make his life more difficult. She would not.

"I'm confident you and your family will make the best decisions for all of you. Please don't worry about you and me. I'm not going anywhere." She'd never put herself between Joe and his son. She hoped they would work things out, but she loved him enough to give him up if it came to that. Maybe this was the answer to her fear over embarking on a full-blown commitment just when she was testing her independence.

He gripped her upper arms. His blue eyes bored into her. "I'm not giving up on us, goddamn it! Don't you dare give up on me. Do you hear me?" He gave her a small shake, his jaws clenched, the muscles jerking.

She shook her head. "Never. I'll never give up on you, but I'll also never pressure you to make a decision not in your son's interest. I couldn't live with that, Joe."

"We'll work this out, baby. We will."

"I know." She put her hands on his beloved cheeks. "I love you. Don't ever forget."

He rolled his face to the side and kissed her palm. "You're my dream come true, sweetheart. I'm not willing to give up my dream." His promise was followed by a gentle kiss on her lips. "I should go."

"Yes." *Go, please. I can't hold back my tears much longer.* She forced a smile and led him to the door.

He stopped. "I'll call you soon. I'll be counting the seconds until you're back in my arms."

Through trembling lips, she answered, "Me too," then closed the door behind him. Clutching her arms tight around herself she rocked.

———

Joe sat in his parked car, cell phone to his ear. Was he nuts? Calling Liz this late? He'd thought to give her a head's up about his conversation with Sandy before the two women crossed paths at the workplace. No, it was too late. He'd catch her in the morning. Punching Cancel with his thumb, he started the engine, checked the side mirror and pulled out onto the dark street. No more than a hundred yards down the road, his phone buzzed. He grabbed it. "Liz?"

"Joey? Why are you calling me so late?" Alarm rang in her breathless voice. "What's wrong?"

"I'm sorry. I'm just leaving Sandy's. I punched your number without realizing it was after midnight." Head swiveling from right to left he scanned the street for a place to park. "Hold a sec. I'm parking the car."

"Joey? Joey!"

He shouted so she could hear him. "Hold on, damn it! I'm parking the car!" He drove into a convenience store lot, turned off the engine and lights.

"Sis?"

"Don't yell at me, you jerk! You woke me from a deep sleep and scared the bejabbers out of me."

He deserved her wrath. He had no business calling her at this hour. "Sis, I'm sorry. I wasn't thinking. Never mind. I'll call you tomorrow. Go back to sleep."

"Go back to sleep? You're one taco short of a combo plate if you think I'll get back to sleep now. Did you and Sandy have a fight? Are you breaking up? Are you ill?"

"No, no, and no. I'm giving you a head's up because you girls work together. You'll be seeing her again before I do." He pressed the bridge of his nose. "She knows." Flashing lights swept the interior of his car. A police cruiser screeched to a halt behind him. "What the hell? I gotta go. A cop just pulled up and an officer is standing behind his open door. He's signaling me to open my window."

"Joey!"

He disconnected the call, dropped the phone on the passenger seat, and lowered his window. Head out, he called, "Officer? Can I do something for you?"

"Put both your hands out the window. Keep them where I can see them."

"Are you kidding me?" What in blue blazes was going on here? He wasn't illegally parked. He hadn't been driving erratically. The cop placed his hand on the butt of his weapon.

He's not kidding.

The officer shouted, "Step out of the car. Walk slowly toward me. Keep your hands where I can see them!" A second patrolman now approached the passenger side of the Beemer, his flashlight shining into Joe's face. The first cop stepped out from behind his door. "Your driver's license and registration." He held out the hand not resting on his gun.

Joe took a calming breath and reached for his wallet. "No problem." He noticed the store clerk standing at a window watching the scene unfold. Joe opened his wallet and held it up so the officer could see the license.

"Remove the license and hand it to me."

Joe removed the license and held it out. The officer took it with two fingers of his left hand, not removing his right hand from his weapon. "Where's the registration?"

"In the console." Joe took a step toward his car.

"Stay where you are!"

Joe raised his arms. "Okay. Okay." The last thing in the world Joe expected was to be standing on a dark street late at night being rousted by two LAPD patrol officers. At that moment, his phone sounded off. "Shall I answer it? It's probably my sister. I was talking to her when you pulled up."

"This your car?"

"Hell yes, it's my car! If you let me get the registration from the console, I'll prove it." The phone rang again. "May I answer my sister's call before she dials 9-1-1?" He backed up a step. "She will. Believe it."

"Felix, keep an eye on him while he reaches for his phone. Go ahead, Mr. Hamilton, answer, and then hand the phone to me."

"Liz? Take it easy!" He looked at the name on the cop's badge. "I'm handing my cell to Officer Bradburn." He drew it away from his ear and handed it over.

"Who is this?" Bradburn asked. "Say again?" He nodded and rolled his eyes. "Miss, Miss, if you give me a chance, I'll explain."

Joe glanced over his shoulder when he heard the other officer choke back a laugh.

"There is no reason to be alarmed, Ms. Hamilton. We pulled him over for a routine check. No, there's been no accident. My badge number? No problem." He recited the number. "Yeah, I'll wait till you find something to write on." A few seconds later he repeated the number then said, "He's fine. Yes. I'm handing him the phone now." He thrust it in Joe's direction. "For the sake of all that's holy, tell her you're all right."

Unable to stifle the smile on his face, Joe took the phone. "Sis. I'm fine. I'm not sure. I'd just parked in front of a convenience store when they pulled up. Hang up now and I'll call you back. No! Do not call 9-1-1. These guys *are* the police. Yes! I'll call you back. I promise! Give it a few minutes." He sighed and dropped the phone in his pocket.

The first officer indicated the store window where the young clerk stood. "Felix, get that kid out here." He motioned Joe to the trunk of his car. "Stand there."

Officer Felix—could have been his first or last name—tapped on the store window and gestured for the guy to come outside.

The nervous kid stared at Joe through huge, black-framed glasses. He approached warily, appearing sick in the halogen parking lot lights.

He shook his head so hard it was a wonder it didn't fly from his shoulders. "That's not him. When I saw him sitting in the car I couldn't tell for sure. It looked like the same car. That's why I called." His face glowed with a garish orange blush. He licked his lips. "Sorry, mister. I was scared. I thought you were the guy who held me up last week."

Felix put his hand on the kid's shoulder. "That's no problem, Samir. You did the right thing. Go back to work. We're done here."

The young man ducked his head and backed away. "Sorry, man."

Joe shrugged. "Don't worry about it." If he wasn't so rattled he'd have thought the situation funny. He leaned back against his car and dragged his hand over his face. "Shit."

Felix slapped him on the back. "Better call your sister, Hamilton."

The two uniforms got in their cruiser and backed away.

Joe took the phone from his pocket and punched redial. Liz answered on the first ring.

"Joey? Are you all right? Do you need a ride? What can I do?" She muffled a sob.

"I'm not hurt, honey. It was a mix-up. I'm going inside to get a drink." He shouldered the heavy glass door and walked to the cooler.

"A drink? No, Joey, don't!"

"Am I allowed a can of ginger ale?" He carried it to the counter and set it down.

The kid backed away from the can like it was a poisonous snake. "No charge, man."

Chapter Twenty-One

Joe canted forward in his chair, elbows resting on his knees. Clint sat across from him between Liz and their mother, Bernice. Don had taken the chair next to Joe, mimicking his son's posture.

"So that's the entire story." Joe's voice held a note of regret. "I wish we'd told you before you found out on your own, but the years got away from us."

"Did you ever plan to tell me, or..."

"Yes, sweetie, we talked about when it would be appropriate. We missed the window of opportunity, more than once, I'm afraid," Bernice said.

"How come my mother—" He flashed a look at Bernice and back to Joe, "—how come she dumped you?"

Liz put her arm around Clint and hugged him close.

Joe raised his hands and shrugged. "We'd only been together one night when I asked her to marry me. She said yes. Why, I'm not sure. I was a nineteen-year-old kid with big plans and dreams and very little money to make them a reality. She was angry I'd joined the Marines without telling her. I'd only been in Iraq a few months when I got her

195

letter. She probably felt she had no real commitment to me. Maybe she was really in love with the guy she married."

Clint snorted and rolled his eyes. "She had enough of a commitment to get knocked up, didn't she?"

Before Joe could answer, Don spoke up. "We've talked about unwanted pregnancy, son. It isn't a commitment, it's impulsive and irresponsible behavior."

Joe squeezed the bridge of his nose and clenched his teeth, ready to say something to his father he'd regret later.

Clint opened his mouth, but Don stopped him with a raised hand. "Fortunately for all of us, the result was *you*. We have not regretted one day since you came into our lives."

Liz and Bernice murmured agreement.

"I became an alcoholic because of her." Joe slumped and dropped his head.

Clint snorted. "That was your fault. Not hers."

Taken aback, Joe said, "You're absolutely right. It was my fault." He stood. "Clint, let's take a walk. I'd like to talk with you one-on-one. You're free to share anything we say with the rest of the family afterward. I'll leave that up to you."

Bernice squeezed Clint's hand. "Go on, sweetie."

Don stood and nodded at his sons. "Good idea. You need a conversation without us popping off." He took his empty glass. "Mother? Lizzie? You want a refill?" He tilted his head in the direction of the kitchen and patio in case they didn't get his meaning.

Joe opened the front door and Clint exited ahead of him. "Look, Clint. You're free to discuss anything with me. I respect your opinions. Please don't hold back your thoughts and feelings until you're pissed. We've always had a great relationship. We have a lot to sort out between us. Let's talk about it."

Clint shrugged. "Yeah, okay. You can say whatever you want too. I'm kinda bummed, but not too bad, I guess. I never thought what it meant to have two dads. It still seems like you're my big brother— but not. You know?"

Hands jammed in their pockets, they strolled down the street in the direction of the park. Joe clenched his teeth. He'd let his kid decide when he wanted to say more. If the shouts and cheers were any indication, a game was in progress. "I thought Cluny coached the kids on Saturdays."

"It's men's softball most Sundays. The Spring Grove Volunteer Fire Department is playing the Ventura County Sheriffs today. Wanna watch for a while?"

A ballgame hadn't been Joe's reason for them to be alone He had a hunch Clint wasn't ready to talk. The baseball game would give him time to get his thoughts together. "Sure, but from the sound of the crowd, it's standing room only. Who you rooting for?"

"The Sheriffs. They're undefeated this season."

"I betcha the fire guys are ahead." He pointed to the third base side of the field. "If we go over there, we can see the scoreboard." Joe broke into a trot. He laughed when Clint zipped past him. He had twenty years on the kid. He wondered what it would be like starting a new family with Sandy, how Clint would feel about it.

"Joe!" Clint gestured to the area behind the Fire Department dugout. "There's Santos and Ric. Coach McPherson is playing outfield and Coach Dempsey is pitching. It's tied three to three." He jumped up and down and waved his arms until Santos looked in their direction. "He sees me. Do you mind if I go over there?"

"No, go ahead. I'll wait here." So much for the brother-father-son talk. Maybe the adults in the family were taking the whole situation too seriously? He shrugged and threw Gunny Dempsey a rude catcall, "You couldn't hit the side of a bus, Dempsey!" Joe heard some angry mumbling and looked to the side. "Hey, it's okay, he's an old Marine buddy of mine."

He'd forgotten how seriously the residents of Spring Grove took their amateur sports teams. Gunny showed him up by striking the deputy out with no more than five pitches. Joe remembered how good he'd been at throwing grenades back in the day. Joe clapped and whistled when the disgruntled sheriff walked out of the batter's box.

At the beginning of the next inning, Clint, Santos, and Ricardo joined him. Ric perched on Santos's broad shoulders as usual. Joe grinned. "How's the McPherson contingent today?"

Little Ricardo pointed across the field. "That's our daddy!"

They laughed as Cluny's little clone bounced up and down on his big brother's shoulders.

"Is that Hot Stick Hawk at the side of the dugout?" Joe pointed. "At the end?"

Santos smiled and nodded. "Yeah, Dad talked him into joining the team this season. He failed the tryout as a player, so he's assistant coach and cheerleader."

The afternoon was looking like a reunion of the Marines who'd served together in Fallujah. "The ladies here?" He scanned the area behind the dugout for Misty Hawk, Graciella McPherson and Marla Dempsey but couldn't spot them.

"Nah, they stayed at Major Hawk's house with the babies. We're having burgers for the team there after the game." Santos poked Joe's shoulder. "Why don't you and Clint come, too? They'll have enough food for a battalion. The only catch is; anybody who isn't on the team has to clean up or be a babysitter." He winked and squeezed Ric's knees. "I'm already doing the babysitter gig."

"I'm not a baby!" Ric complained, kicking his feet against Santos's broad chest. The young man was well on his way to being as tall and brawny as his late father, Marvin Jefferson. The SEAL Beachy's old squad owed their lives to.

Clint cast Joe a hopeful expression. "Can we go…*Dad*?"

Joe's heart stuttered for a second.

Santos poked Clint. "You called your brother, Dad, jabroni."

"I always thought he was my brother, but I found out he's really my dad." He faced Joe. "Can we?"

"Uh." Joe couldn't manage another word. He was still processing Clint's bombshell.

Clint grinned up at Cluny McPherson's tall, adopted son. "You're not the only one to have two dads, *jabroni*. It's kind of, like, cool. Except for your first dad getting killed in the war. That sucked."

Joe's head spun. Clint thought it was *cool*. He'd been ripping himself apart, searching for a way to help Clint keep the family secret. Assumed he wanted it kept. He didn't. Joe cleared his throat. "We should go back to the house and let the family know we want to go to the team cookout, not just leave them hanging. I can't call, I left my phone there. Colonel Dad's still top dog, you know?"

"Yeah, I get it, no prob. There's only one more inning. We'll go tell them when the game's over. The undefeated Sheriffs are getting their butts kicked."

Santos nodded. "We're heading back to our seats. I'll tell my parents we'll see you later."

From his lofty perch on Santos's shoulders, Ric parroted, "We'll see you later."

Gunny Dempsey took the mound at the top of the ninth. He struck out two deputies in a row, then the next batter hit a solid single to right field. By the time the next batter hit a pop fly-out to the infield the fans of both teams were on their feet screaming. The score was still tied, so if the game wasn't going to go to extra innings, the home team needed to score a run in the bottom of the ninth.

"Coach Dempsey's a good pitcher, isn't he?" Clint remarked. "How'd he learn?"

Joe took the chance of another rejection by putting his hand on his son's shoulder and was gratified when he didn't pull away. "Throwing grenades at the bad guys in Iraq. He and McPherson have been coaching you kids every summer as long as I can remember. Could be that, too."

"I'm going to join the Marines in five years. Santos is joining the Navy in three years. Coach McPherson wants him to go to college first, but he doesn't want to. Me either."

"Well, there's plenty of time to make those decisions. McPherson and Dempsey both waited until they graduated with degrees before they joined. Neither of you should be in a hurry." The thought of his kid getting shot at nauseated Joe. But Clint was only thirteen. A lot could change in the next five years.

"Your dad said you joined right out of high school."

"Yes, and he wasn't any too happy about it, either." Hearing Clint refer to Don as *your dad* jarred Joe. "Maybe we should be thinking about what form of address you plan to use when referring to me and Dad. You're correct, he is my dad, but he's been your dad for as long as you can remember. Why not just stick to Joe and Dad for now?"

Clint wrinkled his forehead as if in deep thought. "I could call him Dadpa and call you Dadbro." The spunky kid snickered and socked Joe in the shoulder. "How about I call Lizzie Auntsis?"

"How about you stop being such a snark-ass?" Joe poked him back.

Clint took a boxer's stance, dukes up. "You want a piece of me, big guy?"

Joe rolled his eyes. "God help me." He gave Clint a soft smack on the back of his head and turned toward the family home. "Is there anything you want to talk about before we get to the house?"

"You told me everything already, didn't you?" Clint trudged alongside Joe, at thirteen he was nearly as tall as him. Joe wondered how tall he'd be when he reached his full height. He knew so little about Rita's family, nothing about the average height of men in the last couple of generations. Clint bore him a powerful resemblance, but every now and then something in his eyes or mouth stirred a memory of Rita.

"Yes, but you haven't said what you want to do going forward."

"Do? Like what?"

Joe threw up his hands. "Hell, I don't know! Continue to live at home with our parents? Come live with me? Split your time between me and them. You have a say in this, Clint."

"Why would I want to move? This is where I've always lived. I've gone to the same dumb school with the same dopey friends since kindergarten. Santos and I play baseball with the park middle league every summer. I don't want to live with you. Why would I?"

Momentarily ashamed for feeling relieved, Joe also experienced a flash of regret and rejection. He hadn't known what to expect when he'd arrived at his parent's home early this afternoon. His son had blindsided him at every turn.

"You told Santos it was cool to have two dads. I guess I figured you might want to spend more time with me, do things with me, just the two of us."

"Like going to all the Dodgers games you never take me to?" A hint of snarl accompanied Clint's retort. "Why can't we leave things as they are? It's not my fault if you feel guilty. It *is* cool to have two dads, but that doesn't mean I have to choose, does it?"

"No." Joe jammed his hands in his pockets and shook his head. "You don't have to choose. If I were in your place, I'd pick Dad over me every day and twice on Sunday. But I would like to get closer to you. We've never really talked. If you want to go to Chavez Ravine with me, I'd be happy to take you. I don't go to the games nearly as often as I'd like. I'll get tickets for the next game Kershaw's pitching."

"What about your girlfriend?"

"Sandy? What about her? She guessed I was your father before I had a chance to tell her. Are you worried she wouldn't want you around?" Man-oh-man, this kid was way ahead of him. Clint had spent a lot of time thinking about Joe and his situation. "Sandy likes you a lot. She hopes you'll accept her. In fact, she's feeling more threatened than you, with all this shit hitting the fan."

"I like her. She's super-hot. I wish she was my girlfriend."

Joe glanced sideways at Clint and was elated to see the kid's playful smile. "Don't get any ideas. She's off limits. Anyway, as soon as you're old enough your Auntsis will be on the hunt for females to match you up with."

Clint made a loud snort and rolled his eyes. "That'll suck."

"Tell me about it." They turned up the walkway to the front door.

———

SANDY'S APARTMENT. LATE EVENING, SAME DAY.

Sandy flopped down and propped her aching feet on the rented coffee table. She'd chewed over the Hamilton family meeting while cleaning and rearranging her new condo again. Next, she'd empty the last of the wardrobe boxes she'd filled with the help of her former neighbors, Joy and Mr. Bennett, then sort through them and most likely donate many of her things to charity. Every reminder of her ruined home made her neck and head ache.

She didn't expect to see or hear from Joe this evening. The family conference was foremost on his mind. Clint had to be his number one priority. She understood that and would support any decision he made. Family secrets had the potential to hurt the very ones being protected from them. Not only Joe, but Liz and her parents had their work cut out. Clint seemed to be well-adjusted, but who knew what went on inside the tortured mind of a teen boy? How would he handle the truth? The man he'd thought to be his big brother was his father. His *parents* were his grandparents. Would he feel betrayal, rage? She'd noticed the animosity directed at Joe when she'd met him at the Hamilton family cookout.

Her cell phone sounded off. She had no idea where she'd left it. Standing, she surveyed the room and followed the ringtone to the kitchen, then the guest bathroom. Where had her mind been when she'd left it balanced on the side of the tub filled with soapy water and soaking rags?

She quickly swiped her finger across *answer* on the fourth ring. "Stinky?"

"Muttface, I know it's late, but you should get your butt in gear and head up this way. Our mother's in the hospital."

"What happened!" Sandy's heart squeezed her breath away. She wanted his answer as much as she dreaded hearing it.

"She has pneumonia. She's responding to treatment, but she's fragile. Greg is with her. I came to her house to retrieve a few things she asked for."

Sandy swallowed her fear. "I'll be on my way as soon as I can pack and call my boss to let him know I have a family emergency." She wished Joe could come with her, but that was out of the question. "If I leave in the next hour I can be there late tomorrow. Keep me updated."

"It's not a crisis yet, but I took the precaution to arrange a ticket for you on Southwest out of Burbank tonight. I'll text you the flight details. The plane leaves at nine-thirty. I'll be at the airport when you arrive."

Full of icy fear she answered, "Please tell Mom I'm on my way."

"Yep." Her brother disconnected abruptly. She stared at the phone in her hand, taking several seconds to get her thoughts organized.

First, she had to call her boss, Jordan People, and let him know she'd be out for a few days. She hated calling him on Sunday, but better that than him expecting her to be there Monday morning for yet another strategy meeting.

He answered on the first ring. "Cassidy? Has something happened?"

"Jordan, I have to leave in a couple of hours. My mother is in the hospital up in Portland."

"Is she going to be all right?"

"I hope so. She has pneumonia. My brother just called me. He said she's responding to treatment, but I know he'd never call unless it was serious. I'm sure I told you before, she has MS. She's been going downhill the past several months. I'm very worried."

"Look, kiddo, you take care of family business. I've got everyone in the company working our problems, so we'll manage. Do you have any sales calls I need to cancel or reschedule?"

"Not tomorrow, but I did have a couple on my calendar for Tuesday."

"Go. I'll take care of it. Keep me updated."

"Thanks, Jordan. I'm sorry the timing is so bad."

"Not your choice. Take care." He clicked off.

She had a bag packed and was her way out the door when she got a text from Damon with her flight details. She wanted to call Liz or Joe but knew better. Not today. Liz would find out when she got to work tomorrow, and she'd wait to call Joe until she'd talked to the doctors and had her mother's prognosis.

Scribbling a quick note for the building manager, she grabbed her things and proceeded to the lobby to shove it under the door. Instead of leaving her car at long-term parking, she'd called Uber. The car and driver waited at the curb in front of her complex.

She checked in with Southwest, picked up her ticket, cleared security, and got a boarding pass. Then she grabbed a sandwich and waited.

Her flight was finally called, and she joined the line of passengers anxious to be on their way. The one hour and fifty-two-minute flight time seemed more like four, as concern for her mother built with every mile. She spotted Damon in the baggage claim area and breathed a sigh of relief at the smile on his face.

"She's still not out of the woods." He dropped his arm around her shoulders and lifted her bag as if it were a down pillow. It took less than five minutes to get to his car in the short-term lot. "You had dinner?"

"I ate a roast beef sandwich at Burbank airport. One of those ready-made things. How about you?"

"Janeen insisted on forcing a bowl of soup down my throat when I went back to close the shop after we admitted Mother to the hospital."

"She's what five feet tall, a hundred pounds? From the smile on your face I doubt she had to use much force." Sandy poked his arm.

"You're right." He stopped at a red light and faced her. "How are things with Joe?"

"Things are good between us, but there's been an interesting development, or rather revelation, in his immediate family. How long have you got? I left without telling him, but Liz will find out when she gets to work. Life is never dull, Stinky."

"Yeah. The ancient curse." He drove in silence for several minutes then turned into the visitor parking area of Good Sam medical center. Because of the late hour there were plenty of good parking spaces available. He turned off the engine. "Let's go. Mother is anxious to see you."

Chapter Twenty-Two

Joe sent Sandy a text because she wasn't answering her phone. Liz told him she'd gone to Portland yesterday evening to be with her mother in the hospital. He'd looked for Damon's business card in every drawer of his desk. *Where did I put it?* Dragging his hand down his face, he sat at his kitchen table wondering what to do next.

Good, Good Father, by Chris Tomlin sounded on his phone. He grabbed it. *Sandy. Finally.* "Sweetheart, I've been frantic. How is your mother?"

"I'm sorry, honey. I went straight to the hospital last night and never took my phone off airplane mode. Mom's holding her own."

"Thank God. How are you holding up?"

"I'm doing okay." She paused. "Joe? My mother wants to meet you. Can you can take some time off and come here?"

"Absolutely. I'll leave in the morning. If I drive straight through, I'll be there tomorrow night."

"That's crazy, Joe! It's almost a thousand miles."

"No problem. I was stationed in San Antonio for a while and made the long drive home in one day several times. I want to have my car with me. I'll drive you home when you're ready."

"Joe, I'll worry about you all day. Please call or text me to let me know you're still awake and not in a pile of twisted metal in a ditch somewhere."

"That's a lovely thought."

"Sorry. I'm just telling you the truth."

"Give me Damon's address and I'll put it in the GPS."

"I'm staying at Mom's." Sandy recited her mother's home address and Joe jotted it down.

"I'll see you tomorrow night, sweetheart." She wanted him to come and he wanted to be there for her.

"Oh, I'm so glad you're coming. Why don't you bring Clint with you? I'd love to introduce him to my family."

That stopped him. "Are you sure?"

"Yes. I already told them you have a son. Ask him if he'd like to come, but don't put any pressure on him."

"I'll ask, but, wow, I don't know how he'll react. I'll let you know."

"I love you, Joe."

"I love you more." His worry that she might have been avoiding him evaporated. As soon as he hung up he called his parents' home.

Clint answered. "Hullo?"

"Clint. This is…Joe…uh…your…uh…dad." He sounded like a moron and wondered why this was still so difficult for him.

"Jeez, I know who you are, *Dadbro*. You sound like a crack-head." The smart-alecky kid snickered. "Whadaya want?"

"Right now, I want to poke you, smartass, but I called to ask if you'd like to drive up to Portland with me in the morning. Sandy's mother is in the hospital and wants to meet me. And you."

"Why?"

"Because you're my son."

"No, I mean why do you want to take me?"

"Can we just get past all the crap? Sandy would like you to come with me. If you don't want to, you're under no obligation?"

"Okay. I wanna go."

Surprised, Joe shook his head. He wasn't cut out for this dad stuff. Not when it came to a thirteen-year old. He wondered if he'd make a good father if he and Sandy ever started a family. "Good. Have Mom help you pack. We might be there till the weekend. I'll pick you up in about an hour You can spend the night here because I want to leave early."

"On it, Daddy."

The kid hung up before Joe had a comeback. He sighed and went in search of his garment bag. Just over an hour later he pulled up in front of the family home in Spring Grove. His father opened the front door and stepped out to meet him.

"Joseph."

"Dad." He couldn't read his father's expression. "Is something wrong?"

"On the contrary. This is a good idea. He's excited about going."

"Dad, I'm shooting in the dark here. In the back of my mind, I always knew that someday he'd learn the truth. It happened so unexpectedly, I was caught off guard. I don't want to mess up." He massaged the back of his neck.

"We were all caught off guard. I take full responsibility for letting the deception go on so long. He deserved to know years ago. I confess I enjoyed having him as *my* son, even though it was not the truth." Don jammed his hands in his pockets.

Joe rested a hand on his father's shoulder. "You've been a great father to both of us. I haven't told you and Mom often enough. I owe you a debt I'll never be able to repay."

"Wrong. You don't owe us anything. Mother and I had our own selfish reasons in all this. We're good with any decision you and Clint make going forward." He turned toward the house.

"Dad, wait up." They stopped and Don faced him. "I'm thinking of taking Clint to my AA meeting when we get back to my place. Is that a bad idea? I hate to miss a meeting and I'm not comfortable with dumping him alone in my apartment for a couple of hours."

"Why don't you leave it up to him?"

"Is there too much of me in him, Dad? I made some really lousy decisions when I was his age, right up until I got sober." Jaws clenched, his shoulders slumped.

"Here's the way I see it. If Mother and I haven't done our job right by now, there's nothing else we can do. He'll make mistakes. He'll make bad decisions. We all do. When you were his age, I was absent much of the time on long deployments. You've traveled a rough road to get here, but you're a fine man and I'm proud of you."

Stunned by his father's words, Joe didn't know how to respond. Don's love for him was always a given, but his military minded father seldom spoke words of praise. He usually demonstrated his feelings with actions, not words. At the ripe old age of thirty-three, Joe felt like a kid who'd just made the winning goal on the soccer field while his father was watching. "Dad, I..."

"You two had better get a move on. You'll have a late evening and you're embarking on a long drive tomorrow." He opened the door and went inside, leaving Joe speechless on the doorstep.

Finally, he stepped inside. Mom entered the room, Clint right behind her. "He's all packed. Against his loud protests, I included a nice shirt and his sports coat." She grabbed Clint by the ear and play-fully pulled him close. He couldn't duck the kiss on his cheek without pulling painfully against her. As soon as she let go, he made a big show of wiping it off. Joe remembered how his mother's show of affection had embarrassed him at the same age. He grinned at Clint's discomfort.

"Let's go, pal. I have an AA meeting tonight. You can come with me if you want. Otherwise you can twiddle your thumbs and watch TV until I get home."

Clint hefted the long strap on the soft-sided suitcase over his shoulder. "Epic."

"What's epic? The AA meeting or the TV?"

"The AA meeting. I always wondered what a room full of reformed boozers looked like."

"You may not relish me introducing you to my friends and sponsor."

"Do I have to pretend I'm your brother, or are you telling them you're my father?"

"That's the point." He gave Clint a playful tap on the back of his head of thick, curly black hair and kissed Bernice on the cheek. "See you in a few days, Mom and Dad. I'll call when we get there."

"Clint? Have you got your cell phone and laptop?" Don inquired.

He patted the side of the travel bag. "Right here. I hope they have wi-fi in Portland."

"It's not the other side of the moon." Joe laughed. "It's ten times bigger than Spring Grove, and twice as big as Simi Valley." He shook his head. "Get your butt in the car. We gotta shake a leg."

Don and Bernice walked them to the car and waved when he pulled his Beemer into the street. Joe thought he detected a fleeting expression of loss on his mother's face.

Most every attendee had taken a seat in the church where the AA meeting was held by the time Joe and Clint walked in. "There's my sponsor, Brian. I see a couple of empty seats next to him." Joe pointed across the room just as Brian turned and spotted him. He waved them over and stood when they reached his row. "Joe. Glad you could make it. Who's this handsome young man?"

Clint actually blushed. Joe clamped a hand on his shoulder. "Brian, I'd like you to meet my son, Clint. Clint, this is my sponsor, Brian."

The kid stuck his hand out. "Nice to meet you, Mr. uh..."

Brian grinned. "Just, Brian, son. We don't use last names here. Have you ever been to an AA meeting?"

"No, sir." Clint looked around at the diverse audience and shook his head. "Is it like church?" Tonight's crowd had both sexes and every age range from young to old.

Joe supposed he might have gotten that idea because the meeting was held in a large room at the First Presbyterian Church. Joe's parents were Episcopalian, but usually only went to services on special holidays, when they'd all go as a family.

"Not really," Brian answered. "But like some churches we encourage our members to testify about their successes and failures. We're a very supportive bunch. Our goal is to help through difficult times and celebrate the good times."

"Oh." Clint thought about this. "Um, Mister...uh...Brian? Are you a...I mean...are you...?"

Clint's cheeks blazed, but Brian laughed and immediately put him at ease. "You betcha."

Joe added, "Everybody here, except for guests like you, is a recovering alcoholic. We've all been there, which makes us perfect to help one another. If it goes on too long, or you get uncomfortable, let me know and we'll sneak out." He gave the kid a small nudge with his elbow. "I saw a big plate of fresh glazed donuts from the Vietnamese baker, by the coffee machine. It'd be a shame to miss those."

The meeting had been good and ended right on time. Joe smiled. "What are we waiting for?" They wandered over to the snack table and helped themselves to two huge glazed donuts and hot chocolate. Balancing their plates, they took a seat.

A lovely young woman stood in front of Clint and gestured to the chair next to him, "Mind if I sit here?"

Clint's mouth was full. All he could do was shake his head. He swallowed with difficulty and chased it down with cocoa. "Go ahead."

The girl, who didn't look much older than Clint, smiled and sat. "I'm April." She cocked her head and waggled her finger between Joe and Clint. "You must be Joe's son. You look just like him."

"Yeah." Clint stared at her. "Are your parents here?"

Joe said, "April's our youngest member. How you doing, April?"

"Member?" Clint's eyes rounded. "How, um, old are you?"

"I'm eighteen. Believe it or not. I always wanted to look older, but Joe set me straight. He said I'd be rejoicing when I'm thirty and all my friends were jealous." She graced Joe with an adoring smile. "I'm secretly in love with Joe. But two recovering drunks is a lethal combination. At least that's what he told me."

"He's got a girlfriend," Clint declared as if protecting Sandy from possible competition. "But I don't."

Joe chuckled quietly.

"You're going to be a good catch, Clint, but alas, too young for me." She winked at him and blood rushed to his cheeks. "I met Joe's girl at a meeting about a month ago. That's when I decided I'd better quit looking for love in all the wrong places." Her laugh tinkled like windchimes on a breezy day.

Joe blew on his chocolate. "Dig in, pal. We've got an early morning coming up."

———

On the way to Joe's apartment, Clint said, "I really liked Brian and April. They're cool."

"Yes, they are. It's a great bunch. I hate when I have to miss a meeting."

"Does Sandy go with you?"

"Nah, just the once. She was in a frenzy over a dish she cooked for me using red wine. She panicked and was ready to take me to ER to have my stomach pumped. I convinced her to come to AA and meet Brian instead. He set her mind at ease." Joe's belly bounced with laughter. "She was sure she'd sent me down the road to perdition."

———

Joe and Clint closed the trunk of the Beemer before the sun was up. Being part of a military family, they were both familiar with rising at zero-dark-thirty. Don was always up at the crack, and Mom had breakfast on the table by six.

"We'll get breakfast on the road. There's a good diner up top at Gorman, just before we go down to Grapevine Valley."

"Oh, yeah. I remember stopping there on the way to Fort Tejon for the Civil War reenactment with…um…Dad."

Joe didn't miss the confusion in Clint's voice. "Look, quit worrying about what to call me and Dad, OK? He's always been your dad. Keep calling him Dad and call me anything you want."

"Anything?" A sideways glance by Joe revealed Clint's eyes gleaming with his teasing remark.

"Sure, anything. But if I pop you, you'll know you went too far afield."

Clint's answer was a soft punch in Joe's shoulder. "Sure thing, Big Daddy."

Joe laughed. "Okay, okay, let's change the subject. How are you doing in school?"

"Like Dad gives me a choice? Boy, you are old."

"Hey, I remember! I was the son before you were the son. We're both better off for his discipline. It's how he shows he loves us."

"Yeah, I get it. Tell me about your job. I'm good on computers. Maybe I'll decide to do what you do."

"I thought you were joining the Marines as soon as you turned eighteen." He remembered being all over the place about his future when he was Clint's age. Always in a rush.

"Maybe I will go to college first. I could ace it in three years easy."

"I don't doubt it. You'd be twenty-one when you got your degree. That's a lot better than doing it my way. I was almost thirty when I got mine. But I did enjoy serving. My buddies stuck by me when I started drinking. It could all have turned out different without them, and Dad throwing the fear of Dad into me, which you know is scarier than the fear of God." He sighed hoping Clint would avoid some of the mistakes and bad decisions he'd made. "I owe a lot of good people."

The weather was good, traffic smooth, conversation between them relaxed. As evening approached, they stopped for the night at a brightly lit motel in Marysville, north of Sacramento. They enjoyed dinner in the family sports bar off the lobby and watched a few innings of a Red Sox-Yankees game. They cheered for the Sox because everybody hates those damn Yankees, don't they?

Back in their room, Joe called Sandy while Clint showered. "Hi, baby, how's your mother doing?"

"Good, she's doing good, but they're keeping her in the hospital for a couple more days to make sure she doesn't have any secondary infection. Where are you?"

"Marysville. We made good time today. Clint's in the shower, so I'll take advantage of that by telling you all the hot and steamy things I'm going to do with you when I get you in my bed again."

"Oh, please do. Greg's out tonight, so I have the house to myself. Should I take my clothes off so I can fully fantasize?"

Joe chuckled low and sexy. "Torture me, sweetheart. Oops! The shower just went off. Looks like it'll have to wait until I get there."

"Darn it! How do parents manage, I wonder?"

Clint strolled into the room, a towel wrapped around his waist. "I think Mom forgot to pack my pajamas." He dropped his suitcase on the bed and started digging. "That Sandy?"

"Yes, I was just telling her when to expect us." He felt his face going warm in the face of his fib. "I'll say goodnight, sweetheart. We'll see you at your mother's home tomorrow evening. Don't wait dinner. I'll give you a heads-up about an hour out." He nodded and smiled.

"Yes, you can talk to him, but I usually frown on naked guys talking to my girlfriend." He held the phone out to his outraged, red-faced son.

Clint yelled, "Why'd you tell her that!" accompanied by a look that would kill a charging grizzly. He made no move to take the phone.

Joe immediately regretted his ill-timed tease. The poor kid was thirteen. He'd probably remember this for the rest of his life, and hate Joe for embarrassing him. He put the phone back to his ear. "I'm just teasing. He's in his pajamas and went back in the bathroom to brush his teeth. Yes, see you tomorrow." He shook his head and hung up. "Sorry, that was stupid of me."

"You're a shithead! A real world-class shithead!" He yanked his pajamas from the bottom of the bag and stalked back to the bathroom and slammed the door so hard it rattled the window.

So much for the nice day of father-son talk.

Joe shmoo, that sums it up.

Chapter Twenty-Three

JOE GLANCED AT CLINT WHEN THEY SAT IN THE COFFEE SHOP
the next morning. The boy was silent and surly. Arms crossed, he
stared out the window. Joe had deeply embarrassed his son and
wasn't sure how to make it right. Or if he could. Sitting across from
him in the diner where they'd stopped for breakfast, Joe cleared his
throat.

"Look, I'm sorry for embarrassing you. It was stupid and
thoughtless."

"Ya think?" Clint refused to meet his eyes and continued to stare
out the window.

"Like I said, I'm sorry. I mean it. Can we get past this? We have
hours in the car before we get there." He rubbed the back of his neck
and twiddled his fingers on the rim of his coffee cup.

"Get past it? Every time Sandy looks at me she'll picture me naked.
Every time. I wish I hadn't come with you." A muscle worked in his
jaw. "You're such a tool."

"No, she won't. She was full of tension about her mother's situation. I was making a lame joke to relieve her anxiety. What I said
probably didn't even register. She won't think of you that way."

"Sure." He clamped his lips tight when the server placed the plate
of pancakes in front of him. He looked at her. "I had a side of bacon

with this." His tone of voice was worlds friendlier that the one he'd been using with Joe.

"Comin' right up, honey." She set Joe's omelet on the table. "I owe you sourdough toast. Be right back." She smiled and headed for the kitchen.

Joe slid the syrup caddy across the table to his son then reached for the Tabasco and doused his eggs. He'd let the kid calm down in his own good time. It made no sense to keep apologizing.

During breakfast, he was relieved to see the tension in Clint's posture easing slightly. He figured they'd make it to Yreka by lunchtime, then Eugene for dinner. That should give him time to cool off before they got to Portland this evening. He hoped to God Clint would cool off, otherwise it was going to be hell for both of them, not to mention the trip back with Sandy in the car.

The meal proceeded with minimal conversation, mostly consisting of sniffs and grunts. When the server brought the check, and held up the coffee pot for a refill, Joe shook his head. "No thanks, we need to get on the road."

"Where y'all headed today?" The rosy cheeked woman had a deep southern drawl.

"Portland." Joe checked the bill and placed twenty dollars on top of it.

"Well then, you do need to head out if you're going to make it before dark. You want change? No?" She smiled. "Have a safe trip. I don't often get two good lookin' men sharing the same table to start my day." She winked at Clint and walked away.

His face bright pink, Clint grumbled, "What's wrong with every-body? Is there a sign on my back that says tease me?"

"No, you were blessed with Mom's good genes. Be glad of it. It'll come in real handy in about three years."

Clint emitted a loud snort. "Like Dad would ever let me drive the car or go on a date."

"You want to learn how to drive? You're big enough, but a little young yet. When we get home, I'll take you to Santa Anita race track. You can practice in the big parking lot when there's no racing. Dad said Grandpa taught him to drive in an arena parking lot when he was *twelve*. Don't tell him I let the cat out of the bag."

"Twelve? No shit?"

"No shit. Now let's take it easy on jarhead language. You know how Mom and Liz despise it. Mom used to put a drop of Tabasco on my tongue when she caught me cursing." He chuckled at the memory of her furious and determined face.

"No...sh... kidding?"

"How do you think I acquired such a taste for it? How does she discipline your mouth?"

"She'd doesn't need to. I'm a perfect angel."

"Satan was a fallen angel. Make sure you don't take a fall, smartass."

Clint pointed to the CD player. "You got anything but old fogey music on there?"

"How about Metallica? Or is Green Day or Red Hot Chili Peppers more to your taste?"

"Any Garth Brooks? I don't get it. You have this great X5 sound system. Why do you even have a CD player?"

"I like my old favorites. Have you listened to the Una Día Normal album by Juanes? Sandy loves that one. Five CDs are loaded already. Have a look in the console, or just scan the sound system."

Yeah, the kid could listen to anything he wanted. It would take the pressure off the strained conversation, give them a couple hours to get past it.

———

Joe recognized Damon's Audi when they were looking for house numbers. He turned around and parked in front of the house. "That's her brother's car. I told you she has two brothers, Damon, her big brother and Greg, her little brother. This is their childhood home. Sandy's mother lives here alone now, but they have a woman who comes in and does the cooking and cleaning. Do you know anything about MS?"

"I know I never want to get it." Clint shuddered.

"Sandy tells me Beverly's had it since she was in her late thirties. They've managed it all these years, but now it's taking a toll on her. According to Damon, she often goes for weeks without symptoms, then they hit her hard again. She uses a wheelchair now to avoid falling."

They got out of the car and approached the house. The door opened and Damon stepped out. "Joe! You made good time." He walked forward and extended a big, meaty hand. "You're Clint. Glad to meet you." Clint's hand was completely engulfed by Damon's.

The kid's eyes widened in surprise at the size of Sandy's big brother. "Hey."

Damon spoke to Joe, "Mother's having a good day. She's anxious to meet you both. After you hit the head and have some coffee or soda, I'll take you to the hospital. Sandy and Greg stayed to have dinner with her." He turned and gestured toward the open front door.

"Look, Damon, you don't have to put us up in the house. I can get a hotel room."

"That's nuts. This big house is full of empty bedrooms. Sandy will get you settled in when we get back from the hospital. Don't say any more about it."

Joe grinned. "You're the boss. I'd love a cup of coffee."

"I'll have coffee too," Clint said, and gave Joe a look that dared him to say no.

Joe raised a hand. "I need to get something from the car before we go. I brought a little gift for Beverly."

Damon put a hand on Clint's shoulder. "Bathroom's down the hall on the left. I'll be in the kitchen. What do you take in your coffee?"

"Um…black, I guess."

Damon winked at Joe, then said, "I've got some great French Vanilla creamer you might want to try."

"Yeah. Okay. Thanks." Clint headed toward the bathroom. Joe gave Damon a thumb's up.

Forty-five minutes later they strolled down the hospital hall. Sandy stood waiting at the door to her mother's room. Her face lit up when she saw Joe and Clint. She walked quickly toward them with her arms open, but went straight for Clint and gave him a big hug. "I'm so glad you came, honey. How was that long drive?"

Adam's apple bouncing with shock at her unabashed greeting, Clint grinned shyly. "Long."

Joe moved Clint aside and embraced Sandy. "The good news is we didn't kill each other."

She clung to him and whispered, "You smell so good."

"What do I smell like?"

"My Joe."

He grinned and hugged her again. "How you holding up, sweetheart?" Planting a light kiss on her lips, he stepped back and studied her.

"I'm fine, really. Damon, would you go in and tell Greg and Mom we'll be right there?" She took Joe's hand and Clint's hand and led them to a small waiting alcove a few doors down. "Mom's doing great. We'll be able to bring her home tomorrow after they run her labs. How did you manage to get off work? I know you're deep into an important investigation."

"We ran into a snag, so Yoda's working to clear that up before we can go forward. It was good timing. You never know with my boss, but he's been mellow about me taking time off. As long as I'm back by the beginning of next week. I don't dare push it beyond then. I'm still the new kid on the block."

"What have you got?" Sandy nodded at the bright pink gift bag he carried. "For me?"

"Nope. For your mother. I found something I think she'll like."

Sandy smiled. "If she doesn't like it, she'll pretend she does, so you'll never be sure. Mom always makes a big deal over every tiny little thing we do for her, or gift we give her. It's an inside joke with me and my brothers. We tease about giving her a garlic acifidity bag one of these days just to see how she reacts." She laughed and gave their hands a squeeze.

Clint cheeks reddened when she squeezed his hand. "What's that?"

She grinned at him. "Before modern medicine, some ethnic groups had the practice of making up small bags of various herbs, and sometimes disgusting things, to hang around the neck. They were supposed to ward off evil spirits and disease. A nice strong garlic bag would probably ward of anything and anybody except disease."

Clint raised his eyebrows. "Mom says garlic is a natural antibiotic. She uses a lot of it in stuff she cooks."

"She's right there but hanging it around your neck won't do the trick." Sandy looked at Joe. The love in her eyes nearly floored him. He hoped they'd be able to manage some private time in the next few days. He longed to have his hands all over her.

"Let's go in so I can introduce you to my mother." Sandy stood and tugged their hands. "Come on, my two handsome guys. I want to show you off."

Joe smiled secretly at Clint's blush. The kid was totally in love with Sandy. When they walked in the room, Beverly smiled and waved. "You're here! Come in. I'm so happy to meet you both."

Damon made the introductions. Greg nodded at Joe and clapped a hand on Clint's neck and grinned. "Great to meet you, my man."

"Yeah...uh...me too." He looked from Greg to Damon with confusion. The difference in their physical appearance was dramatic.

Beverly noticed. "Damon takes after his father. Greg and Sandy take after me." She gestured for Clint to come closer. "You look like Joe. Which side of the family do you resemble?

"Liz, my si...aunt, and Joe and me...we take after our...uh...Joe's mom."

"Yes, Sandy tells me your grandparents adopted you after your mother died while Joe was deployed. I can see you're still having trouble shuffling the relationships. But—isn't it great to be part of such a nice, loving family?" She gestured again. "Joe, come here. I've been dying to meet you ever since Sandra first told us about you."

Joe walked to the bed, bent forward and hugged Sandy's mother. He kissed her lightly on the cheek. It suddenly became clear to him how beautiful Sandy would still be when she was this woman's age. "I'm so happy to finally meet you, Mrs. Cassidy."

"Oh, please! Call me Beverly." She cocked her head. "What's that you have behind your back?"

Joe grinned. "I brought you something. I hope you like it." He held out the small bag. "If you don't like it, you can blame your daughter. She clued me in on some of your favorite things."

Beverly glanced at Sandy and took the gift. Her lovely smile mirrored Sandy's. "What have we here?" She removed the tissue and peeked inside. "Oh, my." She lifted a lovely decorated jar of sweet pea scented hand cream. "Where on earth did you ever find this?" She handed it to Joe. "Open it for me please. I'm not much good at opening things."

Joe opened the jar and took a sniff before offering it back to Beverly. "Nice. I'll keep it if you don't like it." He grinned and handed it to her.

Beverly took a whiff of the scented cream. "Joe this is just wonderful. I love it!"

Joe winked at Sandy, and they shared a private look. She rolled her eyes and grinned.

When Beverly began to show the effects of the visit, Damon said, "Mother, you're tired. You need to rest because we want to take you home. Joe and Clint had a long drive and I bet they're ready to crash. We'll head out and be back around noon tomorrow." He leaned down and kissed her on the top of the head. "Janeen's cooking dinner for all of us to welcome you home."

"Oh, isn't that nice! You're right, honey. I'm pooped, but so happy you're all here. I'm looking forward to seeing my future daughter-in-law and her darling Isabella." She smiled at Joe. "Little Belle is so adorable. You'll fall in love with her, I promise you."

"That's what Sandy tells me." He gave Beverly's hand a gentle squeeze. "Clint and I want to thank you for allowing us to stay in your home."

"I love having company. So nice to finally meet you, Clint."

"Me too, ma'am." He looked at his shoes and nodded.

Greg put his hand on Clint's shoulder. "Hey, how about riding back to the house in my car? I was planning to stop at my favorite bakery and pick up tomorrow's breakfast, and maybe a treat for tonight. You can help me decide."

"Yeah, sure." Clint looked at Joe.

Joe nodded and slapped him on the back. "Good, that's good. I'll bring your bag in and put it in the room you'll be using. Pick something that's delicious and totally bad for us. You know some of my favorites and Greg knows Sandy's. We'll see you shortly."

———

Sandy slid in next to Joe in the backseat of Damon's car. He caught her eye in the rearview mirror. "What am I, your chauffer?"

"Just drive and keep your eyes on the road. We'll behave, I promise." She'd maneuvered past Belle's car seat and took the center, her hip firmly against Joe's, and fastened the belt. She had no intention of behaving, and once they were on the road, she pressed her hand in Joe's lap and whispered in his ear. "You'll have your own assigned room, but you'll be sleeping in my bed tonight."

"You're killing me," he hissed through gritted teeth, then covered her hand and pushed down. His head dropped on the headrest. His sigh had an audible waver.

She whispered again, "Not exactly what I had in mind." Evidence of his passion sent her reeling. She loved him more than she ever thought possible. Whatever hurdles they encountered, they'd conquer together. She wanted this man in her life for as long as she lived.

Glancing up, she caught Damon's smirk. "She crowding you back there, Joe?"

Joe removed her hand and placed it on her leg. "I can handle her."

Damon shook his head, cranked up the volume on the radio, and kept driving.

When they pulled into the Cassidy driveway, Joe shifted and tugged at his waistband. Damon stepped out of the car. "You coming?"

Joe cleared his throat. "Be right there. Gotta tie my shoe first. You and Sandy go ahead."

Sandy slid across Joe's lap and exited the car on his side. She felt a little, only a little, guilty for causing his discomfort. "Okay, honey. Don't take long." She looped her arm in Damon's and they went inside.

Damon elbowed her. "I thought you loved the guy."

Her brow went up. "I do, Stinky. Why?"

"You know why. Janeen would never pull a dirty trick on me like that." He unlocked the front door.

"Sticking to that story, are you?" She grinned and took her cell phone from her purse and set it on the charger in the entry hall.

"Well, not when anybody else is around." He dropped his jacket on the coat rack. "Let's get the coffee going. Give the poor guy time to get his act together."

"He's wearing loafers." Sandy winked at Damon. "How do you think he'll explain that whopper?" She stopped talking at the sound of the front door opening and closing.

Joe joined them in the kitchen in his stocking-feet. Neither of them asked him where his shoes were. "Anything I can do?"

"I've got it covered. Muttface can show you where you and Clint will be sleeping while you're here. I left your bags in the back hallway. Go ahead and settle in."

"Sounds good. We'll make it fast." He gripped her hand and dragged her down the hall. "Which rooms?"

"Clint can have the boys' old room." She pushed a door open to reveal a large bedroom with bunk beds, desk and TV. Several model spacecraft hung suspended from the ceiling, and Star Wars posters covered one entire wall. "Greg sleeps here when he overnights, but now that I'm home he stays at his house."

Joe walked into the room and placed Clint's suitcase on the bottom bunk. "And mine?"

She gestured across the hall. "The guest room is there. My room is the one beyond it. "Would you like to see my room?" She couldn't miss the dangerous glint in his eye.

"Love to." He left his bag just inside the guestroom and followed her to the next door. She opened it to reveal a very girlie sanctuary. Her mother must not have changed a thing about it since Sandy left home. The four-poster, white-lace canopy bed had a flowery duvet with layers of ruffles floating over the sides of the double mattress. Mountains of frilly pillows were banked against the headboard. White end tables on either side carried matching lamps with the shades decorated with a fringe of crystals.

A large chest of drawers, next to a frail looking white, mirrored vanity, the top covered with dozens of antique perfume spray bottles took up the wall facing the bed. On one side wall were large framed posters of Luke Perry, Mark Wahlberg and the Backstreet Boys.

"My God, it looks like Disneyland in here." He chuckled and turned completely around to take it all in.

Sandy sighed. "It is a little over the top, I admit. Damon built all this furniture in his first wood shop in Mom's garage. Isn't it wonderful? I thought if I ever had a little girl, she'd get a big kick out of it."

Joe locked the door. "Something else is going to be over the top right now."

She took a step back. "What do you think you're doing, Joseph Hamilton?" For every step he took toward her, she stepped back until she was stopped by the bed. The next thing he did was enclose her in a tight embrace, and his mouth slammed down on hers. They fell on her bed, knocking the wind from her, but that didn't stop Sandy from gripping his neck and kissing back with the same level of passion. "Joe, we can't."

"Like hell. You started it." He kissed her again and fumbled with the hem of her skirt. When she clamped her knees together, he growled, "I need you, sweetheart."

Sandy sighed and ran a hand down the side of his face. His intense blue eyes burned through her. "I need you too, honey lover. But we don't have much time."

"I'll have this mission completed to your satisfaction in no time." When he kissed her again, she wrapped her arms around him and moaned. Joe's hands were magic. She wanted all of him and she wanted him now.

Chapter Twenty-Four

Sandy closed the door behind Damon and Greg around 11:00 p.m.

Clint was fading fast. They'd been on the road since before six in the morning. Joe stood from the table. "Come on, son, I'll show you where your room is. I had a quick shower before you got here so you can have the shower all to yourself in the morning."

Clint picked up his plate and carried it to the sink. He came back for hers.

Sandy gave the tall boy an affectionate smile. "I'll put the plates in the dishwasher, honey. You go ahead with your dad and I'll see you in the morning. Sleep late. We won't be leaving the house until after lunch, until the doctor signs Mom's hospital discharge."

His shoulders drooped. "Cool. I'm so tired it sucks dust."

Sandy laughed. "I hate that feeling." She exchanged a look with Joe. He was tired too. Both Hamiltons yawned when they walked down the hall, leaving her to finish clearing up the dishes. She was setting up the coffeemaker when Joe returned and embraced her from behind.

"He's already halfway out. I hate to admit it, but so am I, sweetheart. I doubt I'll be any good to you tonight. I gotta catch up on my Z's." His lips brushed her ear. She shut off the water and turned in his embrace. "You're always good to me, you tired old man. What say we both catch up on those Z's. Together. In my bed?"

"You read my mind." He took her hand, switched off the overhead light and led her down the hall to her bedroom.

Joe's arms gave her the sense of being snug in a warm, safe place. She leaned into his side wondering if it were in the cards for her to share a future with this special man. She tried not to let lingering doubts spoil the moment. Now she'd crawl into bed with him and enjoy the comfort of his body cradling hers through the night. She still had so much to accomplish to get to a firm sense of her own security and independence. She needed to get there first in order to move forward. Once she was confidently in that place of self-sufficiency, once she'd regained the ability to trust herself to make the right decisions, then she'd be ready to put her demons behind her, not bring them with her into Joe's life.

In the meantime, they could be together, enjoy each other, and become friends as well as lovers. Joe had a lot on his plate. His altered relationship with Clint was paramount. Once he and his son resolved their issues, he could devote more time to considering a future with her. If he desired one, Clint would be part of that future. Joe was strong and confident, but she was acutely aware of his convictions about trust. His complete trust in her could make or break them.

It was barely light when Joe stroked her leg and nuzzled her neck. She rolled over and smiled. "Good morning, honey lover."

Joe pulled her tight against his chest and growled. "I thought you'd never wake up."

"Really? I don't usually rise before the cock crows, but I never went to boot camp or was a military brat. Is this what I have to look forward to if you decide to hang around?" His touch set her on fire from her heels to her eyebrows. Joe put his knee between hers and nudged her legs apart. Heat warmed her in all the best places. His hand glided up and down the inside of her thigh until she lost patience, reached down and placed it where she knew he could perform the most incredible magic. "Joe."

His mouth found hers and the blazing kiss had her moaning with anticipation. He raised his head and scowled. "Where are my pants?"

"What?" She stopped breathing. "You getting up?"

Joe raised on his elbows and shook his head. "Only as long as it takes me to find my pants before I get past the point of no return. We have hours for some slow, real slow. I'm going to show you just how much I've missed you, sweetheart. As you can tell, the cock grows when the sun comes up."

"Your whimsical, romantic phrases make my heart go pitter-pat." She gripped him where it counted and smiled when he winced. "That's a taste of your punishment. Don't make me hurt you."

He laughed and nodded across the room. His pants had barely made it inside the door last night. "Hold that thought."

———

The fragrant, woodsy smell of coffee woke Sandy. Joe was still wrapped around her, their legs intertwined. Who made coffee? Damon and Greg wouldn't be here this early. "Joe? Honey?" She untangled her legs.

He dragged a hand down his face and squinted. "Yeah?"

"I smell coffee." She pushed back until she rested against the headboard. She couldn't reach the sheet to cover herself and felt shy.

Joe rolled toward her and nipped her breast. "Do not cover these up for my sake. I could drool over them all day. Mmm-mmm-mmm."

"Stop it! I need to get up and check out the kitchen. See who's in there."

"Whoever it is, I'm going to kick his ass right out the door." Joe got up and pulled on his boxers and pants. He raked fingers through his hair and scratched his bristly chin.

Sandy jumped off the bed and grabbed a robe. "Oh, no you don't. Me first." She pulled open the door and headed down the hall, Joe right behind her. She stopped abruptly at the kitchen door. He bumped her back, and had to grab her to keep both of them from tumbling on their faces.

Clint glanced up from his laptop. "What? Am I tapping the keys too loud?" He smirked at Joe and went back to whatever it was he was doing. "I made coffee." He jerked his chin at the sink counter but continued to stare at the screen. "I'm talking to Dad. I promised to stay in touch. I was too tired last night." He tapped a few more keys, then raised his arms above his head and stretched. "Now that you're finally up, I'll go take my shower."

Sandy felt Joe's fingers squeeze her shoulders. She smiled at Clint. "I'll warm those muffins you and Greg bought last night. They'll be just right when you get back." When Clint attempted to slide around them she grabbed his arm. "You're not leaving until I get my morning hug." She wrapped her arms around his wide, bony shoulders. "Thanks for the coffee."

Clint hesitated for a split second, cast a startled look in Joe's direction, then quickly raised his arms and hugged her back. "Welcome." He stepped away and made a hasty retreat, cheeks glowing.

Joe chuckled quietly, shook his head and dropped into one of the kitchen chairs.

"Coffee, honey lover?"

He slapped a hand on the table and winked. "Put it right here, woman."

Sandy shook her head and sashayed to the counter. "Maybe I'll just put it in your lap."

Joe jumped up, streaked across the kitchen, and grabbed her from behind. He lifted her off her feet. She screeched with surprise and struggled against him. He crushed her to his chest. "What did you say? Hmm?"

She wiggled loose and elbowed him away. "Behave yourself!"

"That's not what you said a couple of hours ago." He pretended to bite her neck and smacked her on the bottom. "Is it?"

"I'm gonna puke," a voice behind them muttered. "It must run in the family."

They stopped playing and spun around. Sandy clutched her robe tight across her body. Clint stood in the doorway shaking his head with disgust. "Don't mind me. I came back to rescue Sandy when I heard her scream. Guess I'll have to take Dad up on his suggestion to start wearing bells on my Nikes. Sheesh." He glared and grabbed his laptop. His snickering echoed down the hallway.

"That certainly broke the mood," Joe groused, unable to suppress a smile.

Yes, Sandy thought, Clint was a lovable complication for them. A sure-fire mood breaker.

———

Sandy smiled and hugged herself because her entire family, including Joe and Clint, were seated around the large dining table celebrating Beverly's return home. In rosy, good health and spirits, she praised Janeen's delicious dinner. Joe held Belle on his knee while she chattered away telling a long, involved story about her day at preschool.

"And then my daddy came to pick me up and when we got back to the cabinet shop, he put my painting right on the front of the filing cabinet by his desk so everybody who came in would see it."

"What did you paint?" Joe winked at Damon across the table. The big man's eyes were full of unabashed love for the tiny girl.

"I painted a pichur of the dog my daddy is going to get me and the dog house Daddy is going to build for it. Then when the doggie has a nice warm house my daddy is going to build me a playhouse right next to it. He's going to paint it pink with green shutters next to the windows."

"So, will your doggie be a girl dog or a boy dog?" Joe was trying to keep up his end of the amusing conversation. He'd never spoken to a three-year old girl and wasn't confident he'd have all the right questions and answers for Belle.

She scowled and puckered her lips. "I don't know. Why?"

"Well, I could be wrong, but if it's a boy dog, he might want to have a blue house instead of a pink one."

"Dogs can't see colors." She shook her head at his ignorance. "Didn't you ever have a dog?"

"I did. He lives with my parents now because my apartment building doesn't allow pets."

"They're not very nice, are they? What's your dog's name?"

"Major. He's retired from the Marines, and happy to be living a very good life in Spring Grove with my mother taking good care of him. Someday maybe you'll get to meet him."

"OK." She hopped off his lap. The conversation was clearly over and she was ready to move on. She skipped behind Joe's chair and crawled into Clint's lap. "We're getting ice cream for dessert. Do you like ice cream?"

Crimson faced, Clint mumbled, "Um, yeah, doesn't everybody?"

Damon took pity on his discomfort. "Belle, come sit with me. Daddy's lonely."

She grinned and hopped off Clint's lap. "OK, Daddy."

Janeen leaned sideways and put her lips close to Sandy's ear. "Your brother is going to spoil that child rotten."

Sandy smiled, shook her head and whispered back. "You can't spoil a child by loving it."

———

Sandy's happy and tired mother said she needed to get to bed, Joe gave Beverly a hug and told her how much he and Clint had enjoyed meeting her. "We'll be pulling out pretty early, so we'll say our good-byes now. I hope we see you again before too long."

"Oh, me too, honey. Thank you for making my daughter so happy. She's glowing from head to toe. You and your son are very special to her."

"Sandy makes me very happy too."

"I'll help you get ready for bed, Mom." Sandy pulled back the wheelchair and directed it to her mother's bedroom. She tossed a kiss over her shoulder and Joe reached out to grab it, "That one was for Clint." She and Beverly laughed as they turned into her bedroom.

Joe chuckled and walked Damon, Janeen and the sleeping Belle to their car. "I'm guessing the next time I see you will be at your wedding?"

Janeen stood tiptoe and kissed his cheek. "Absolutely. Don't disappoint us, Joe." She looked around. "I don't know where Clint got off to but tell him we expect him to come with you."

"I'll pass it on." He waited while Damon buckled the sleeping child into her car seat, then shook his hand. "It was great seeing you again."

"Same here." He opened his door and slid inside. "Take care on the long drive home."

"You bet," Joe answered with a quick nod.

He went back in the house marveling how he already felt like a part of Sandy's family. In the kitchen, he found Clint and Greg finishing the dishes and cleanup while laughing at something.

"Great timing, Dadjoe." Clint pursed his lips and nudged Greg. "Didn't I tell ya he'd show up when we were all done?"

"You got a smart kid here, Joe." Greg folded the dishtowel and neatly hung it on the bar next to the sink.

"Takes after his old man." Joe laughed at Clint's sour expression. "You about ready to head home, Greg? We'll be leaving early tomorrow. Will Beverly be all right here by herself?"

"Her nurse will be here by six. She comes in every other day to assist Mom with her bath and then prepares her breakfast. I'll be back to check on her by ten. She's dying to get to the hairdresser, so I made an appointment for her at eleven."

"You're a good man, Greg."

"That's what I keep telling the rest of the family." Greg gave Clint a one-armed man-hug and gripped Joe's hand. "Hope you'll be at Damon's wedding next month."

"Wouldn't miss it. We'll walk you out after you say goodnight to your mother and sister." He smiled to himself at Greg's wording: 'The rest of the family.' The Cassidys behaved as if he and Clint were a given.

Clint followed Greg out of the kitchen. "I'll say goodnight to your mom too, then I gotta get on the laptop and let Dadpa know when we're leaving in the morning so he can start worrying. He'll say it's Mom who's worried, but that's a big fat lie. He's the mother hen."

Joe smiled at the accuracy of his son's comment and went to his room to lay out tomorrow's clothing and finish packing before he got in the shower. They'd be on the road south at first light. His text message signal sounded off when he stepped in the room.

Puzzled, he took the phone out of his back pocket, surprised by a message from Yoda.

Been putting in some overtime and think I've triangulated the leak. We'll knock this puppy out on Monday morning, Mr. Hamilton. I'm taking a couple vacation days until then. Y.

Joe nodded and sent a reply. *Good news, Hotstuff. Monday.*

Chapter Twenty-Five

JOE WAS SURPRISED SANDY TOOK THE BACKSEAT IN THE BEEMER after they loaded their luggage at dawn. He smiled and rolled his eyes when she yawned then immediately reclined on her side.

"Don't wake me up until we get to breakfast. I'm not used to keeping Hamilton hours." She placed a rolled-up jacket under her head and closed her eyes.

Clint grinned, shrugged and slid into the passenger seat next to Joe. "Don't forget your seatbelt."

"Done," she grumbled. "Be quiet and let me get some sleep."

Two hours later Joe pulled into the parking lot of the same restaurant where he and Clint had supper on their way to Portland.

Sandy sat up, stretched and ran her fingers through her tumbled hair. "Where are we?"

"Eugene, sleepyhead." Joe switched off the engine grinned at her in the rearview mirror. "You want to eat or sleep some more?"

Clint opened his door and snapped off his seatbelt. "While you two decide, I'm going in and get a booth. There's an empty one by the front window." He threw his long leg out the door and unfolded his lanky frame to exit the car.

"I think he grew a couple of inches this weekend, honey lover."

"Yeah, pretty soon I'll have to stand on my toes to look him in the eye. Come on, I could use come coffee and chow."

When they stepped inside, Clint waved to them from the booth by the window. Sandy waved back then pointed to the restrooms sign. "Be right there. Order me a coffee."

"Your wish, my command."

She rolled her eyes and snickered. "Uh huh." She turned and dodged his swat. The two Hamiltons were in animated conversation when she slid in next to Clint, across from Joe. She bumped Clint's elbow. "What looks good?"

Poor Clint was unable to put a sentence together.

Joe raised an eyebrow and slid her coffee across the table. "We had supper here on the way to your mother's. If that was a clue about the food, you can't go wrong, whatever you order."

Clint cleared his throat. "The eggs Benedict look good."

"I love a man with a sophisticated palate." Sandy sighed and bumped shoulders with him. "I'll have that too."

———

Joe said, "Yeah," when Sandy took the front passenger seat in the car. Clint buckled himself into the backseat and immediately opened his laptop. She reached across the console and squeezed Joe's knee. He covered her hand with his and winked, once again realizing he was totally gone for the woman. They headed out.

Before he had a chance to think about it, he blurted. "Marry me."

Sandy went still. She turned her face to him. "What did you say?"

From behind them, Clint's voice, so much like Joe's, intruded. "He said 'marry me.'"

Joe took a deep breath, pulse throbbing his throat. "Yeah, I'm pretty sure I said that."

She pointed to a convenience store just short of the freeway onramp. "Pull over, please."

Joe jerked the steering wheel and turned his car into the pot-holed driveway, his thoughts a whirlwind. What was she going to say? He cast a quick glance at her just before she yanked the door handle and stepped out of the car. "Sandy, sweetheart, wait! Where're you going?"

She shook her head and threw out her arm as she walked away and disappeared around the back of the building.

Joe parked and yanked on his emergency brake. He gave no thought to stepping out of the vehicle, motor running, keys in the ignition. All that mattered was getting to Sandy, making sure she was all right. Explaining…

He raced around the side of the building. "Sandy!" He stopped at the sound of sobbing coming from behind a giant green dumpster. He rushed toward the pathetic sounds. "Sweetheart, don't cry. I'm sorry. I love you."

She coughed. "You're sorry you love me, or you're sorry you asked me to marry you?" She shoved against his chest when he attempted to embrace her, then dropped her head and turned her back on him. "Go away. Leave me alone."

Joe wrapped his arms around her and pressed his mouth against her ear. "Never. I'll never leave you. I want to spend the rest of my life with you."

She sagged against him, and he kissed her neck, his lips brushing her throbbing artery. Her heart pounded against his chest, in the same thundering rhythm as his own. Emotion clogged his throat and he was unable to say another word.

They stood like that, the myriad smells of the dumpster drifting around them. Not exactly the ideal place or time to propose marriage. He began to chuckle and was rewarded by her calming breaths when she elbowed him in the stomach and dropped her head back on his shoulder.

"Joseph Hamilton." A deep sigh escaped her. "Your timing stinks almost as much as this garbage. What a lame marriage proposal. I don't know whether to kiss you or kick you."

He tightened his arms around her shoulders. "Say yes?"

"Where's the ring?"

He shifted and his neck and cheeks grew hot. "Uh… The ring. I uh…"

"Uh huh, that's what I thought." She twisted out of his arms. "Joe, you—"

"What the…?" Joe looked over his shoulder when he heard an approaching vehicle, the smooth hum of the motor familiar. Clint was behind the wheel of his Beemer creeping slowly forward and getting dangerously close to the chain link fence on the edge of the lot. He slammed the brakes so abruptly the car lurched, and the engine jolted to a stop.

He stuck his head out the window and grinned. "Can you finish this in the car? Teen Wolf comes on at six-thirty, and if we're late to the motel, I'll miss it."

Sandy giggled. "I thought you didn't let anybody drive your precious car."

The proposal wasn't mentioned again on the long drive to their motel, but Joe and Sandy exchanged many glances. He couldn't translate them. "What say we order pizza when we get there and watch Clint's favorite TV show in Sandy's room?"

Early Sunday evening they completed the last leg of their drive. Clint moved to the front seat after Joe walked Sandy to her door and kissed her goodnight. "Did she say yes yet?"

"You're a troublemaker, you know that?"

"It's hereditary."

———

WORLDWIDE SECURITY PARTNERS, MONDAY MORNING

Joe hung his jacket on the back of his chair and took his and Yoda's coffee mugs to the break room. He smiled to have beaten her to work for once. He poured coffee for both of them and carefully carried the steaming mugs back to their tandem desks.

"Good morning, Mr. Hamilton. I'm happy you managed to get in on time." Yvonne smiled her inscrutable Yoda smile.

"How long have you been here? I thought I'd beat you in for a change." He set her mug down, careful not to drip on the keyboard. "Do you live in this place?"

"Indeed no, but at times it would seem I do. You win, Mr. Hamilton. I just walked in the side door. Thanks for the coffee." She dropped her huge purse under the desk and sat in the chair that made her look even more diminutive.

"You're welcome, gorgeous. Is that chair comfortable? It looks too big for you."

"Sadly, they've never made a chair to fit my body, so I make do. Shall we begin?"

She spent the next half hour, between sips of the strong coffee, filling him in on her progress. "The bottom line here is the leak definitely came from inside the ad agency. The leaker is no pro and has left clues. Once I found the first one, it became easier. We're not there yet, but we should have it wrapped up by the end of the day."

Joe made a face and shrugged.

"What?"

"I never wanted to be involved in this investigation in the first place. Both my sister and my girlfriend work there. I'm very uncomfortable about discovering who sold or gave away proprietary information."

She pressed a finger to her upper lip and scowled. "You don't suspect either of them, do you?"

"No! No, I don't, but it's somebody they work with. Maybe a friend." He stood. "I'm going back to Chambers' office and ask if he'll reconsider and take me off it. Let you finish up alone."

Yoda took her coffee cup. "Let's get another cup of coffee and step outside the building to have a little chat first. Chambers is very touchy about having any of his assignment decisions questioned."

Joe and Yvonne grabbed a fresh cup of coffee and walked to the side door leading to the parking lot. The door locked automatically behind them. "Dammit. I don't have my key card, Yvonne. I hope you brought yours. Otherwise we have to walk clear around the block and go back through the lobby."

"Not to worry. I have mine. Anyway, a walk around the block sounds like just the ticket to me." She waved to the security camera, put her small hand in the crook of Joe's elbow and tugged him.

"OK, good point." Joe's shoulders gave a resigned shrug as they approached the front of the building for the second time. He stopped at the lobby doors and looked down at her. "You're right. I'll finish the project with you today and tomorrow we'll move on to a new assignment. I do have a favor to ask of you though."

"Ah, a fly in the ointment. What's the favor, Mr. Hamilton?"

"I need to buy an engagement ring. I don't want to involve my sister or my mother. Would you go with me after work?"

"Congratulations!" She tilted her head back and grinned up at him, Joe got a hint of how cute she probably was when she was a young woman. He had no idea of her age, or her life before they were paired up as a team. He laughed.

"Did I make a joke?"

"I'm laughing because I can imagine what you're going to say when I tell you about my proposal."

"I'm all ears."

He pressed his thumb and forefinger against his nose. "We were standing next to a garbage dumpster in the middle of nowhere. Sandy gave me a *look* and asked where the ring was. Not a well-planned or romantic proposal."

She rolled her eyes and laughed. "But memorable. I wondered when I'd hear a name other than sweetheart." She preened. "I'd be honored to go ring shopping with you. You've been in love with the young lady for some time. I got a hint when you first requested Chambers to reassign you to a different investigation." She stepped back and took her time studying his face. "Yes, Mr. Hamilton. No mistake about it. Now, we've used up more than our allotted coffee break. Let's finish up this job and knock off early. The best place to shop is the Jewelry Exchange in downtown L.A. It so happens I have two brothers who have competing stores there. I'll give them a call." She pointed to the door. "Shall we?"

Joe grinned. "You've made this my lucky day, Yvonne."

"Good. Now let's get back to work, and then later we'll make this Sandy's lucky day."

———

"No. No. No. No." Joe's stomach clenched, and his head felt weightless. Yoda's words about making this Sandy's lucky day came back to haunt him. He barely made it to the men's room before losing his lunch. This couldn't be. It was a mistake. It wasn't possible. He splashed water on his face and took several calming breaths while staring at himself in the mirror. Unable to think clearly, he somehow found his way back to his desk.

He and Yoda had analyzed on the same data, but Joe had the task of matching the results with a name.

Yvonne watched him as he came through the door and slumped in his chair. "Is something amiss, Mr. Hamilton?" When he stared vacantly at her she asked, "Did you corroborate my conclusions, or was I off in the weeds?"

"No." Joe cleared his throat and shook his head. "My conclusions matched yours. I checked and double-checked. There's no discrepancy." He sat heavily and closed his eyes, took a steadying breath to stop the ringing in his ears.

"You're not looking well. Do you need to leave?"

"Yes. I should go. I tossed up my lunch." He stood unsteadily and pulled his jacket off the back of his chair. "I'll...uh...I'll check in later. You can finish up and pass our results to Chambers. Everything points to a single individual. No doubt about it." Shrugging into his jacket, he handed her the confidential employee file showing *Sandra Cassidy* highlighted, and bolted from the office.

How could this happen? Was there a sign on his back reading; the world's biggest fall guy? First Rita, now Sandy?

I sure know how to pick'em.

He slid into the Beemer and stared at the concrete wall in front of the car. It was blank except for the small company logo and his space number. *Now what?* He fired up the powerful engine, backed out of the roomy space then headed for the exit. The security guard flashed a cursory wave as he left the garage.

Joe drove to his neighborhood, right past his apartment building and kept going. He spotted a liquor store and pulled into the lot. He bought a six-pack of Coors out of the cold case and told the clerk to get him a bottle of Jack. Purchases clenched under his arm in a paper sack, he got back into the car and drove for another thirty minutes before he realized where he was headed.

Three hours after he left Worldwide Security Partners, he turned onto the narrow dirt road leading up a small rise through pine trees and parked under the covered space next to stacked firewood. He retrieved the key to the family vacation cabin from a slot in the bottom of a movie rock by the back door and stepped inside the dark, stale interior. He couldn't remember the last time he'd been here. But why was he here now? What was he planning to do? Cry like a baby and get shit-faced?

Joe threw open the front and back door and struggled to raise all the stubborn windows. The electricity was on, but the only heat in the structure was the large central fireplace he and his dad had built when he was Clint's age. The two-sided fireplace opened on one side to the great room, where they all slept on a combination of fold-up cots and sofa beds, and the kitchen on the other. He plugged in the refrigerator then went outside and crawled under the house to turn on the water valves, trashing the knees of his suit slacks. His father always drained the water and turned off the valves to prevent pipes from bursting when the temperatures dropped below freezing in these mountains.

He slapped dirt and pine needles off his knees, stripped off his tie, stuffed it in the pocket of his jacket, and took a ratty sweater from the pegs by the front door. It was cold. He needed to build a fire. He retrieved the liquor store bag from the trunk of the car, placed the beer in the refrigerator and set the bourbon on the drainboard. He stared at the bottle imagining the taste he loved and the mellow feeling it would impart once he'd had a nice big pull. That could wait. First, he had to get a fire going and see if there was any edible food in the place.

The cabin filled with smoke. Joe doused the fire and dragged the partially burned logs into a metal bucket, cursing the entire time. He'd forgotten to open the flue. Now he had to wait until the smoke cleared out and the flue chain cooled down before he could start another fire. As the sun lowered behind the pines, the cold mountain air filled the interior. Self-loathing overcame him as he sat in a small wooden chair in the kitchen and stared at the bottle of bourbon.

His initial shock and bewilderment at Sandy's betrayal was replaced by seething anger. Liz's first instincts about her were right on the nose. Sandy could not be trusted. She used men. Whether to buy her dinner with false expectations or to find some sap to propose marriage. He'd gone against his better judgement to take it slow. Saturated with sexual desire for her, he had fallen into her craven trap hook-line-and-sinker. *What a fool.* The lying little schemer had taken full advantage of him. He blamed himself. He'd been thinking with the little brain instead of the big one.

He had a good brain. He was cool in combat and high-pressure situations, but his instincts about women were on junior high school scale. His thirteen-year-old son was probably more level headed than him. How would he ever face Clint and his parents and sister? *You're a nincompoop, Hamilton!*

He reached for the bottle and struggled to open it. Once the top was off, he put his nose to the neck and took a deep, dizzying whiff. Heaven.

––––––

PEOPLE & PRODUCTIONS ADVERTISING AGENCY, TUESDAY MORNING

Seconds after Sandy got to her desk a secretary from Jordan's office leaned close to her ear. "Jordan wants you in his office right away."

"Good morning." Sandy smiled. "I have a couple of customer calls to make first then I'll be right there."

"Now." The woman's face unreadable, Sandy felt a flutter in her chest.

"Okay, sure."

"Bring you purse." The woman waited.

"Is something wrong?" Sandy slung the purse strap over her shoulder. What in the world? Yesterday she'd brought in a new account, and Jordon had thanked her with the promise of a bonus. She repeated, "Is something wrong?"

The woman turned and left her office without a word. Sandy had no alternative but to follow her down the long hallway to Jordan's conference room. Other employees stared as she walked past. Liz looked up, a puzzled frown on her face. Sandy shrugged with an I-don't-know raise of her eyebrows.

Inside Jordan's office, half a dozen stone-faced people were seated around the oblong table. Sandy recognized everyone except a small, older woman. More confused than ever, she stood waiting for instructions from her boss.

"Sit, Cassidy." He only addressed her by her last name if the subject they were to discuss was serious or she'd committed some infraction.

"Is something wrong, Jor…Mr. People?"

"Sit, please."

Sandy placed her purse on top the shiny walnut surface and dropped into a chair. Her glance at the faces around the table added to her anxiety.

"Cassidy, this is Ms. Yvonne Pennington. She's an investigator with Worldwide Security Partners. They've been conducting an investigation for us to find the source of the proprietary information recently leaked to our competitor."

Sandy's eyes widened. "Oh, well, that's good. Isn't it?" Her head spun. Worldwide Security Partners? That was the company where Joe worked. She wondered if he'd been involved in the investigation. He'd been very closed-mouth about it. This had to be a coincidence. He'd probably been working on something else. His sister worked here. Why would his employer create a conflict of interest like that?

Oh, my God. Liz couldn't be involved. She couldn't be the source of the leak. No. That was not possible. That was insane.

Jordan's sigh was weary. "Yes, it's a good thing, but disappointing to learn one of my most trusted employees betrayed us." He sat back and clasped his hands against his chest. Was he waiting for her to speak? The silence stretched uncomfortably.

"Who is it? Is that why you called me here? To tell me?" Her confusion grew. The sharp burn of acid rose in her throat. *Please don't let it be Liz.* Joe would be devastated if it turned out to be his sister.

"I think you know. We all know who it was now."

"I know? How could I know?"

Jordan rose, leaned forward on his fingertips. "A security guard is waiting in the hallway. He'll observe while you remove any personal items from your office and will escort you from the building. Go directly to personnel and pick up your severance check. Leave the name of your legal representative and we will contact them when we're ready to file charges."

"Charges? I'm not following you." This couldn't be happening. Somebody had really screwed up the investigation. She attempted to stand, but the loud buzzing in her ears warned her she was close to fainting. She sat back in the chair with a thud and lowered her head onto her arms and tried to breathe.

"Cassidy. Please leave the room."

"I...I...it wasn't me, Jordan. I don't understand what's going on. I didn't—"

"We have proof, Cassidy. Ms. Pennington and her associates have confirmed the information leaked to our competitor came from your desktop computer."

He looked at the woman. She nodded.

"Please do as I asked and do it now. I don't wish to further humiliate you."

Drawing to his full height, he stared at Sandy and pointed to the door.

Numbed, dazed, Sandy picked up her purse and backed toward the door. All eyes in the room were now staring at the table except for the woman from Worldwide Security, who had a pained expression in her eyes. Sandy fumbled the door handle attempting to open it. Someone from outside pulled it from her hand. The person waiting to escort her was Thomas, her friend.

Avoiding her eyes, he gestured for her to precede him back down the endless hallway to curious stares from her coworkers.

Chapter Twenty-Six

SANDY SQUEEZED HER EYES SHUT. SHE HOPED LIZ WOULD STOP knocking on her door, give up and leave. She didn't have anything to say. Curling up on her couch and hiding in her apartment was the plan for one of the worst days of her life.

"Sandy! Sandy, open up, it's Liz."

Sandy put her eye to the peephole, relieved the hallway was clear of any neighbors.

"Sandy," Liz said in a lowered voice, "I know you're home. Your car is outside. Please, let me in. Come on, please."

The deadbolt made a quiet snick when she opened the door a crack. "Is Joe with you? I don't want to see him."

"No, I'm alone. I haven't spoken to him. It's unusual because we usually talk a couple times a week."

Sandy slowly opened the door, turned her back and walked away toward the living room. "I'm a mess. You don't want to be with me right now."

Liz pointed to the overnight bag at the end of the sofa. "Are you going away?"

"I don't know." Sandy flopped into a chair and covered her face with a small throw pillow. "I don't know what to do." She moaned. "I wish I was dead."

Liz tugged the pillow away and stifled a gasp. "You look awful. Tell me what happened. The office is in an uproar. Jordan is unbearable."

Sandy shook her head and pulled up her T-shirt to wipe her face.

Liz pressed on. "Sandy?"

"I didn't do it. Jordan can't believe I'd betray him."

"Do what?" Liz dropped her purse on the floor next to the suitcases and sat on the arm of the sofa across from her. "What does he think you did?"

"He didn't tell anyone?" Her red-rimmed eyes grew wide.

"No, he isn't saying a word. I have to know what's going on. Why you were escorted out by Thomas. The poor man looked like he'd rather have confronted and armed assailant than lead you out of the office. The clock moved so slowly today, I was sure the battery was dying. Everyone is on edge, afraid to talk or speculate. At five-thirty the office cleared out like an emergency evacuation drill."

Joe's sister paced then asked, "Do you have anything cold to drink?"

"There's iced tea in the refrigerator. Help yourself."

"Come in the kitchen, I'll pour some for both of us."

"Liz, you've been looking forward to your weekend in San Diego with Joe's buddy, Cole. He's made meticulous plans for you, and you told me you'd talked for an hour on the phone last night. Now this morning's events are spoiling it for you. I don't want that."

Liz flapped her hand dismissively. "Why did you say you didn't want to see Joey? Are the two of you having a row about something? Did you break up?"

Tears brimming, Sandy shook her head. "No. He asked me to marry him Saturday afternoon." A sob racked her chest. "I love him, but now…with what happened this morning…"

"What happened? Tell me, Sandy." She handed her a box of tissues from the table. "Wipe your face. Sit still and talk to me."

Her voice so shaky, Liz had to lean forward to hear, Sandy related the events that occurred in Jordan People's conference room shortly after she arrived at the agency this morning. As the story unfolded, she realized it was her brother's company that had conducted the investigation and presented the results to their boss. The apartment was quiet except for the tick of a clock above the kitchen window facing the inner courtyard.

"Sorry, I have to ask." Liz gritted her teeth. "Did you do it?"

Desolated, Sandy stared, horror must have shown on her face. "How can you ask me that?"

"This is important. Just answer the question please." She studied Sandy's expression.

Sandy pushed back from cheery table she and Liz had painted and decorated. The chair made a loud thump as it tottered and nearly toppled when she jumped to her feet. "No!"

Liz raised her hands. "I believe you."

"You believe me?" A range of emotion erupted. She pressed a hand to her mouth and fell into her seat.

"Yes." Liz reached for her hand. "I don't care what proof they supposedly found, I know you wouldn't do such a thing. It makes no sense. We need to find Joey and ask him who at his firm worked on the investigation. Ask him if it was only the woman who left Jordan's office shortly after you. He'll know. He can help us get to the bottom of it, exonerate you."

"Don't you get it? It was Joe who did the investigation. The woman was his partner on the project. I recognized her the minute Jordan said her name." Sandy shoved hair back from her forehead. "He told me on the way home from Oregon, they were sifting through the facts of an important job the two of them would finish on Monday morning. He was careful not to mention any details or the company under scrutiny. Joe didn't like me asking questions about the confidentiality of his work. I never dreamed it had anything to do with our agency. I even had a horrible fleeting thought, when the woman began to lay it out for everyone, it might be you they were planning to accuse."

"Me!" Liz slapped a hand to her chest. "I'm his sister, why would they have him working on an investigation involving his sister? That's insane."

"That's exactly why I never imagined he'd be working on behalf of P&P. What kind of security company would put an analyst on a project that could implicate the employee's family member?" She straightened. "This is a nightmare."

"That's an understatement." Liz sipped tea and raised her eyes. "I'm calling Joey." She shook her head at Sandy's horrified expression. "I know my brother. We need to talk to him."

"Think, Liz. Why hasn't he called me? Or you? Where is he? He promised to phone me last night, but when he didn't, I figured he got busy or forgot. But now?"

"Good point. I expected him to call after he and Clint returned from Portland. He promised to take pictures of your family and the area where they reside and email them to me after he dropped Clint at home. Neither has happened. I'll call Mom. Maybe she's heard from him." She fished in her pockets for her cell phone. Dialed and put it on speaker.

Clint answered. "Yo, Aunt Sis."

"Is Joey there, smarty pants?"

"Nope. Why?"

"He said he'd call me when he got back in town and tell me about your trip. He promised me pictures too, but I haven't heard from him."

"No sweat. I downloaded the pictures from his phone to my laptop. I'll shoot them over to you. We had a good time, but I got bored with that long drive there and back."

"I'm glad you enjoyed it otherwise. So...Joey hasn't talked to Mom or Dad?"

"Nah, it was late when he dropped me off Sunday night. Maybe they eloped."

Liz detected Clint's derisive snicker. "They wouldn't do that. Anyway, Sandy was at work yesterday and today. She would have said something."

"Ask *her* where Dadbro is. Like they say on the cop shows: She was the last person to see him alive."

"Not funny. Talk to you later. Bye." She clicked the End key and faced Sandy. "I'm worried. Where could he be?"

"I left him a mushy text message before I went to work this morning, but he never answered." She pressed fingers to her temples. "I have to lie down. I feel sick."

"Go ahead. I'll warm soup or scramble eggs for us. Maybe he'll drop by."

Sandy sighed. "I don't know whether that's good or bad."

Liz opened the pantry and rooted around for a bit then selected a can of corn, a potato and an onion. "I'll make vegetarian corn chowder."

"All right. Maybe I'll be able to think clearly after I get some food in my stomach."

———

Sandy forced down the fragrant chowder Joe's sister had set before her. After the drama at the office this morning, and the way the two of them had got off on the wrong foot so many months ago, she wondered why Liz believed in her innocence now. She shook her head and stared at the half-empty bowl.

"What?" Liz asked. "No good?"

"The chowder is fine. I'm still in shock and can't understand why you're defending me. Taking my word that I wasn't the source of the proprietary information leak."

"First of all, there's no rhyme or reason for you to do such a thing. You love your job, you're good at your job, and if you were unhappy at P&P you could have gotten hired by any number of our competitors. Why Jordan accepted the so-called proof of your guilt baffles me. Surely, he could have come to the same conclusions I have. I'm going to try and talk to the woman, the one Joey calls Yoda."

"What good would that do? She wouldn't divulge whether or not Joe was involved in the investigation."

"We have to start somewhere. Maybe Joey was on a different job and we're just assuming he had anything to do with this." She reached for her phone.

"You wouldn't be able to reach her now, it's after eight."

"I'm calling Dad."

"Liz, maybe…"

Liz held up her hand. "Hi, Dad. Have you spoken to Joey?" She glanced at Sandy and shook her head. "No, he promised to call me when he got back but I haven't heard from him. If you hear from him, tell him to call me, please. Love you too." She shrugged and put the phone on the table next to her glass.

———

Joe sat on the porch step of the cabin until the cold evening sent him inside. He had to get a fire going. It would take an hour to warm up the place. The nights were frigid in these mountains. First, he needed to root through the big trunk in the corner and find something to wear. A suit and tie weren't going to cut it. The family had an assortment of clothing that had accumulated over the years. Things they no longer wanted at home. Memories of past good times with his family were stirred as he dug through the trunk. He finally came up with a torn pair of expensive ski pants he hadn't been able to part with and one of Dad's heavy sweatshirts. They'd be the height of fashion with his lace-up dress shoes.

He changed and got to work on the fire, doing his best to block out the horror of their discovery. The discovery that caused him to flee the office so abruptly and to leave town without informing Yoda and Chambers. He'd be lucky if he still had a job at WWSP when...if...he went back. A gob of hot sap popped off a big log and landed in his hair. He batted at it frantically, ran to the sink, and put his head under the cold-water faucet.

"Godammit!" He didn't know what was worse, the burn on his scalp, or the icy blast of water that exploded out ahead of the air gap in the pipes and rattled the rudimentary plumbing like an earthquake.

He yanked off the sweatshirt and used it as a towel. Joe stumbled on one of the kitchen chairs and nearly planted his face on the linoleum before he caught himself. "Suffering Christ!" He grabbed his suit jacket off the coat hook and pulled it on. He was shivering, furious, sick to his stomach, and heartbroken. He spewed a torrent of foul language he hadn't used since the last time he'd been in combat.

The open bottle of Jack taunted him. He reached for it, took a deep whiff, then strode to the door, flung it open and hurled the bottle like a grenade. It shattered against a granite boulder on the perimeter. The rich golden liquid slid down the rock face, no longer a temptation.

You dodged that round, Hamilton. Now what?

———

Hunger drove away Joe's fitful dreams of making love to Sandy. The way her chest and neck turned rosy and migrated to her cheeks just before…He cracked an eyelid and scowled into the gray morning light. Time to put another log on the fire and find something to eat. Last night's beans and stale saltines hadn't provided more than a skimpy snack. His mother usually kept a good-sized supply of dehydrated food and canned goods in the wooden storage box in the woodshed. But first, he'd stoke up the fire and get the morning chill out of the lonely cabin. His stomach clenched when he remembered telling Sandy he'd like to bring her there for a private weekend.

He had the IQ of a forty-watt lightbulb where women were concerned.

Chambers would have sent Yoda to the ad agency with the results of the investigation by now. Sandy would be out on her sweet ass and might be facing criminal charges. Instead of satisfaction, he was stung by regret. This was the woman he'd imagined himself spending the rest of his life with. How had she managed to take him in so thoroughly? Maybe her ex, Phil, hadn't been as bad as she'd painted him. Had she been looking for greener pastures once she'd tired of him? She'd said they had been divorced for years before his accident, but maybe that was another of her lies.

He got the fire going and found a big jar of instant coffee on a shelf above the kitchen stove. The stainless-steel teapot sat on the cold electric burner covered with a sheen of dust. Joe wiped it away and took off the lid. It was clean and dry. No spider had taken up residence. After a quick rinse, he filled the pot and turned on the burner. Coffee would help him think. Plan. Figure out how he'd been so naïve.

He could shower, but he'd forgotten to turn on the electric water heater last night. He'd have to wait another hour or so before there'd be any hot water in the bathroom. He'd been able to endure cold showers when he was on active duty when necessary, but those days were gone forever and he'd been young, fearless.

It was time to brave the chilly morning and check that supply box in the woodshed. The only thing he'd brought with him was beer and whisky. *Another brilliant move, Hamilton.* The whisky was history, but the beer waited for him in the refrigerator. Joe didn't know how long he'd be here. Perhaps he'd better get himself down to the village store and pick up some supplies.

He juggled the boxes and cans in his arms, struggling to get through the door and silence the shrieking whistle of the teapot. He'd left the burner on high and walked away. It's a wonder he hadn't burned the damn place to the ground. He dropped the supplies on the table and turned to the stove. "Dammit to hell!" Joe yanked back scorched fingers from the handle. Had his brain turned to mush? What had he been thinking? He grabbed a mitt and moved the pot to a cold burner then made his second trip to the sink to stanch a painful burn. At this rate, he was headed for the nearest ER. Or psych ward.

He'd found enough basic supplies to make it a few days before he'd have to go shopping. In addition to the selection of canned and dried food, his mother had left a gigantic bag of M&M's in the food locker. He could live on M&M's if it came to that.

Feeling like a new man after a hot shower and a clean T-shirt, he stuffed his underwear and his dad's sweatshirt in a laundry bag in the bathroom. He choked down a large bowl of dry cereal with canned milk then took his coffee mug out to the porch. It was time to quit feeling sorry for himself and think about what he would do.

Not today.

Tomorrow.

He was racked with doubt. Maybe he should have stayed in the Marines. He wasn't sure why he'd made the decision to retire. Sure, he wanted to have a good paying job, independence, spend more time with his family. And start a family of his own, if he was lucky enough. His situation with Clint was unresolved. Maybe a good place to start was with the family he already had.

He walked to the woodshed and found an old fly-fishing rod and a creel with some moth-eaten flies he'd helped Clint tie for one of his Cub Scout projects. Fishing was a good way to think. He grabbed a can of beer, dropped it in his pocket and made his way through the woods to the small creek leading to the lake, passing a few deserted cabins on the way.

He couldn't hide out here for long. He'd have to call work, let his family know he was all right, and sooner or later he'd have to talk to

Sandy. He'd tell her face to face when he broke it off and say what he thought of her lies and dishonesty. It was something he'd do after he cooled off.

Chapter Twenty-Seven

"Liz, go home and finish packing for your trip to San Diego." Sandy was miserable and didn't see any point in dragging Liz deeper into her real-life soap opera.

"I'm not leaving until we make a plan to get your dismissal reversed, Sandy. There must be a way to disprove what implicates you in the data leak." She tapped her cellphone.

"Who are you calling?" She wrung her hands. "Don't call Joe, please. I'm not ready to talk to him."

Liz waved her hand. "Hello, Cole? Look, an emergency at work erupted today. I'm not going to be able to make it this weekend." She shook her head. "No, I want to come. Is it possible to reschedule it for a couple of weeks from now?" Liz slumped back in the chair. "How long will you be gone?"

Sandy got up and went to the sink for a glass of water. This was not good. Liz and Cole had been planning and looking forward to their weekend adventure for weeks. She was aware of their many phone exchanges and suspected a budding romance. The last thing she wanted, well almost the last thing she wanted, was to throw a monkey wrench in their plans.

"Oh." A deep sigh accompanied by a disappointed expression shook Liz. "Wait, Cole. Could you come up here instead? Yes, you can stay at my place. We'll figure something out. Great." She grinned. "I'll see you tomorrow night around ten? Me too. See you then." She tapped the *End* key and put the phone on the top of the table.

Sandy didn't know what to say. She stared at Liz, marveling at her good fortune to have found loyalty. "Liz, I feel bad about you changing your plans for me, you've been looking forward to your weekend with Cole."

Liz waved her off. "Don't worry about it. We'll still have our weekend. There's a method in my madness. Cole and Joey go way back. He'll come in handy when we put our heads together. I'm going to try Joey's cell again. I won't tell him I'm here. Sooner or later the two of you will have to sit down and face this."

Sandy had been thinking along the same lines. Instead of running away, which was her first instinct, she had to face reality. She was in love with Joe. She hadn't heard from him and could only assume it was because he believed the worst about her. "You're right. Even if he doesn't believe me and never wants to see me again, he has to hear my side of it. I love him. He needs to know I'd never betray his trust. I just hope he'll give me a chance." A warm tear tracked down her cheek and she swept it away.

———

THURSDAY, MID-MORNING

Sandy raised her hand to knock on Liz's door. She hesitated when she heard laughter and what sounded like a friendly tussle from inside the apartment. Taking a calming breath, she rapped her knuckles on the heavy oak. The laughter morphed into murmurs. A couple of seconds later Liz opened the door and invited her in. Cole sat on the couch with a mug of coffee in his big hand. An undisturbed stack of folded sheets and blankets rested on the floor near his feet.

A warm blush heated Sandy's cheeks when Liz brushed past her, straightening her T-shirt on the way to the kitchen. "Coffee? We got a late start this morning. I just brewed a fresh pot."

"I'd love some, thanks."

Cole stood and grinned. "Nice to see you again, Sandy." For a large, grown man, he wore the expression of a naughty boy who'd been caught with his hand in the cookie jar.

Well, well, well.

"Nice to see you too, Cole. I apologize for ruining your weekend."

She accepted the coffee from Liz, who'd pulled her hair back into a tight ponytail, hastily wrapped with a rubber band.

Cole indicated the chair across from the sofa. "Couldn't be further from the truth." He patted the spot next to him and Liz sat close. He touched her knee and smiled. Her eyes sparkled and her cheeks flamed.

"Um, what time did you get here last night?"

Cole grinned again. "Not soon enough."

Liz poked him. "Stop it."

"Stop what, sugar?"

Sandy stood and carefully set her brimming cup on the table and retrieved her purse. She had clearly interrupted something. Something completely unexpected in the sense it seemed to be happening very fast. Based on what she'd deduced from their first meeting at the Hamilton family home, she thought they were a good match.

"Where are you going?" Liz raised her eyebrows.

"Three's a crowd. I've messed things up enough." She took a step toward the door.

Liz jumped up. "Oh, no you don't."

Cole stood. "Don't leave, Sandy. We have important business to discuss. Liz and I have the rest of the weekend to...visit."

Liz reached for Sandy's purse and placed it back on the table. "We're all adults here. Cole and I want you to stay."

Sandy hesitated then resumed her seat. "I'm embarrassed."

Cole winked. "Don't be. Liz and I won't pretend. We're in to each other and intend to enjoy it. She's my best bud's little sister. If I don't treat her right, there will be hell to pay." He stepped to the kitchen. "You want a refill, honeybun?"

"No, I'm good." Liz sighed and stared at his retreating back.

An impressive back, Sandy had to acknowledge. "Oh, boy. I'm glad I didn't get here an hour ago," Sandy whispered.

"Me too. He's...wonderful." Liz sighed.

Liz's happiness brought back images of her own complete fulfillment whenever Joe's arms had been around her. She choked back useless tears. Either she and Joe would be OK, or they wouldn't. She'd never regret loving him or making love with him. No matter what happened.

"Joe will be here this evening," Cole said. He sat next to Liz. "I didn't tell him you would be here, and based on what we discuss, the three of us will decide if it's a good idea for you to stay or leave before he comes."

At the mention of his name, Sandy's heart had leaped into her throat. A jolt of fear and uncertainty filled her. "I don't...I..."

"Liz doesn't believe for a minute the accusations leveled against you. That's good enough for me. I have some ideas that might help get to the bottom of the situation. There is an explanation. Liz asked you to bring your personal laptop. Where is it?"

Sandy pressed cold hands to her hot cheeks. "In the car. Shall I go and—"

Cole shook his head. "Give me your keys. I'll get it. You ladies relax and enjoy your coffee. We have plenty of time." He took the keys from her and headed out.

When the door closed, Sandy took calming breaths and lifted the cup to her lips. "You're right, Liz. He's wonderful. Don't let him get away."

"No chance of that happening. I've never felt this way about a man. Cole is open and honest. He fills up the whole room. I wish Joey had introduced us years ago. I have to pinch myself to be sure I'm not dreaming."

"I'm happy for you." Sandy meant it from the bottom of her heart.

Seconds later, Cole returned with her laptop.

"Why did you ask me to bring it? I was told the desktop in my office was where they traced the security leak." Cole and Liz were trying to help her, but she had no idea what they had in mind.

"I'll explain later," Cole answered. "First, I'd like to walk you through Monday. Everything you did that day leading up to your dismissal Tuesday Morning. I can see it doesn't make a lot of sense to you now, but it's important not to leave anything out, even if you think it's unrelated."

Liz sighed. Sandy squeezed her hand. "Give it a chance, all right?"

They spent the next two hours going over her activities at home and the office. Using the meticulously kept calendar on her laptop. All her phone calls, customer visits, paperwork, emails, work she'd done on both her laptop and her office desktop. Everything. Going back for a year. Then they went over it again while Cole took notes.

She covered her face and threw her head back. "*Gah.*"

Liz stretched. "Let's take a break. I don't know about the two of you, but I'm starving. Why don't we go to Jake's and have an early dinner? It's only five minutes from here."

"I'm in." Cole grinned and closed his notepad. "You read my mind, honeybun."

Sandy got to her feet. "Me too. My head is swimming, but I'll follow you in my car and go home from there. I don't want to be here when Joe comes over. I hope you understand." Joe's silence since that horrible day at her office broke her heart. She'd rather have suffered his rage than his stony silence.

———

Liz's apartment, later that evening.

"Joey, what were you doing up at that cabin for the last few days?" His sister was not happy, and she didn't try to soften it for him. He didn't blame her.

"Nice to see you too, sis." He nodded at Cole.

"I'd like an answer," Liz insisted. She crossed her arms to emphasize her determination. Joe had to smile.

"What was I doing? Moping around feeling sorry for myself. Wondering what I should do, if anything. Thinking of quitting my job and rejoining the Marines. Planning on giving Sandy a piece of my mind. Realizing I'm still in love with her and don't want to believe she's a clever and deceitful liar. Satisfied?"

Cole stepped forward and stuck out his hand. "That's a mouthful, bud. Let's sit down and decide where to go from here. Liz and I went over Sandy's story for hours with her this morning. We're both convinced she didn't do what she was accused of."

Joe dropped into a chair. "I can't believe she's guilty either, in spite of the evidence we uncovered."

"What are you going to do about it, Joey?"

"For starters, I am going to quit my job, but not until I've had a chance to go back in and analyze the data again. Yoda can help me look at some new angles. When I figure I don't need access there any longer, I'm going to give notice to Chambers. He's got an ego the size of Everest. I'll tell him what I think of his bonehead decision to involve me in an investigation with serious conflicts of interests. If he continues his stubbornness it could lead to some serious lawsuits in the future.

"It wouldn't be wise for me to quit until I've explored other job opportunities though." He looked around aimlessly. "Liz, you got anything to drink? Something cold."

She rose from the sofa and went to the kitchen without answering him.

Cole leaned forward with his elbows on his knees. "Do you remember my friend Curt from DHS? Didn't he tell you a couple of years ago there was a real good possibility you could get a job with them?"

"Yeah, but I have reservations about working for the Department of Homeland Security or any other federal agency. If I wanted to work for the government again, I'd re-up for the Marines."

Cole chuckled. "You're a little over the hill for that, pal."

"Look who's talking."

"Hell, I'm career. That's different. You already rejoined once. That's enough in my opinion."

Liz handed Joe and Cole glasses of sweet iced tea. "This should hold you for a while. I made it yesterday before Cole got here." The look she gave Cole caught Joe off guard.

Joe took an assessment of his buddy. "Where you staying while you're in town?"

Liz and Cole exchanged glances. "He's staying here, Joey. Do you have a problem with that?"

He pressed his lips together. "Nope. You could do worse."

Cole grunted and covered Liz's hand. "Thanks for the vote of confidence."

Joe would leave it at that. "So—what new information did you come up with today?" Was it possible they'd found something both he and Yoda missed? If so, would it exonerate the woman he loved? It seemed unlikely.

"Nothing new but have a look at this." Cole took out his notes and the three of them spent the next hour analyzing. The information Joe and Yoda came up with seemed airtight, but enough questions were raised by their discussion to give Joe welcome, serious doubts about Sandy's guilt. He knew what he had to do.

"I'm going back to work in the morning. If I still have a job, I'll put my head together with Yoda's and ask her if she'd mind going over the data again. Maybe we'll get pointed in another direction. She's been at this a lot longer than I have, and she has contacts with many computer nerds in the civilian world. Both black hat hackers and white hat folks. They tend to find one another to socialize. Nothing connects people better than a shared interest. I'm hoping we missed something, or at the very least need a new approach."

"Will your coworker get in trouble?" Liz asked.

"I wouldn't ask her to do anything unethical or against company policy. Maybe she'll agree to work off the books on this with me. She knows about my relationship with Sandy." He huffed. "You'll appreciate the irony—I asked her to go ring-shopping with me after work Monday, then we finished the investigation, and everything went to shit."

Liz bristled at his revelation. "Why didn't you ask me to help you select a ring? I'm your sister."

"Exactly. I didn't care to involve anyone in the family before I'd given Sandy the ring and she'd either accepted or rejected my proposal. I doubt she would have appreciated you being in on it." He raised his hands to belay further protests. "Let's talk about the immediate problem, not my private life, OK?" He raked his hands through his thick curly hair. At times like this he missed his Marine baldy.

"Joey, this *is* your private life, and this is us trying to help you salvage it." She leaned toward him and touched his knee. "Call Sandy?"

"No, not yet. She's hurting. We both need time to reflect."

"We're on your side, pal," Cole added.

Joe rose and shoved his hands in his pockets. "I know. Thanks."
He paced around the cozy room for a few seconds then came to a decision. "I'm going home." He picked up Cole's notepad. "I'll take this
with me. Did she leave her laptop here?"

"It's on the kitchen table. I'll get it for you." Liz sprang to her feet
and hurried to retrieve Sandy's computer.

Cole lifted Butterfly off his lap and walked over to Joe. He looked
him directly in the eyes. "I care for your sister. I won't hurt her. You
have my word."

Joe couldn't help his protective, brotherly instincts. Liz was a
grown woman, she didn't need a big brother looking after her. While
he'd been on active duty, they'd been separated many times, for long
periods, over a year more than once. "Yeah, I get it, but like it or not,
I'll have my eye on you."

"I'd expect nothing less." Cole squeezed his shoulder.

———

Joe realized his sister hadn't included the power cord for the laptop
when he was almost home. He hoped he had one that would work,
otherwise he'd have to make a trip back there. He didn't want to do
that because he was still sorting out his feelings after seeing Cole and
Liz together. No doubt about it, it was more than a casual friendship.
He told himself he was responsible for them meeting in the first place,
and he wouldn't have introduced Cole to his sister if he hadn't considered him worthy of her. *Let it go.*

———

His first and most urgent task was doing whatever he could to exonerate Sandy. The more he thought about it the surer he was she
couldn't have been guilty. He was ashamed of himself for doubting
her. Instead of walking out of his office last Monday like a whipped
dog with his tail between his legs, he should have insisted they start all
over and review every step of the investigation. On reflection, it had
seemed almost too easy when they got to narrowing it down.

Sandy wasn't stupid. If she was smart enough to concoct a scheme to steal corporate information from her employer, it stood to reason she was smart enough to cover her tracks better. It seemed as if she was asking to be caught. Everything they'd found pointed directly to her guilt. But then, why would she hand over her laptop if she was guilty? That didn't sit right with Joe.

He spent a couple of hours after he got back to his apartment, going over Cole's notes, reviewed their conversation, and took a lengthy look at the laptop for the possibility someone had managed to get past her password using her wi-fi connection. It could have happened. He hadn't considered it until now.

He'd have to call her or go see her, but a thorough investigation would probably take weeks. He wasn't ready to face her. He had nothing encouraging to offer, Not yet.

Chapter Twenty-Eight

JOE SETTLED AT HIS DESK BY SIX A.M. THE NEXT MORNING, AND had already consumed two cups of coffee when Yoda walked in. He looked up. "Good morning, Yvonne."

"Well, well, look who's here bright and early. Good morning Mr. Hamilton. We need to talk." She shoved her oversized purse under the desk and settled in her too big chair, looking more inscrutable than ever.

Joe shoved his chair a short distance back from his keyboard. "I'm in trouble, right?"

"Not particularly with me, but Chambers is not happy." She cocked her head. "I doubt that surprises you."

"Do I still have a job?" If he didn't, he had no one to blame but himself.

"I wouldn't be privy to that information." She leaned back and interlaced her fingers in front of her chest. "What are your plans?"

"I left a note on his secretary's desk, asking for an appointment to see him as soon as he gets in. I'm going to tell the truth. If he doesn't can me, I'll go from there." Joe leaned forward on his elbows. "I have a favor to ask."

260

"Would this favor have anything to do with a certain Ms. Sandra Cassidy? The young woman I assume you planned to marry?" Yvonne's eyes reflected several emotions from speculation to regret.

He didn't want to picture the events Sandy had experienced on Tuesday morning. Heaviness crushed his chest. Instead of verbalizing a response, Joe pressed his lips together and nodded.

"I suspected as much within minutes after she was called into Mr. People's office. He asked me to confirm the identity of the computer that had been the source of the leak prior to her arrival. There was no question it was the desktop at her workstation. Weren't your conclusions the same?

"Yes."

"But?"

"If there's any other explanation, I intend to track it down. What did she say when her boss confronted her with the proof?" As much as he'd like to go back to square one and begin the cyber investigation again, he was certain the results would be the same.

Yoda narrowed her eyes and tapped her clasped hands against the tip of her nose. "Her shock was evident. She was bowled over, and it had a ring of sincerity. As I studied her reaction, I was less confident of her guilt. The public nature of her abrupt firing struck me as unnecessary. I don't believe her boss handled it in a professional manner. It was very uncomfortable to witness."

Joe pressed his temples and squeezed his eyes closed. Even if it turned out she was guilty, it was a brutal experience for her to endure. "God." Dropping his hands, he sighed.

"Yes." She met his eyes. "Where do we go from here?"

He was deeply heartened when she said "we." He wouldn't ask Yvonne to put her neck on the line, but he'd welcome her help. "I have her laptop. She gave it to my sister. Liz gave it to me. I want to see if it could have been breached, hacked or infected with malware that would allow access to her desktop at the workplace."

"I'm assuming she'd download work from her laptop to her desktop on a regular basis, like so many employees who call on clients, or work from home occasionally." Yvonne nodded. She gazed at the wall behind him.

Joe detected the familiar gleam her eyes took on when she weighed possibilities. "Exactly." The slight warmth of hope in his gut was welcome. "She took extensive notes after every sales call and downloaded them to a flash drive so she could add them to the customer data on the company network. I've seen her do it a few times when we've been together, and she remembered a detail she needed to document."

Joe racked his brain for any other time he'd seen Sandy using her laptop. She emailed her brothers on a regular basis. Other than that, she left it on the small table inside her front door where she kept her purse and keys.

The silence between them was broken when Joe's desk phone buzzed. "Hamilton." He rolled his eyes when Yoda gave him a questioning look. "Be right there." He put on his jacket and cocked his head at his investigating partner.

"Chambers?"

"Yep."

"Good luck, Mr. Hamilton."

Half an hour later, Joe reentered his workspace and hung his jacket on the back of his chair. He dropped into his seat, put his elbows on the desk and lowered his head into his hands. He racked his fingers through his hair and groaned.

"I don't see you clearing out your desk. How did it go?"

Joe did a quick scan of the room before answering. "The nasty little Munchkin ripped me a new one but didn't show me the door. He pitched a fit when I told him he had no business assigning me to an investigation where my sister and a friend were employed. I'd protested the conflict of interest at the beginning of the investigation, so he shouldn't have been surprised when I walked out after we nailed down the source."

Joe hadn't experienced such a personal attack since he'd been called to account by a less-than-competent superior officer in the Marines. The difference then—he had kept his mouth shut and taken the unjustified shellacking. He wouldn't do that any longer. "What a total…"

"I get the gist, Mr. Hamilton." She handed him a folder. "We have a new assignment. We can't revisit the People and Productions matter during office hours. I'm going to write down an address. Be there at seven tomorrow evening. I know some people who might be of help. Bring the young lady's laptop."

He watched her scribble the information on a sticky note and reached across the desk when she pulled it off the pad. "Thanks, beautiful. I owe you one."

"And I will collect. Shall we get to work? This new investigation looks interesting."

"Gimme the skinny." He opened the folder and scanned the contents while she went into the details.

———

That evening he couldn't stop thinking about Sandy. He wanted to touch her, hold her and say he was sorry for what she'd been through as a result of his investigation. He picked up the phone to call her a couple of times then thought better of it. He needed to separate his heart from his head for the clear and objective thinking required to dig further into any information or leads he'd need to follow up on. This could be the most important sleuthing he'd ever done and their future, if there was one, would depend on him having a clear head.

An AA meeting in the next few days was next on his list, after that close brush with disaster in the mountain cabin. He'd give Brian a call and ask if he'd like to have dinner beforehand.

The new job he and Yoda had been assigned was interesting and intense. It involved a government contractor and possible security leaks. They'd provide their findings to the FBI and DHS. Those agencies were notoriously stingy with feedback, so it would mostly be a one-way street. Their reward would be uncovering one or more traitors. Joe knew very well the danger such leaks could be to military in country.

He was about to call it a day when he changed his mind and decided to take a walk. He nearly bumped smack into Seth when he stepped out the front door of his building. "Hey."

"Hey, Joe. Where you been? You owe me a handball game. Or are you too old to play anymore?"

Joe laughed at the incorrigible kid. "Cute. Headed to work?"

"Yep. Got the late shift tonight. Where you going?"

"Taking a walk. I'll go with you and pick up the latest copy of Wired. What kind of trouble have you been in lately?"

"As much as I can between work and school. How's the gorgeous redhead? Or did she dump you by now?" He punched Joe's shoulder lightly then dodged out of his reach.

Seth's remark was a little close to home, but Joe just smiled and smacked him on the back of the head. "You a professional student, or are you planning to graduate any time soon?"

"I got one more semester, then Dad says I have to get a full-time job and start paying rent." He put on a tragic poor-me face followed by a fake sob.

"You can always join the military if that doesn't work out. They'd make a man out of you."

"And give up Mom's cooking? No way. I plan to hang around with them until I find a rich woman who's also gorgeous and a good cook, who'll turn me into her eager boy toy." He grinned. "What?"

Joe had to grin back. He'd have to get the kid over to his parent's house for his dad's barbeque one of these days. His folks would love Seth. Instead of answering the question, he shook his head and shoved his hands in his pockets. If nothing else, Seth had put a smile on his face. He followed him into the drugstore, bought his magazine and then continued around the block.

———

At seven the next evening, Joe stood outside the address Yoda had given him. He wondered if she'd written it down wrong. A young guy with purple hair and a ring in his nose, gave him the once over.

"You lost?"

"Ah, I'm not sure. I'm supposed to meet a coworker here. She's going to introduce me to some friends."

"What's her name?"

"Yvonne Pennington."

"You're in the right place. Come on, we'll find her." He hauled open the scarred metal door to a cavernous and noisy room. He pointed to a far corner. "She usually sits over there with Calvin and

Hobbs. Follow me." The young man weaved his way through the crowd, glancing over his shoulder to make sure Joe was behind him.

People chatted, gestured, and laughed as they crowded around laptops on every table in the room. The perimeter was lined with booths. Waiters dressed as Star Wars characters wended their way through the mob carrying drink-laden trays. Every walk of life seemed to be represented, teenage punks like the one he was following to grandmotherly women to Wall Street types in impeccably tailored suits and thousand-dollar Barker Blacks, all mingling together, no pattern to the assortment. *So much for the birds-of-a-feather theory.*

Yvonne sat on the outside seat of a booth next to a guy with a shaved head and tattoos covering his arms from his wrists to his shoulders. They were both engaged in conversation with a wisp of a blonde who looked like she'd just come from her first communion. Joe wondered what Yvonne was getting him involved in. His tension eased slightly when he noticed all the drinks on the table were of the soft variety.

His purple-haired guide shouted, "Yo! Ma! Here's the guy you were waiting for."

The little blonde brightened when they approached. "Hey, Penn."

"Hey, Hobbs." He nodded to the bald man. "Hey, Cal." Then slid in the booth next to the girl.

The bald guy tipped his root beer can, smiled and slid over so Yvonne could make room for Joe. She gestured for him to sit. "These are my friends Calvin and Hobbs, and you've met my son, Penn." She held her hand toward Joe. "This is my colleague, Ham."

Joe got the message, everyone at the table used a pseudonym.

Calvin extended his hand, "Nice to meet you, Ham. Yoda said she was expecting you." He waved to catch the attention of one of the wait staff. "What's your poison?"

Joe shook his hand and sat next to Yvonne. "Yoda?"

"You're sworn to secrecy, *Ham.*"

He grinned and leaned low to kiss her cheek. "I'll have what she's having."

"Cherry cola it is." The waiter reached their table. "Another round here and a cherry cola for my new friend."

"Coming right up, Cal." He picked up some damp napkins and left a dry stack.

Cal tipped his head at Joe. "Next round's on you, pal."

"You got it."

Hobbs extended her small hand. "Can I have a look at the laptop?"

Joe handed it over. She opened it and put her head close to Penn's. It was the beginning of one of the most interesting and enjoyable evenings *Ham* had ever spent.

Over the next two hours, Joe learned Penn was a senior at Cal Tech, Calvin was in charge of IT systems at a well-known Catholic Women's college in L.A. and Hobbs worked in the computer animations department at Disney Studios.

"I hope you're not in a hurry," Calvin said. "This could take as long as two months. It looks like some amateur's been spoofing but did a pretty good job covering his tracks."

———

Sandy, determined not to fall into victim mentality, had spent the day doing a deep-cleaning of her apartment. She'd removed everything from the kitchen cupboards, washed and dried the shelves and installed a colorful lining before replacing her dishes and supplies. She was good and tired but determined to tackle her bedroom closet before she stopped working.

She separated the clothing into three piles on her bed; summer, winter and thrift shop. Her mom told her many years ago, "If you haven't worn it in over a year, you don't need it taking up space in your closet." Some of the clothing she found would be moved closer to the center of the deep u-shaped rack. These were garments she loved but had forgotten about. Sandy decided she wouldn't buy a new piece of clothing unless she was willing to remove one she already owned.

Always in the back of her mind were thoughts of Joe. They moved forward and receded like a tide. She was deeply hurt by the fact he hadn't been in touch. Not even an email. The one thing that kept her bruised heart beating was Liz's report that he'd expressed doubts about her guilt and had set out to get to the bottom of it. He'd told Liz he was in love with her even though his first reaction to the result of the investigation was betrayal.

It hurt that Joe would think she'd lied to him. But what was he to think when they traced the leak of privileged information directly to the computer on her desk? He'd told Cole and Liz no trace was found on any other device in the company. The information had been stolen from Jordan's password protected files, and then released to a competitor from her desktop. The entire episode was beyond her understanding.

She reached the end of the hanging bar for the last garments. Among them was a shirt of Joe's. Tears threatened when she saw wrinkles at the elbows showing her the shirt had been worn and rehung. The hanger slipped from her hand and his shirt puddled at her feet. She went down on her knees, grasped the shirt, pressed it to her face and breathed in his scent. The floodgates opened. She curled into a ball on the floor of the closet clutching it to her chest and face. The bottomless sense of loss was more than she could bear.

Chapter Twenty-Nine

SANDY WAS SKEPTICAL BUT ADMITTED IT COULD BE TRUE. SHE checked her watch. Was it too late to call Liz? She crossed her fingers and tapped Liz's icon on her cellphone.

"Sandy?" Liz's voice was breathless.

"Am I calling too late?" She heard a muffled male voice in the background.

"No, you just caught me. I'm taking Cole to Union station for his train back to Camp Pendleton tonight. We've cut it close. Can I call you back?"

"Yes. Go. I'll wait." Sandy put her phone on the kitchen table and rose to put the teakettle on the stove. She hadn't been sleeping and hoped a cup of chamomile tea would help. The thought she'd just had, filled her with hope and doubt. Was it possible? Could he have had anything to do with it? The kettle shrieked. She clutched her chest and realized she'd neglected to add more water to the almost empty pot. "For heaven's sake!"

While holding the pot under the faucet, something nagged at her brain. *What?*

Then she made a dash for her phone. Scrolling through the list she tapped the name and Call. "Yes, hello. I'm looking for Zack Graham. Is he there?"

"Zack is off tonight. He'll be back in at six tomorrow morning. Would you like to leave a message?"

Disappointment burned in her throat. "No, I'll call back in the morning."

"Miss? He's got a full schedule tomorrow. It would be better if you left your name and number so he can return your call when he has a break. Unless you'd like to speak to someone else?"

"Oh. In that case please tell him Sandra Cassidy called regarding Phil Rice, a former client of his. I'd appreciate a couple of minutes of his time."

"No problem. Is this the number where you can be reached?"

"Yes. I'm available any time he can take a moment. Thank you." Yes, she was available twenty-four hours a day now that she had no job. She had more time on her hands than she knew what to do with.

Her phone still in her hand, sounded off and startled her. "Hello, Liz?"

"No, honey, it's Cole. Liz is driving. What can we do for you?" The man had a wonderful, deep voice.

"Hi, Cole. I probably should wait until I have more information, but I remember something that might be important." She took a breath. "Gosh, I've reached the anger stage and I'm ready to punch anyone who looks at me sideways."

Cole laughed. She heard him tell Liz, "She's fine. Madder than a wet hen." Liz laughed and said, "Good for her!"

"What did you come up with, Sandy?" Cole was still chuckling. "Sorry, honey, but mad is good."

"I'll take your word for it." She lifted the heavy pot and set it back on the still-flaming burner. "Phil, my ex-husband, attended several weeks of digital marketing classes at Fremont Community College a couple of years ago with a friend he met at physical therapy. I wonder if there's any chance this means anything."

"Who knows? It's something. Is it possible for you to reach the friend?"

"I don't remember his name, but I left a message with Phil's old therapist. He's out until tomorrow, but I'm pretty sure he'll call me back."

"You might be onto something, and trust me, if he's a guy, he'll call you."

"Thanks for the vote of confidence, Cole. I may be grasping at straws, but I don't want to leave a single stone unturned. Tell Liz I'll contact her tomorrow if I get any useful information. Wait a minute. I thought you were being deployed to the Middle East for a few months. What happened?"

"I'm shipping out tomorrow. Managed to catch some time with Liz beforehand. You take care. I'll check in when I get back."

"You take care, Cole. I mean it."

"Always do. Gotta go. We're pulling into Union Station. I'll pass on the message to my honey."

Her troubles were insignificant compared to Cole heading into a hot war zone. He was going as an adviser to Afghan army forces in the field. Based on news from the front, some of the American Marines were in as much jeopardy from the *friendly* forces as they were from ISIS. She'd say a prayer for his safety. She wondered if Joe knew Cole was on his way. Probably. He was in touch with his sister and family even though he'd made no attempt to contact her. She sighed and went to the sink and reached for her tin of tea bags. Staring at the container, Sandy decided she didn't want tea.

She went to bed, and stared at the ceiling, running every name she could think of, starting with R, trying to hit on the one for Phil's friend from rehab. "Reston. Rogers. Reynolds. Reese, was that it? No. Rivers. Rivera. Rizzo. Rizzo? No. "Dang it!" She slammed her arms on the top of her quilt.

———

Her phone rang. It felt like minutes after she'd finally fallen asleep. "Hello?"

"Ms. Cassidy? I hope I'm not calling too early."

She glanced at her clock. Five-forty-five. "No, Zack? Thanks for returning my call."

"Is there something I can do for you?"

She cleared her throat and ran a hand through her tangled hair as she sat up straight. "I hope so. Do you remember the name of Phil's friend who took him to computer classes at Fremont?"

"Curt Rizzoli. They were in rehab at the same time. They weren't what I'd call friends, but Curt took an interest in him. Once Phil started the classes I believe they went their separate ways. Curt works for the Department of Homeland Security and had doubts about Phil's character."

"Yes! Rizzoli. I've been driving myself nuts trying to remember his name."

"Do you mind me asking why?"

"It's just a hunch I had about some strange data that shouldn't have been on my laptop. I doubt Curt will have any information for me, but I'll never know unless I contact him."

"I have his phone number, but it wouldn't be appropriate for me to give it out. If it's OK, I'll contact him and give him your number."

Wide awake now, Sandy threw her legs over the side of the bed and opened the blinds in her bedroom. "That would be great, Zack. Thank you so much."

"Happy to be of help, Ms. Cassidy."

The second she disconnected she received a text from Liz. *If ok I'll come over aft work. 2 bz 2 talk now. L.*

Sandy sent an immediate response: *Yes, dinner here. S.*

———

She'd just finished setting the table and opening a bottle of mellow red wine, when her doorbell rang. She peeped to make sure it was Liz then opened the door. "Come in. How was your visit with Cole?"

"I don't know how I'm going to make it six months until he comes back. At least we can stay in touch regularly by email and cell phone. I'm head-over-heels for the big lug. I'd like to smack Joey for taking so long to introduce us." She hugged Sandy.

"I'd like to smack him for different reasons."

She laughed and held up her hands as if to fend off an attack. "I'll be careful what I say around you. The question is: How are you doing?"

"Good." Sandy grinned. "Come to the kitchen and I'll pour some wine. Dinner will be about half an hour." Her affection for Liz brought a warm calmness to her. She'd get through this regardless of the outcome.

"Smells fantastic! What is it?" Liz took a chair and reached for the glasses to push them close to Sandy.

"Crockpot chicken piccata. I hope it's good. I've never made it before." She poured generous portions of wine and sat across from Joe's sister and shrugged.

Liz held her glass aloft. "I'm sure it's delicious. Here's lookin' at you, kid." She took a healthy swallow and sighed. "Just what I needed. What a day!"

"I'm afraid to ask."

"Jordan is still on a rampage. He's assigned your accounts to others in the sales department and the results have been spotty. One of the salesmen quit after getting chewed out. He yelled at Jordan so loud we could hear it all over the office. I have a feeling if you walked through the door, he'd rehire you on the spot in spite of what happened."

Sandy pressed her lips together she shook her head. "Not interested."

"I don't blame you, even a tiny bit." She took another sip. "Good wine." Liz picked up the bottle and studied the label. "I'm going to get some of this. By the time my man gets home I'll be attending AA meetings with my brother." She started to smile then stopped. "Sorry."

"Don't worry about it. I have calluses on my ego by now."

They chatted for a few minutes about Clint's latest adventures learning how to drive. Liz told her their father started teaching him, then their mother took over before there was a bloodletting. Imagining Clint behind the wheel reminded her of him driving Joe's car to the back of the convenience store and interrupting Joe's clumsy proposal. "Dinner is ready. I'll serve it up. While we're eating, I'll explain the hunch I mentioned to Cole."

———

"Are you kidding me? I know Curt Rizzoli." Liz put down her fork and stared wide-eyed at Sandy.

"You know him?"

Liz waved her hand. "No, I don't *actually know him*, but I do know he works for DHS and wanted Joey to apply for a job there. I remember his name because it's the same as one of the characters on the TV show. The one with uh, uh," She raised a finger. "Angie Harmon." Liz put both hands on the table and leaning forward declared, "They say there's no such thing as a coincidence, but wow, this sure seems like one to me."

"I wonder if he'd be of any help, you know, if he thought Phil could be involved?" Sandy felt a ray of hope warming her chest. If only this information would lead to something.

"I have no idea, but I'm definitely going to call Joey. How did you learn about Rizzoli?"

"I remembered Phil went to computer classes a couple of years ago. Another man in rehab told him it might lead to a good job when he became proficient." Could it be possible that Phil had so much anger toward her that he'd try to destroy her character and her career? "I learned his name when I called the therapist at the PT facility to ask if he knew who it was."

"Sandy, this is great." Liz held up her hand. "Don't get your hopes up, but it seems to me there could be something here. At least it's a lead we didn't have before."

"Thank you for saying '*we.*' I'm so glad you're on my side, Liz." Tears pooled in her eyes and she ducked her head too late to hide them. "Lord! I'm such a sob sister." She dabbed her face with a crumpled paper napkin.

Liz reached across the table and placed her hand on top of Sandy's. "I think you're very brave and you've been wronged by everybody, including Joey."

"No, Liz, don't blame him. He was doing his job. I'm beginning to understand his reaction even though I was horribly hurt by it. He thought I'd betrayed him, lied to him like the other woman he asked to marry him, I'd like to pop him in the nose, but I forgive him."

"I wish the two of you would talk."

"Not yet. He's doing what he can for now. I accept that. I doubt we'll ever be able to get back together after this, though. Hurt and misunderstandings are deep on both sides."

"Don't say that! Joey loves you. He told me. He told Cole and Clint and our parents. He's got a lot to sort out, so don't give up on him."

Sandy sighed deeply. "It might be best for me if I leave the area, sub-let this place and move up to Oregon to be with my mother. She needs me now. Damon and Greg have been great, and I've spent enough time feeling sorry for myself."

"I feel so bad for both you and Joey. This never should have happened. I hope when they get to the root of this you'll consider taking legal action against whoever is responsible. It's just not fair." Liz's eyes shone with sympathetic tears.

"Trust me, if I'm still as angry when the truth comes out, I'll make sure whoever did this to me pays dearly. I'm fed up with being Ms. Nice Guy."

A smile trembled on Liz's face. "There's the Sandy I know."

———

Sandy lay awake for a long time. Her heart was broken, her spirit had taken a nasty thumping. She loved Joe, but the damage this ordeal had done to their relationship probably finished them. She hadn't shared any details with her family and decided to send a text to Damon.

Taking vacation from work. Leaving day after tomorrow. Plan to stay with Mom for a couple of weeks. Will advise arrival details later. S.

Chapter Thirty

JOE'S PHONE VIBRATED AS HE WAS PARKING HIS CAR IN THE company lot. "Sis? Everything OK?"

"Joey, remember the guy who wanted you to apply for a job at DHS?"

"Rizzoli? Yeah."

"You're not going to believe this." She proceeded to tell him everything she and Sandy had talked about the night before. Why in hell hadn't he thought there might be a connection between this mess and Sandy's rotten ex before? Who else would have more of a motive to get her in deep trouble? *What a vindictive bastard.*

"It makes sense to me now, sis. And here's a zinger—I've seen Rizzoli at the hacker's hangout a couple of times. He goes by C-Riz, and he moves around in the club between the black hats and the white hats. He has friends on both sides of the law. I'm definitely going to corner him and have a conversation." He wanted to kick himself for never going down the Phil Rice path before now.

"Will it be soon? Tonight?"

"I have an AA meeting tonight. Can't afford to miss it. But this week for sure."

275

"OK."

He let the silence hang between them.

"Joey?"

"What?"

"I wish you and Sandy would have a conversation."

"Can't happen yet. We'll have time to sort it out soon, I hope. Just so you know, Clint called and asked if I had any objection to him calling her. I didn't know what to say. I hope you don't mind, but I asked him to talk to you about it first."

"When did you become such a wimp?" Her disgust came through loud and clear.

"I've always been a wimp. Think about it."

She didn't answer for a few seconds, then said, "Yeah, you always were too soft-hearted. Fifteen years in the Marines should have toughened you up."

"Put a weapon in my hand and send me outside the wire at a FOB, and I'm your man. But I'm hopeless when it comes to women. Isn't that why you tried to protect me from Sandy?" He chuckled at his little sister's attempt to run interference for him.

"I guess the bone I had planned to pick with you can wait."

"Don't keep me in suspense." She always had something to say about his private life.

"Why did you wait so many years to introduce me to Cole? I'm not getting any younger, you know. He's on deployment again. I'm beside myself."

Not what he'd been expecting. "I never felt the need to try to run your love life the way you try to run mine." He didn't mask his annoyance.

Her deep sigh came through the phone. "Oh, Joey, I don't want to fight with you."

"Why'd you pick one then?"

"Because I'm missing him."

"Got it bad, huh?"

"You don't know the half of it."

"Ain't love grand." It wasn't a question. "Look, sis. I've got to get to my office. We're deep into a new privileged information breach investigation for a fellow private security firm. It'll be a long day, and like I said, I'm going to AA tonight."

"What should I tell Clint?"

"You figure it out. I'm a wimp, remember?" He disconnected, locked his car and hurried to join Yoda.

––––––

"That was too close, Joe. Why didn't you call me?" Brian gave Joe a stern look across the small booth in the coffee shop. It was late. The AA meeting had dragged on until the church custodian asked them to wrap it up so they could clean and rearrange the meeting room.

"It crossed my mind, but I was up in the mountains. It was dark and cold and I was trying to get the temperature in the cabin above freezing." He'd related the fallout from his investigation implicating Sandy as well as what he looked back on now as a comedy of errors at the family cabin.

Brian shook his head and sighed. "At least you got through it on your own. That's good." He lowered his head and traced the rim of his glass. "I really liked your young woman. I hope you'll be able to repair the damage and get back together."

"It'll be hard to overcome the hurt and anger on both sides." The thought of losing Sandy was something he didn't want to face. "I blew it. I should have known she wouldn't be involved in a scheme to defraud her employer. But I let my initial shock overshadow clear thinking."

"Alcoholics have a tendency to make bad choices during a crisis." Brian shook his head sadly. "We've all been there. Don't beat yourself up over it. Be grateful you had the clarity of mind to think twice about falling off the wagon. You've made good progress. I'm confident you'll continue to do well." He raised his glass in salute.

Joe wished he had as much confidence in himself as Brian had expressed. He'd get back on a regular schedule of AA meetings, help himself by helping others in the group. "I'm giving myself a Brownie point for overcoming that near fall." He smiled at his sponsor and nodded.

———

At the end of the next workday he asked Yvonne if she was going to the hacker's hangout that evening.

"Not tonight, Mr. Hamilton. I'm having dinner with my mother."

His eyebrows went up in surprise. *Her mother?* "Did I hear you right? Your mother?"

"Yes, Mr. Hamilton. We all have mothers and I'm fortunate to still have mine. She's eighty-eight and I can't beat her at Scrabble or chess." She laughed at his reaction. "Penn will be there with the usual crowd."

Clearly, Yoda was younger than he'd assumed. When he thought about it now it made sense. Penn, her son, couldn't be more than early twenties. "I never asked before, but where does Penn work?"

"He's living off his mom for now while attending Cal Tech. I fully expect him to become a successful and prosperous scientist so he can take care of said mother in her old age. At some point, he'll probably have to give up the purple hair and a few piercings, but for now I consider it a harmless form of self-expression. He's disappointed his appearance doesn't, as the younger generation like to say, 'Freak me out.'" Her small smile was precious. Penn was lucky to have her as his Mom.

———

On his way to the club, Joe puzzled over Clint's request to call Sandy. All he needed was another member of his family mucking around in his private business, but Joe decided he'd call his son after the meeting tonight. Except for Clint's brief call to ask Joe's permission to contact Sandy, they hadn't talked since the investigation blew up in his face. What a coward he was to pass the problem on to Liz. Clint's acceptance of Joe as his biological father was tenuous at best. He'd take responsibility for calling the teenager, and work to reassure him they were good.

———

Sandy's phone rang and she didn't recognize the number. She let it go to voicemail then pushed the Talk button immediately when she recognized Clint's voice. "Hey, uh, Sandy, I wanted to—"

"Clint? Hi honey. Is everyone all right?" She pictured the blush no doubt coloring his young cheeks. Then she had a horrible thought something might have happened to Joe.

"Yeah. We're good. I wondered if you'd like to get a hamburger and go to a movie or something with me?"

She felt a big smile bloom on her face. "Are you asking me on a date?" She realized her blunder when she was greeted by silence. "Clint? I'm sorry. I don't know why I said that. I didn't mean to embarrass you."

"Uh, it's cool. I guess I kinda was…asking you on a date. But not a love-date or any junk like that. A friend-date."

She breathed a sigh of relief. "I'd love to go on a friend-date with you, but it would have to be tonight. I'm driving up to Oregon to my mother's tomorrow."

"Are you moving away?" He was so alarmed his voice squeaked.

"No, no, I'm going to spend some time visiting family." She wasn't entirely truthful because she wasn't sure what she would do. She'd been considering making a permanent move.

"But you're thinking about it, right?" Joe's man-child son was very perceptive. "Dadbro really blew it. Didn't he?"

"It's not that simple, Clint."

"Yeah, I get it." A couple of beats, then he said, "So what about it? Superbad is playing at the three-dollar movie house in Spring Grove. I never saw it when it first came out. Santos and his dad saw it though. Santos said it was super tope and full of emo."

She had no idea how to interpret his teen-speak, and she felt old, old, old. She laughed. "You'll have to translate. What did his dad think?"

"He said it was funny. Made him glad he and Mr. Dempsey weren't teenagers any more. So, if you want to, I could go tonight, but, uh, you'll have to meet me and Santos at the mall. He has a driver's license, but I don't."

"It would be the three of us?"

"Yeah, he wants to see it again. Snooky's burgers is right next to the movie theater. We could meet there. We'll pay for our own burgers. We're not barnacles."

That one she understood. "OK, I'd love to have a burger with you and Santos and go to the movie. What time shall we meet?"

———

Hamilton Home, Spring Grove, Sunday evening

"You what?" Joe stared at Clint. "You and Sandy went on a date? What the hell are you talking about?"

"Joseph," his dad said. "Take it down a notch."

Clint, looking more like Joe every day, even in his mannerisms, raked his hands through his hair and jammed them in his pockets. "Me and Santos and Sandy got a burger and went to the movies. It was no big freakin' deal."

"When were you planning to let me in on this?" Joe glared. His life had gone to shit. He hated his job. Sandy left town for who the hell knew how long. Now he finds out his kid brother—correction, his son, went out with his girlfriend. Former girlfriend.

"Today." Clint leaned close to his face. "I'm telling you now. Anyway, I didn't need your permission."

Joe rose from the lawn chair, hands clenched at his sides. He took a step toward Clint. The boy stood his ground and glared back, mirroring Joe's posture.

"Put a lid on it!" Don inserted himself between them.

Liz and Bernice walked out onto the patio. "What's going on out here?"

Clint raised his arm and pointed in Joe's face. "You suck, asshole!"

Don gave Clint the Colonel-Dad stare. "I said, put a lid on it." He turned to Joe. "You, too. Is that clear?"

Clint and Joe mumbled surly replies.

Don's voice went quieter. "Is that clear?" Nobody dared challenge their father when his voice went quieter.

Joe sighed and stiffened his spine. "Yes, sir. That's clear."

"Yeah," Clint grumbled.

"Yeah what?" Don cocked his head at the boy who was now as tall as himself.

"Yeah. Crystal. Can I leave now? Sir?"

"Leave."

Don, Bernice, Liz and Joe watched Clint's receding back as he slammed out the side gate.

"Explain yourself, Joseph." Don pointed to the chair Joe had vacated and took the empty one next to him.

"Dad, he…" Liz stepped closer.

"Keep out of this, Lizzie. You and your mother go back inside. This conversation is between your brother and me." When they didn't move, Don waited in silence. Finally, Liz and her mother turned and went back in the kitchen.

Joe put his elbows on his knees and rested his head on his fists. "I wish I *could* explain myself, Dad." He rolled his head from side to side. "I'm trying to learn what really happened. Liz doesn't believe Sandy did what our investigation uncovered, and I don't either. I thought I was so goddamn smart on computers. I'm a novice compared to those kids at the geek hangout. I'm trained to do one thing, investigate. Follow a trail. Beyond that, pah!" He waved his arms and slumped back in the chair. "Shit. She lost her job because of me."

Joe chose not to reveal to his dad that he'd also been having mortar attack dreams again after more than three years. He'd hoped he was done with combat nightmares.

"And the outburst with your son just now?" Don chuckled and held up a hand when Joe scowled. "Take it easy."

Joe bolted upright and scanned the yard. "Where's Major? I haven't seen him all day." He got a sinking feeling in his gut. Not his dog too. Were the fates lined up against him? "Where's my dog?"

"*Your mother's dog* spent the last two nights at the groomer's. He blunders around just like you do. Went after a skunk. It'll take days to get the stink off him. He's had more baths in the last few days than in his life up to now."

"Jesus, what next?" He looked at his dad and they both broke out laughing.

Going after a skunk would have been preferable to what had happened. He could eventually wash off the skunk smell. It would take more than a few baths for him and Sandy to wash off the stink of betrayal. If it was her ex, Phil Rice, who'd brought down this shit storm, it would take a squad of recon Marines to keep Joe from beating the living crap out of him.

He stood. "I gotta go find my kid. He didn't deserve to have me dump on him."

Don got up. "I'll go with you."

"This is between him and me, Dad."

"No, it's between the three of us. There's too much simmering below the surface. It needs to be aired."

Joe shrugged. He could use the backup. Or, maybe Dad going to be there to give Clint backup? "Where do you suppose he went?"

"He's either at the park or over at McPherson's. He knows to stay close to the reservation." Don preceded Joe to the gate and looked over his shoulder to see if he was following. Just as Don reached for the latch, the gate swung in and Clint stood on the other side of it. Don twirled his finger. "About face. We're taking a walk to the park."

"Why?" Clint asked with a sneer.

"It's time to settle a few things." Don gripped Clint's shoulders and turned him around. "Move it. You too, Joseph. This could take a while." He waved them through the gate.

Chapter Thirty-One

CALVIN AND HOBBS HAILED JOE ENTHUSIASTICALLY FROM ACROSS the room in the hacker's hangout. He worked his way to their table. "Hey. What have you got?"

"Ham, my friend, this laptop has a very interesting piece of malware on it. This stuff is so clutch we almost missed it. Have a look." He turned Sandy's laptop so Joe could see the screen. "This noob had just enough knowledge to be dangerous. Took our best sniffer app to find it."

Joe scowled at the screen. "Sorry, I don't see what I'm supposed to be looking at." More than ever he realized his limitations. He still had plenty to learn, especially if he was going to be of value to a different employer after he told Chambers where he could put it. "Enlighten me."

"This malware allowed someone to take an image of her computer and programs and work with them on a virtual computer. Once that was accomplished, he was home free to do whatever dirty deed he wanted." Calvin tapped a few keys and displayed some icons Joe didn't recognize. "All this bozo needed was a little more smarts and we'd never have found this."

"Does this mean what I think it does?"

"Yes. Nothing was a secret on this system once he established the virtual clone. Now that her company, with your help, de-linked her permanently from their system there has been no new activity from the amateur hacker."

Joe winced at *with your help*. "So, is it possible to trace the source?"

"We're going to show *you* how to do it." She handed Joe several pages of hand-written instructions. "Read it. If there's anything you don't get, we'll go over it with you."

Joe got to his feet. "I'm going to take this out to my car and study it. There's too much going on in here. I'll make notes as I read and bring them back inside the club."

"We have to be someplace else in half an hour. We've already shown this to Penn. He should be here around eight. That'll give you time to digest it."

Joe reached across the table and shook hands with them. "I don't know how to thank you." He rolled up the pages and stuck them in his jacket pocket. "Drinks are on me next time."

Hobbs chuckled and saluted with his soft drink can. "That'll do it." He held up Sandy's laptop. "Better take this with you." `

Joe turned to leave and bumped into C-Riz. "Whoa, sorry, man." Rizzoli was dressed in a business suit. He'd been in the process of pulling off his tie when Joe nearly knocked him over. "Just the person I was hoping to see tonight." He stuck out his hand. "Nice to meet you, name is Ham."

Curt grinned. "Change your mind about submitting your job app at DHS, *Ham?*"

Joe grinned back. "I might. But I need your help on a personal issue. Not entirely personal, business and personal." His tongue was in a knot.

"Over there." Curt pointed to a couple of empty seats at the far end of the bar. "It's too noisy in the middle of the room." He led the way, took a stool and ordered a bottle of Mexican beer. "What'll you have?"

"Make it club soda with lime." He nodded to the bartender. "On me."

"How can I help?" He picked up the cold beer and took a healthy swallow. "This about Chambers? He's a pain in the ass."

"Agreed, but do you remember a guy named Phil Rice? You were in physical therapy at the same time as him a couple of years back." Joe knew from the eye-roll and sour expression on Rizzoli's face that he remembered.

Rizzoli lowered his chin warily. "I did." He shrugged. "How do you have the misfortune to know him?"

Joe pressed the cold glass to his forehead. "He's my girlfriend's ex-husband. Very ex."

"Whoa." Curt opened his eyes wide. "That knockout redhead is your girlfriend? You have my congratulations, pal." He grinned and made a low whistle.

"That's the personal part." Joe went on to describe what had happened with his investigation of Sandy's workplace and their find-ings. How he was working off the books with the help of Calvin and Hobbs and Penn to dig deeper. "They found evidence of malware."

"Those kids are phenomenal. Don't torture yourself, there's no way you could have found that during your investigation. Without her laptop, it was impossible."

"Even then I would have missed it. Yoda and I never considered it could have happened any other way. Everything pointed directly to her desktop computer at the office. Do you think it's possible Phil Rice could be behind this? He's a bloodsucking bastard who took advantage of her generosity. When she finally threw him out after discovering he'd been lying about going to therapy after he'd been released for months, he paid her back by knocking her around and trashing her house and all her belongings."

"That guy belongs in jail, but I don't know how you'd prove he engineered the data leak. It's all circumstantial." He took a swallow of his beer and shook his head. "I remember how she used to chauffer him to his sessions when Zack was working with both of us. I lost track of him when I got a clean bill of health."

"Sandy told me you encouraged him to take some IT classes so he could get a good paying job when he regained his mobility. It dawned on her Phil could be behind the f-up and she informed my sister. Liz contacted me right away. Penn mentioned you came here now and then. I'm glad I bumped into you." Joe raised his glass. "So, where do I go from here?"

C-Riz opened the laptop and took the instructions Calvin and

Hobbs had given Joe. He went over them then handed them back to Joe. "It's pretty clear cut. I don't think you'll have any problems, but a piece of advice. If you want to be a hero, you'll go back to her employer, tell them what you've found and advise them there might be further intrusions into their proprietary customer data. Now that you've got evidence she wasn't behind it they'll probably think twice about legal action against her."

"I'll talk it over with Yoda, then contact them tomorrow. They'll probably want their entire IT system gone over with a fine-tooth comb." Joe inhaled deeply, took a swallow of his drink. Hope expanded in his chest for the first time in weeks. His yearning for Sandy grew stronger every day. He needed her in his life.

Joe spent the rest of the evening with Rizzoli going over the instructions Calvin and Hobbs had supplied. His heart raced at the prospect of pinning Phil Rice to the security breach at People and Productions, but what really mattered to him most—Sandy would be proven innocent. Deep in his heart he'd known it all along which was why he'd been so destroyed. He wanted to kick himself. He shook hands with Rizzoli.

"Thanks for your time, *C-Riz*. I'm going home and work non-stop on this. I don't care how long it takes."

Rizzoli cocked his head. "Don't rush it or you're sure to miss something. This will take a while. If you get stuck, call me. I'm happy to help out a friend, especially if I can talk him into meeting with my supervisor for a job interview. We need good people at DHS. You're one of the good guys." He tapped the table. "I gotta get home." He held up a hand with his index finger and thumb a centimeter apart. "Anita's patience goes just so far." He laughed. "I never realized how much time I spent in cyberworld until I got married last year. She keeps me grounded in the real world. All she has to do is flutter those great eyelashes of hers and I wonder why I didn't come home sooner."

"Married life good for you, huh?"

Rizzoli slapped him on the shoulder. "Oh, yeah. You should try it."

———

Greg leaned close to Sandy. "So…you're going back tomorrow?"

"Yes. I love it here, but my heart is in SoCal. I'll be looking for a new job first thing."

"Where's Joe? What's really going on?"

"What's the matter? Your radar on the fritz?" She didn't want to talk to anyone in her family about what had happened. She'd come up to Portland to get away from it for a while. "You know I'll find out, right?" He used his arm to put her in a gentle head-lock.

"I don't doubt it for a minute." She loved both of her brothers so much and maybe they could help her, but she'd failed miserably at her marriage to Phil. To let them know she'd blown it again was more than she cared to face. She'd figure this out by herself. She had to.

They entered the cool entry hall just inside the building housing Greg's condo. To her horror, tears threatened, and she swallowed, trying to squelch them. She turned her face to the side so Greg couldn't see. It was no use. There was nothing wrong with his radar today.

"OK, that does it." He took her elbow and led her to his door, unlocked it and drew her into his arms. "You're not leaving here until I know the truth."

Sandy collapsed against him and sobbed into his neck. Her body trembled from head to toe as the floodgates opened. She wasn't sure how long they stood there, but Greg never stopped holding her tight against his chest. He was a rock that could stand up against as many waves of her crashing emotions as needed.

Her brother's hand rubbed soothing circles against her back while he whispered soft comforting words in her ear. "Breathe, honey. We'll fix whatever this is."

Sandy pushed back and stamped her foot. "Love stinks! Don't ever fall in love, I'm warning you, it isn't worth it." Her eyes swept the room frantically. "What have you got to drink around here?"

Greg chuckled. He led her to his beautifully decorated living room and urged her to sit. He picked up a nearby box of tissues and thrust them into her hands. "Don't get snot on my new upholstery. I'll be right back."

Sandy flopped back against the cushions, grabbed a handful of tissues and pressed them against her face. She blew her nose noisily, not caring whether or not it sounded ladylike. As she wiped away infuriating tears, she began to giggle. "Damnit. This isn't funny. Why am I laughing?"

Her brother walked back in the room carrying two fancy crystal classes. "You might not need this after all." He handed her a frosty martini with three olives. "Slug it down anyway."

She held the icy glass by the stem and sipped Greg's specialty. "Oh, God, that's good." She took another sip and sighed. "What would our mother think? It's only ten-thirty in the morning."

Greg winked and took a healthy swallow. "I'm not planning on telling her, and if you say anything, I'm claiming you couldn't force me to join you in your blatant debauchery."

Sandy gazed at her brother's movie-star handsome face. "I love you so much."

He held up his glass. "The feeling is mutual. Now drink up. I made a double batch. We're having martoonys for brunch and lunch today. Our dark and dangerous secret."

They were feeling no pain an hour later. Sandy had kicked off her shoes and sprawled across Greg's sofa like a confirmed lush. It gave her some insight to Joe's downward spiral into alcoholism, and how admirable his determination to be clean and sober had been. Oh, how she wished she could be angry with Joe, but no matter how hard she tried to convince herself she just couldn't do it.

Greg had stretched out on the floor in front of the couch and put his stocking-clad feet next to Sandy. He'd whined until she gave up and consented to giving him a foot rub. This was a ritual they'd often enacted while they were growing up. She'd always shove his feet away, wrinkle her nose and grump, "Pee-you, get those stinky clodhoppers out of my face!" In the end, she always relented. His feet didn't stink, in fact she was sure he was the cleanest male on the planet.

Greg moaned with pleasure. "Oh, God, oh, God. You have the touch."

She snorted drunkenly. "Oh sure, you'd say that to anybody who'd rub these disgusting things." The sting was taken out of her words by the sloppy grin on her face.

"Don't be mean or I might change my mind and not call out to La Petite Maison to deliver our dinner. You have any idea how much that's going to set me back?" He shifted so she'd start on the other foot. She stuck out her tongue but continued.

They were silent for a while as Sandy worked her magic. Greg lazily fumbled for his cellphone on the coffee table and finally got ahold of it. He stared at the screen, trying to sharpen his focus, she assumed, and then tapped it. "Franco, darling, Greg here. I'm spending the evening in my condo with a beautiful, sexy woman who needs my advice on her love life. What miracle do you suppose Maurice could whip up and have delivered around six?" He nodded a couple of times then rolled his eyes. "She's my sister, you brute. You have nothing to worry about, so get cracking." He disconnected the call and winked at Sandy.

"Who's Franco?"

"Presently, he's somebody I like, but who knows?" He waggled his eyebrows knowing he could be as outrageously gay around her as he chose.

She shoved his feet away and sat up. "Have you been listening to me?" She slurred then giggled inappropriately. "I'm telling you to never, never, ever fall in love." She pushed herself up and wobbled to catch her balance. "I gotta pee."

"Need any help."

"Bite me."

———

Now sober, and halfway through dinner, Sandy swooned and pressed a hand to her heart. "Oh-my-god-oh-my-god. This food is so sinfully delicious, I think we're headed straight to hell for just eating it. You have to marry this Franco guy for sure, before I do."

"Sorry, sugar cakes, it's me he's interested in, not my sister." He took a bite of the decadent chocolate dessert concoction and rolled his eyes. "But I would need to be in love with the man I marry, and you've convinced me that's a road I never want to go down."

On the contrary, Greg had spent the better part of the day convincing her to face reality. She was in love with Joe, and if there was any way to repair the breach between them, she owed it to herself to try. She wrinkled her nose and made a face at her brother. "You are such a pain."

"I'm only bending to your vast experience in the field of relationships." He polished off the last bite and licked the spoon.

She'd done her best to belittle herself all afternoon, by lamenting her bad judgement in her marriage to Phil, trying to convince herself more than her brother that she was deficient in the way she sized up men, blundering into a rotten marriage, and then falling into blind love with Joe.

Greg nodded and agreed with every bad thing she had to say about herself and her inability to make good decisions then laughed when she got mad at him for doing it. She knew very well his method of madness and had walked right into it.

"My dear sister, you are so lucky." He cocked his head and gazed into her eyes, golden brown twins of his own.

"I'm lucky?" He could always turn a discussion on its head. She admired how quick he was on his feet, but his question puzzled her.

"Yes, lucky. Sometimes I feel like I'm the only one in the world who's never been in love. Almost everyone I know has been, or is in love. Can you believe Damon? Our steady-as-she-goes brother falling so deeply in love. I'm supremely happy for him, but it baffles me. You've been in love twice."

Sandy sniffed. "The first time doesn't count." When had she turned into a crybaby?

"Oh, I beg to differ. They all count. You can't imagine how I've longed to experience that rush, that deep feeling of euphoria, that sense of lightness and worth. That state which nobody who's been lucky enough to experience seems able to explain. I want that for myself."

"Oh, honey." Sandy touched his hand. "You will. I'm sure of it. I need to quit feeling sorry for myself. I apologize."

He flipped his hand. "Forget it. All I ask is if I'm ever in a similar situation, you'll be there with your shoulder for me to cry on. What's a big sister for anyway?" A smile spread on his face and he winked. "Now—what are you going to do? Are you going to talk to Joe? You're still in love with him. It's worth saving, isn't it?"

"Yes. As soon as I get back, I'll call Liz and see if he's still trying to help me. If we think the timing is right for me and Joe to get together, I'll take the first step."

"Now you're talking."

"Um." Sandy winced and touched his hand. "There's one more person you know who's in love. Liz is on cloud nine over a Marine captain friend of Joe's."

Greg sighed dramatically and slapped a wrist to his forehead. "Oh, mercy."

Chapter Thirty-Two

"JOEY, WHAT WERE YOU DOING FOR HOURS IN JORDAN'S OFFICE today?" His sister's voice brimmed with anxiety.

"I was planning to call you. I wasn't sure you were home from work yet." He pulled over and put his car in Park. "I'm five minutes from my place. I'll call you back as soon as I get there."

"But, Joey..."

"I'll call you in five minutes." He disconnected the call, tossed his phone on the passenger seat next to his laptop briefcase, and drove to his building's parking area.

He unlocked his apartment door, tossed his jacket on the back of a chair and toed off his loafers. He needed something cold to drink. His throat parched from hours of conversation with Liz's boss had him digging in the refrigerator for the bottle of sweet iced tea he purchased the previous day. Eschewing a glass, he tipped the liter bottle up and drank almost half of it before pausing for a breath. *God what a day. Jordan People is an exasperating guy.*

He wondered if all bosses were the same. Starting with Gunny Dempsey, Master Sergeant Beachy, then every other commanding officer, and now Chambers and Jordan People. He couldn't imagine what his Marine subordinates thought of him. *Christ!*

Joe grabbed two chocolate cookies and gobbled them down with the help of another gulp of the tea, then picked up his phone.

Liz answered on the first ring. "That was eleven minutes, Joey, not five."

"Give me a break, sis! I'm up to my eyeballs in assholes. I don't want to add you to the list." He exhaled and flopped into a kitchen chair, the bottle of tea in his other hand.

"Sorry." True contrition permeated the word. "I don't know why I went off on you. Can I come over? I'll bring dinner."

"God, yes. I need a shower and a drink, but I'll settle for the shower. See you when you get here." He ended the call and stared at the bottle of tea in his hand and polished it off. It would be at least forty-five minutes before Liz got there. That was plenty of time to decompress, have a long-hot shower and change into sweats.

His doorbell rang an hour later. "Come on up." He took his finger off the intercom and unlocked his entry door and left his open. He stepped into the kitchen to set the table. When he heard her come in, he yelled, "In here." The door closed, but Liz didn't come in. "You need help?"

"Liz doesn't, but I do."

Joe spun around at the sound of Sandy's voice and he dropped the silverware he'd been holding on the floor. His nerves clattered as loud as the metal when it landed and scattered.

They stared across the short distance, neither moving. Finally, Joe found his voice. "Sweetheart."

They met in the middle of the room and Joe grabbed her in a fierce hug, then kissed her with urgency. Flooded with mixed feelings he was unable to make sense of, he paused and deepened the kiss. He couldn't think, only feel. Sandy in his arms again. Her mouth on his, her body pressed against him, her slender fingers tangled in his hair.

Sandy stiffened and pushed away from him. Before he had a chance to react, she pummeled him in the chest and shoulders with her fists. Sobs tore through her and her eyes glistened with tears. He caught her wrists easily and held her at bay. "Sweetheart, honey, I'm so sorry."

She sucked in a ragged breath and unclenched her fists. He let her go.

Sandy slumped into his chest and clutched at his back, trembling from head to foot. "Damnit, Joe, damnit, damnit, damnit."

He tightened his arms around her, stroked her back and murmured quiet shushing sounds. Burying his nose in her hair, he inhaled her unique scent. His eyes dampened with unshed tears. He hadn't admitted to himself these past awful months of their separation, his fear of never being this close to her again. He'd rather die than never to feel her soft body, run his fingers through her beautiful hair, while surrounded by her sweet scent.

Now she was here. No more need to agonize over how he would approach her, how he would attempt to mend the terrible breach. She'd taken the lead, put him out of his misery. That she loved him as much as he loved her filled him with gratitude and wonder. *Thank you, God.*

He placed his finger under her chin and tilted her head back so he could look into her eyes. He wiped away her tears with his thumbs and smiled. "I love you, Sandra Cassidy. I love you so much. Don't ever doubt it."

"I know." Her soft palm stroked his cheek. "That's the only thing that kept me going. I don't want to talk. I want you to kiss me, make love to me. Let's put all this behind us and start over."

"You want to start over?" He grinned and cocked his head.

"More than anything, Joe."

He held up a finger. "Hold that thought." He hurried toward his bedroom.

"Where are you …? Joe?"

"Wait. I'll only be a minute." As soon as he closed the bedroom door, he yanked his shirt over his head and hopped out of his sweatpants. In the closet, he found the pants and shirt he was looking for and quickly donned them. A quick look in the mirror, a brush of his hands over his hair and he was out the door.

"Come on, sweetheart." He grabbed her hand. "We're going out."

"Out? Where are we going?" Her precious face was filled with confusion, but she trotted after him. "Joe? Stop!"

He faced her. "You want to start over, right?"

She nodded, still confused. "Yes, but…"

He grinned and dropped a light kiss on her lips. "If you want to start over, we have to go back to the beginning. Come on, it's getting late." He tugged her toward the stairs. "Hop on." He slapped his hip. "I'll give you a piggyback ride."

She laughed. "You're crazy. How come I never knew that before?"

"You always knew it." He waggled his butt. "Hop on."

She yanked her hand away and stood her ground. "Only if you tell me where we're going."

"Caliente Latino, where else?"

———

They swayed on the dance floor, barely moving their feet. They'd been there for hours, the orchestra had quit playing and were quietly packing their instruments. The nightclub lights blinked. Sandy looked up. "Oh. Looks like we've overstayed our welcome."

Joe sighed and reached into his pants pocket. His hand around all the bills he found there, he stepped to the bandstand and passed them to the conductor. "Muchas gracias, mi amigo. Buenas noches." The man bowed and smiled.

"Let's go, honey lover. We're out of time and now money." Sandy rested her temple on Joe's shoulder and lifted her small purse from the table where they'd been sitting. Around the large room, all the chairs had been turned upside down and placed on the tabletops in preparation for the cleaning crew waiting off to one side. A plump Latina crossed her hands over her heart, nodded and grinned as Joe and Sandy made their way to the door.

The street was dark except for one light in the deserted parking lot at the side of the club. Sandy shivered in the cool air and Joe took off his jacket and pulled it around her shoulders. His blue eyes gazed into hers with such intensity she could feel the love they conveyed as a physical force. She reached up and ran her fingers over his lips as softly as the flutter of a moth's wings. Words were unnecessary. She kissed him instead.

"Do we really have to go back to the beginning?" She asked, a feisty smile playing across her mouth, still tingling from the touch of his lips. "Because as I recall, it took weeks before I was able to lure you into my bed."

Joe's big hand slid down to caress her bottom. "I'm not so sure who did the luring, but I believe we could manage to nudge the fast-forward button a bit. The parking lot light blinked off. "Looks like they're trying to get rid of us."

"You think?" She squeezed his fingers as they made their way to Joe's Beemer.

He got behind the wheel and buckled up. "You know, sooner or later we need to have a long discussion."

"Later works for me." She locked her buckle. "I have other plans for what's left of this night. Step on it, Marine."

He snapped off a salute. "Yes, ma'am."

It took the better part of an hour to drive back to Glendale. Finally, they were inside his apartment again. Joe leaned back against his door and drew her into his arms. They stood that way for several minutes, holding each other, absorbing each other, acutely aware of each other. Making up for lost time.

Joe turned and walked backward, she followed as if it were another dance step.

Inside his bedroom he proceeded to slowly remove her clothing, piece by piece. Stopping after each piece to fold it neatly and set it on top of his dresser. When she chafed with impatience, he removed her hands from his collar, smiled and shook his head. He placed a finger on her lips when she opened her mouth to speak.

The last garment was placed on the tidy stack.

Joe stepped back and gazed at her.

She felt extremely shy because he was still fully clothed. A warm blush rose from her chest and burned its way to her scalp. "Joe." She covered her breasts with her hands.

He softly stroked her cheeks, neck, shoulders, and then swept his hands down her sides, stopping to rest them on her hips. Joe dropped to his knees before her. He put his arms around her hips and rested his face on her abdomen. A powerful thrill swept through her, moist heat invaded her lower torso. She gasped at its intensity. "Joe, what are you doing?"

Lips on her stomach, he murmured, "Taking my time." He tilted his head up to gaze at her and took her breasts in his hands. "Taking my time."

She mewled and dropped her head back, wondering how much more she could take before her knees gave way. "Oh, God. You have to stop, please."

"You want me to stop?"

"Yes. No, but..."

He rose and stopped her words with a soft kiss that morphed into one of near savagery. He held her tight against him. "I've got you," he said over and over. "I'm never letting you go again. Never."

"I love you, Joe. You don't know how much." She gasped when he lifted her and carried her to his bed. Laying her down with excruciating gentleness, he ran his hands over her body again.

Abruptly he stood and unbuttoned his shirt, his eyes never leaving hers while he stripped off his clothes then lowered himself next to her. "I'm taking my time," he repeated. "We're going to go slow, real slow."

Sandy knew to her bones that she'd climax the second he touched her between her legs, and she did. Tears of joy slipped from her eyes when she opened them to his intense blue gaze.

He grinned. "Hang on, sweetheart. I haven't even begun."

———

Sandy stared into her nearly empty mug of strong black coffee and tried to bring some order to her sleep-tousled hair with her fingers then gave it up as a lost cause. She leaned forward on her elbows and gave Joe a murderous glare. "I don't want you to ever touch me again!"

"You can count on it, baby. I don't ever want to." He returned her glare, sticking out his chin for good measure.

The stare-down lasted several seconds as Sandy tried very hard to conceal a smile by putting her hand over her mouth. Joe grabbed her wrist and pulled it away from her face. "You got something to say to me? Huh?"

She yanked her hand away from him and jumped to her feet. She stuck a pointed finger directly at his nose. "Yes! You..." She shrieked when Joe stood to his full, totally naked, height. *My Lord, he's magnificent. He belongs on the cover of Men's Health.*

She slowly backed up as he made a move in her direction. She put out her hand. "Oh, no. Don't even think about it."

He raised his hands into claws and growled menacingly while continuing his stalking approach. "Don't tell me what to think, you wicked hussy."

She shrieked again and ran to the bedroom, Joe hot on her heels before she could reach for the door. He grabbed her around the waist and tossed her on the bed where she collapsed into a helpless puddle of giggles. Giggles stifled when he dropped on top of her, effectively pinning her to the pile of disordered sheets and blankets. She knew what she was in for as well as she knew Joe was more than ready for it.

It was a while before they came up for air again.

Sandy stroked Joe's chest and dropped her leg over his. "Don't you have to go to work?"

"Screw work." He raised his head and squinted at the clock. "Ugh. I'm feeling sick. I don't want to spread it around the office. I owe it to them to take a sick day. You know, so they don't get it."

She raised on her elbow and put her hand on his forehead. "Feverish. No doubt about it. Am I in danger of getting it?"

"I doubt it. I probably got it from you. I was feeling fine until you came over last night. No symptoms, no fever, no loss of appetite. You're a regular Typhoid Mary."

"How's your appetite now?"

"Improving."

"Good." She slapped his belly and headed for the bathroom. "I'm going to shower. Either cook me some breakfast while I'm in there or figure out where you're taking me." She blew him a kiss over her shoulder and wiggled her fingers.

"I'll shave while you shower. I already decided where we're going." He hopped out of bed and followed her into the bathroom. "Ever been to Foxy's on Colorado Blvd? I can taste that cinnamon roll French toast already. Mmm, mmm, mmm."

———

They were on their second pot of coffee when Joe finished bringing her up to date on his investigation, with the help of Yoda and the great geeks at the hacker's hangout. When he brought the proof to her boss and warned him about possible further intrusions in their systems, Joe advised him to consider digging deeper, finding the actual culprit and press charges against whoever it turned out to be and quit considering her as having anything to do with it.

Jordan had been beside himself. Now he'd have to go to greater expense to dig deeper, but he would hire a different security firm. He was outraged when he learned Joe's boss had insisted he pursue the investigation even though he had a serious conflict of interest with his sister and fiancée both working for him. Joe recommended hiring Penn as an independent contractor instead of going to another commercial enterprise. "He's a certified ethical hacker," he reassured him. "Has the certificate and everything."

"Rizzoli asked me again about coming to DHS."

"Is that something you'd want to do?" Sandy dabbed her mouth. "I remember you mentioned it a long time ago."

"No. I'm toying with the idea of going into teaching. I have a degree in physics. I've always enjoyed teaching kids when the Marines hosted an event at the base. I don't have a credential, but I should be able to accomplish that without too much trouble."

"Gosh, that came out of the blue. I had no idea."

"What do you think? Doesn't pay much compared to what I'm making now." He pushed back his chair and picked up the check. "I haven't made any decision. Just mulling it around in my brain." He put her sweater around her shoulders. "Let's shake a leg. We have to go shopping."

She looked puzzled at the sudden change of subject. "Shopping? Now?"

"Yep. Now." He winked and handed the check to the cashier. Once the bill was settled, he led her outside. "It's a perfect day for shopping."

"What are you up to, Joseph Hamilton?" She stopped on the sidewalk and faced him. "I know that look. Where are we going?"

"To get that damn ring. I'm not going to be put in that spot again."

Epilogue

SANDY STOOD IN THE FLOWER-BEDECKED CHAPEL IN THE Oregon woods with her right hand in the crook of Clint's elbow and her left hand in Joe's.

Today was the special day they'd anticipated.

Clint whispered, "This place is totally rad."

Early afternoon sun filtered through the stained-glass windows, beaming shafts of soft color over the wedding guests. Her big brother Damon stood at the dais. His sappy smile brought a big grin to her face. Greg, his best man, flashed a broad stage wink as only he could pull off.

Joe raised Sandy's left hand to his lips and kissed the finger wearing his beautiful, too extravagant, engagement ring. They strolled to the front.

Clint fidgeted. She squeezed his arm, and he took a deep breath. "I don't know how men get through this stuff." He looked pointedly at Joe.

"Hey, kid, I can't speak for the others, but I could do it. I'm a Marine, remember."

They'd just made it to take their place next to Beverly, in the front row, when the wedding music commenced. Sandy's mother sat with her hands crossed on her heart and beamed with happiness and love at her sons.

Little Belle, in a frothy cloud of organza, carried a white wicker basket of deep red rose petals. She flung them haphazardly as she skipped down the aisle, then hopped with excitement and tossed a handful of petals at Damon Cassidy's feet. "Hi, Daddy."

He bent forward, took the basket from her hand, lifted her in his arms, and held her against his broad chest. "Hi, baby." Tears glittered on his lashes as the little girl reached up and circled her arms around his neck.

Sandy's heart swelled, she couldn't help it, she choked back a sob. Joe put his arm around her shoulders and kissed her hair. "Hang in there, sweetheart," he whispered softly. "We're next."

She nodded and trembled a sigh.

The wedding guests turned at the first notes of the traditional wedding march. Damon's bride, Janeen, glowing in an aura of radiance, began her walk down the aisle on the arm of her father.

Sandy had never seen a more beautiful bride. She leaned into Joe's side. "Oh, my God. She's gorgeous."

"She is indeed." He spoke close to her ear so he wouldn't be overheard, "She's the second most beautiful woman in the room."

THE END

———

Don't miss out on your next favorite book!

Join the Satin Romance mailing list
www.satinromance.com/mail.html

THANK YOU FOR READING

Did you enjoy this book?

We invite you to leave a review at the website of your choice, such as Goodreads, Amazon, Barnes & Noble, etc.

———

DID YOU KNOW THAT LEAVING A REVIEW…

- Helps other readers find books they may enjoy.
- Gives you a chance to let your voice be heard.
- Gives authors recognition for their hard work.
- Doesn't have to be long. A sentence or two about why you liked the book will do.

About the Author

I wrote my first novel at the age of six. It was titled "The Mouse," and was two pages long—including illustrations! My mother saved that *first edition* and every now and then, I take it out and smile over it.

When my beloved husband of many years suddenly died, I'd come home after a long day of work and write. Writing allowed me to pour out all my sadness. Then, the more I wrote, the more I realized I would go on. I would be happy, I had a lot of living to do, and love stories to tell.

I'm published now in Romance novels and an anthology of short stories. But my first two manuscripts still reside on a CD somewhere in my house. I can't bear to erase them because they're mine, they're loved, and like a crazy relative one hides in the attic, they reside in a quiet, safe place.

www.pattycampbell.com
pattycampbellauthor.blogspot.com

facebook.com/Patty-Campbell-Author-536855299661241

goodreads.com/goodreadscomuser_PattyCampbell

Also by Patty Campbell

WITH MELANGE BOOKS

Wounded Warriors Series

Love of a Marine

Soul of a Marine

———

Novels

Risky Business

www.ingramcontent.com/pod-product-compliance
Lightning Source LLC
Chambersburg PA
CBHW031109030726
47496CB00002BA/453